The fire was destroying her area. Suck it up, Westin. Raising the Pulaski, she stumbled toward the glowing edge. She'd kill it for sure this time. *Vengeanth ith mine*, sayeth the fat-lipped firefighter.

An hour later, the fire was out. Only a few acres lay in smoking gray ruins. Most of the firefighters, including Joe and Lili, had gone home, but the ones who remained divided the devastation among themselves and tromped through it toward the lake, stirring ashes and turning over smoldering chunks of wood to ensure the flames wouldn't spring to life as soon as they departed. Sam was pulverizing a smoldering ember into ashes when Mack yelped from fifty yards away.

"Holy shit!"

It took her a minute to locate him in the moonlight among the skeletons of trees. He was on his knees beside a charred tree trunk. Had he hurt himself? After making sure she had permanently blinded the glowing eye on the ground, she trudged toward him. Side by side, they stared at the blackened log, still smoking on the forest floor.

It was wearing boots.

Berkley Prime Crime titles by Pamela Beason

ENDANGERED
BEAR BAIT

BEAR BAIT

PAMELA BEASON

BERKLEY PRIME CRIME, NEW YORK

THE BERKLEY PUBLISHING GROUP
Published by the Penguin Group
Penguin Group (USA) Inc.
375 Hudson Street, New York, New York 10014, USA
Penguin Group (Canada), 90 Eglinton Avenue East, Suite 700, Toronto, Ontario M4P 2Y3, Canada
(a division of Pearson Penguin Canada Inc.) • Penguin Books Ltd., 80 Strand, London WC2R 0RL,
England • Penguin Group Ireland, 25 St. Stephen's Green, Dublin 2, Ireland (a division of Penguin
Books Ltd.) • Penguin Group (Australia), 250 Camberwell Road, Camberwell, Victoria 3124, Australia
(a division of Pearson Australia Group Pty. Ltd.) • Penguin Books India Pvt. Ltd., 11 Community
Centre, Panchsheel Park, New Delhi—110 017, India • Penguin Group (NZ), 67 Apollo Drive,
Rosedale, Auckland 0632, New Zealand (a division of Pearson New Zealand Ltd.) • Penguin Books
(South Africa) (Pty.) Ltd., 24 Sturdee Avenue, Rosebank, Johannesburg 2196, South Africa

Penguin Books Ltd., Registered Offices: 80 Strand, London WC2R 0RL, England

This is a work of fiction. Names, characters, places, and incidents either are the product of the author's imagination or are used fictitiously, and any resemblance to actual persons, living or dead, business establishments, events, or locales is entirely coincidental. The publisher does not have any control over and does not assume any responsibility for author or third-party websites or their content.

BEAR BAIT

A Berkley Prime Crime Book / published by arrangement with the author

PUBLISHING HISTORY
Berkley Prime Crime mass-market edition / October 2012

Copyright © 2012 by Pamela Beason.
Excerpt from *Undercurrents* by Pamela Beason copyright © 2012 by Pamela Beason.
Cover photos: *Olympic National Park* © Pat O'Hara / Getty Images;
Black Bear © Glowimages / Getty Images; *Paw Print* © Hemera / Thinkstock.
Cover design by Judith Lagerman.
Interior text design by Laura K. Corless.

ISBN: 978-0-425-25165-2

BERKLEY® PRIME CRIME
Berkley Prime Crime Books are published by The Berkley Publishing Group,
a division of Penguin Group (USA) Inc.,
375 Hudson Street, New York, New York 10014.
BERKLEY® PRIME CRIME and the PRIME CRIME logo are trademarks of
Penguin Group (USA) Inc.

PRINTED IN THE UNITED STATES OF AMERICA

10   9   8   7   6   5   4   3   2   1

ALWAYS LEARNING   PEARSON

For my mother,
Ruby Gardner,
with all my love.

ACKNOWLEDGMENTS

I want to express my gratitude to my agent, Curtis Russell of P. S. Literary Agency, for his support and efforts on my behalf. Thank you to my Berkley Prime Crime editorial team and promotional staff for all your work in making my new series a success. And to all my critique partners over the years who kept me from wandering too far astray in the literary wilderness, I cannot say "I appreciate you" often enough.

1

THE leaves rustled on the bushes ahead. Sam took a few steps backward, expecting that a bear might emerge. She had followed Raider's tracks from the release site in the parking lot to this dense thicket of Himalayan blackberries. She was anxious to lay eyes on her problem bear, to make sure he was adapting after being relocated to the Marmot Lake area. She hoped he was prowling for berries and digging for grubs like any self-respecting black bear should. As opposed to hightailing it back to the Hoh Rain Forest campground to ransack his favorite garbage cans.

The leaves stilled. Silence reigned. No bear. The movement might have been a raccoon, a Douglas squirrel, or even a bird. Whatever it was, she wasn't wading through those thorns to see it. Making a mental note to remove the nonnative berry bushes, she turned to look for another route, and then her breath caught in her throat.

A hunter stood in the clearing behind her. The intruder had silently materialized from the forest in full camouflage gear, including a fatigue cap and green and gray paint on his face. On his belt was a huge knife in a sheath. In his arms he cradled what looked to her like an automatic rifle. His gaze traveled rudely down her park service uniform.

Sam forced herself to inhale, and her heart started again, beating double time now. To her amazement, her voice sounded remarkably calm as she said, "This area is now part of Olympic National Park. It's off-limits for hunting."

The intruder glared and shifted the rifle as if he was contemplating shooting her, and then silently turned and melted into the woods like a malevolent specter.

She heaved a sigh of relief and dried her sweaty palms on the thighs of her uniform pants. Thank God the hunter had taken her word as truth. With this contract assignment in the park service, she finally had some authority to back up her instructions, even if the situation was only temporary. Jerks tended to pay more attention to a woman wearing a government uniform.

Only after she'd taken a few steps on her way did she realize that it wasn't hunting season anywhere, for any creature. Which made the encounter even more sinister. In her experience, illegal hunters were like snakes: if you saw one, there were probably a dozen hidden nearby. Had she plunked Raider down among them? That would be bitter irony. She could envision the headline all too easily: WILD- LIFE BIOLOGIST DELIVERS EASY PREY TO LOCAL SPORTSMEN.

Good thing she wasn't working in the sound-bite world of Internet news at the moment. It was so nice to be unplugged for a few months.

". . . so then Rocky chose Deborah because her dad has a plane."

Plane? Sam's brain snapped back to the fire lookout and the scene that was actually before her eyes: endless acres of black spiky Douglas firs silhouetted against a star-spangled sky. To the east, a full moon peeked over the Olympic Mountains. Soon the black spot to the north that marked Marmot Lake would shimmer like molten silver.

Sam lowered her binoculars to the window ledge, scribbled *OK—Westin* in the 11 P.M. slot in the logbook, and then swiveled on the high wooden stool to gaze down at the rough-planked floor where thirteen-year-old Lili Choi sat cross-legged on top of a sleeping bag. Her caramel-colored eyes were raised in Sam's direction. She clearly expected some sort of reaction.

"Hmmm . . ." Pressing her lips together, Sam dipped her chin in what she hoped was an interested but noncommittal expression. She had completely tuned out the girl. How did Joe and Laura and all the other parents in the world follow the stories of their offspring? Their tales went on and on and on.

"I don't think that's fair, do you?"

Picking up on the cue, Sam leaned away from the hiss of the Coleman lamp at her elbow and said, "Not really, but . . ." But what?

"We can't all have planes, can we?" Lili pulled at the fountain of curly black hair that sprang from an elastic band on top of her head. "And it's not even like it's Deborah's plane, or like she can fly it or anything."

Sam had the gist of it now. "Well, no, it's not fair for . . . Robbie—"

"Rocky!"

". . . for Rocky to like Deborah better just because her family is rich, but unfortunately, a lot of people are like that—they pick their friends for what they own, not for who they are."

Lili frowned. "That's exactly what Martian says."

"Martian?" People named their kids after aliens now?

The girl laughed. "That's what we call Mr. Murtinson. He teaches earth science. He's my favorite teacher." She reached for another brownie from the plastic container on the floor. "Rocky doesn't like him much, but that's probably because Martian's the soccer coach and Rocky's only the assistant."

"Sounds like Rocky's pretty shallow."

"Got that right," Lili said between bites. "But he's the most interesting guy around here. He's got ideas, unlike most boys. Well, there is one other who's even more interesting." Her eyes went dreamy as she added, "He's *fine*." Lili washed down the brownie with a gulp of iced tea from the plastic cup in her hand.

Sugar and caffeine at 11 P.M. If the girl's father was here, he'd have Sam's head on a platter. Joe Choi, one of Olympic National Park's law enforcement rangers, was a new friend. Still, she shouldn't have let him coerce her into letting Lili sleep over in the fire tower. Joe feared Lili was having trouble adjusting to life in rural Washington. He begged Sam to talk to Lili "girl-to-girl," discourage her from wearing "slutty tops and skirts shorter than shorts," and "set her on the right track," whatever that meant.

"Why me?" Sam asked. She'd never imagined herself as a role model to anyone, let alone an impressionable child. Lili had a perfectly good mother.

"Lili doesn't talk to Laura or me anymore," Joe said. "She's taken to you. Maybe you can find out what's in her head these days."

Sam suspected Joe really wanted to know if his thirteen-year-old was contemplating—or God forbid, had already indulged in—sex. So far, Sam had unearthed no real hanky-panky. Midriff-baring T-shirts and microskirts were simply what Lili thought would impress the local boys, just like the henna tattoo on her left ankle—a circular leafy stamp that reminded Sam of a Tree of Life quilt.

Of course, even the idea that Lili wanted to impress the boys might be enough to send Joe up in flames. He didn't think thirteen-year-olds should have thoughts about the opposite sex at all. But he needed to take a good hard look at his oldest child. Lili, as Sam's grandmother would have said, had "blossomed early," with swelling breasts, pouty lips, and almond-shaped eyes designed by nature to drive even prepubescent boys wild. Although Lili was as American as Kentucky Fried Chicken, her one-quarter Korean heritage gave her an exotic attraction that girls would envy and boys would lust after.

"What? Is there a big zit on my nose or something?" Lili scrubbed her hands across her face.

"I was just zoning out," Sam admitted. "It's been a long day. Let's brush our teeth and hit the sack."

She showed Lili how to pump water from the collapsible plastic container. They went outside onto the balcony with cups and toothbrushes in hand. The night air was cool and soft with humidity. A chorus of Pacific tree frogs hummed in the thick Douglas firs beneath them.

Lili spat a mouthful of toothpaste over the wooden railing. She watched the frothy white droplets fall to the ground a hundred feet below. "Sweet," she said. Then she glanced at Sam from beneath her long lashes. "Can I call you Aunt Summer? Aunt Sam sounds like a transvestite."

Sam laughed. Thirteen-year-olds knew about transvestites? "How about just calling me Sam? Or Summer? We're both independent women."

Lili grinned. "But only in private. Dad would have a cow."

"Then Aunt Summer's fine with me."

People rarely used her given name. As a teenager, she'd started calling herself Sam to stop the high school boys from crooning "Cruel Summer" and "Summer breeze, makes me feel fine." The oldie-moldy "Hot time, Summer in the city" kept cropping up, along with a lot of imaginative tales about "hot Summer nights." Lili was no doubt due for a lot of innuendoes involving sniffing and plucking and pollinating.

"So, Summer," Lili said, trying the name out with a shy smile, "for this school project, I have to write a report on two careers." She took a deep breath and plunged on. "And I figured, since you're a wildlife biologist and a writer, you could help me with two at once." She hesitated uncertainly. "I mean, if you want to."

Sam blinked at her, not knowing whether to be flattered or appalled. "Is it okay to interview the same person for two different careers?"

Lili shrugged. "Ms. Patterson didn't say we couldn't."

"Wouldn't it be good to get more than one person's point of view?"

The girl's face clouded. She looked down at her toes and mumbled, "You don't have to help. It's all right. I'll try to find someone else."

Oh, for heaven's sake. "Okay. I'll help you, Lili."

"Yes!" Lili pumped her fisted toothbrush toward the star-spangled sky.

It was nice to be the source of someone's excitement, even a thirteen-year-old's. "When is this paper due?"

"August seventh?" Lili shot a quick glance at Sam as if expecting an objection. "Dad told me I had to get started in plenty of time for once."

"It's due in two weeks?" Sam only had three weeks to finish her environmental survey and write up her recommended management plan. Now she'd agreed to help Lili, too? Deep breath, she told herself. It was a junior high project—how hard could it be? "What's the first step?"

"I'm s'posed to come up with questions about each career," Lili said. "I'll do those tomorrow." She sighed. "I thought I'd hate summer school. But it's sort of okay."

There was a possible segue back to Lili's social life. Sam jumped at it. "Are there any cool boys?"

A loud boom rocked the fire tower. Sam grabbed the railing, knocking the tube of toothpaste from the rough two-by-four.

"Aunt Summer?" Even in the dim light, Sam could see that Lili's eyes were wide.

"It's okay." At least she hoped it was. She dashed inside, grabbed the binoculars, and focused them on Marmot Lake.

Like an anxious cocker spaniel, Lili followed close on her heels. "What *was* that?"

"I don't have a clue." Sam lowered the binoculars to look at Lili. Then lights flashed through the forest near the lake, and she raised the binoculars again. A set of headlights. No, two. Two vehicles. The road to the lake was now closed to the public, barricaded with a steel gate and lock. Nobody should be in there.

Should she call in the violation? The trespassers were leaving; the odds against catching them were high. The explosion was most likely local teens setting off fireworks. M-80s could sound like cannons, especially on a quiet night like this. The Quileute and Quinault reservations were still hawking firecrackers, although the Fourth of July had passed weeks ago.

A yellow light bloomed from the darkness near the lake. Then another. The brightness splashed and spread. She grabbed the radio on the desk and raised it to her lips.

"Three-one-one, this is three-two-five. Come in, three-one-one." She raised her finger from the Talk button. Nothing. She looked longingly at her cell phone on the shelf, but knew that it didn't work in some areas of the park. She tried the radio again. "Three-one-one, this is three-two-five."

"Three-one-one." The voice of the night dispatcher was hoarse. "Did you say three-two-five? Cat Mountain Fire Lookout? Where's Jeff?"

"Jeff went home. His mother's sick. This is Sam Westin."

"Oh, yeah. What's up, Sam?"

"I've got fire at Marmot Lake." In the distance, a dead tree caught with a sudden rush, a knife blade of orange light in the darkness. The headlights strobed through thick evergreens as they raced west toward the highway.

The dispatcher's reply was clipped, all business now. "Copy that, three-two-five. Fire at Marmot Lake."

"I see at least three sources. Roll everyone you can get. Send them in on"—she checked the map beneath her fingertips—"Road 5214. Over."

"Roger that—5214. I'll wake everyone up. Over."

"I'm heading for the blaze now. Over."

"You're a temp. Stay at the lookout. Over."

"I'm fifteen minutes away. I'm a trained firefighter; I have equipment."

"You are? You do? But "

Sam cut her off with a press of the Talk button. "It'll be at least an hour before you can get anyone to the lake. Over."

The dispatcher chose not to debate that point. "It's against the regs. Don't do anything stupid. Three-one-one, out."

Sam dumped the radio on the countertop and pulled on her boots. She heard the radio call to Paul Schuler, the law enforcement ranger who patrolled the west side campgrounds at night. The rest of the calls would be made via telephone; other staff members would be asleep at home. If all went smoothly, the west side crew might reach the lake in forty-five minutes. Most of them lived in the small town of Forks, less than fifteen miles away. But in that time, a fire could consume acres of forest. With luck, she might be able to extinguish a couple of small blazes before wildfire dug its ugly claws too deeply into the forest.

Lili jammed her feet into her own hiking boots.

"No," Sam said. "You're staying here."

The fountain of dark hair bounced as Lili's chin jerked up. "You can't leave me here! What if the fire comes this way?"

Good point. If the fire turned in this direction, she might not make it back to get Lili. Damn! "Then I'll have to drop you—"

"Where?" Lili's voice was shrill. "There isn't anywhere."

Sam stared at her, trying to think of a safe place to deposit the child. Her mind was filled with visions of flames licking through the forest, a small fire growing larger by the second. Panic growing as birds and deer and bear circled within the smoke, tree frogs frantically searching for twigs that wouldn't scorch their skin.

"The trees are burning right now," Lili said, as if reading her thoughts.

Sam didn't need to be reminded: her imagination was loud with screams of terrified animals.

"I'll do *exactly* what you say." Lili made the sign of the cross over her chest.

"You bet you will." Sam blew out the Coleman, stuffed her flashlight and first-aid kit into her daypack. Her fire-retardant suit, along with shovels and Pulaskis, were locked into a metal toolbox in the park's oldest pickup at the bottom of the tower.

Lili worked in silence, throwing gear and water bottles into her own pack as Sam picked up the radio again. When the dispatcher finally answered, Sam informed her that Lili Choi would be riding with her to Marmot Lake. She heard a sharp intake of breath on the other end.

"No choice," Sam said into the radio void. "Three-two-five, out."

2

THE old pickup fishtailed in soft dirt at the turnoff to the logging road, jerking Sam's hands on the wheel. Lili braced herself against the dash, but said nothing. Sam drove with her window rolled down, analyzing the night air for smoke. So far, she detected only a faint acrid scent that might well be her imagination. The heavy steel gate arms that should have barricaded Road 5214 sagged on their posts, wide open, the padlock dangling from a length of chain. There was no need for the key in her pocket. Had the chain had been cut? She couldn't spare the time to check.

Armies of hemlocks, red cedars, and Douglas firs flashed by in the headlights, occasionally reaching out to rake the speeding vehicle with spiky branches. A bottle-brush of needles whipped through the open window, stinging Sam's neck and shoulder.

The air along the road was still clear, the forest quiet with dappled moonlight. The summer had been typically rainy on the Olympic Peninsula: the vegetation was lush and green. Maybe the fire would fizzle out before they even got there.

The acrid odor grew stronger near the water. Sam skidded to a stop in the tiny gravel parking lot on the east bank of Marmot Lake. Ghostly fingers of smoke glided over the silvery water. A tongue of flame burned orange along the west shore, its reflection bright in the lake surface. The blaze looked reasonably small. Potentially manageable.

Jumping out, Sam ripped open the tailgate of the pickup,

yanked out the fire gear. She extracted one shovel and one Pulaski. She stepped into the heavy firefighting pants, hauled up on the suspenders. Lili frowned at the strange axe-hoe head of the Pulaski, then clasped her fingers around the shovel. Sam squelched her protest—if she couldn't leave Lili in the fire tower, she certainly couldn't leave her in the truck. At least the girl was willing to carry her share of the load. Sam shoved her fireproof jacket into Lili's hands. "Put this on."

The jacket hung down almost to the girl's knees and covered her hands. Sam shrugged on her spare, a medium size that swallowed up her slender frame in a similar fashion. She had no fireproof pants that would even remotely fit the child; her own were so huge the rolled-up cuffs collected more debris than they shed. Thank heavens Lili wore heavy jeans and leather hiking boots, not the popular rubber and foam sneakers that so easily melted.

She knelt in front of Lili, snugged her only helmet onto the child's head. "You've got to do exactly what I tell you."

"Duh," Lili muttered impatiently. "I already promised." Her face gleamed with excitement, but her brown eyes were calm.

Sam hoped her own gaze was as steady. "The radio will be right here in my pocket. If anything happens to me, you grab the radio and run back here, okay?"

The girl dipped her chin in response.

"Do you know how to work the radio?"

Lili rolled her eyes. "Of course."

Sam tucked the radio into her jacket pocket, shouldered the Pulaski, pulled out her flashlight, and started down the trail. Lili's footsteps stayed close behind as they jogged along the root-gnarled path that bordered the small lake. As they neared the west shore, the smoke thickened.

Then the enemy was in sight, and providing enough light that Sam flicked off the flashlight. The fire was larger than she'd hoped. Waves of flames lapped at the thick cushion of duff under the evergreens. Dead twigs on lower limbs burst into sparklers. One isolated cedar was fully engulfed, a fountain of fire that lit up the surrounding forest. The Biblical burning bush rose in her imagination. She snorted at the absurdity.

"Over here, Lili." Sam paralleled the blaze, weaving her way to the far side of the fire between spindly evergreens and ferns nearly as tall as she was. Smoke hung dense and foglike; so far the air remained still. If they could contain the flames to the lakeshore, the conflagration should burn itself out.

She attacked the line of flame at her feet, using the hoe side of the Pulaski to claw loose dirt over burning fir cones and needles. Beside her, Lili coughed as she beat the backside of the shovel against flames at the base of a tree.

"Use the dirt," Sam shouted above the crackle of flames. "Make a bare strip that the fire can't cross. Throw dirt on the flames." She choked on the last word. Puffing, she dragged mounds of duff away from the hungry flames. Beneath the usual forest detritus, the ground was rock-strewn glacial till, requiring teeth-jarring jabs to loosen even a tablespoon of soil.

Lili gamely scooped a shovelful of pebbles and managed to smother the glowing embers at her feet. She stepped forward to tackle a larger bloom of flames.

Sam lunged after her, pulled her back. "Don't worry about anything between here and the lake. Stay beside me. We've got to hold this line, keep the fire from spreading."

Hold the line—the mantra of the firefighting course. Surround the enemy. Confine the conflagration, make it eat everything it has now so it will starve to death later.

Beating back a fire had been much easier during training, back when, right out of college, she'd rehearsed for the ranger job she'd never landed. But that was—jeez, fifteen years ago? Sweat coursed down her neck to join the swamp of perspiration coating her entire body under the heavy fire suit. In what she knew were minutes but seemed like hours, she and Lili managed to beat back only a few yards of flames.

She hated fire. When there was fire, there was nothing

else. The scent of cedar and wildflowers, the melody of
bird calls and tree frogs vanished, leaving only smothering
smoke and blistering heat and the popping and crackling
and hissing of death. And just when you thought you had
finally beaten it into a flat still blackness, fire could spring
to life again like a relentless villain in a horror movie.

The forest behind them was still cool, green, quiet. The
landscape in front cackled and spat like a battalion of
demons. Every smack of the Pulaski radiated pain up
Sam's arms and neck into her skull. Her sinuses burned. A
section of downed limb flared up in front of her, yellow
flames bright against blackened ground. She stabbed her
axe blade into the rotten wood, flung the burning chunk
into the flames a couple of yards away, clearing the zone at
her feet.

The wind was rising; the acrid air licked across her
sweaty brow and stung her eyes. She hazarded a quick
glance at Lili. Tears streaked glistening channels through
black smudges on the girl's face. How long could the child
keep up the hard work? For that matter, how long could she
herself keep it up? Where was the rest of the crew?

To her left, an arrow of fire snaked up the skeleton of a
dead cedar. With a whoosh like a sudden intake of breath, a
limb overhead burst into flames, a Fourth of July sparkler
that showered them with fiery bits of bark and needles.
Sam curled her fingers into Lili's collar and yanked her out
of the rain of embers. Caught off-guard, the girl stumbled
against her. Sam stepped back to recover her footing.

The ground disappeared beneath her boots. What felt
like solid rock slammed first into her spine, and then collided with the back of her skull. Her jaws snapped together.
Her teeth sliced into her lower lip. The Pulaski crashed
down across her thighs. With a great roar, the flame-lit surroundings transitioned into nothingness like the screen
pixels between photos in a computer slide show.

Was that Lili shrieking? The surge of blackness threat-
ened to engulf her. *No! Shake it off, no time to pass out.
Lili's counting on you. Breathe. Now. Just do it. Now.*

With Sam's first painful intake of air, feeling and vision rushed back. The earth beneath her was cool. Far above the chaos of the fire, stars winked through thin streams of smoke. Lower, toward the ground, Lili's smoke-darkened face peered anxiously down at her. And then there were other faces, rangers Paul Schuler and Mack Lindstrom and a gray-haired fellow whose name she couldn't remember. The roar in her head drowned out all other sounds.

A stinging bumblebee of pain registered in front of her left ear, and she raised a hand toward it. Mack's heavy boots thudded onto the ground beside her. He swatted a glowing ember away. As if the burning coal had blocked her ears, her hearing suddenly returned.

Mack's square face blotted out everything else. "You shouldn't move."

Groaning, she pushed herself to a sitting position.

"Okay, so don't listen to me. You okay, Sam?"

"Think so." The air hurt her lip and tongue and the inside of her cheek, where her teeth had torn into the soft flesh. Her mouth filled with bitter liquid. She spat onto the ground. Blood ran down her chin. A quick exploration with her fingertips revealed a gash in her lip and a lump already growing at the base of her skull. Sam sucked in another deep lungful of air, coughed once, then gasped, "Just knocked the breath out of myself."

Taking Mack's extended hand, she pulled herself to her feet. "I'm too old for this shit."

The last words came out "thith thit." She spat again, dug a toe into the dirt, grabbed a root that spiked out of the earth wall overhead, and pulled herself skyward. Mack's hands pressed against her buttocks, a gesture she would ordinarily have protested. Under the circumstances, she was grateful for the boost. On her hands and knees, she crawled out of the crater, feeling like a drunk who had just come to after spending the night on the barroom floor.

A low wolf whistle sounded from behind her, and she glanced over her shoulder to spy a man leaning on his shovel, leering at her, his teeth unnaturally white in his smoke-darkened face. Just her luck, the only firefighter paying attention would be Arnie Cole, a smarmy forest service ranger she'd been trying to avoid since their first meeting over two months ago. A few yards away, Joe Choi, in full fire gear, clasped Lili to his chest. Catching a glimpse of her over Lili's head, he raised a hand and gave Sam a thumbs-up sign. In a line that stretched into the hazy distance, ghostly yellow-and-green-clad figures wielded shovels and Pulaskis. Over the crackling and hissing, she heard the loud whine of the portable pump on the lakeshore. Its racket added a treble note to the pounding in her head.

Mack clambered up beside her, one fist clamped around her Pulaski. She stood on the edge, swaying slightly as she stared into the dark void. The crater was easily fifteen feet across and at least seven feet deep. Why hadn't she noticed it before? "Was that always there?"

Alwayths theah? The three syllables stabbed. Blood streamed down her chin, and sudden tears blurred her vision. She covered her lips with cupped fingers to smother the pain.

"How would I know? This is *your* area." Mack pressed her Pulaski into her hands and reached for the shovel he'd left on the ground.

Ah yes. The fire was destroying her area. Suck it up, Westin. Raising the Pulaski, she stumbled toward the glowing edge. She'd kill it for sure this time. *Vengeanth ith mine*, sayeth the fat-lipped firefighter.

An hour later, the fire was out. Only a few acres lay in smoking gray ruins. Most of the firefighters, including Joe and Lili, had gone home, but the ones who remained divided the devastation among themselves and tromped through it toward the lake, stirring ashes and turning over smoldering chunks of wood to ensure the flames wouldn't spring to life as soon as they departed. Sam was pulverizing a smoldering ember into ashes when Mack yelped from fifty yards away.

"Holy shit!"

It took her a minute to locate him in the moonlight among the skeletons of trees. He was on his knees beside a charred tree trunk. Had he hurt himself? After making sure she had permanently blinded the glowing eye on the ground, she trudged toward him.

Side by side, they stared at the blackened log, still smoking on the forest floor. It was wearing boots.

3

THEY both dug out flashlights to take stock of the situation. The body, dressed in ash-smudged camouflage trousers, khaki shirt, and leather boots, lay mostly in Elk Creek, which was now a slow trickle of sludge. The face was turned into the scorched ferns along the bank, the visible portion a mass of blisters interrupted by a singed eyebrow. Blackened hair was clumped into snarls by congealing blood that flowed from a gaping wound at the back of the head.

Sam's stomach lurched at the odor of charred flesh. Not even an illegal hunter deserved this end. "Is he—"

A dribble of blood slid over her lower lip. She wiped it on her sleeve and pressed her lips together to lessen the flow from the gash her teeth had cut.

Mack pressed his fingers to the victim's neck. After a few seconds, he said, "Can't feel a pulse." He placed his hand in front of the blistered lips, then, after another interval, shook his head. "We're going to need a body bag."

Slipping his fingers under the web belt at the broad waist, he tugged. With an obscene sucking sound, the body broke free of the mud and flopped over onto its back. A hand, its fingers curled, came to rest on the toe of Sam's boot.

The transformation made her gasp. The side of the face that had been pressed to the ground was untouched by fire. An ivory cheek shone through streaks of gray mud. The wisp of hair that hung over the half-moon eyebrow was a warm honey blond. Gold loops threaded both earlobes.

"Holy shit," Mack said again. "It's Lisa Glass."

The name didn't mean anything to Sam. "Who's Lisa Glass?"

"Trail crew," he murmured.

The trail crew, a group of seasonal workers Sam hadn't met, had started work about ten weeks earlier in the north section of the park. The job—clearing existing trails of debris and hacking new paths out of the mountainous terrain—was grueling physical labor, most often performed by teenage delinquents working off community service sentences from juvenile court. It surprised her that this girl had been among them, although judging by her long muscular body, Lisa Glass would be physically able to wield a pickaxe and sledgehammer. Sam regretted not getting to know this tough young woman.

Mack's head jerked up. "She's alive! I just saw her take a breath."

"What?" Sam knelt and gently pushed up an eyelid.

The pupil that stared back at her flashlight beam was an unmoving black well surrounded by ice blue iris. Suddenly the victim's chest moved with a jerky breath

"She's unconscious," Mack confirmed. "And I moved her. Oh God." He wadded his jacket front in a fist his sooty brow creased with anxiety. "I couldn't feel a pulse or breath, I swear."

"It's okay, Mack, I would have done the same. You didn't know she was still alive." Sam brushed a tangle of burned hair away from Lisa's blistered face. A wedge-shaped piece of skin from the girl's cheek peeled away with the strand, and Sam froze, paralyzed by the horrible sight. In Lisa's case, life might not be a blessing.

IT was midmorning by the time Sam arrived at Mack's apartment building. In its first life, the structure had been a rambling farmhouse, as evidenced by its wide covered wooden porch and cedar plank floors. The flower-stenciled front door opened onto a tiny lobby with a sitting area and mailboxes for the three tenants. After stepping into the interior gloom, Sam raised her eyebrows at the unexpected sight of a lanky form sprawled across one of the two chairs.

The man had stretched out his gray-trousered legs and slouched down into the faded brown velvet armchair until he could rest his head atop the back cushion. A lightweight gray sports jacket had hiked up around his shoulders and waist. At least twenty-four hours' worth of beard darkened his square jaw line, lending the olive skin a bluish cast above the neckline of his navy shirt. A loosened gray-and-white tie hung limply around his neck like a broken leash. His eyes were closed.

As she approached on tiptoe, the hand that had been lying relaxed on his thigh slipped back beneath the jacket. One eye opened a crack, revealing a deep brown iris and alert pupil.

She held up both hands. "Don't shoot."

His fingers slid away from the holster at the back of his belt out onto his thigh. "Sorry." He pushed himself into a more upright position. "Reflex action."

Special Agent Starchaser J. Perez rose and wrapped his arms around her. She tilted her face up. Their lips met briefly, a not-unpleasant pressure on her lidocaine-numbed mouth. He tasted like coffee. Suddenly she craved an espresso from Mack's stovetop maker. "Come with me." She motioned toward the stairs.

"Blake told me I could find you at this address. What gives? Last time we met, you were a writer."

Sam grimaced. "Try to keep up, will you, FBI? The life of a freelancer is hectic. When we met, I was writing for the Save the Wilderness Fund. Then I had a weekly gig writing articles about hiking and outdoor equipment for an e-zine called *The Edge*, but a few months back they decided there's not enough money in GORE-TEX jackets and hiking socks. In an attempt to fool us into believing that the economy's recovering, they've switched from rugged individualists conquering the great outdoors to beautiful people conquering luxury spas. Now they're selling designer yoga wear."

The last three words were especially difficult to enunciate, but her mangled mouth must have worked better than she thought, because Chase said only, "Really?"

"Really. So, courtesy of the park service, I'm a biologist again. A big area of national forest land is being added to Olympic National Park to create a protected continuous wildlife corridor from the mountains to the coast. They hired me to do an environmental survey and management plan for the new area. It's only a twelve-week contract, unfortunately, and I'm already more than two-thirds of the way through it." She dreaded the end of her contract. She had always wanted to be a park ranger, but her timing had never been right. After college, she was too short and too female; now the NPS budgets were too small.

"You're living in this . . . place?" She could tell that he really wanted to say *dump*.

"It belongs to my friend Mack. We shared a cubicle during my online encyclopedia days at Key Inc."

Chase raised an eyebrow.

"Another job I had before we met," she explained. "Mack was botany; I was zoology." Post-lidocaine talking was definitely easier than her pre-lidocaine efforts, although she still slurred the plosives. "We commiserated about seeing plants and animals only on computers. Then he up and abandoned hi-tech for Olympic National Park. He lets me crash here once in a while."

"You outdoor adventure types do like to sleep around." His steps echoed on the wooden treads behind her.

"What about you?" she asked. "Why are you here?"

"I just happened to be in the vicinity."

"Chase, there's *nobody* in this vicinity except hunters and fishers and hikers. I figured you were hot on the trail of those robbers in Salt Lake. The armored car bandits?" She'd seen the story on the news two weeks ago. Or was it three? Four?

"I was. I am. The trail led to Boise, and now it looks like the perps have moved to Washington State. We've been chasing these guys across three, no, four states for months. Now they're taking on banks, too."

Sounded like a major crime spree. "How are they getting away with it?"

"There's always a distraction for the local police at the same time. We're beginning to think it's a huge group, not just a few individuals. It's become a road show." He sighed wearily. "On a tip, we staked out a First Interstate in Olympia through the wee hours, but nothing happened."

That explained the whiskers. The "we" reminded Sam of Chase's partner. "Where's Nicole?" she asked.

"Some fancy resort in the San Juan Islands. Hubby picked her up in his private plane for a romantic weekend."

The plane reference made her think about Lili's school friend. Just how many people had their own planes, anyway? Was she living that far out of the mainstream?

She unlocked the door, pushed it open into the foyer off Mack's compact kitchen. Although a pair of blue jeans dangled from a chair, she was relieved to see that no jockey shorts or balled-up socks littered the front room this time.

Opening the freezer door, she rummaged for the bag of coffee. She poured the last of the dark-roasted beans into the grinder and pressed the button.

Perez put his hands on the countertop, leaning close to be heard over the racket. His lips tickled her ear. "I was hoping for a romantic weekend myself." His tone promised steamy embraces. He inhaled deeply. Wrinkling his nose, he drew back.

She released the grinder button, grinning. "I know. Smoke. Singed hair. Sweat. I even find myself disgusting. I wondered why you didn't comment on my appearance."

He blinked. "Why? Have you done something different?"

"As well as ruining my coiffure"—she patted a few sticky strands for effect—"I banged my head and cut my tongue and lip. I'm surprised I can talk at all." She balled up the empty coffee bag and aimed it at his nose.

He easily caught the bag and crumpled it into a smaller sphere. "I thought you were trying to seduce me with a sexy lisp." His last two words came out "thexy lithp."

So much for sympathy. She placed the double pot on the burner and turned up the heat. "Watch that, will you? When it stops hissing, it's done. I'm off to the shower."

He smiled. "I'll join you."

"Not this time, FBI."

She closed the bathroom door behind her. Her relationship with Chase Perez consisted of a kidnapping drama they'd floundered through in Utah, and a handful of encounters here in Washington State when he was passing through. They'd dated off and on for nearly ten months, but hadn't yet progressed to mutual nakedness. Something always prevented the time from being right. Like now; filthy, thick-lipped, and headachy, she felt far from sexy.

She pressed her face into the shower spray, wincing as the water glanced off her blistered cheek. With a liberal application of almond soap, her greasy coating of perspiration and smoke disappeared down the drain in a dark swirl.

"So tell me about your bad hair day." Chase's voice came from the other side of the shower curtain, in the direction of the vanity. He probably had his handsome backside perched on the beige Formica.

She gingerly rubbed shampoo over the sore spot at the back of her head, enjoying the vanilla scent. No wonder Mack smelled like a candy bar.

"It was night, not day," she told him. "You would have loved it. Just your kind of thing." Her lower lip still felt like a block of wood. She hoped she wouldn't dribble her coffee.

"Murder? Mayhem? High-powered shoot-out?"

"Definitely mayhem. Some firebugs lit a couple blazes. While we were putting out the flames, we found a body." She shivered, remembering Lisa facedown in the ashes.

"How old?"

How old was Lisa Glass? No. He was asking how recently the victim had died. "This body was still alive. Barely. A girl from the trail crew. Head injury, smoke inhalation. Second- and third-degree burns." Sam raised a hand to her own face and was reassured to find the skin was for the most part still smooth and intact, except for that dang blister on her temple. She turned off the shower and squeezed the excess water from her long rope of silver-blond hair.

"So, what's the story?"

"The espresso's done, Chase. Go take it off the burner." She raised her hand to the shower curtain. "I'm coming out now."

Silence.

"Get out of here!"

"Spoilsport," he mumbled. She heard the soft thud of the door closing.

When she emerged into the kitchen, he had poured the espresso into decorated mugs, a great white shark for him and a wolf howling at the moon for her. To hers, he added a small dash of milk, just the way she liked it. He'd only seen her prepare coffee once, but his mind recorded every detail. A remarkable talent. Her thoughts constantly strayed away from the here and now like dogs that wouldn't stay on the porch.

His gaze traveled from the new Band-Aid on her temple down her uniform to the thick hiking socks on her feet. "You keep clothes here? You've moved in with Mack?"

She raised an eyebrow at his tone. "Why not? He's a good-looking guy and—"

"At least a decade your junior."

"Watch it," she hissed. "That gap is a piddly eight years." She finished French-braiding her hair, secured the end with an elastic band. "Actually"—she dropped her voice to a stage whisper—"it's not Mack I've got the hots for. It's his couch."

The sagging, stained brown futon clearly dated from Mack's college days. Chase looked at her, tried to keep a straight face but failed, and they burst into laughter simultaneously. She pressed her fingers over her lips to quell the resulting pain, then bent her aching head and struggled to pin her park service ID onto the khaki shirt.

"Uh-oh," he groaned, coming over to help. "You're still on duty? I assumed that after fighting fires all night, you'd get the rest of the day off."

"That's because you feebs are pansy-asses. We outdoor adventure types don't need rest breaks." She couldn't stop a wistful sigh at the thought of lounging around with Chase. A strand of inky hair slipped onto his forehead as he fastened her pin. She had the urge to caress it back into place, but was afraid of starting something she didn't have the energy to finish. "I have to go back; the usual fire lookout's off on emergency leave. There's nobody else to fill in. Besides arson, there are other hinky things going on."

"Kinky things?" He raised an eyebrow. "Then I better come for sure."

"Hinky things. Strange, weird things."

"Well, kinky or hinky, sounds like you could use a trained special agent at that fire lookout." When she didn't protest, he grinned. "It'll be like old times—getting in trouble together in the wilderness."

SHE fired up the truck.

"Four U.S. troops were killed when a roadside bomb detonated near Kabul," the radio informed them. Sam quickly turned off the NPR news station she normally listened to, not wanting the latest grim details from the Middle East to intrude on her time with Chase. She didn't like to think about the billions of dollars that had drained into that sinkhole instead of flowing into wildlife conservation or education or health care or anything worthwhile. She hoped those four soldiers had not died in vain.

As she drove from Forks to the new section of the park, Chase questioned her about the fire and the discovery of Lisa Glass.

"No chance of identifying the vehicles, I suppose?" he asked.

"I was five miles away; it was night." Her mouth seemed to be working fine, but now that the lidocaine was wearing off, she could feel the ragged bite marks on her tongue and the insides of her cheeks. "At least six vehicles have driven up and down that road since the firebugs took off, so there's virtually no chance of identifying tire tracks."

She stole a quick glance sideways. He'd changed into jeans, boots, and flannel shirt. The informal clothes made him look less intimidating, less hard-edged. Was his gun in the pack he'd brought or in the pocket of his jacket in the backseat?

"How did the fire first get your attention?"

She slapped a hand against the steering wheel. "I completely forgot about the explosion!"

He perked up. "Explosion?"

"A big bang."

"The creation of the universe?"

She groaned at his humor. "It seemed earth-shaking at the time. And then came the fire."

He considered for a second. "Could it have been a Molotov cocktail?"

She wasn't even sure what a Molotov cocktail was. "They explode?"

He shrugged. "Frequently."

"Then it might have been that. Or maybe a firecracker. It sounded powerful." A suspicion flashed through her thoughts. How could she have forgotten? "Raider!" She gripped the wheel with both hands and applied her foot more forcefully to the gas pedal.

Chase braced a hand against the dashboard. "What?"

She hit a chuckhole head on. They bounced hard, but she didn't slow down. "It could have been a high-powered rifle. The bastards might have been after my bear."

4

IN daylight, the burned area seemed small and pathetic, totally lacking the menacing majesty of a blaze under a full moon. The tops of many blackened trees were still green, but their scorched trunks were sad skeletons. Birds flitted among the naked branches, exploring the new spaciousness of their forest. Sam watched a red-shafted flicker skitter up a ruined pine, its rust-colored feathers bright against the charcoal bark. The bird stopped and cocked its head, displaying a red blaze beneath its bill that marked it as a male. It let out a shriek, then hammered a violent staccato tune on the blackened trunk. A black-and-white hairy woodpecker landed just above the flicker. A noisy squabble ensued as the flicker defended his hunting ground.

"Poor things," Sam murmured. "I hope they nested outside the burn zone."

Chase gave her a look that told her his thoughts were not stuck on birds. Hers should probably be on other issues, too, like arson and unconscious girls. And bears. After a night of no sleep, she wasn't processing too well. At the edge of the burn line, she paused to run her fingers over a patch of missing bark on a Western cedar.

"Looking for woodpecker holes?"

She shook her head, and instantly regretted the motion. Pain sloshed over her, leaving nausea in its wake. Maybe she did have that concussion, after all. "I'm looking for fresh bear marks. We moved Raider here a week ago."

He raised an eyebrow. "Raider?"

"A two-year-old black bear, most often seen on top of picnic tables or butt-side-up in garbage cans. Usually with an audience of screaming campers. He has a white scar on the back of one ear."

"If you say so." He pulled her around so she faced him.

"This is prime bear habitat," she continued. "We hoped he would find female bears more fascinating than picnic leftovers." She rubbed a spot on her cheek, remembering the struggle to get the bear into the cage. Would Chase think it was too weird if she told him it had been fun?

He drew the tip of his index finger across the faint pink line left from one of Raider's claws. A pleasant ticklish sensation quickly spread to more sensitive areas of her body. How much would it hurt her mouth to French-kiss this FBI agent?

"My wild woman," he murmured. "You still haven't learned to give the beasts enough tranquilizer? I'll never forget having to sit on your mountain lion last year."

My wild woman? Why did men always have to *own* women? Why couldn't Chase be different from the typical possessive male? "Tranquilizing wildlife is not an exact science. I'd rather end up with a few claw marks than a dead animal." The words came out with more frost than she'd planned.

His eyes clouded and his hand dropped back to his side. *Great.* Now she'd hurt his feelings. She definitely needed more practice with this man-woman-relationship dynamic. She still felt like a sap for the way that her previous boyfriend, newscaster Adam Steele, had used her to further his own career. Now she worried that she would misread Chase Perez, too. It was hard to figure out where their relationship was going when they met only a few times a year.

Feeling uncomfortable now, she turned to survey the blackened woods. Joe and another ranger were out here somewhere; there had been two NPS trucks in the parking lot.

Thankfully, Chase changed the subject back to wildlife. "Black bears aren't endangered, are they?"

"Not yet." Give the human race enough time, she thought grimly, and all wild animals will be endangered.

"Is it bear season now?"

"No." But now that she thought about it, the season on the Olympic Coast was only a week away. Oh, goody. More armed men in the woods. Something to look forward to. "Poachers work all year round," she told him.

He nodded. "The gall bladder business still going strong?"

"Yep. The Chinese still make medicines out of them, still pay big bucks for them." She made a face. "Bear paws, too—rich Asians eat them on special occasions, like wedding banquets." It was too easy to envision Raider sliced and diced. A horrible thought. She almost shook her head again, but caught herself just in time.

"There will be no bear hunting here. This is *my* area," she said.

He looked surprised.

"Well, it's my area right now," she explained. "Wildlife is protected in the national park. That's one of the reasons we barricaded the road, so I could do my survey, and to have a transition period, to let the regular national forest users know that this area is now off-limits to hunters and off-road vehicles and such."

"That must piss them off."

"Got that right. It doesn't stop all of them, either." She told him about the armed intruder she'd encountered.

He frowned. "Sounds like that hunting guide in Utah— the one we investigated after your friend Kent was shot? Ferguson, wasn't it?"

"Buck Ferguson." Even saying his name raised her blood pressure. She had glued his photo to a dart board in her home office. "There are plenty of guys like him around here, too. You've heard of the spotted owl controversy in the eighties?"

"Sure. Endangered species regulations shut down local commerce—that's not unique to the Pacific Northwest."

"The logging community over here was particularly

enraged. A tavern in Forks used to host a spotted owl bar-beque every Friday night."

"Sounds hostile."

"It was chicken, of course." She sighed. "Very few people have seen an actual spotted owl." She still hoped to catch a glimpse of one.

He frowned. "Watch your back, Summer."

"It's not so bad now. Forks mostly depends on tourism these days, not logging."

"I hear there are vampires in the area," he said.

She laughed. "Werewolves, too. Serving as the setting for the Twilight Series was the biggest thing to hit Forks in decades." She moved on down the trail. "Keep an eye out for anything that might be a bear carcass."

"Yuck."

Hardly the response she would have expected from a man who had examined dozens of human corpses. She approached the edge of the burn. Yes, there was the crater, dropping away in front of her toes. Before the fire, she'd walked through this area a dozen times. There might have been a slight depression in that spot, but she was positive the crater hadn't been there before the fire.

Chase balanced beside her on the edge. "Is this the hole you fell into?"

"Uh-huh." It was embarrassing to think about it. She had a bruise on her hip that exactly matched that knob of protruding black rock on the bottom. As she rubbed the injured area, her lower lip began to throb in sympathy. She turned away, pulled a tiny bottle out of her pants pocket, and pumped anesthetic spray into her mouth, working it around with her tongue. The initial sting brought tears to her eyes, but the pain was followed by a welcome dullness.

"What is this pit, anyway?" Stepping down from the rim, Chase slid into the hole, dislodging a large rock that rolled away from beneath his boots. He hopped agilely over the avalanche he'd created and came to rest at the bottom of the crater. A fog of fine ash swirled up in her direction, and she sneezed painfully.

"This is a frame of some kind." His personal rockslide had collapsed one side of the pit, revealing thick blocks of wood wedged into the dirt. He knelt to examine two pieces of lumber joined with a thick spike.

Sam clambered down to join him. They clawed and kicked dirt away until a ragged opening about three feet high was revealed. The sides and ceiling of a rough tunnel were supported by insubstantial-looking lengths of weathered gray wood.

Chase said, "Looks like an old mine shaft."

"Damn," she said. She pulled a kerchief from a pants pocket and wiped her hands on it.

Chase was staring at her, waiting for her to continue.

"Used to be that almost any yahoo could stake a mining claim on National Forest land," she explained. "But I'm not sure what the rules are now, and I'm not sure which side of the line this mine shaft falls on."

She held the kerchief out to him. He spread the kerchief between his fingers. Finding a clean spot on the cloth, he scrubbed at his hands.

Every few years someone in the American Congress brought up the idea of reforming the Mining Law of 1872, but as far as she knew, only a few minor amendments had been passed.

She'd have to research this old claim and deal with it somehow in her management plan. With the price of minerals these days, some entrepreneur might try to blast it open over and over again. Could she hide the mine? She rubbed her hand across her aching stomach, which seemed to be suddenly awash in acid. First, illegal hunters; now, a mine.

"You mucking up our scene?"

Looking bleary-eyed under his gray-green NPS cap, Joe Choi stood on the crater rim, a clunky Polaroid camera slung around his neck. Beside him stood another ranger with a neatly trimmed goatee, one latex-gloved hand resting on his service pistol and the other holding a small wooden sign by its stake.

Sam wasn't sure whether Joe was kidding or not; he knew that she had no real authority to be digging around here. She and Chase climbed out of the crater. Joe introduced Norm Tyburn, the other law enforcement ranger; Sam introduced Chase.

Joe glanced at Tyburn. "Management called the FBI?"

"Chase is a friend," Sam explained, wanting to head off any weenie-wagging between macho cops.

Chase shot her an indecipherable look and then said, "I'm out of the Salt Lake office, up here investigating a string of robberies around the area. I found out Summer was in the area and stopped by to say hello."

Trying to be surreptitious, Joe waggled his eyebrows suggestively at Sam.

Ignoring him, Sam pointed into the crater. "It's an old mine, guys."

"Uh-oh," both rangers said simultaneously.

Then Tyburn said, "It just gets better and better. Check this out. We found it out by the road." He held up the plywood sign in his hand. Blue stenciled letters had been spray-painted across the plywood surface.

THIS IS YOUR LAND
WELCOME ATV'S & HUNTER'S

"Not another one," Sam groaned. "I've pulled down a dozen from all around the perimeter of the transferred section. But they keep reappearing."

"That's defacing federal property," Joe said.

Sam pointed a finger at the sign. "It's defacing the English language, too—the nincompoops don't even know the difference between plurals and possessives."

All three men stared at her as though she'd suddenly sprouted a horn in the middle of her forehead. Maybe this was not the time for a grammar discussion.

Tyburn finally cleared his throat. "You should have told someone about these signs. What did you do with them?"

"Superintendent Carsen told me to store them in the district HQ building," she told him, answering both questions. Just because she was working on her own out here didn't mean she was some kind of loose cannon.

Tyburn stroked his goatee and tapped the sign on his leg for a second, then murmured, "Well, all righty then."

All righty then. She asked, "Did you two see any signs of illegal hunting around here?"

Joe looked surprised. "No. You reported an explosion and then the fire."

"The explosion could have been a rifle shot," she explained.

From his right jacket pocket, Tyburn produced a ziplock bag full of spent cartridges. "Plenty of rifles have been fired around here. But wait!" He changed his inflection to sound like a television huckster as he pulled another plastic bag of debris from his left pocket. "We also have fireworks of all types and sizes!"

"And we have definite signs of arson," Joe added. "Smells like kerosene."

"Containers?" Chase asked.

Joe rubbed his eyes. "No such luck."

"Think the injured girl was involved?"

"Hard to say," Tyburn responded. "Looks like she was kayoed by a falling branch during the fire. We've got the likely culprit in the truck; weighs a good twenty pounds."

Joe yawned. "Technically, even though this area is off-limits to the public, Lisa Glass wasn't trespassing because she's a park employee. And she was off-duty, so nobody was keeping track of her whereabouts. But she didn't come alone, because she left no car behind. The trail crew dormitory is way over by the hot springs, a good fifteen miles from here as the crow flies, and a lot more by road." He yawned again. "I suppose we won't know anything more until she comes out of her coma."

Sam raised a hand to massage her aching temple. "*If* she comes out of her coma. That poor girl—" She accidentally brushed her fingers across her blister and ended the sentence with an involuntary yelp.

Chase's dark eyes filled with concern. Joe asked, "You all right, Sam?"

"I'm okay," she reassured everyone.

Radios crackled to life on Sam's, Joe's, and Tyburn's belts. "Five-nine-two. This is three-one-one."

Tyburn pulled his radio from its holder. "Five-nine-two, three-one-one. What's up?"

"Vandalized vehicle, west side campground. Site twelve."

Tyburn groaned. "Roger that, west side campground, site twelve. I'm on my way. Five-nine-two, out." He shoved his radio back onto his belt. To Joe, he said, "I'll check the campground registrations, ask around to see if any of the campers saw anyone leave or return in our time frame. Then I'll grab Koch and we'll hit the other campgrounds in the area and the houses on the periphery of 5214. Oh, and someone needs to interview the trail crew. They're up north breaking rocks, six miles in on the Rain Mountain trail."

Joe groaned. "Think it can wait till they come in tonight? I'm not up for a hike."

"Blackstock rides herd on them pretty close, so that ought to be okay. They usually get back to the bunkhouse around five."

"I'll be waiting for them," Joe said. "Probably asleep in my truck."

"Sounds like a plan. Later, alligators." With a wave of his hand, Tyburn turned and headed in the direction of the parking lot.

"How's Lili?" Sam asked Joe.

He rolled his eyes. "The fire is the most exciting thing that's happened to her, ever. She's got plastic wrap around a lock of singed hair so she can save it to show off at school on Monday."

"She's going to talk about it at school?" Sam asked, horrified. That's all she needed, for the whole town to know she'd taken a child to a forest fire.

"Not if I have anything to say about it," Joe assured her.

"But it's not like she listens to me these days. She'll probably start a trend of local teenagers setting fires so they can
be heroes when they put them out."

She stared at him. "You're kidding, right?"

"I hope so." He checked his watch, and then yawned
again, this time so widely that he displayed several gold-
crowned molars. "I've been on overtime for more than ten
hours. I'm going home now, grab a few hours of shut-eye
before I catch up with the trail crew."

"Mind if we look around some more?" Chase asked.

Joe had already turned to leave. "Knock yourself out,"
he said over his shoulder. "If you find anything of interest,
you know what to do."

"Roger that," Chase responded to his retreating figure.
Turning to Sam, he said, "Where was Lisa found?"

"I'll show you."

A strip of startlingly green grass marked the area where
Lisa's body had shielded the ground from the fire. Surrounding the green strip, the soil was smudged with footprints and
indentations where their knees had rested in the mud.

"Her head was at this end." Sam pointed. "The rest of
her was in Elk Creek here." It made her a little queasy to
think about how she and Mack had manhandled the
charred corpse before they realized it was a living woman.

She spotted a partial paw print on the creek bank.
Impressions from two long toes, possible claw dents at the
end. It could have belonged to a black bear, and she couldn't
help thinking of Raider. The print was overlaid by a heavy
boot tread. Impossible to tell when it had been made.

Chase paced a spiral out from the area, examining the
ground as he walked. At one point he stopped, knelt down.

Sam hastened to join him. "Find something?"

"They missed one." He pulled a pen from his shirt
pocket and used it to pick up a brass tube lying in the dirt.
The metal was blackened, but the bullet casing was easily
recognizable. "Looks like a three-oh-eight."

Sam's mind leapt back to the illegal hunter she'd
encountered. "Powerful enough to bring down a bear?"

"Yes." Chase spiraled the pen, watched the casing twirl. "Blow a hell of a hole through a man, too. Or a woman."

Sam's thoughts had been on guns and bears. She hadn't yet considered guns aimed at humans. "Lisa wasn't shot."

"But she wasn't alone. Maybe she was running from someone."

Horrible thought. But maybe he was right; maybe Lisa had stumbled across criminal activity. Like bear poaching. Or someone dynamiting an old mine.

After a short blast of static, her radio announced, "Three-two-five, this is three-niner-niner. Come in, three-two-five."

She unclipped the instrument and held it to her lips. "Three-two-five."

"Where are you? They told me you were en route over an hour ago. I'm due at Hurricane Ridge in fifty minutes. Over." The voice sounded annoyed.

With a pang of guilt, Sam pictured Ranger Glen Crowder's sun-lined face peering out the lookout window. "I'm at Marmot Lake, three-nine-nine. Just wanted to make sure no hot spots had flared up," she lied. "I'll be there in ten. Three-two-five, out." She shoved the radio back into its holster on her belt.

Chase raised an eyebrow. "Checking for hot spots?"

"See any smoke anywhere?"

"No."

"So, we checked. And we'll come back later, or someone else will. I think the park service even has fire investigators now. Unless the budget deficit's erased those positions, too."

He wrapped the bullet casing in his handkerchief and handed it to her. "Have a ranger hold this in case you need it for prints. You never know how things are going to play out."

Sam pocketed the tiny bundle. She hoped the casing was from a long-ago legal hunter, and that Lisa was going to wake up and tell them exactly what had happened. But it couldn't be good.

5

AT the base of the lookout, Sam parked the truck in the shadow of a huge boulder, a few yards away from Crowder's pickup. She turned off the ignition and put a hand on Chase's arm. "Could you hide in the woods for a couple of minutes?"

"Ah, subterfuge. My specialty." He silently opened the door and melted into the shadows of the forest.

Shouldering her daypack, Sam trudged up the rise. She hadn't reached the foot of the lookout's ladder when Glen Crowder leaped down the last few rungs. He landed with a thump before her, a scowl darkening his face.

"Sorry I'm late," she said.

He snugged his cap lower on his brow. "Sure." He trotted toward the parking area.

After she heard the gravel thrown by his departing pickup, Sam returned to her truck. Chase stood by the open rear door, a knapsack slung from one shoulder, a sleeping bag tucked under an elbow. "I take it I'm not here."

"You dropped by, but then you had to leave." She picked up the sack of groceries they'd brought. "I'm already going to be in hot water for taking a kid to a fire scene; I'm certainly not going to admit to mixing my love life with the job."

His grin was broad. "Love life. I like the sound of that."

THEY spent the rest of the afternoon in the fire tower, catching up on what they'd been doing since they last saw each other. Sam couldn't help feeling that her tales of flora and fauna surveys didn't quite measure up to tracking scam artists and armed robbers. She struggled to think of something that might sound interesting.

"The Save the Wilderness Fund invited me to a photo shoot in India."

"That's great!" he said. "When are you going?"

She wrinkled her brow. "It's in December, but I don't know *if* I'm going. They purchased some of my cougar photos from last fall for their website."

"Congratulations!"

"The money wasn't much." She'd already ruled out professional photography as her next career.

"You shouldn't measure success by filthy lucre alone. India would be an adventure. I think you should go."

Easy for him to say. He had a decent job to come back to. SWF hadn't mentioned travel expenses, which could easily amount to a couple grand. Why couldn't she ever land a long-term job like a normal woman? A job with health care benefits. Paid holidays. Vacations. Unemployment pay if she got laid off. Her job history was a patchwork quilt of odd assignments that didn't add up to a career by anyone's measurements. She closed her eyes, raised her face to the setting sun, and said a silent prayer for inner tranquility. And for a bottle of aspirin. Her head was starting to ache.

By suppertime, her head and lip throbbed like the base beat of a rock song. The anesthetic spray had long ago been used up. She momentarily envied Lisa's unconscious state, then cursed herself for such a horrible thought. Silently, she watched Chase mix stewed tomatoes, mushrooms, onions, and spices on the ancient Coleman two-burner on top of the lookout desk. Her stomach churned; she couldn't decide if she was starving or too nauseous to swallow a bite. But she knew he loved to cook, and she certainly wanted to encourage that.

"That spaghetti sauce smells good."

"Liar." He stopped stirring to study her face. "You look a little green. Didn't the doc give you any pain pills?"

"Yeah, but I've got to take them with food."

"And you will." He uncorked the Chianti they'd brought and poured her a third of a glass. "But in the meantime, this might help."

She eagerly reached for the wine. "Couldn't hurt." Well, it did, but the sting on the inside of her mouth was only temporary. She held her glass out for more.

He hesitated. "You promise not to drive or operate heavy machinery?"

She crossed her heart dramatically and then put her hands together in a begging gesture.

He handed her a full glass. "And you're not going down that ladder alone, either."

"You can carry me," she told him, taking a sip. "All sixty-two steps."

Sitting cross-legged on the balcony with plates in their laps, through the railings they watched the western horizon transition from gold to orange to crimson. The pain pills made Sam feel light-headed. It seemed vaguely wrong to bask in the glory of sunset when she knew that Lisa Glass was fighting for her life in the hospital, but Sam couldn't tamp down the rainbow cotton filling her brain enough to make room for guilt or sadness.

The sky darkened to a deep purple. An occasional breeze fluttered the wisps of hair on her forehead, but the air rising from the forest below was still warm and gentle. Chase's pasta was surprisingly delicious. Years ago she'd grown sick of her own cooking. Noncooking was more like it; at home she usually left food chores up to her housemate Blake. Nice to have someone make dinner for her again.

If only Chase lived closer, they could do this more often. She'd be thrilled to have a handsome Latino-Lakota FBI agent in her kitchen. And in her bedroom, too. Or in his. *Oh yeah.* She couldn't wait to see every muscular inch of his lean body. She should find a way to tell him that. A romantic way. But she was fading fast. She was grateful for the rough cedar plank wall supporting her back; otherwise she might have fallen over.

With a flutter of blue feathers, a Steller's jay thumped down onto the railing. The bird hopped toward them, chirping its bright *"chek-chek-chek-chek."* Chase tossed a bit of bread over the railing. The jay shrieked and snapped, just missed the morsel as it sailed by, and then leapt off the railing in swift pursuit.

"Wouldn't you like to be a bird?" She turned to him, smiling. "Hop off into space, knowing you'd be fine when you land on the ground a hundred feet below?"

He leaned toward her, took the plate out of her hands, and stacked it on top of his on the deck. "If you're thinking of hopping off into space, you're either feeling worse or a whole lot better."

"Much better. Oh, yeah."

His laugh told her that she sounded as fuzzy as she felt. She sat forward and reached for the balcony railing. "I've got to do the logbook." While she was still conscious. "You don't see any fires, do you?"

He pulled her back down onto the deck, positioned his long legs on either side of her. "In a minute," he murmured into her ear. He smelled so nice. A little wood smoke, a faint trace of citrus aftershave, a little perspiration—so manly. His fingers kneaded the stiff muscles of her neck, gently but firmly worked outward to her sore shoulders.

"Chase, did I ever tell you"—she wanted to purr like a cat—"that I think you're *fine*."

She leaned back against his chest and closed her eyes.

THE Rushing Springs Roadhouse was cool and dark, the way Ernest Craig thought bars should be. The varnish of the oak counter was worn away in spots, but the surface was clean. The Roadhouse was nice and quiet, too, with only the TV news turned down low and the clink of pool balls on the table near the back. He hated those watering holes where you had to shout over the music just to say hi to your neighbor. Besides, it was the only place in walking distance and the battery in his old station wagon was deader than the mouse in the trap under his kitchen sink.

Other than the two pool players, there were only a couple of fellas in the place, sitting at the bar. He took the stool next to the one who had gray-streaked hair like his. With his mustache, pockmarked face, and baseball cap, the guy seemed more approachable than the younger man in sports coat and tie. He wouldn't know what to say to a yuppie. Ernest hitched his bad leg up on the chrome foot rail with a grunt.

"How you doing, Ernest?" The bartender was a skinny grizzled guy, name of—Rob, was that it? No, that wasn't quite right. In the light of the bar, his skin looked gray. Ernest sometimes wondered if the man looked any healthier in daylight, but he'd never seen him outside of the place.

"The usual." He couldn't wait through chitchat for the whiskey. The pain in his leg was like a hot knife. When the bartender brought the glass, Ernest tossed it back like a college kid on a bet. "'Nother."

The bartender fixed his sad eyes on him. He resembled a basset hound Ernest once had. The guy's name suddenly came to him. "No worries, Bob," he said. "I got the dough."

When the next whiskey came, he sipped it slowly, savoring every drop. His leg was already feeling a little better, so now he focused on the reason he'd come here. "Tell you the truth, Bob, I ain't doin' too good today. I'm lookin' for my daughter. You seen her round here?"

Bob pushed a rag up into a newly washed shot glass, wiping off water spots. "Allie? She doesn't come in here, Ernest. You know that. Is she missing?"

"Seems like it. I'm worried about her. She's got herself a good job with a landscaping company over in Seattle during the week, makes real good money." She was so happy to finally find a job that paid more than minimum wage. It was Allie's money that paid for most of the whiskeys, too, but that was nobody's business. "Stays over there durin' the week, but she always comes home on Friday nights, spends the weekend with her ol' man. 'Cept this morning, when I got up, I seen her bed ain't been slept in. I asked down at the grocery and at the Quik Stop, but they ain't seen her."

Bob put the glass on a tray and wiped down another. "Does she have a boyfriend?"

Ernest snorted. "If you could call him that. Owns that little woodworking place next to the highway." He ran a hand through his wavy hair, which was an odd length now. He'd have to take himself in for a cut or band it back in a ponytail soon.

Having polished the shot glasses, Bob pulled open a cabinet door and slid the tray onto a shelf and said, "Well, there you have it."

"Have what?" He wished the man would stop fussing around and just talk to him.

"She probably spent the night with her boyfriend."

Ernest groaned. "No. Allie's not like that. She's a good girl. I brought her up right. 'Sides, I saw Jack—that's the kid's name, Jack Winner. But let me tell you, he's not. A winner, that is. His business is barely getting by. Allie could do better. She's a smart one, a lot faster than her ol' man."

He shook his head, thinking about her. "She should be in college, but we ain't got the money just right now. You know how things are these days. They got scholarships for country club kids and minorities and all kinds of gimps, too, but not a cent for us hardworkin' folks."

He stared sadly into his nearly empty glass. He was getting way off the subject. It was just that he hadn't had anyone to talk to all week. "Anyhow, Jack said that he ain't seen her, either, not since last weekend."

Bob shrugged. "She's what—twenty?"

"Just turned twenty-one."

"Aha. Legal drinking age. She probably decided to spend Friday night celebrating with friends and forgot to tell you. I'm sure she'll be home tonight."

One of the pool players whistled from the back of the

room. Bob flipped up a section of the counter to let himself
out and went to check on them.

Ernest glanced out of the corner of his eye at the heavyset man beside him. The man's eyes were on the news on
the television screen. The sound was muted, but Bob had the
captions turned on. "Fallen Heroes," it said at the top of
the screen over a photo of a black woman in uniform. What
a waste they'd been, those stupid wars in Iraq and Afghanistan. That was the government for you, repeating the same
stupid mistakes over and over again. And now girl soldiers
were getting killed along with the men. But at least this
time nobody was spitting on soldiers when they came back.
This time, nobody much seemed to care one way or the
other what was going on over there.

He thought about saying something about the war to the
man on the next bar stool. Touchy subject, though. If he
said the wrong thing, the guy might get riled up. He shot
another glance at him. The stranger wore a black baseball
cap with HAWKEYE TOURS stitched across it in fancy silver
letters.

"You with a tour group?" Ernest asked.

"Nope," the man answered, pulling his gaze off the TV
to look at Ernest, "I'm trying to start my own business up
in Forks; doing hunting, fishing trips, stuff like that, in the
forest around the park." He took a sip of his beer. "You
know Olympic National Park?"

"Of course. It's all around here." Ernest had driven Allie
all over the whole place years ago, right after they'd come
up here to live in his brother-in-law's backyard, when she
was just a little girl. It wasn't like just one park. The parts
weren't even all connected. There was the Hoh Rain Forest
down south, and the Olympic Mountains over to the east;
roaring rivers everywhere, and to the west, ocean beaches
with driftwood logs bigger than any trees you saw standing
upright these days. He hadn't been to any part for years,
though, except for where Highway 101 passed through.
After Allie showed up, maybe tomorrow they'd go for a
drive to someplace pretty. That'd make a nice change.

Where was she? Maybe she had to work overtime. Maybe there was a message from her on the answering machine waiting for him right now.

The man held out a business card. "Name's Garrett Ford; you know anyone who needs a hunting or fishing guide, send them to me, okay?" He shook hands with Ernest, then turned back to the TV. Abruptly, he tensed up and slapped a hand on the counter. "Goddamn it!"

Ernest jerked his gaze to the set. On the screen he saw a silver-blond woman with a scrape on her face and a little boy in her arms. Then the picture changed to show the same woman, this time sitting on the ground with what looked like a dead cougar in her lap. The words at the bottom of the screen said something about a conference in Seattle, which didn't seem to have anything to do with the pictures. Ernest had a hard time tracking the story, but he didn't see what had made Ford so angry. "You know her?"

"She's one of those so-called environmentalists that's out to ruin my business!" the man snapped. "Her and the rest of the goddamned feds! First the government took all that land in Utah and Arizona years ago, said we couldn't hunt there anymore, said all the animals were 'protected.'" He made angry air quotes around the last word. Then he picked up his beer and slurped it before continuing, "And now they're doing the same thing here."

Ford made it sound like protecting something was akin to stealing it. His loud rambling attracted one of the pool players, a burly young guy with a blond crew cut, who now stood a few feet behind Ford, smoking a cigarette while he stared at the TV and listened to Ford's rant. Ernest thought he'd seen that same guy over at Jack's place a few times. Bill, was that his name? Something like Bill.

"Just six months ago, the government took the land *I've* been hunting on up here for the last ten years! Just grabbed it, without asking anyone. The feds've locked up Utah and Arizona, and now they're doing it to Washington State!" Ford thumped the bar with a fist.

This was an old song in the area, whining about the government. A lot of the whining was horse shit, but then Ernest had found long ago that if he wanted to fit in, he'd best put on his hip boots and wade in it, too. "Yeah," he said, "I read the president made some new monuments and such."

"It's nothing but a goddamned land grab! The government thinks it can take away anything you have nowadays. The national forests are supposed to belong to the people. They've got no right to take them away to make a park bigger. The last thing we need is a bigger park! How the hell are you supposed to make money out of a park where they won't let you shoot a deer or chop a little firewood, for chrissakes?"

The crew-cut pool player, smiling and nodding like he'd just heard something funny, went back to his game. Privately, Ernest thought that making any park bigger sounded like a pretty good idea. God knew the land around his double-wide was being swallowed up by tacky little summer cabins, and Rushing Springs wasn't anything close to a big city.

He and Allie used to see all kinds of birds and even elk and martens, and one time a fox, but nowadays he was lucky if anything more than a stray cat walked through the backyard. Made his days even lonelier, with nothing to look at. It was the end of the road, this place. Always had been, always would be. He sure hoped Allie would be there waiting for him tonight when he got back, ready to tell him all about the landscaping business and the wider world of Seattle. And about whatever she'd been up to all of last night and all day today.

His whiskey was gone, and he had no money for another. He looked longingly at Ford's mug, still half full of Budweiser on the countertop. Maybe he could get the guy to buy him a beer. "I know what you mean about the feds," he offered. "I was in 'Nam, too, right at the tail end. Got this bum leg now, and is the government takin' care of me? A long time ago, the doc said I should get an operation, but is the VA gonna pay for it? No way. Hell, ask any of these poor jerks comin' back from the Middle East—nobody even knows where the VA is these days."

"I heard the VA got their act together," Ford said.

"Yeah?" Ernest was surprised. "How so?"

Ford shrugged. "They opened up some new clinics and stuff. Maybe you should check into it."

"Huh," Ernest huffed. He thought about the pile of unopened mail on the kitchen table and the computer that was so slow it was useless. "If they got a new clinic, it'll be all the way over in Seattle and you'll have to make an appointment on the computer."

The guy shrugged again. "Maybe."

Ernest decided to get off the vet thing. "And jobs?" he said, snorting for effect, "When I moved up here, I asked the forest service and the park service for jobs. Nothing but trail crew, they said."

Ford nodded. "Yeah, there's always trail crew jobs in the summer. Pay's not bad, but it's damn hard work."

Ernest shook his head. "Do I look like I can bust a trail? That's a job for kids." He placed a hand on the counter. "But that's the government for you. They just use a man till he's all used up, don't give nothin' in return."

Ford's gaze remained locked on the news program. He curled his fingers around the beer mug, gestured with it in the direction of the television, which now showed a bunch of kids on skateboards whizzing around with juice drinks in their hands.

"You know that blond gal, she was down in Utah bugging a friend of mine last year," Ford growled. "And now she's up here! She's one of those tree huggers who think animals are more important than people." He leaned toward Ernest, wafting the heady scent of Budweiser beer his way. "Well, I'm going to beat her at her own game. I know how to fix her wagon. I know how to fix all their wagons."

6

THE brightness of sun on her eyelids woke her up. Sam yawned, rolled her head to the left, and was startled to find Chase's face only inches from her own. He lay on his stomach, his face mashed into the pillow. The sleeping bag had fallen away from his bare shoulders. They were nice muscular shoulders, tapering to a lean bronze back. It was weird how they'd been through so much together and yet she had never seen him without a shirt before.

His black hair was ruffled, for once not parted knife-straight with FBI rigidity. His lips were slightly parted, pale against the dark sheen of whiskers. Relaxed in sleep, his features looked softer. It was easy to picture what he'd looked like before kidnappers and extortionists and bank robbers had sobered him. But it was still hard to picture him as the accountant he'd been before joining the FBI. She raised herself up on an elbow.

The movement woke him. His eyes snapped open, focused on her, and then crinkled at the corners. "Good morning." His voice was husky. He smiled and rolled over on his back, stretching his arms above his head. His bare leg grazed hers beneath the covers, startling her. He had zipped their sleeping bags together.

Trying to be inconspicuous, she slid a hand down into her own sleeping bag. She was wearing a T-shirt, bra, and panties. She could feel Chase's gaze on her face. Damn the blush creeping up her cheeks!

He cupped his hands behind his head. "How are you feeling this morning?"

"Okay," she mumbled. Confused was more accurate.

"How's the head?"

Actually, her head felt surprisingly good, considering. She searched her memory for the night before, remembered wine and pain pills and his hands on her shoulders, then couldn't come up with anything beyond leaning back into his arms. She turned her eyes away from his. "Uh, last night . . . Did I . . ."

"Still having trouble with the mouth?" His expression was deadpan, but a gleam lurked in his dark eyes.

Damned smart aleck.

"You called me *fine*." He used the same inflection that Lili had, and batted his eyelashes at her.

"When exactly did I do that?" Had she finally tangled the sheets with Chase and not even remembered it?

A pained expression took over his face. "It was that forgettable?"

Her cheeks burned. "Well, I . . ." She remembered wanting to kiss him and see him naked, but she didn't remember actually doing either of those things.

Clapping a hand to his jaw, he focused his gaze in the direction of his feet. "Jeez," he sighed, using her slang, "I guess I'm going to have to study the manual again." He leaned back against the pillow, rolling his eyes. "I practice and practice . . ."

She jerked the pillow out from under his head and pressed it down over his face. "You . . . you . . ." She fumbled for an appropriate term. When she took the pillow away, he was laughing. "You're an exasperating man, Chase Perez," she told him.

He rolled over, pushed himself up on his elbows, and moved his head close to hers. "I don't take advantage of unconscious women, Summer."

Pulling himself out of the sleeping bag, he stood up. She had long wondered whether he'd wear boxers or briefs.

Trust him to choose something in between, a close-fitting type of gray knit underwear that hugged his buttocks and muscular thighs.

He retrieved his jeans from the floor. "Keep staring like that and you're going to see more than just my shorts."

"A little more?" she teased. "Or a lot?"

"Hey, they don't call me a special agent for nothing."

"You do gymnastic tricks or something?"

"More like magic."

"Show me."

He groaned. "Hold that thought. I'll be right back." He jammed his feet, sockless, into his boots. "If the President calls, I'll be in the small conference room, the one with the half moon on the door." The door slammed behind him. It sounded like he was descending the ladder three rungs at a time. She should have told him that it was all right to pee off the balcony.

Should she take her T-shirt off? Wait for Chase to do it? A delicious thought. Then she had a sudden vision of the tight neckline getting hung up on her chin or nose. Decidedly unsexy. She ripped the T-shirt off, tossed it in a corner, studied her bra and panties with dismay. White cotton. She wished she were wearing the peach-colored lace set at the bottom of her underwear drawer.

She crawled to her daypack, pulled out the tiny mirror. Surprisingly, the face that looked back was not too bad. Her lower lip was still swollen and dusky, but if she ignored the stitches, the injury gave her kind of a sexy, hard-kissed look. She squeezed a dab of mint toothpaste onto her tongue and ran it around her mouth, sniffed her armpits, finger-combed her tangled hair. Then she slid back into the sleeping bag, pulled the quilted nylon up to hide the utilitarian bra, arranged herself as if casually lounging against the pillow.

It was finally going to happen. She and Chase. Actual lovemaking. Sex. Anticipation—or was it anxiety?—tingled throughout her body. Did she even remember how to do this? It had been nearly a year since Adam. You never forget, she told herself, like riding a bike. Well, no, not a bike. Riding a horse? Hardly. Well, sort of like riding, any-way . . .

A couple of clomps thundered against the ladder. "So you're the guy who usually mans this tower?" Chase said loudly.

What the heck?

More clomps. "She'll be *so* glad you're back." Chase's voice rose in volume. "Not to mention—*surprised* to see you so *soon!*"

Goddammit! Sam dove for her T-shirt, found the wad of her uniform in the corner. She jammed a splinter into her bare foot as she hopped one-legged into her pants. Damn, damn, damn! She buttoned the waistband just as Perez walked into the room, accompanied by a red-haired, mustachioed fellow. The redhead carried a loaded back-pack, which he dumped onto the floor before extending a hand.

"Greg Jordan," he said. "I'm back."

The firewatch volunteer. She pumped his hand. "Glad to meet you, Greg," she lied. "I'm Sam Westin, the temporary bio-study hire. And I guess you've already met my friend."

Behind Greg's back, Chase pantomimed choking the younger man. Sam pressed her lips together to keep from laughing. By the time Greg turned around, Chase was reaching for his flannel shirt, which dangled from the back of the solitary chair.

"How's your mother?" she asked Greg.

He swiveled to face her again. "Back to her usual criti-cal self, in spite of the heart attack. I couldn't wait to get back here, out of range."

Chase fired an imaginary pistol at the back of Greg's head. Three shots.

Sam laughed aloud. Greg, assuming her response was due to his wit, chuckled along with her.

While Chase jammed sleeping bags and pillows into stuff sacks, she made a pot of coffee over the small propane two-burner stove. The three of them drank it and chewed granola bars as Sam told Greg about the fire.

"I wish that'd happened on my watch," he said wistfully.

Sam rolled her eyes at Chase.

"You may still get your chance," Chase said. "People that get a kick out of starting fires usually do it more than once."

"I heard about that poor trail worker," he said. "What happened there?"

"Nobody knows yet," Sam told him. "So keep an eye out for anything suspicious going on."

She described her fears about Raider and the illegal hunter. Greg promised to keep a lookout for bears as well as fires, and listen for gunshots. "Call me if you even suspect hunters might be crawling through the woods," she told him.

He looked happy to have a mission. "You got it."

Chase frowned. "And then you'll both call the rangers, right?"

Ignoring his tone, she followed him to the door. "Happy rhymes," she said over her shoulder.

"Oh, I almost forgot," Greg blurted out. "You're supposed to check in at headquarters. The main HQ, not the district building."

"Now? I'm supposed to drive all the way to Port Angeles?" Seemed like she'd been at the hospital there only hours ago. "Why didn't they call me?" She pulled her radio from its holder on her belt. The power light didn't show even the faintest glimmer of life. "Well, crap."

Chase peered over her shoulder. "Looks more like a dead battery to me."

Not checking her radio: another demerit on her record. Good thing there hadn't been another fire last night. She'd find her spare battery as soon as they got down to the truck. "Do me a favor, Greg?"

"Sure."

"Don't report in for twenty minutes, and . . . you never saw my friend."

"Perez? Never heard of him." He gave them a two-fingered salute.

As they neared town, Chase's cell phone trilled from his shirt pocket. After answering and listening for a moment, he sighed heavily, then said, "On my way," before clicking the phone closed.

She was about to ask him if it was the bank robbers when he turned to her, one eyebrow raised, and asked, "Happy rhymes?"

"He won some sort of grant," she told him. "He's a poet."

"Aha. That's how he stands it up there by himself."

Chase didn't appreciate the solitude of the fire tower? A spark of anxiety flared in her gut. "That boring, huh?"

"Not for a short time. And that sunset was certainly worth a verse or two."

Well, at least he'd enjoyed that. She focused on the road ahead, trying not to think about what he would say if it had rained last night.

His hand crept onto her khaki-covered thigh, his fingers hot. "And then there was your body—"

"Don't start that again," she groaned. "Not now."

She stopped at Mack's apartment building in Forks, where Chase had left his car.

He kissed her gently as they said good-bye in the parking lot. "Be careful out there in the woods. Call me if there's any more trouble. Watch out for vampires."

She laughed.

"And come see me in Salt Lake, okay, Summer?" He pressed her more tightly to him. "Make it soon."

She wrapped her arms around his waist. "As soon as I can. After my contract is up here." Pressing her ear to his chest over his heart, she murmured, "I want to see these special-agent magic tricks."

"I'll study the manual."

Putting on a disappointed expression, she looked up into his eyes. "I thought you had it memorized."

He snorted, licked his index finger, and theatrically

marked a point in the air for her, then turned and slid into his car. Her chest pulled tight at the thought of what almost happened between them this morning. So close. She swallowed hard, waved, and watched him drive away before she turned her truck toward Highway 101 and park headquarters.

SAM entered the park's central administration building forty-five minutes later. Mack Lindstrom was lounging in the dilapidated lobby, shooting the breeze with the park's geologist, Jodi Ruderman, as they waited for the crowds to gather at the visitor's center for their afternoon lectures.

"Yow." Jodi stared at Sam's lip. "Does that hurt?"

"It looks worse than it feels," Sam told her. Were the stitches *that* ugly?

"Sam frequently looks like she's been in a bar brawl," Mack said helpfully. Then, to Sam, "Hoyle's waiting for you."

Uh-oh. She'd expected to be cross-examined by Tracey Carsen, the superintendent, not Peter Hoyle, the assistant super. This didn't bode well. Carsen was all about conservation and promoting public appreciation for wilderness; Hoyle was all about rules and regulations. Sam had heard that he'd been an officer in the Army Quartermaster corps before joining NPS, and that seemed to fit his officious personality.

"Joe's in there now," Mack added.

This didn't bode well at all. Joe should have been at home with his family. Sam reluctantly changed course to Hoyle's office. Mack murmured in a low voice, "I wouldn't want to be in your shoes, prima donna."

Joe was slumped in one of Hoyle's folding metal visitor chairs. Catching her eye, he mouthed the word *sorry* before focusing again on his lap. Peter Hoyle sat ramrod straight, his hands folded together on top of his immaculate desk. Overhead, the cheap fluorescent light fixture buzzed like a trapped bee.

"How are you, Peter? What's the word on Lisa Glass?" Sam asked, hoping to head off whatever unpleasantness was planned.

Hoyle waved at the empty chair. "We'll get to that in a minute. I want to talk about this situation with Lili first. Sit."

Sam slid into the other chair. "I know I shouldn't have had her up there."

"Damn straight, you shouldn't have. You got the manual, you signed the contract, you know the regs."

"But the volunteers—"

"Have guests all the time, I know." He leveled a finger at Joe. "And I know that Choi asked you to invite Lili. That was the first mistake. You can go now, Choi. Close the door behind you."

Joe slunk out of his office.

Behind his wire-rimmed glasses, the assistant superintendent's eyes were fierce. "The volunteers are beside the point, Westin. They're *volunteers*. The park service doesn't pay for their health care, doesn't pay for insurance, and doesn't have to answer for their irresponsible actions. Lili is a dependent of an employee. And you—you may be just a temporary hire, but you still have to obey the regs. What if Lili had been hurt out there? We've already got one employee on the critical list."

Sam squirmed in her chair.

"You had no business tackling that fire on your own. You seem to think that just because you're a celebrity, you've got some sort of special status around here."

Celebrity? And Mack had called her a prima donna. "What do you mean, celebrity?"

Hoyle stared angrily at her, his lips pressed into a thin line, then shook his head. "You don't know?" He unclasped his hands, leaned back in his chair, and folded his arms across his chest. "You were on the news last night."

"The news?" Sam had a sudden fear of a TV news helicopter zeroing in on her and Chase in each other's arms. No, that was ridiculous—they would have heard the roar of chopper blades, or at least Chase would have. She leaned forward. "That's impossible. I was at the fire tower all afternoon and evening."

Hoyle sighed wearily, as if trying to reason with a three-year-old. "They used photos from that Zack Fischer story in Utah last year. You with the boy and you with the cougar."

No wonder Mack had called her a prima donna. "Why did they dredge that up?"

"I was going to ask you that." Hoyle selected a black government-issue pen from an Olympic National Park mug on the desk, and then squeezed it between his thumb and index finger as if measuring its thickness. "They flashed a photo of you in uniform, too. Your park service ID photo."

"My ID photo? How—"

"I'm checking into that. You haven't loaned your ID to anyone, have you?"

"Of course not." Sam fervently hoped it was in her day-pack right now. "So this report was about the Zack Fischer story?"

"No, it started with the Western Wildlife Conference. It's in Seattle this year, with the focus on the Endangered Species Act. But you know that."

None of this made any sense. "Why would I know that?"

"Well, you're speaking there, aren't you?"

"What?" Sam raised her chin.

"Cougars, the ESA, and the new addition to Olympic Park—all in the same damned report. The nutcases are crawling out of the woodwork. We had another death threat this morning."

"Excuse me, but did you say *I'm* speaking at the Wildlife Conference?"

Hoyle jerked open his desk drawer, pulled out a facsimile page, and handed it over. The message was from Richard Best, marketer at *The Edge*.

Wilderness Westin is invited to deliver a paper on Environmentalists as Endangered Species at the Western

Wildlife Conference in Seattle (August 28–30). Usual
rate, contract to follow. Congrats!! Great publicity for
your future assignments!!

Environmentalists as Endangered Species. A timely
topic. She folded the fax, her brain battered by a flurry of
conflicting emotions: she felt honored about the recogni-
tion of her expertise, pissed off about Best's assumption
that she'd accept the assignment, pleased that he had promised her future work at the e-zine. Well, sort of pleased.
Because he'd only sort of promised. Only four months ago
he'd told her they no longer required her services. Now he'd
changed his tune? Was it real? *The Edge* was famous for
dangling tidbits only to jerk them away at the last minute.
What happened to luxury spas?

She'd never done any sort of public speaking. As she
tried to visualize standing in front of a huge audience, her
current boss's last statement registered. She looked up.
"Did you say something about a death threat?"

"The newscaster said that you were now a ranger at
Olympic Park, so some anti-Endangered Species crackpot
called headquarters. Said that for every man sacrificed for
an animal, one of us—I presume he meant the park staff—
would die."

Die? Sam leaned back into her chair, crumpling the fax
in her fist.

"Don't take it so seriously," Hoyle told her. "The locals
are upset that the government turned their personal play-
ground into a wildlife sanctuary instead of a hunting refuge. We've received at least one threat a week ever since
the annexation was announced."

"Really?" This was getting creepier by the second.

Hoyle jabbed a finger at Sam. "Don't get off the subject.
Just because you're on Channel 8 doesn't mean you have
special rights around here. You're not a ranger. You're just
a tech, and a temporary one at that. Don't meddle in dangerous situations."

Sam was tired of this refrain. She *was* responsible for

one small area of the park, at least right now. "You hired me to do an environmental survey and write a management plan for the Marmot Lake area, correct?"

"Yes." A hint of wariness crept into Hoyle's expression, but he quickly recovered. "That, and only that."

"Doesn't that mean that you want me to identify problems there and recommend solutions? So I can develop a plan that truly protects the wildlife and the resources?"

Hoyle hesitated a second as if suspecting a trap, then finally conceded, "Yes." He leaned forward. "But don't ever, ever let any guest accompany you when you're on duty."

Sam tried to look humble. "Got it." She prayed that Greg Jordan would stay mum about Chase's visit.

"Don't let your publicity stunts interfere with your work here."

Sam's mouth opened in protest. She shut it before something spilled out that she'd regret. She couldn't wait to get back to the woods.

"Now." Hoyle smiled, but the warmth didn't quite reach his eyes. "We're all taking turns sitting with Lisa Glass at the hospital. I've put you down for one to five today. Okay?"

Sam peeked at her watch. Five after twelve. It would take her a good forty minutes to drive to the hospital, and she hadn't even had lunch. Damn, damn, damn. She could hardly say no after she'd just been chewed out, and the assistant super knew it. "Glad to," she chirped.

"Thanks. You never know when she might come around, and we wouldn't want her to be alone."

"I'd better hit the road then." The folding chair squeaked when Sam stood up. Crap! Four long hours staring at an unconscious girl in a hospital room. If Lisa woke up, what could she say to her? What kind of comfort could she be to a perfect stranger?

She'd already spent too much of her life huddled beside an inert body, inhaling the miasma of chemicals and disease, with only the beeping and whistling and clicking of cardiac monitor and respirator for company. Had her mother appreciated the company? Had she even known Sam was there? But at least she'd had some relationship, however strained, with her mother. She'd never even met Lisa.

Joe was leaning against her truck in the parking lot. "Sorry, Sam."

She shook her head. "Don't worry about it. If it hadn't been the fire, it would have been something else. Hoyle's never liked me for some reason."

"You don't grovel sufficiently."

"Compared to what? Or whom?"

"He wanted his nephew to get your contract."

"Why didn't he?"

"Forestry degree, not wildlife biology. Besides, you're a name." He grinned.

"Hardly." She was only well known with the staff of Heritage National Monument in Utah. "Well, maybe within the park service . . ."

"How did your talk with Lili go?" His deep brown eyes searched hers. "Did she say anything I should know about? She never talks to me or Laura anymore. I don't even know who her friends are these days."

Sam thought back. Seemed like weeks since she'd talked to Joe's thirteen-year-old daughter. She dragged her mind past Chase and Lisa and fires and explosions back to the evening with Lili at the fire tower. "Lili mentioned some girls. Deborah was one, I think."

"I know Deborah. Lili's always wanting something Deborah has. Shoes, bracelets, a smart phone, for heaven's sake." Joe snorted. "Only problem is that the Rosemonts own the bank, while the rest of us have to actually work for a living. Did she mention any boys?"

"Some boy—Robbie?" She frowned, trying to remember.

"Rodney? There's a Rodney who's her assistant soccer coach."

"That doesn't sound quite right, but it was something

close to that. Shallow but interesting, she said. But it didn't sound to me like she really had the hots for him."

Taking in the dismay on her friend's face, she said, "You know what I mean. Oh, and she mentioned that she thinks a lot of her science teacher—Martinson?"

Joe appeared surprised. "I'm glad to know Lili likes one of her teachers. She had a hard time after we moved here from Flagstaff. She was embarrassed that she had to go to summer school to move on to eighth grade this year."

"She said summer school was okay. And she said Martinson was fine, if I'm remembering right."

"Fine?" Joe's dark eyes grew worried. "She talks about him a lot, now that I think about it. Thanks, Sam." He walked away, running a hand through his straight black hair, muttering to himself. "Martinson?"

THE Winner Woodworking shop was quiet, now that they'd finished hammering all five podiums together. The pine structures, one already stained dark, stood scattered about the room, making the huge empty space appear as if it were waiting for a political rally.

Looking at the sad state of his shop tightened the knot between Jack Winner's shoulder blades. He knew from experience that the pain would only get worse as the day went on. Only a couple of years earlier, he'd been raking in the dough, well known in the business, creating custom home theater setups for rich homeowners and wired desks for high-powered execs. But now business had slowed down to this, one puny contract for five damned podiums and one upcoming bid for a custom restaurant counter. All the money flowed right out of the country these days—to those ragheads in Iraq and Afghanistan or to those poor slobs in Haiti or Africa.

What little money Winner Woodworking did bring in got ripped off in taxes. Other countries got things for their taxes, like health care or endless paid vacation. But not

Americans: no, every day, the damn American government just handed *their* taxes to millionaire bankers at home or camel riders or Jews overseas. At the same time, the feds cooked up more ways to be sure hardworking Americans couldn't make a decent living anymore. Now they were talking about taking away Social Security, and everyone he knew had been paying into that since they were teenagers. And the reporters didn't even have the guts to call it robbery.

Hurricane Katrina had been the perfect example of how little the U.S. government cared—leaving all those poor people to die. He would have thought that would finally make people wake up and see how bad things were in this country. But no, they continued to vote in the same government that bailed out bankers and Wall Street brokers and gave tax breaks to millionaires. The feds didn't do one damn thing to help out the common man who couldn't find work or couldn't get enough to pay the mortgage. Small business owners like him couldn't even get unemployment pay. They were just shit out of luck. Americans needed to wake up. This government that was supposed to be of, by, and for the people was of and by the big corporations, and for everyone else *except* the American people.

He and Allie talked about this all the time. She'd been so angry about the way the Veterans Administration had treated her dad, refusing to consider his knee problem service-related just because it'd gotten worse later. She'd had to go all the way to Seattle to find a job that paid more than starvation wage. His vision blurred with sudden tears. He gritted his teeth and tried to think about something else. Like the money that he was going to come into in a few weeks. Should he use it to try to improve his business here or to finally escape from this place?

"What's this for?"

Jack looked up from the Sunday paper he'd stretched across his drafting table to see Philip King tracing the indentation in the front of a podium.

"A plaque goes in there. Stewart's in Port Angeles is

making them up; they'll be ready at the end of the month."
Jack pulled the design from beneath the newsprint and
waved it in his friend's direction.

"You mean like a carving? I could have done that."

King's carvings were hardly professional quality. Jack
ignored him and turned back to scanning the news section.
His throat was dry, and he wished he'd brought a Mountain
Dew to the shop with him.

King moved over behind him, breathing down his neck,
trying to read over his shoulder. "Anything?"

"Get off me, man." Jack elbowed him away. "I'm
looking."

Finally, in the section reserved for local news, there was
a tiny blurb on page two. FIRE IN OLYMPIC NATIONAL PARK.
"Here it is."

"What's it say?"

"The fire burned fourteen acres."

"Is that all? I thought it'd be bigger."

King pointed to the paper. "Is there anything about . . ."

Jack quickly summarized. "The fire was intentionally
set, a park service employee was severely injured. There's
nothing here about Allie." He was surprised he could say
her name so easily. He rubbed his fingers over his arm. It
was chilly in the shop this morning. He should go find his
sweatshirt.

King ran walnut-colored fingers through his close-
cropped hair, leaving a dark stripe through the blond stub-
ble. Jack examined his own hands. There was a little stain
under the nails, if you looked close, but otherwise they
were clean.

"The fire musta burned everything up," King said.
"That's good, that's real good." He stopped himself. "I'm
sorry, man; I didn't mean that . . ."

Jack shrugged, scratched his nose. "She should have—"
His voice cracked, and he swallowed hard before saying,
"We couldn't have done it any other way." But he wondered
about that. He'd been completely stunned when King and
Roddie told him Allie was dead. Then they were setting

the fires and yelling the cops were coming and running through the dark forest, leaving her behind.

King punched him in the arm. "There are always casualties, man."

"I guess." It felt wrong to dismiss Allie so easily. Was there any chance that she'd made it? The paper hadn't mentioned anything about a body. But that could be a trick. He couldn't go back to check, not yet. Rangers would be crawling over everything out there. He looked at King. "What did you do with the lantern?"

"It's back in my garage where it belongs."

That made sense, Jack guessed. Coleman fuel was everywhere; a lot of people had those lanterns for camping.

"Old man Craig's been wandering around town looking for Allie. Did I see him in here yesterday?"

"Yeah." Jack folded the paper, rose from his stool, and tossed it into a nearby trash bin. "Don't worry, he doesn't know shit."

"What'd you do with her car?"

Jack glared at the other man. The less he knew, the better. King was a fair carpenter and a good marksman, but he was none too bright, and he had a tendency to shoot off his mouth when he'd downed a six-pack. "Don't worry about it. I took care of it."

"This little glitch doesn't change anything, right?"

Little glitch? He clenched his fists and considered slugging King for calling Allie that.

"We've got the perfect target now. Much better than a stupid old VA office. The plan's still on, right?"

King was right. It was more important than ever to be part of it now. "The plan's still on."

7

THE hospital was every bit as depressing as Sam had thought it would be. A tiny dark-skinned nurse led her to Lisa's room while telling her that Lisa had not regained consciousness, but might at any moment. Or might not for days. One eardrum was broken, and the girl had a severe concussion in addition to her bruises and burns.

An oxygen mask covered Lisa's nose and mouth, but thankfully she was not on a respirator. There'd be no mechanical breathing to listen to. The hissing and clicking always made Sam feel as if the device was trying to breathe for her as well as for the patient.

"Press the call button if anything changes, yes?" The tiny woman's English was heavily accented—Philippines, India? Sam couldn't tell. The nurse came up only to her shoulder making Sam's five-foot-two seem tall.

She ate a stale ham-and-cheese and greasy chips, sipping her Diet Dr Pepper slowly to make it last. She hadn't seen any signs about not using cell phones, so she pulled hers out to call her housemate Blake. Maybe he'd seen last night's news story and would fill her in. The recorder answered in Blake's cheery voice. *Hi, Sam's out of town and Blake's off doing God knows what right now. Leave a message and we'll call you when we get back.*

A great message for would-be burglars. She left a snide suggestion that he should at least add a statement about pit bulls on patrol.

The hospital room had a damp, oily smell. Body fluids

seeping through Lisa's gauze dressings? Or maybe the burn ointment? She hoped it was the latter.

She spent two hours alternately staring at the bandaged body on the bed and trying to wade through the first chapter of the mystery she'd purchased. Finally she put it down and tried to imagine delivering a speech in front of hundreds of people in Seattle. Or would it be thousands? The thought of standing at a podium looking out into a sea of faces made her stomach churn.

How had this all come about, anyway? What had prompted the television station to air the old news clips? Her cell phone was blinking its low battery warning, so she pulled out her reserve phone card and used the hospital room phone to call directory info and then KSTL, Channel 8, in Seattle. After being questioned by a series of gatekeepers, she found herself talking to an assistant producer who sounded like she should be in middle school with Lili instead of working in a TV station.

"The lead-in was the Western Wildlife Conference," the high-pitched voice told her. "Not much by itself, but there's a lot of controversy right now about the Endangered Species Act, and then when we found out you were the featured speaker, we knew it could be a public interest story. A lot of people still remember the Zachary Fischer incident and—"

"Who said I was the featured speaker?"

"Just a minute." Sam could hear the faint clicks of keystrokes in the background. "Well, the conference organizers said you were invited—hmmm—oh, here it is. Someone at your place of employment—a Richard Best— told us you accepted."

Damn the man. "He didn't have my permission to do that. I haven't agreed to speak."

"Really?" The producer sounded concerned. More clicking sounds, then, "Oh, good. We just said you were scheduled. So we're okay." She gave an audible sigh of relief.

Sam gritted her teeth. Modern media. As long as they

couldn't be sued, they didn't care what they put in front of the public. "Where did those photos of me come from?"

More key clicks. "Those belonged to the network. I see ten seconds from archived wire-service tape labeled ZACHARY FISCHER CASE, from last year. We made stills from the video."

"Okay. But I understand that there was a photo of me in a national park uniform? Where did you get that? I'm not a ranger, you know."

"Oh. Well." A pause. "Oh, here. The photo was from an NPS employee record book dated several years ago. From Utah."

The summer she'd been a seasonal ranger in Heritage National Monument. Her first brief stint in NPS green.

"That's a government document, so it's public record. And we didn't say you were a ranger. We just said that you were currently working in Olympic National Park. You are, aren't you?"

"Yes."

Another sigh of relief. "Is there anything else I can help you with?"

Sam considered for a second. There wasn't anything she could do about this, was there? She'd just have to hope that the locals would quickly forget they'd seen her face on TV.

"Ms. Westin, are you working on that incident where the girl was injured in the forest fire? Because we'd love to talk to you about that."

Sam's breath caught in her throat. She shot a guilty glance at Lisa's sleeping form in the bed. It was bad enough that KSTL was showing footage of her involvement in the old Fischer case on TV, but if she was outed on this case, Peter Hoyle might look for a way to cancel her contract before she finished her twelve weeks.

"I'm not a ranger, remember? I'm only a temp. You need to talk to the park's public relations officer."

"But I see that you're calling from the Port Angeles hospital—"

Sam slapped the receiver back into its cradle. Damn

caller ID. She glanced at the door, half expecting a tele-vision camera and reporter to dash in, stick a microphone in her face, and demand that she tell what she knew about this incident. How did she always end up attracting the attention of the news? She was nobody.

And now her name was on some conference schedule as a featured speaker. They'd be expecting Wilderness Wes-tin, the intrepid beauty who had been promoted with slick marketing language and a doctored photo. And they'd get short, insecure, thirty-seven-year-old Summer Westin who was beginning to sag around the edges.

If she didn't accept the invitation, this would all fade away. The few who saw the television broadcast had proba-bly already forgotten her latest thirty seconds of fame. But then again, the invitation was an honor, the biggest she'd ever received in her life. And if she didn't make the speech, it was a good bet that *everything* would fade away. She'd certainly never work for *The Edge* again.

She didn't like either choice. Her plastic chair grew increasingly uncomfortable as she squirmed on it. When she stood up to stretch, the form on the bed moved.

Lisa Glass opened her eyes to narrow slits. At first, the girl's gaze didn't seem to focus; she stared blearily in Sam's direction. Then her eyes flew open, her jaw dropped, and her whole body tensed under the sheets.

Sam hastily leaned forward to place a hand on the young woman's exposed wrist. "It's okay, Lisa."

She tried to make her voice sound soothing. "I'm Sam Westin, from the park."

Lisa pulled her wrist away and tugged the oxygen mask down onto her neck, keeping her gaze fixed on Sam. Her irises were ice blue. They were disquieting, those piercing eyes, one lashless, nestled among puffy lids and yellow-stained gauze, the other framed by long lashes, a light brown eyebrow, and pale freckled skin.

"You're in the hospital," Sam told her. "You had an acci-dent." Then, thinking that Lisa's reaction might be from her own appearance, she said, "There was a forest fire. I

was there when we found you. That's why I look like this."
She gestured to her lip and the Band-Aid on her temple.

Lisa's gaze broke away from hers and she glanced nervously around the room. Remembering the girl's shattered eardrum, Sam asked, "Can you hear me, Lisa?"

A quick dip of the chin.

"Good."

Sam scanned the area above Lisa's head for the call button, but didn't see it. Two electrical leads snaked over the mattress and disappeared under the sheets. Sam peeled the sheet down a little, and saw that the lines paralleled Lisa's neck and disappeared under the hospital gown. Leads for the monitors. The girl inched away from Sam's prying fingers. Sam leaned back. "We called your aunt in Philadelphia, but we haven't connected yet. Is there someone else we should call? Do you want to call someone? I could hold the phone for you."

Lisa lay so still that at first Sam thought she hadn't heard her, after all, but then the girl slowly shook her bandage-swathed head. She licked her blistered lower lip.

"Are you thirsty?"

With lips pressed together, Lisa slowly moved her head up and down, just a fraction. Poor thing. It probably hurt like hell.

Sam poured a cup of water from the pitcher on the bed table, then held the bent straw to Lisa's lips. "Do you remember what happened?"

The girl swallowed painfully, took another sip before answering in a barely audible croak. "No."

Sam told her about the loud bang and the fire, about Mack finding her facedown in the dirt beside Elk Creek. The pale eyes remained fixed on her throughout the story. Didn't this girl ever blink? Maybe she really couldn't hear at all; maybe Lisa was reading lips.

She should go call the nurse. But how long would Lisa be conscious? Sam was afraid to leave her.

"Do you remember the fire?" she asked.

Again, the barely discernable shake of the head.

"What were you doing at Marmot Lake, Lisa?"

The icy gaze remained firmly on Sam's face for a moment longer, then Lisa looked away.

"Were you setting off firecrackers? Because that's okay; but you need to tell me."

Lisa seemed to be considering. Or trying to remember? Or maybe making up her mind whether to tell. A white coat flashed by the doorway and Sam thought about chasing down the wearer. But then, the girl looked at her again. Through swollen lips she whispered hoarsely, "Kidnapped."

Kidnapped? Sam had a wild urge to grab the girl by the shoulders and shake the story out of her. She grasped the bed rail, forced herself to take a deep breath. *Go slowly. Don't scare her off.* She reiterated, "You were kidnapped, Lisa?"

"Made me go."

"Who? Why?"

Lisa's eyes stared at the twin hills formed by her feet under the sheets. Her chest rose as she inhaled deeply. The blue eyes closed.

"You're not going to get anything more from her now."

The deep voice startled Sam. She hadn't realized the doctor was there in the doorway. He was a handsome man, with sideburns silver against his walnut brown skin, contrasting with the tight ebony curls that covered the rest of his head. He strode into the room.

"Did you hear what she said?" Sam asked.

"Something about going with someone." He stood beside Sam, looking down at Lisa. "I'm amazed she spoke at all," he said. "You should have called a nurse immediately." Reaching down, he pulled Lisa's oxygen mask back into place. "Why didn't you press the call button?"

"I couldn't find the dang thing."

The doctor slid his hand along the lowered bed railing, plucked off a tiny gray rectangle with a lighted button. "It's clipped to the rail. That way it doesn't get lost."

Assuming you knew what the thing looked like and that it could be clipped to anything. "Aha," Sam muttered.

"Did she seem oriented? Coherent?"

"She didn't say much. But she seemed to be thinking as she talked." As a matter of fact, it seemed to Sam that Lisa had thought too long before she said anything.

"Hmm. I wouldn't put much stock in what comes out of her mouth just yet. Smoke inhalation makes people very disoriented. And that was a powerful blow she took to the head. Do you know what she got hit with?"

"Looks like it was a falling branch."

The doctor nodded, his eyes on the page in front of him. "That would fit with the debris we found in the wound."

"Will she wake up again soon? We really need to know what happened."

He looked at his watch, made a notation on the page, then flipped the chart closed. "It's impossible to say. Head injuries are unpredictable. And then there's the smoke inhalation. She could sleep for minutes or hours. She could slip back into unconsciousness and stay that way for days."

Days? Now Sam had the urge to shake the doctor. She chewed on the knuckle of her index finger instead.

"Waking up is a good sign," he said. "Press that button if she comes to again." His foam-soled shoes didn't make a sound on the tile floor as he left the room.

She paced back and forth at the foot of the bed, her thoughts lurching and colliding with each other like insects trapped in a jar. Kidnapped. By whom? What the hell for? Why the fire? Then there was this morning's phone threat. Did that have anything to do with Lisa? Would the threatener kidnap a park employee? Start a fire? Did the old mine figure in here somehow? The bear? Had they captured or killed Raider?

She used the room phone to call park headquarters and, unfortunately, ended up with Hoyle. Sam repeated what Lisa had said and what the doctor had told her, summing up with, "It's probably just delirium, but maybe we should have a guard at Lisa's door, just in case. Whether or not she's hallucinating about the kidnapping, the arson's a crime, and Lisa might be the only witness."

Hoyle's reply started with a heavy sigh. "We don't have the budget for that, and the Port Angeles Police won't do it. That's why we have our volunteers sitting with her around the clock. Let me know if she wakes up again so I can send a ranger to interview her."

Frustrated, Sam hung up, then paced impatiently next to Lisa's bed. Chase! She'd call Chase. Kidnapping a federal employee was certainly FBI business. She reached for the phone, but stopped before her fingers picked up the receiver. *Get a grip.* As the doctor had said, Lisa might have spoken from delirium or confusion. Brain-damaged victims mixed up their words, blurted out one thing when they meant another.

She stared at the sleeping form on the bed. She had a million questions for Lisa. Whatever the criminals had been up to at Marmot Lake, so far they'd gotten away with it. And they were still out there. The only movement was the girl's chest rising and falling under the white sheets.

Please wake up. Sam took hold of a foot that formed a small tent near the end of Lisa's bed. She tweaked a toe. Lisa groaned. Guilt instantly washed over Sam. *Now you're torturing a severely injured girl, Westin?* She fled as soon as Mack appeared to take her place.

BY Sunday evening, Ernest Craig was frantic. Nobody in town had seen Allie. He'd searched her room at their trailer, but he couldn't find any trace of a work number. He called Jack Winner again, and her friend Susan Plinsky. Neither of them knew the name of the company she worked for in Seattle.

He sat at the chipped table in the kitchen, cradling his aching head in his hands. She'd been so proud to finally land that job, after almost a year of looking for *anything* better than Best Burgers in Forks. She was so smart, but a high school diploma didn't get anyone far these days. The best she could do was a job at a landscaping company. Or was it a nursery?

Why didn't he keep track of these things? Shit, how could he call to see if she was all right if he didn't even know the name of the company? He couldn't even file a missing person on Allie; he could imagine the smart-ass county sheriff laughing at the holes in his story. Leaning forward, Ernest let his forehead drop to the tabletop, let it thump against the cool Formica. He deserved the pain. His ex-wife was right; he spent his life with his head up his ass.

The paper reported that a young woman, a park service employee, had been severely injured in the park in a forest fire. They had girls fighting forest fires now. Girl soldiers, girl firefighters. Well, Allie was strong, especially now that she was doing landscaping. He guessed she could be a firefighter if she had to. But he hoped it would never come to that. He remembered the way the guys in his unit had talked about the nurses in 'Nam. He didn't like to think about his girl out in the woods with a bunch of rough men.

He raised his head and checked the paper again. Lisa Glass, that was her name, the park service employee. From Philadelphia. Crap, she was only nineteen years old, two years younger than Allie. And in serious condition. He felt sorry for her parents. He knew what it was like to worry about a daughter. If he had any money, he'd send some flowers to that poor family.

It was a dangerous world out there for girls, especially blond lookers like Allie. And the damn cops were as useless as the feds. They wouldn't do anything to protect her. He had visions of her old Nova breaking down, of her hitchhiking and being picked up by a group of perverts, of them beating her and raping her and leaving her for dead in some clear-cut or drainage ditch along the highway.

She could be lying there right now.

8

THE forest was already in evening shadow by the time Sam drove into the parking lot at Marmot Lake. When she saw the gate standing wide open, her pulse quickened. But only another NPS truck faced the lake. As Sam pulled hers into place beside it, Ranger Paul Schuler emerged from the trail, shovel in hand, stomping and brushing ash off his clothes. She climbed down to greet him.

He held up a hand in greeting. "All clear," he told her. "No flare-ups."

"Anything else of significance?"

"Such as?" His steel-rimmed glasses were so smudged she wondered how he could stand to look through them.

"Blood. Bear skin. Weapons. Tools."

He gave her a surprised look, so she told him about the illegal hunter she'd encountered a couple of days ago, and then about the old mine shaft.

Paul's eyebrows rose. "The plot thickens. Maybe we'd better start running patrols through here once in a while to remind the public that this is NPS property now."

"I just came from the hospital," she told him. "Lisa Glass woke up for a few minutes."

"That's good news."

"She said she was kidnapped."

"Hmmm. Not such good news." He turned away and leaned on his shovel, considering, and they both stared at the lake for a moment. The evening light reflected lavender in the water's quiet surface. Finally, he murmured, "The best laid plans of mice and men are often gone awry."

She stared at him. Did he always talk in code? "You lost me there. Care to explain?"

"I meant that anything could have happened. Stay out here long enough, and you'll run into everyone from Big foot trackers to meth cooks."

She didn't want to hear that. She had enough to think about with arsonists and potential poachers and miners. "And where do you think Lisa Glass fits in?"

"Lisa works on the trail crew," Schuler said. "And the trail crew is not the most trustworthy bunch."

"I hear they're mostly JDs," Sam commented.

"Yep. Trail work counts as community service with juvenile court judges, so we have a bunch of delinquents slinging pickaxes every summer."

"But Lisa wasn't a delinquent." She'd found out that much from Joe.

"True." He rubbed the back of his neck. "At least not a convicted one. But she's got to be a tough cookie. Trail crew pays twelve dollars an hour, but hardly anybody signs up after they find out they've got to break rocks and get up at the crack of dawn and bunk out in the middle of nowhere."

Sam bristled. "You think Lisa's a criminal just because she's tough?" Would he say the same about a young man?

"I'm saying she hangs out with criminals *and* she's a tough character. Is she telling the truth about what happened out here?" He shook his head as if to answer his own question.

"She nearly died, Paul. She's a victim."

He shrugged. "Maybe. But meth cooks set themselves on fire; hunters accidentally shoot their partners. Stay out here long enough; you'll see what I mean."

Sam wished she were going to be there long enough to discover all the park's secrets. Across the lake, a creature was moving at the water's edge; she squinted, trying to determine what it was.

Schuler followed her line of sight. "Canada goose," he said.

He was right—the creature turned and now she could make out the slender neck and black-and-white head. "Did you see any sign of bears?" she asked.

"Nothing but a couple of paw prints. There were plenty of hoofprints—the elk came through here last night." His stomach growled then.

Hers gurgled in response. She pressed a hand over her belt buckle.

"Dinnertime. Time to lock up." He looked pointedly at the exit road, then at her.

She hesitated, still wanting to look for Raider. But Schuler was observant enough to notice bear tracks and identify geese from a distance. If he hadn't seen bears or anything else unusual, she probably wouldn't, either. And dinner sounded awfully good right now. She climbed back into her truck and drove toward Forks, leaving him to lock the gate.

Her thoughts turned to provisions for the fire tower. In the middle of her mental grocery list, she remembered that the tower wasn't hers anymore. She braked to a stop.

When she'd first landed the job, there'd been an offer of a rustic bunk somewhere in the park. All the summer rangers were currently filling the main park dormitory building, so that hadn't been it.

The trail crew bunkhouse—that was it. It was a dilapidated old boardinghouse a few miles from the Sol Duc Hot Springs. A bit of a drive, but . . . A spark of excitement rose through her fatigue. Bunking with the trail crew could solve two problems: it would give her a place to sleep and a chance to check out Lisa's compatriots, satisfy her curiosity about Lisa's kidnapping story. If they still had a bed for her.

But it was probably not wise to show up unannounced and it was getting late. If she was going to spend the night in town, she might as well embrace civilization. She was dying to use a computer. Since the Forks library and the district headquarters building were closed, Mack's was closest. She still had his spare key on her key chain.

She stopped by the Best Burgers drive-in in Forks and
ordered The Twilight on the Beach Special, which tonight
was scallops and coleslaw. The place was busy, as usual.
One of the joys of small-town life, she thought to herself,
remembering all the hours she'd hung out at the Burger
Corral in her tiny Kansas hometown.

Two booths were full of teens shooting the paper covers
from plastic straws at each other. Another booth held a
family of four tourists huddled over an Olympic Peninsula
map. In the corner were another mom and pop and two little girls, but they looked local. And was it just her imagination, or were both adults glaring in her direction?

She ran her tongue over her lower lip. The stitches were
ugly, she knew, but enough to make strangers frown at her?
Her uniform shirt was clean, her ID tag straight. Even her
hair was reasonably neat, imprisoned in a French braid at
the back of her head.

The bell above the door jangled, and a gray-haired man
with a mustache entered. He wore heavy work boots and
well-worn jeans. He nodded at the local couple, placed his
order at the counter, and then leaned against it to survey
the room. When his gaze met Sam's, his forehead furrowed
and his eyes narrowed. What the heck?

Had they all seen her on the newscast? Was that it? Did
they think she was a prima donna, too? I didn't ask to be on
television, she wanted to tell them. Damn Richard Best,
anyway.

The ponytailed counter girl placed a paper bag on the
scarred Formica and called out Sam's order number. She
slid out of the booth toward the counter and the glowering
fellow. He took the booth she'd been occupying. Was that
it? She was in the seat he wanted? She hoped it was that
simple. She smiled at him.

He glared back.

THE seafood was still warm when she dumped it onto a
plate at Mack's. She savored the scallops along with a

chilled Negra Modelo and a slice of lime. As far as beer sharing went, Mack was her idea of perfect: a die-hard Budweiser fan that wouldn't dream of touching the imported beer she'd stashed in his refrigerator. Her housemate Blake's tastes were too close to her own; anything she put in the fridge was fair game to him.

But Blake would never leave that stack of the dishes in the sink. Or the gray-ringed bathtub. She never needed to clear a path through Blake's dirty socks. When the guy wasn't baking bread, he was vacuuming. A sudden pang of homesickness struck. She wanted to walk barefoot across her own Navajo rugs. Hear her cat Simon purr. Sleep under the sunflower quilt her grandmother had made. She even wanted to hear the latest episode in Blake's eternal quest to meet the perfect partner.

The urge to forgo Mack's futon in favor of her own bed was strong. It was only seven thirty: with luck, she could make the nine fifteen ferry out of Kingston, be home by eleven thirty. She picked up her keys, considering. Yeah, right. And then get up at four in the morning to make it back in time to work tomorrow. She threw the keys down again. Simon and Blake and good housekeeping would have to wait until next weekend.

She parked herself in front of her friend's computer and turned it on. Mack's Internet connection was only dial-up out here, but at least he had one. She called up Google and typed in *black bear poaching*.

A list of articles assured her that, just as she feared, bear poaching was still thriving in the United States. And the Pacific coast, with constant Asian trade moving through its ports, was bear parts central. Nothing would keep her from looking for Raider tomorrow.

Next, she researched mining on public lands, and fell into a morass of articles and links to web pages. The overload of information made her eyes cross and each page took forever to download, but she read enough to determine that any American citizen or corporation could still stake a claim for mining rights on most forest service and

BLM lands. Thankfully, it looked like the national parks
and wilderness areas were off-limits, except where active
mining claims existed at the time of the area's designation,
which didn't seem so bad until she read one document,
which reported that in 1995, national parks in the United
States contained over 13,000 mining claims.

The different rules for different areas were so confusing. She really needed to determine the history of that
mine she had literally stumbled into, as well as which side
of the forest service–national park boundary it was now on.

There had apparently been a few minor reforms to the 1872
law, but they didn't seem to accomplish much. A 2007 reform
set royalties for new mines at 8 percent and old mines at
4 percent, and established a cleanup fund. Before that, there'd
been no royalties and no protection, and the Bureau of Land
Management estimated that in the year 2000 alone, more than
$982 million dollars worth of minerals had been extracted.

Next she came across a map of Western states with dots
marking hundreds of thousands of abandoned mines, along
with shaded areas indicating water polluted by minerals.
Large sections of southern Oregon and a good third of California were nearly obliterated with dots and shading. The
entire state of Nevada was freckled and blotched. Utah, Arizona, western Montana, and much of Idaho were disaster
zones as well. And the top half of Washington State looked
as if it had a severe case of measles. Several of those blem-
ishes were close to her present location. The map was dated
2002. A note included with the map stated that two out of five
watersheds in those areas were polluted by mines. Yeesh.
Given the hands-off political climate and the downturn in the
economy since the map had been created, it seemed unlikely
that many of those sites had been cleaned up.

She gritted her teeth. Supposedly federal lands belonged
to *all* the American people. The public had been getting
ripped off for more than a century, not to mention getting
stuck with the cleanup bill. Why didn't the media ever do a
story on this atrocity instead of plastering her photo across
the television screen?

Her head ached, more from outrage now than from the injury she'd received less than two days ago. She shut down the computer and stood up, her muscles knotted with anger, and moved to the window to stare at the darkness.

Her mind wouldn't stop racing in circles. Poachers, mines, arson. Kidnapping? What had happened at Marmot Lake two nights ago, and what threats were still out there? Right now, she knew the area better than anyone else. She should have ignored Schuler and explored the place earlier this evening. At first light tomorrow, she'd be in those woods, looking for clues.

Not only did her head throb, but the stitches inside her mouth were smarting again. If only Chase were here to massage her neck now. She rubbed a finger across her lips, trying to remember the feel of his kiss. Instead, she felt only the rough seam of stitches.

Was he in Seattle, or on his way back to Salt Lake? She picked up her cell phone, punched in his number, and immediately got his voice mail. Which could mean anything: he was in a meeting, he was on another call, he was in a shoot-out in a dark alley.

"Chase, it's Sam, I mean Summer." He always called her by her given name, insisting that it was perfect for her. And it sounded that way when it came from his lips. "Well, you know who it is. Just wanted to say that I'm thinking of you, and I hope you're safe, and I hope I see you again soon." She pressed the End button, feeling a twinge of frustration at not getting to talk to him.

Was his partner Nicole with him, or was he by himself now, too? That question led her to a less pleasant thought, one of Chase having an evening out with a woman decidedly more elegant than Summer Westin. In her mind's eye, this woman was a luscious brunette in a black lace cocktail dress and heels, drinking whatever cocktail was in vogue, eating an elegant seafood meal with Chase over a white tablecloth.

White tablecloths had always made Sam nervous. She was more comfortable eating out of tin pots and sleeping on the floors of fire towers.

Chase had hinted that the fire tower had been boring. In her vision, the brunette shared a tinkly laugh with handsome Agent Perez.

Sam rubbed the frown line creasing her forehead. She was letting her imagination run away again. Chase did keep coming back to see her, didn't he? And so far, every female he mentioned had turned out to be either another FBI agent or one of his extended family of Lakotas and Latinos. But then again, those were only the women she'd heard about. Special Agent Starchaser Perez was an expert at keeping secrets.

CHASE sipped his Blue Moon pinot gris. The Oregon wine was a perfect accompaniment to the linguini with clam sauce. Naturally, Nicole had picked them both. Even in the smallest, most rustic hamlets like this ferry landing on the Kitsap Peninsula, she had a knack for sleuthing out the best food and drink that fit within their meager FBI expense budget.

"Where next? What's your vote?" Nicole's sleek auburn hair swung forward as she bent her head to take a sip of water.

On the table between their plates lay a folded map, copies of police reports, computer printouts, communiqués from the SACs in Salt Lake and Seattle.

"Despite the fact that this one was a wash, I still think the pattern generally holds. Small towns with big money and small police forces. Diversionary tactics minutes before the robbery. I choose La Conner." He tapped the dot on the Washington map. "Small town, a lot of well-to-do citizens and vacationers. Most available law enforcement preoccupied with a bomb threat at the local high school at the time the bank was robbed." He pushed the map back toward his partner and wound up another mouthful of linguini.

Nicole nodded. "Agreed. I'll let Seattle know we're headed there. Like the pasta?"

"Perfect choice."

Chase had spent his childhood in cookie-cutter housing developments in Montana and Idaho. With his Lakota mother, his Mexican-American father, his brother and sister and all his parents' relatives, his home had been happy and stimulating. But it was never immaculate, and rarely quiet. He'd dreamed of marrying an elegant, refined woman with a decent salary. They'd both have interesting careers and a home that was a refuge of peaceful sophistication. They'd talk about books and go to lectures and concerts.

It was probably some sort of lesson in humility that he'd been partnered with just such a woman. She made being an FBI agent look easy. He'd learned a lot from Nicole over the last six years. She seemed to manage a happy home life, too, if the persistent smile on her husband's face was any indication. But Chase was not the least bit sexually attracted to Nicole.

He took another sip of the pinot gris. How could it be that this expensive, delicate wine was not nearly as delicious as the cheap Chianti he'd shared with Summer last night? The time he spent with her always seemed so . . . refreshing. Which was a ridiculous thought, now that he stopped to analyze it, because when he was with her, they were forever scrambling over rocks or wading through rapids.

How had he gotten involved with a woman who slept in fire towers and tramped around in the wilderness for a living? Had he ever seen her without a smudge of dirt or a scratch or bruise on her face? Damn that Greg Jordan! If he'd only shown up at the fire tower a couple of hours later.

"Chase?"

He looked up.

Nicole's eyebrows lifted. "You're thinking about *her*, aren't you?"

It was embarrassing, how easily his partner could read him.

"How long have you two been playing this game? It's been nearly a year now, hasn't it? Just go for it, partner," she told him. "Take her on a romantic vacation."

A snort escaped his nostrils. "Right. That's worked out well so far."

He'd scheduled a rendezvous last November, but then the Bureau sent them to Boston on a supposed emergency that turned out to be totally bogus. Then he'd set up a ski trip in March, but Summer had been sent off to write up a bird-watching event in Oregon and he'd been shipped off to Homeland Security training at Quantico. The two of them seemed destined to revolve around each other like two moons locked into separate orbits.

"Well, keep trying," Nicole advised. "In the meantime, send her a fantastic gift to show you care."

Easy for Nicole Boudreaux to say. Jewelry, clothes, art would suffice for her. But what could he buy for Summer Westin, who was more impressed by sunsets and bears than gold and silk?

Although she wasn't nearly as tough as she liked to believe, Summer was a strong woman. He worried about the hazardous situations she jumped into, but the truth was, she could handle herself pretty well. She didn't really *need* him. He understood that: he didn't really *need* her, either. But sometimes he *wanted* her so badly it hurt.

Nicole's cell phone chimed. She slid it from her purse, glanced briefly at the screen, and mouthed "SAC" to him before answering in a low voice, "Boudreaux."

She listened quietly for a moment, glanced at her watch, and then said, "We'll be there before midnight." As she slid the phone back into her purse with her right hand, she used the left to wave to the waitress across the room, then pointed to herself and to him and mouthed *Coffee*.

The waitress nodded and headed for the counter. Chase hurriedly shoved another forkful of pasta into his mouth and chewed.

Nicole turned back to him and explained, "Hot off the press—bank robbery in Rock Springs, Wyoming, minutes after the train derailed in the middle of town."

"Sounds like our guys," he said. "I suppose they got away?"

"You suppose right."

"So we're off to Wyoming?"

She shook her head. "We just caught an attempted armored car robbery near Blaine, up by the Canadian border, called in fifteen minutes after an arson fire at a local hospital."

Either coincidences were spreading like fungus or they were definitely following a large group of operatives. He poured the last of the pinot gris into his glass.

She raised an eyebrow. "Didn't you hear me say we're off to Blaine?"

"Yep. It's your turn to drive."

As she glowered at him, he tossed back the wine, swallowed, and wound up another forkful of pasta. "You said an attempted robbery. Cops in Blaine catch the perps?"

Nicole shook her head again. The waitress arrived with coffee. He asked for the check as she poured. Nicole waited until the waitress had moved away. "The robbers escaped into the countryside; cops are still searching. But they captured their vehicle."

"The key," he murmured wishfully through the last of his linguini.

"Let's hope. We're getting closer." She checked her watch. "The next ferry leaves in twenty minutes."

They both reached for their coffee cups.

SAM shook her head at her mental meanderings about Chase. They lived hundreds of miles apart. There'd been no promises made between them; the man was free to go out whenever he wanted, with whomever he desired.

As was she. Unfortunately, she couldn't think of any other man she'd recently been attracted to. Every time she thought about men, she thought about Chase. And he wasn't there.

But it wasn't as if she was cloistered or anything. She knew plenty of males, even if most of them were just friends. Blake was gay, but he still counted. Kent and

Rafael in Utah, Joe Choi here. She was in a man's apartment right now, even if the man wasn't there. Mack was sitting with Lisa Glass until 9 P.M.

The light was blinking on Mack's answering machine. The Play button activated Peter Hoyle's voice. "Lindstrom, this is a message for Westin. I assume she's staying with you." The pause that followed was probably meant to indicate Hoyle's disapproval.

"Westin, I need you to sit with Lisa from seven to nine tomorrow morning; the regulars have a staff meeting then. You can work late to make up for it. I left this message on your voice mail, too."

Sam grimaced. Damn! She wouldn't be at Marmot Lake at first light, after all. The message continued, "If either of you know anything more about Lisa, now is the time to spill it. The emergency contact number we have on file for her isn't valid. And Lindstrom, about the meeting tomorrow, try to be on time for once—it begins at seven forty-five, not eight, not eight fifteen."

Sam reset the machine. As she was writing a note for Mack, her cell phone began its distinctive wolf howl. "Westin," she answered.

"Hi, sweetheart."

Hearing Mark Westin's voice surprised her; her father usually called on Sunday afternoons. "Hi, Dad."

"I was sitting here reading before I went to bed and thinking about you when suddenly it occurred to me that I could check on you, now that you have a cell phone."

Oh, great. She struggled throughout the week to think of safe topics to talk about on Sundays and now he was going to start calling at other times, too? She'd finally bought a cell phone for business reasons, but carrying one around had its drawbacks.

"You're still coming to the wedding, aren't you?"

"I wouldn't miss it for the world." Although a formal wedding in the August heat in Kansas wasn't an event she could actually look forward to, even if it was about time her father and his "lady friend" tied the knot. In western Washington, it was easy to forget that summer was proceeding full blast in the rest of the country. She'd compared temperatures in the paper yesterday: Seattle, 72; Wichita, 99. She wilted just thinking about jetting into that oven.

"And remember, Zola wants you to come a couple of days early. She's made you a dress in your size, but she says there's a final fitting. I know how you girls are."

Sam winced at a mental picture of herself in a lavender chiffon spaghetti-strapped concoction, with her half-tanned, muscular arms exposed for the church ladies to critique. "I've made reservations for August twentieth, Dad, so there'll be plenty of time. Is Zola there?"

"Of course not, Summer. It's after ten o'clock here."

She felt like a naughty teenager, to have imagined that his fiancée would be in his house that close to bedtime. He'd always had a way of reprimanding her with only a few words. "I know it's late, Dad. Anyhow, tell her I'll be there on August twentieth."

"Give me your flight number. We'll come and pick you up."

"I'm not home right now, Dad, I don't have it with me."

"I'll get the flight number later, then."

"No, Dad, it's too far to Wichita. I'll rent a car." She'd go berserk trapped there without transportation of her own. At least she could drive herself out to the lake and howl at the moon when she needed to. "My plane gets in around noon, so I should be there around two."

"If you're sure you don't want me to come . . ."

"I'm sure, Daddy. It's too much trouble." There was a brief, uncomfortable stretch of nothing but background static, and then she said, "Well, good night, Dad. Say hi to Zola for me."

"I will, Sugar. Good night. God bless." He hung up.

She sat cross-legged on the carpet, listening to dead air for an instant, then sighed and pressed End. That air of unspoken dissatisfaction had always existed between them. She was nearing forty, unmarried, childless, flitting from one peculiar job to another, sharing her small home with a gay man.

She knew it was hard for Reverend Westin to find anything about his daughter's life that he could even mention to his friends, other than the stories and photos she had published.

If she were a featured speaker at the wildlife conference, that would be a source of pride. She could send him a brochure with her name in it. A soft groan escaped her lips. She had to take that offer.

Her cell phone began its wolf howl. That had to be Chase. She eagerly raised it to her ear again. "I hope you're studying those special agent tricks, FBI," she breathed into it.

"Uh." A childish voice. "Is Summer Westin there?"

Lili. "It's me, honey," Sam said, embarrassed. "I thought you were someone else." She *had* to start checking the caller ID before answering.

"I guess so. You know someone in the FBI?"

"I have a friend who's an FBI agent." She wasn't about to share her love life with a thirteen-year-old.

"Sweet." Then there was a hesitation. "But an FBI agent is a fed, right? So maybe that's not so sweet."

"Trust me, Lili, he's pretty sweet." And then she was exasperated at herself, because now she *was* sharing her love life with a thirteen-year-old. "But I'm sure you didn't call to talk about that."

"Remember my career project? I wrote down a lot of questions about being a wildlife biologist. So I was wondering, can we get together tomorrow after school?"

Sam planned to spend most of tomorrow looking for more signs of trouble at Marmot Lake. "Well, Lili, I have to work."

"And *I* have to go to school," Lili retorted, her tone long-suffering.

Good point. She *had* promised to help. "You're right. What time is 'after school'?"

"I get out at two."

Well, that was darn inconvenient—smack in the middle of prime survey time for her. "Lili, how'd you like to come out and do some fieldwork with me?"

"Really? That'd be cool! Maybe we could find a bear."

"Maybe we could; I'm looking for one. Think your mom or dad might be able to deliver you around three?"

"I'm walking over to Dad now; you can ask him."

"Wear your boots and bring a water bottle."

"I will. Thanks, Aunt Summer! See you tomorrow."

After making a deal with Joe to rendezvous with him and Lili at a forest service campground, Sam ended the call and wandered around the living room. She pulled the power knob on his old TV. Nothing happened. She checked the plug and gave the antique device a solid whack, clicked it on and off a few times. Nothing.

She perused Mack's book collection, which consisted of military thrillers, truck catalogs, and botany textbooks, reminding her again that her friend might be a fellow outdoor enthusiast, but he was a guy, and a young guy to boot. She felt like a salmon that had leapt the wrong waterfall and ended up in an alien pond.

She plopped onto the floor, pulled her duffel to her, and rummaged through it, finally extracting a plastic bag that contained an embroidery hoop, fabric, and a small stack of quilt blocks. She dumped the bag's contents out on the floor. The finished blocks were the beginning of an album quilt. Her grandmother had made one for her mother: a record of the milestones in Susan Crawford Westin's short life. Squares commemorating childhood events, high school graduation, engagement, marriage, and the birth of her only child, Summer.

Her mother's album quilt was traditional. Her own would be a record of a very different life. And with her mother and grandmother both in their graves, Sam would have to finish it herself.

The top square had been stitched by her mother. Sam couldn't remember ever seeing her with a needle and thread, so she must have sewn this shortly after Sam was born, before ALS had robbed her hands of their strength. A yellow-haired baby sitting cross-legged on a Bible, reaching toward a black-and-red butterfly that fluttered just out of reach. Sam knew that she was the baby, that the Bible represented her father. And the butterfly her mother? Had the poor woman been that perceptive? Sam sighed. She'd never know.

The next four squares had been pieced together by her grandmother. One showed a small figure in a tree filled with birds. Until her grandmother had produced this, Sam believed that her favorite hiding place was a secret. There was a square showing a girl on a galloping pinto, the horse's mane and tail and the girl's hair flying in the wind. Just looking at the appliqué image made Sam remember the happiness she'd felt riding Comanche through the prairie grass and wildflowers.

The next square was a girl in cap and gown: high school graduation. Then one of a college diploma clasped in the huge paw of a grinning grizzly bear. Her grandmother's gentle humor, representing Sam's college degree in wildlife biology.

Sam had sewn the last square herself, as evidenced by its uneven stitching. But at least the subject was original: a blond woman standing with a shovel in hand, shadowed by an ostrich. This square stood for her brief stint as a zookeeper. She'd added a malevolent squint to the ostrich's embroidered eye. The giant African birds were not to be trusted; she still had a scar on the back of her neck to prove it.

She fingered the plain-colored squares of cloth at the bottom of the stack. What next? Did she really want to memorialize her first Internet reporting gig for the Save the Wilderness Fund? She'd certainly never forget it, and both a ranger friend and a cougar bore old bullet scars as permanent reminders. Several people had almost died, including a two-year-old boy. She shivered. No.

She didn't really feel like sewing or even thinking about a design for a quilt block. She stuffed the squares back into her bag, went to the kitchen, and poured another Negra Modelo for herself. Ten forty-five. Mack should have left the hospital at nine. He was probably out with Jodi or one of his buddies. Or maybe avoiding his apartment because he feared she was there? Tomorrow, she'd take herself out of his hair.

Yawning, she dumped out the last third of the beer. She took a shower, and after leaving Hoyle's message on Mack's pillow, she folded out the futon and made up the lumpy mattress with the same wad of sheets she'd used a week ago. She woke only once, a little after midnight, when a square of light from the hallway spilled onto her face as Mack opened the door.

9

THE next morning, Sam found Lisa reclined in a half-sitting position in her hospital bed, cradling her head in her hands. Twenty questions for her immediately leapt to Sam's mind. Take it slow, she reminded herself. She smiled. "I'm glad to see that you're awake this morning, Lisa." Thrilled was more like it.

Lisa looked at Sam, her gaze unfocused. She didn't smile back. Sam plopped into the visitor chair. It hadn't gotten any softer since the previous day. "Remember me? Sam Westin? How are you feeling?"

A tiny moan escaped the blistered lips, then Lisa croaked, "Head hurts. Bad."

"Did they give you something for it?"

Another half nod.

"Well, then, it'll probably get better in a little while." Sam slid the chair closer. "If it doesn't, we'll see if we can get the nurses to give you something else."

The chair creaked as she leaned forward. No wonder the previous visitor had had a hard time meeting the girl's gaze. Some of Lisa's bandages had been removed, and her skin had been cleaned or scrubbed, or whatever torturous thing they did with burns these days. The right side of Lisa's face was smooth white skin; the left half was blood-red jelly overlaid with white cream. Sam clasped her hands in her lap to keep from patting her own cheeks to make sure they were okay. "Lisa, last time I was here, you told me that you'd been kidnapped."

The girl's gaze moved to the far wall. "Yes."

So it hadn't been just delirious rambling. Sam stood up, curled her fingers around the side rail of the bed. "Can you tell me what you remember?"

Lisa cleared her throat before starting. "I was walking . . . before I went home." The words sounded tentative, her voice hoarse. It seemed like she didn't want to move her lips any more than she had to.

"Where's home?"

Lisa's eyes darted back and forth. "Oh . . ." She licked her lips. "I don't really . . . have a place now. Weekends, I camp out . . . in my car. Save my money."

"Can't you can stay in the dorm on weekends? I think most of the trail crew does."

Lisa's gaze now seemed to be fixed on her toes under the sheet. "I don't want to." She swallowed. "Not with . . . those guys."

"Why? Did they do something to you?" They were mostly convicted delinquents, after all.

Lisa shook her head. The motion caused tears to well up in her ice blue eyes. She blinked and said, "Nothing I could prove."

Strange answer.

Lisa's pale eyes connected with Sam's. "I'm not one of them. They'd be in jail if they weren't working there."

"Yeah, I heard that. So, you left work, decided to take a walk. Where did you park your car?"

Lisa looked startled at the mention of her car. "I don't know."

"What kind of a car is it?"

"Chevy. Don't know the license."

That seemed an odd thing for her to volunteer, but now Lisa's expression was so troubled that Sam just shrugged. "That's okay. You parked it somewhere, and then what?"

"I was just walking." She looked down at her lap again. "Then . . . three guys came out of the woods."

Sam's heartbeat sped up. "What did they look like?"

Lisa fidgeted, smoothing the sheet over her thighs. "I

didn't see. They threw . . . something . . . over my head, then put me . . . in a car trunk."

"You don't remember anything about them?"

"They were dark."

"You mean black? African-American?"

"No. But black hair. Greasy. Dark skin . . . swarthy." Her brows knitted together in a frown. "One had a big nose. Maybe a Jew."

What an odd, bigoted thing for a young girl to say. Squelching her irritation, Sam pulled a lined yellow tablet from her daypack. "Mack Lindstrom told me you were an artist. Could you sketch this guy with the big nose?"

Lisa's blistered lips twisted into a grimace. "I'm not really an artist."

Sam placed the tablet and pencil in Lisa's lap.

The girl curled her fingers stiffly around the pencil. "I could try." The IV tube taped to the back of her hand whispered across the rumpled sheet as she made a few tentative strokes.

"Why do you think they took you, Lisa?"

"I don't know. Maybe . . ." The smooth side of her face reddened.

"For sex?" Sam guessed.

Her chin dipped again. "'Cause I'm tall. Fair." Her fingers patted the charred remains of her hair, then touched her burned cheek. The ice blue eyes filled. "Least I was. Now I'll be . . . a monster." A tear escaped her lashless eye and trickled over the ruined side of Lisa's face.

"I doubt that," Sam murmured. But what the hell did she know? Lisa's scars might make little kids run for the rest of her life. But she didn't know how to comfort the girl, and she was determined not to get derailed. "Lisa, we found you near Marmot Lake."

The girl thought about it for a few seconds. "Where?"

"It doesn't really matter right now. Near where we found you there was an old mine. It looks like dynamite blew it open. There was a big explosion on the night we found you. Do you know anything about that?"

Lisa's eyes widened. "No. This thing was over my head."

"You thought they had rape in mind," Sam stated bluntly. Lisa winced at the word. But the question had to be asked. "Did they rape you?"

Lisa's attention shifted back to her lap. She drew another tentative line on the tablet, then stopped. "Something . . . hit me. I don't know anything more."

Sam noticed the momentary eye-to-eye contact after each question, then the girl's averted gaze as the words came out. Had Paul Schuler guessed right? Was Lisa lying? Or was this just a very hard story for her to tell?

Sam pressed. "You didn't have anything over your head when we found you. Did these guys have guns? Explosives? Gasoline?"

"I don't know."

"Can you estimate what time it was when you got hit?"

"I don't know—everything's black!"

A nurse cruised by the doorway, gave Sam a sharp look. From the bedside table, Sam picked up a plastic glass full of water and angled the straw toward Lisa. "I don't want to badger you, Lisa," she said softly. "But we need your help to catch these guys."

After taking a sip, Lisa closed her eyes and clutched both hands to her temples. A tear rolled down her cheek. "My head's going to explode. Make this bed flat?"

Sam set down the water glass, retrieved the tablet from the girl's lap, and reached for the controls on the hospital bed. "Do you want me to get the nurse? Ask if you can have some more pain medication?"

"No. I just want to sleep."

"Of course you do." Sam patted the girl's hand. "Thanks for telling me about the three guys. You did the right thing."

The girl turned her back to Sam. "No. I shouldn't talk." A soft moan, then what sounded like, "'Specially not to you."

"OLD man Craig was by here again," Philip King said.

"Glad I missed him." That was the last thing Jack

needed. He bent over his drafting board, trying to calculate the proper curve for the restaurant counter he was designing. Tears pooled in his own eyes when he looked at Ernest Craig's mournful face; when he heard the guy's voice break, his own throat closed up. He felt a lump growing there now.

King was going on and on about how they needed to get rid of Ernest Craig. Jack didn't ask the psycho what he had in mind. Could open up all sorts of possibilities he didn't want to think about, just like the two long scratches on King's left cheek this morning. He wasn't going to ask where those had come from, either.

"This'll do it." King stuck a postcard under Jack's nose.

Swallowing hard, Jack pulled the postcard out of King's hand and forced himself to focus on it. It was a photo of that famous Hollywood sidewalk with the handprints of the stars.

"My ma brought a bunch of these back from visiting her cousin. I wouldn't be caught dead in faggot land, even if Schwarzenegger used to run the place, but her cousin's married. To a man. I mean, her cousin's a woman, married to a regular—"

Jack interrupted, "How's a postcard going to help?"

King rolled his eyes, "You write on it, like Allie—you got some of her writing around you can copy, right?"

Jack's thoughts leapt to the note in the drawer of his bedside table. The one where Allie had written in big loopy letters that the times they spent together were the best times of her life. Turquoise ink. She'd signed her name with a heart over the letter *i*.

"We mail it to Craig. And he thinks she's run off to Los Angeles."

If only Jack could make *himself* believe she'd run away, that his golden girl was living down in the California sunshine. "But the postmark—"

"Port Angeles." King slapped a stack of envelopes down in front of him. "Check these out."

They were window envelopes—the kind he typically

received invoices or checks in—from one of the restaurants in Port Angeles. He eyed King suspiciously. "Where'd you get these?"

"Around." King tapped a corner of the top envelope. "Check out the postmark."

Clearly, the Port Angeles post office needed to clean their stamping machine. The word *Port* was only a smudge. On one envelope, he could make out *geles*, on another, *Angel*. A Port Angeles postmark could easily be mistaken for Los Angeles.

"Besides, you think old man Craig's going to check a postmark?"

Ernest Craig would glom on to a postcard from Allie like a drowning man would grab a life preserver. Jack looked up at King, who was grinning. Sometimes, for a dim bulb, the guy had some pretty bright ideas.

CHASE Perez sighed in exasperation when he got Sam's voice mail. He was happy that she finally had her own cell phone, but she wasn't much easier to get hold of now than she'd been before. At least half the time she was out of range or had the dang thing turned off to save the battery. Knowing her, she probably subscribed to the cheapest cell plan with the lousiest coverage.

Yawning, he turned his back to the window of Starbucks and studied the cloudy sky overhead. He and Nicole had been up half the night watching crime scene techs take apart the Ford Explorer the would-be robbers had left behind, making sure the fingerprints and hair samples went to the front of the processing queue in New York. They'd caught a few hours' sleep at a Days Inn, but not nearly enough to face the mountain of papers recovered from the vehicle.

After the beep, he said, "Summer, it's Chase. I'm thinking of you, too. I'm still in Washington State, and I'm sure going to try to find the time to see you again. I've been

studying the manual, and believe me, the first chance I get,
I *am* going to show you my special agent tricks."

"I'd like to see them, too." Nicole stood at his elbow.

He straightened, flipped the phone closed, and stuffed it
in his pocket. "Stop sneaking up on me."

"Who's sneaking?" She thrust one of the two lattés she
held in his direction. "I'm just delivering coffee." She nodded toward the car. "It's your turn to drive. I want to have a
look at this manual you mentioned."

He pretended not to see his partner's smirk as he followed her back to the car.

THE lobby of the main park headquarters was empty. As
Sam passed the assistant superintendent's office, she
noticed Hoyle hunched over the desktop, staring at a computer screen.

She stopped at the park superintendent's office. It was
empty, the lights off, the desk far too neat; the room looked
as though Tracey Carsen had not visited it for several days.

"Westin." Behind her, Peter Hoyle had come out into the
hallway. He pointed into his office like he was ordering a
dog to lie down in the corner. Reluctantly, Sam obeyed.
They settled into their respective chairs at the same time.

"If you want to communicate with management, then
you need to talk to me. Superintendent Carsen will be out
for a while. She just had knee surgery and will be out on
medical leave for six weeks." Hoyle narrowed his eyes.

"Okay." This explained a lot. Sam had been hired by
Tracey Carsen. Now Peter Hoyle was stuck managing a
project and a person he had probably never approved of in
the first place.

"Why did you want to see Superintendent Carsen?"

Sam slung her daypack into the adjacent guest chair,
pulled out the sketch Lisa had penciled. "I want to talk
about this." She thrust the drawing across the desk. With
only a few lines, the girl had captured the likeness of a

hawk-nosed man. The drawing depicted an intense-looking fellow with slick-backed hair, bushy brows, piercing eyes, Fu Manchu mustache, and pointed goatee. Add horns and you'd have the devil, Sam thought.

Hoyle's eyebrows dipped into a vee as Sam told him about her conversation with Lisa. His frown deepened with each added piece of information, plowing horizontal furrows across his forehead.

"Like I told you yesterday, you should have called me. A law enforcement ranger should have interviewed her."

"I was afraid that there wouldn't be time for one to get there." Plus the fact that she wanted to hear Lisa's story for herself.

Hoyle stared at the drawing. "This is all I need."

The assistant superintendent seemed immobilized by the course of events. Sam prompted him, "First there was deliberate fire setting, and now an alleged kidnapping on federal property. I thought you might want to call the FBI."

Hoyle slapped the drawing down on his desk. "Are you sure about this, Westin?"

Sam raised an eyebrow. "Why would I make this up?"

"Publicity stunt for another Internet drama?"

Sam chose not to dignify that with a response. "Do you want *me* to call the FBI?" she asked.

All the way from the hospital to headquarters, she had struggled with the urge to phone Chase. But the park service was an entrenched federal bureaucracy, not unlike the military. Skipping the chain of command would anger the management and make her remaining contract time miserable. Like many other law enforcement agencies, NPS rangers tended to view FBI agents as glory-grabbing snobs.

Hoyle sighed heavily. "You have an environmental survey to complete in three weeks. Not to mention writing the management recommendations; be sure to copy that form I gave you. I don't need you sit with Lisa until"—he checked a page on the top of his out-box stack—"four to eight P.M. Wednesday."

"Got it." Sam stood up.

"And another fax from that Best guy came for you. I never know where you'll show up, so I sent a copy to the west district building, too." Hoyle glared at her as if it were Sam's fault that she was a roving temp.

What was she supposed to say here? "Uh, thanks, Peter."

"Get back to work, Westin. Write me a confidential report about everything Lisa said to you, and I do mean everything you learned about her. I'll take care of the rest."

THE trail crew was hacking out new switchbacks up the mountain on the way to the first of the pools in Seven Lake Basin. When she first arrived in the park, Sam met the trail crew supervisor, Tom Blackstock. He was a burly Army Reserve sergeant as well as a seasonal worker with the park service. Word was that he ran his crew like a military unit, although today it looked more like a chain gang. The seven youths rhythmically hacked at the rock with sledge-hammers and shovels.

She made it a point to stand clear of the flying rock chips while she announced herself. "Yo, trail crew!"

The closest youth stopped working to stare at her. Then the others fell silent as well. Blackstock peered around his workers. "Hi, little lady! Come to pay us hardworkin' guys a visit?"

She decided to ignore the "little lady" bit, just this once. "A short visit. I wanted to talk to you all about Lisa Glass."

From beneath his bushy brows, Blackstock gave her a skeptical look. "Why'd they send you?"

"When I was sitting with her in the hospital, Lisa said some things that didn't make much sense. We were hoping you'd be able to help." She hoped he wouldn't ask who else was included in the "we."

Blackstock leaned his shovel against the side of the cliff. "Good a time as any for lunch break, guys. Grab your bags and meet under the cedar." He nodded toward a massive red-barked evergreen that spiked up from a group of boulders fifty feet below them.

Sam climbed down and straddled one of the sun-warmed boulders, leaving the shade under the overhanging boughs for the trail builders. It couldn't be more than seventy degrees out, but they were sweating. As a short muscular youth passed, Sam noted with surprise the protrusion of breasts under the damp T-shirt. That's right, Mack *had* mentioned two females on the trail crew.

The workers arranged themselves around Sam, catching quick glances at her out of the corners of their eyes as if they feared trouble if they examined her directly. None looked older than twenty. The still air was thick with the smell of sweat. She was glad she'd left her own lunch three miles downhill in her truck.

Blackstock removed his hard hat and lowered himself onto a flat rock across from Sam, their knees almost touching. He pulled a mashed sandwich and a thermos out of a tattered daypack. "How's Lisa doing?"

"Her head was hurting her a lot this morning. And the burns on her face and body are pretty bad."

"Do they know what happened?"

Sam shook her head. "It's still not clear. That's why I wanted to talk to you guys."

The youths looked uncomfortable, their eyes shifting nervously as they chewed. Most of them had records; they probably worried they'd be blamed even if they'd committed no recent crimes.

Sam strove to reassure them. "Lisa seems confused, and we don't know whether she can think clearly right now. I need to know what she was like; what you thought of her."

She noticed that several pairs of eyes strayed to a thin-faced boy.

"Lisa was a good worker, had no trouble keeping up," Blackstock volunteered. The group nodded in unison, still chewing.

"Did you all get along with her?"

Various gazes flicked back and forth among the group, many aimed at the same youth. Nobody spoke.

Sam smiled at the boy. "What's your name?"

He peered at her from beneath his hard hat. As he tipped his head, gray eyes under thick brows, a sunburned face, and a thin nose emerged into the sunlight. "Rosen. Ben Rosen." The kid needed a shave: about two days' growth of beard peppered his narrow cheeks and chin. A silver skull earring dangled from one lobe.

"Why does everyone keep looking at you?"

Ben grinned, revealing a chipped front tooth. "Lisa didn't like me much."

"Why not?"

He shrugged, his eyes now focused on the sandwich in his hand as if trying to determine what it contained.

A youth with a sparse mustache and ponytail spoke up. "Ben was always hittin' on her."

Ben waved his sandwich at his accuser. "No more than I hit on any other girl."

"I can vouch for that," the girl said. "He's always hitting on me, too." She'd taken off her hard hat. Her auburn hair was very short, almost a buzz cut. But despite this and her unisex work clothes, she oozed sexuality. The top of a tattoo was visible in the vee of her T-shirt. She jerked a thumb toward a blond-haired boy sitting behind her. "Jason here hits on me, too."

"And on Lisa?"

The blond boy stared back defiantly. "Of course."

Something going on there, Sam thought. "Did Lisa get along with you, Jason?"

"She liked me just fine," he retorted.

Judging by the glare that passed from Ben to Jason, Sam guessed that Jason's last statement was true.

"Maya! Jason!" Blackstock's posture was stiff. He was clearly appalled at his crew's revelations. "We can't be—"

Sam interrupted the inevitable speech on politically correct behavior. "It's okay. I want to hear the truth about Lisa."

She asked them about Friday evening. Jason said that Lisa had left in her old junker after their shift ended.

"Know where she was headed?"

They all shook their heads.

"What do you know about her family, or her friends away from here?"

"She doesn't talk," Ben explained.

"Not even to me," Maya threw in, "and we share a room."

Jason snorted. "She thinks she's too good for us."

"Guys!" Blackstock objected again.

"She said she wanted to hear the truth," Ponytail argued.

"Lisa acts all bougie because *she's* never been in trouble," Maya said. "Just because she's working for money, not donating her time like we are." She ran her fingers through her close-cropped hair.

"Bougie" was a new word for Sam, but she could deduce what the teenager meant by the context.

Maya continued. "When we go to town, she never even gets out of the truck. She wouldn't be caught dead in public with us. That . . . girl is cold."

Sam was sure that Maya would have used the word *bitch* had Blackstock not been present.

She stood up to leave. "Thanks, guys. One final question. I need a place to stay for the next three weeks. Is there a free bunk in your dorm? I remember an offer of one in May when I first got here."

Blackstock scratched his head. "We got two extra bunks in the ladies' room. Think Lisa will be back soon?"

Lisa's burns and bruises loomed large in Sam's memory. Even the medicinal odor came back. "I don't think she'll be back this season," she said.

"Then I guess you can have your pick of three bunks. Right, Maya?" He turned to the red-haired girl.

Maya shrugged. "You couldn't be any worse than her."

10

JOE Choi searched the knots of departing students for the red blouse that Lili had been wearing when she'd left the house that morning. He finally spotted a flash of scarlet. His daughter had tied the long-sleeved blouse around her waist and now sported only a tight tank top above her short jean skirt.

Was that his little girl? One hip thrust out like a model, her little black leather pack slung over one arm and a gym bag at her feet, Lili stood between Gale Martinson and a tall boy with an armload of books. She tossed her head back, laughed at something Martinson said. The boy laughed, too. Joe squinted. How old was that kid? The grades were confusingly mixed together in summer school. Martinson put a hand on Lili's shoulder. Joe felt his chest tighten. Was that a friendly teacher's touch, or something more?

"Lili!" Joe yelled out the open window.

She raised a hand to shield her eyes from the sun, spotted his truck, and frowned. Several kids glanced at him, then at Lili, who shouldered the gym bag and ran to the truck. Today she wore her hair loose, except for a red ribbon tied around her special charred lock of hair.

She reluctantly hauled herself up into the truck, shoving her gym bag onto the floor. "Why are you here, Dad?"

"Did you forget you're meeting Aunt Summer this afternoon?"

"Of course not. But you're not supposed to pick me up until two thirty; I was going to hang out with my friends."

"The school was on my way to the office. You can hang out with me instead."

"So, let's go already!" She groaned and slid down in the passenger seat. "Why'd you have to bring your work truck? Everybody's staring."

"Put your seat belt on." Joe pulled away from the curb. "You expect me to go home and swap cars just so I won't embarrass you?"

"Crapola," she half whispered.

"I heard that. Where are your hiking boots and jeans?"

"In the gym bag, Dad. Duh."

Joe gritted his teeth. It was really annoying how she acted these days as if he were an imbecile for asking the most basic questions. "Why'd you take your blouse off, Lili?"

She shrugged. "I got hot."

"That was Mr. Martinson you were talking to, right?"

She nodded. "My science teacher. And his son, Michael."

"Why did he put his hand on your shoulder, Lili?"

His daughter stared at him for a long moment, and then sighed dramatically. "I didn't even notice."

"Was that the first time Martinson put his hands on you?"

Shock passed over her face. A flush of color rushed into her cheeks. "I can't believe you said that about Mr. Martinson. He's my teacher! Just because you're a cop—"

"Ranger."

"That's a government cop. You think that just because you arrest some pervs in the campgrounds, that everyone's like that. Mr. Martinson's nice. He teaches us all these cool things about science, about nature." A smile crept onto Lili's face. "And Michael's nice, too," she added. "He tells the greatest stories about bears. He's going to let me help him catch one sometime." She looked up at him from under her long lashes.

Thirteen years old, and boy, did she know how to flirt! Those warm caramel eyes, rosebud lips. Just like his wife, Laura, who could still make his blood race with one of her sultry glances. And why was that Michael kid talking to Lili about catching bears? Was that only teen-boy bragging?

He decided to change the subject. "What are you going to do with Aunt Summer today?"

"Learn how to track animals and stuff," Lili said. "I'm interviewing her for my school project." Then, under her breath, she muttered, "At least I can talk to *her*."

SAM dipped a test tube into the nameless creek. Although it was a lot less interesting than following bears, determining the health of all water sources was a necessary part of doing an environmental survey. The water was clear, but now she couldn't help wondering about possible pollution from old mines in the area. There were no mines pinpointed on her map, but then, that was just the point, wasn't it? The mine near Marmot Lake wasn't on her map, either.

She stoppered and labeled the tube, stuck it back in her pack, and stood up, brushing the dirt from the knees of her pants. She was two miles from the closest road. It was blissful to get back to her survey assignment; to be away from people for a while. The summer day was pleasantly warm under a canopy of high clouds, and for once she was glad her uniform shirt had short sleeves. Following the readings on her handheld GPS device, she walked the border of the newly transferred park land, enjoying the fluting songs of wrens and the high-pitched warning chatter of chipmunks.

She surprised two gangly Columbia black-tailed bucks that crashed away through the woods ahead of her. Close to a clump of cattails in a seasonal wetland, she found tracks that could have been Raider's. But she never caught a glimpse of a black bear.

Just before she exited a grove of Sitka spruce trees, a

flash of striped wings whirred through the boughs overhead. She watched in awe as the bird disappeared into the
canopy. Without her reference book, she couldn't be sure,
but it looked like a spotted owl.

She started to document the sighting in her notes, but as
her pen touched the page, a doubt crossed her mind. In this
area, the known presence of this particular endangered
species might entice illegal hunters into the woods. She
decided to ask Peter Hoyle's advice, maybe gain a point or
two with him. Tucking the clipboard under her arm, she
walked on.

The owl still thrived out here, along with the elk and
bears, the salamanders and the squirrels. It always made
her feel good to realize that humans had not yet irrevoca-
bly screwed up the entire planet. They hadn't even irrevo-
cably screwed up this area, although it had been designated
multi-use for decades. She hoped her management plan
would help to make sure humans wouldn't ruin the place in
the future.

The fifth NPS boundary sign she came across was six
feet off the ground, nailed to a large Douglas fir.

OLYMPIC NATIONAL PARK BOUNDARY
NO HUNTING BEYOND THIS POINT.

The sign was intact, just as the previous four had been;
that was good. However, on the next, a couple hundred
yards down the invisible boundary line to the east, three
bullet holes punctuated the message. And nailed beneath it
was one of the blue-stenciled THIS IS YOUR LAND signs.
Some creep, or maybe more than one, had stood at the base
of this tree, right where she was now.

She heard a soft thud behind her, and swiveled to search
the woods. A chattering squirrel bounced across a limb
nearby. Beneath the tree was a large pinecone. That must
have been what she'd heard, the pinecone dropping to the
ground.

Taking a hammer from her pack, she peeled off the

remainder of the bullet-ridden NPS marker and pounded in a new one from the small supply she carried. Then she pried off the offending YOUR LAND sign. It gave her a chill just to touch the dang thing. It was spooky how these signs kept cropping up all over the area.

She heard a cracking sound up ahead. Peter Hoyle's voice abruptly played back in her head: *We get at least one death threat a month.* Sam's pulse quickened as the sneering camouflaged hunter suddenly materialized among the trees in front of her. She pulled her radio from her belt and held it to her lips.

She looked up again. No hunter in camouflage gear. Just a piebald tan-and-white alder amid the evergreens. Damn it. She was letting a few nutcases make her paranoid. With her neck prickling now, she turned to survey the area behind her. For a moment, the only movement was a white butterfly flitting among the salmonberries. Then, not more than thirty feet away, a cedar sapling twitched. Her breath caught in her throat.

When she spotted the mountain beaver at the cedar's base, she laughed at herself for imagining someone was out to get her. She shoved the radio back into its holder. The rabbit-sized rodent didn't move when she approached, but continued to chew steadily on the sapling. The creature didn't even startle when she prodded it with the toe of her boot. Mountain beavers were not only inappropriately named—they weren't beavers and they lived in lowland forests—but incredibly dumb animals. They had another name, sewellels, but nobody ever used that for some reason. The forest service routinely killed them because of the damage they did to young trees. But in Sam's opinion, even the dumbest animals didn't deserve death just for doing what they were biologically programmed to do. And this dumb animal was on the forest service side of the boundary line.

She scooped up the gray-brown herbivore. It squeaked once and then froze in her arms. No survival skills whatsoever. It was a miracle the primitive beasts were not extinct.

She carried the mountain beaver into the woods well beyond the NPS boundary, and set it down near a group of young cedars sprouting from a nurse log. "Now you're in the park. Stay here and you'll be safe. Lots of baby trees to gnaw on."

The furball huddled in the same frozen position it had taken in her arms. Except for its rapid breathing, it could have been a stuffed toy. As she stood up, a scar on the landscape beyond the nurse log caught her eye. She stepped over the log and walked to a disturbed patch of ground.

Her steps came to an abrupt halt when she found the toes of her hiking boots resting in a primitive track that was not on the USGS map. Unofficial trails seemed to be common in the national forest; she'd already found several. She really shouldn't be surprised; television commercials regularly featured four-wheel drives blithely tearing up hillsides and crashing through pristine mountain streams, and those damn THIS IS YOUR LAND, WELCOME ATV's & HUNTER's signs invited local drivers to do as they pleased. These tracks were new, not more than a week old. The damp dirt held recent impressions of heavy tire treads. She dragged a few limbs across the track to make it less attractive, but by herself she couldn't build much in the way of a barricade.

She compared the readings on her GPS device with the USGS map on her clipboard, deduced that the track's origin was probably just a little farther down the forest service road she'd parked on. Most troubling, it disappeared through the trees in the direction of Marmot Lake. Shit. The good ol' boys didn't need to break the chain or climb over the gate on the south side of the lake; they'd blazed their own route in from the north.

The radio hooked to her belt rasped out her call code, startling her. "Where are you?" the dispatcher queried.

"Due north of Marmot Lake, approximately one mile south of Forest Road 4255." Was Hoyle checking up to see if she was working? "Who's asking?"

"Joe Choi. He says to remind you of your appointment, whatever that means."

Uh-oh. She checked her watch, saw that she was going to be late. "I'm on my way."

Damn. Did she dare bring Lili back here? No, she decided. Anything—or anyone—could be at the end of the track. Further exploration would have to wait until tomorrow. She made a hasty sketch of the tread marks, drew in the track's position on the map, and jogged back to her truck.

MORE than two hours later, as Sam was describing how she knew there were owls in the area they were exploring, Lili interrupted, throwing back her head as she looked up from her notes. "Wait a minute! That's poop!"

Sam kept her expression neutral as she pointed toward the droppings on the ground. "Wildlife biologists like to call it scat. See how there's fur and tiny bones in here?" She broke apart a grayish sausage with a stick and leaned back so Lili could look.

Lili fingered her charred lock of hair. The wrinkling of her nose gave away her opinion of scat investigation.

Sam struggled not to laugh. "If I don't know what kind of animal produced the droppings, I collect it."

"*Collect* it?"

"I scoop it into a plastic bag so I can study it later. There are whole books about scat. You can find out a lot about the animal it came from; about what it's been eating. Like this"—she poked at the droppings on the ground—"I can tell that this critter has been eating mostly mice, and I see one bird beak. So I deduce this came from an owl."

The expression on Lili's face was a mixture of horror and incredulity. "I may never eat again," she said.

"Oh, you get used to it," Sam told her. "Every job has something you don't like about it."

Lili tilted her head and studied her notes, brushing a fingertip across her lips in a sensual gesture that seemed older than a thirteen-year-old should make. "I think I'll be a hair stylist, after all. That'd be fun, fixing hair."

"Maybe you should interview a stylist. It's not all clipping and arranging. How about all that ammonia in dye and permanents? How about dandruff and ringworm?"

"Ringworm?" The girl's mouth was open.

"It could happen. And dandruff is common."

Lili groaned. "Now I *know* I'll never eat again. You've been a *big* help, Sam."

Sam laughed. "Glad to be of service. You know, if you have a career day, I could bring different kinds of scat for the kids to look at."

"Uh." Lili ran her painted fingernails through her curly black hair, which she wore loose today. Then she said in exactly the same way Joe did, "I'll get back to you on that."

They walked on. Lili pointed out a butterfly Sam couldn't identify, so Sam stopped to make a sketch of it. Sam showed Lili a salamander waddling through the long grass. The girl seemed impressed with the amphibian, so Sam glanced at the trees to see if she could find a tree frog. And spotted instead another THIS IS YOUR LAND sign.

"Damn it!" She stalked toward the sign, shifting her daypack from her shoulder so she could dig out the hammer. "These idiots just won't stop."

Lili's face turned bright red. Was it because she'd said *damn*? As she pried off the offending sign, Sam tried to remember if she'd ever heard Joe or Laura swear. Should she apologize? She stuck the sign in her pack.

"Do you throw them away?" Lili eyed Sam's daypack.

"The signs?" Sam shook her head. "I'm collecting them in a locker at the division building. One of these days, the park service might get around to lifting fingerprints from them."

Lili's eyes widened. "Why?"

"Because it's a federal crime to deface government property. And these signs are encouraging people to commit crimes. You know that hunting and ATVs aren't allowed in the park, and now this area is part of the park."

The girl continued to stare at the daypack, and the blush

on her face darkened. A suspicion flared in Sam's mind. "Do you know who's been putting up these signs, Lili?"

Lili shook her head, darted a hasty glance at Sam, and then stared at her boots. "Why are you asking me?"

"I just thought that you might—"

When the girl's head came up, her eyes were defiant. "I thought you liked me. Now you're accusing me of things, just like Dad and Mom."

Sam stiffened. Was this guilt talking, or just normal teenage paranoia? "I didn't accuse you of anything, Lili. I was hoping you might be able to help me out."

"Well, I can't." The girl pulled out her cell phone and checked the time. "Dad's going to be here any minute, and we didn't even see any bears." Lili started walking back to the rendezvous point.

Sam dashed to catch up. "Sorry about the bears. They aren't that easy to find, unless you leave food out for them regularly, and of course that's not a good idea. Why do you want to see a bear?"

Lili shrugged. "I just think it would be cool. A boy at school talks about them sometimes."

Sam's internal antenna shot up. A poacher, or the son of one? "How does this boy know so much about bears?"

Lili's shoulders lifted and fell again. "He just does."

"I'd love to meet this boy," Sam said eagerly. "Find out what he knows. What's his name?"

Lili's eyes narrowed with suspicion.

"He could probably teach me a few things," Sam said, trying to allay Lili's fears of ratting out a friend. "There's nothing better than a good bear story."

"Yeah, I know what you mean." Lili brushed her hair out of her eyes and shifted her gaze toward the road. "That guy, though, he just moved. I'm really going to miss him."

IT was dark when Sam arrived at the trail crew bunkhouse. She might have had trouble finding the building if the road hadn't ended there. A park service pickup outfitted with a tall cover and benches in the bed was parked in front of the building. The thick-planked front door didn't have a conventional knob and lock, just a brass handle and a hasp for a padlock to secure it for the winter. She pushed open the door and stepped into the hallway, inhaling the odors of stale cooking and decades-old dust. "Hello?" she said uncertainly.

There was no answer. The wood floors were no longer level, but that wasn't surprising in a building originally constructed in the 1930s to house WPA workers. The furniture, a hodgepodge of worn armchairs and scuffed tables and mismatched lamps, looked nearly as old. In the kitchen, dishes had been washed and stacked in a drainer to dry, and in the communal area, magazines, books, and boxes of board games had been gathered into a brick-and-board bookcase along one wall. She had to hand it to Blackstock; he kept his crew in order.

Four doors led off the hallway. The first door on the left had a hand-painted sign above it: EL QUESO GRANDE. Sam smiled, recognizing the Spanish version of the "big cheese." Tom Blackstock had taken over all four bunks there; one was neatly made, the other three full of papers and notebooks and items of outdoor gear.

In the room across from Blackstock's, and in the next one down on the left, three bunks were occupied. Various items of male clothing hung from the ends of the beds and the backs of chairs. The swimsuit edition of *Sports Illustrated* lay on one lower bunk. That accounted for the six boys on the trail crew. In the final bunkroom on the right, each of the lower bunks was neatly made up, and the top beds were filled with personal paraphernalia. The girls' room.

The top bunk on the right was littered with an MP3 player and headphones and a tube of hair gel. Maya's, Sam guessed. The opposite bunk held a box of tissues, a sketch pad, two romance novels, and a worn black Bible. Lisa's?

Sam let her duffle bag drop from her shoulder onto the lower bunk, and then reached for the sketch pad. The first drawing was remarkably skillful, a chipmunk on a rail. The next drawing depicted a scene from the bunkhouse's common room, three youths gathered at the table over a game board, two in the background washing dishes with Blackstock looking on. She flipped that page to find only a pair of eyes staring out from the next page. Creepy; they gave her the same chill she'd felt on encountering the illegal hunter. But all she learned about Lisa was that the girl was quite talented with a pencil.

The Bible didn't provide much information about Lisa, either. The inside front cover held a puzzling inscription. *From your loving family. Together forever.* If Lisa had a loving family, where were they? Why didn't anyone answer the phone at her contact number? Sam thumbed through the pages. A few had been highlighted with a marker. The Old Testament, the line about God giving Man dominion over all the creatures of the Earth. Several more having to do with either God or some ancient patriarch smiting various people for various injustices. Sam had always despised the Old Testament, with all its eye-for-an-eye violence and women-as-possessions attitudes. It was depressing to think that a young woman like Lisa might look to it for guidance.

A corner torn from a manila envelope marked a spot in the New Testament, and she opened the book there, hoping to find a more uplifting verse highlighted. On the brown triangle of paper was written, *F. Frazier, P.O.B. 103, Carbonado, WY,* and farther down, an address in Seattle.

The scrap marked Psalm 23. *The valley of the shadow of death.* Sam felt a chill, thinking of what had happened to Lisa. In the hospital, the girl's body language had hinted that she was not telling the truth, or at least not the whole truth. Did Lisa have a reason to fear death?

She wondered how the girl was doing. Sam dug out her notepad and cell phone. Surprisingly, the phone showed a signal here, although it was only half strength. She punched in the number of the phone in Lisa's hospital room. After listening to it ring three times, she ended the call. She didn't want the girl trying to reach for the phone. Why wasn't the volunteer answering? Was Lisa okay? She called the hospital information line, ended up at some sort of volunteer desk. "I'd like to inquire about the status of a patient, please. Lisa Glass," she told the young voice that answered.

"Lisa Glass? She's not—" A voice in the background interrupted the speaker. When she came back, she said, "I'm sorry, ma'am, we can't give out that information."

"Look," Sam told her, "I'm a friend. I work for the park service. I was sitting with Lisa just this morning, and I'd like to know how she's doing."

"We can't give out that information."

"Can't you tell me anything?"

"I'm sorry, ma'am. It's the rules." Another voice in the background said something, and then the girl said, "It's the law."

Frustrated, Sam pressed End. Oh, well. She'd take the Bible and sketch pad to Lisa in the hospital tomorrow. Maybe they'd perk her up, or prompt her to talk. Sam could ask her about the name and address in Wyoming, if those were family members or friends Lisa would like to call.

A squeak followed by the thud of the door drew her attention. A thunder of booted feet proceeded in her direction, no doubt drawn by the light spilling from the girls' bunkroom. The herd of hulking boys looked her over once again.

"Hi, guys," she said.

They parted, and the earthy aroma of wood smoke accompanied Maya into the room. She crossed her arms and leaned against the wall. "You're here."

"Yep," Sam said, unable to read the girl's expression.

The cluster of boys shifted again to let Blackstock through. "I see you found your bunk all right," he said. "We were out back. We do a campfire circle on days that the weather's decent; toast marshmallows, tell stories. You should have joined us."

Ben Rosen rolled his eyes.

"Sounds like fun," Sam said. Tom Blackstock had a nice touch with these kids, and the group probably provided more of a supportive family than most had at home. "I'll be there next time. Are s'mores allowed?"

Blackstock winked. "You betcha. You bring the chocolate and the graham crackers."

"I will," she promised. "Any word on Lisa? I just tried to call, but the hospital wouldn't tell me anything."

Blackstock's craggy features took on a grim cast. "I talked to Peter Hoyle about two o'clock. He said Lisa's been out cold most of the day."

"I'm sorry to hear that. But maybe sleep is what she needs most right now."

At least Blackstock didn't say Lisa *wasn't* sleeping. But where was the line between being deeply asleep and being unconscious? Sam made a mental note to ask the nursing staff about that tomorrow.

"Can we talk for a minute?" she asked him.

He eyed her carefully. "Meet me in my truck in half an hour."

That sounded like a sexy rendezvous. Then Sam realized that a vehicle was the only place the two of them could discuss anything in private. It was a truck or the woods. She nodded and checked her watch.

Blackstock moved toward the boys behind him, making herding motions with his hands. "Hit the bathroom, guys, so the ladies can have it when Ranger Westin here gets unpacked."

"Call me Sam," she said. I'm not a real ranger, her conscience added.

"Call her Sam, then," Blackstock told them. "But get a move on. We got a long day tomorrow."

Six young men turned and shuffled down the hall in front of him.

Sam turned to Maya. "There's only one bathroom?"

The redhead shrugged. "Don't worry. Queso makes them clean it up so it's not too disgusting. And there's a sign on the door we can flip so they won't come in when we're in there."

Unpacking took two minutes. Sam hung up her spare uniform, dumped out her duffle bag onto the top bunk, and laid out the T-shirt she slept in on the lower one, along with a headlamp and the mystery novel she was reading.

The bunkhouse was dark and Maya was already snoring softly when Sam donned her jacket and slipped out to Blackstock's truck. The night was turning chilly, not more than fifty degrees out, but the tree frogs were awake and singing nonetheless. Stars glittered overhead in the patches of sky she could see between spires of firs.

The truck cab was nearly as cool as the outdoors. The windshield was already fogging up, and Sam squirmed inwardly, thinking of how this must look from the outside. She wished it was Chase she was meeting on this beautiful night.

Blackstock held out a bottle of whiskey and a paper cup. "Join me?"

"Just a little." Whiskey was not her drink. It tasted as bad as she remembered, like rubbing alcohol, but the warmth as it slid down her throat was welcome.

"Are you from around here, Tom?" Maybe he'd have an insight about the hostile stares from the locals.

"In the winter I live over near Shelton," he said, naming a town on the east flank of the Olympic Peninsula. "But I've been running trail crew for the park service in the summer for years now. Whether these kids have been in trouble or not, they need someone watching out for them."

He sounded like he expected an argument from her. "They're lucky to have you, Tom. Or should I call you *El Queso Grande*?"

"Tom will do." He cleared his throat, embarrassed. "You saw Lisa this morning?"

Sam told Blackstock about Lisa's allegations of kidnapping and rape. As she talked, his expression changed from shock to sadness to worry.

"Of course," she added, "Lisa could be hallucinating, too; the doctor said that was possible."

"I hope so." He took a sip from his cup. "These guys don't need any more problems."

Sam looked toward the quiet bunkhouse. "You can account for all of them in there?"

"Joe Choi asked me that yesterday." He thought for a minute. "Well, I guess there's always the possibility that any of these kids could slip out after I was asleep, but there's no way they could start up this truck without me hearing. And there are no other vehicles."

Sam rubbed a patch of condensation off the window with her elbow and stared out. Nothing but woods for miles around. She wondered if there were illegal tracks blazed through the forest around them. There weren't enough rangers to patrol thousands of acres. "Think they could meet a vehicle in the woods?"

He shrugged. "I suppose. But how would they arrange it? I'm the only one with a cell phone."

Sam considered the timing on Friday night. "Did you get the call about the explosion and fire?"

"Nope. First thing I heard about it was midmorning on Saturday."

So nobody in the bunkhouse had been roused during the night. The boys could have snuck out and back without his notice.

"Lisa drew a picture of one of her attackers," Sam told him. "It looked like a combination of Ben Rosen and the devil."

Blackstock snorted. "Poor kid."

"Lisa?"

"Well, her, of course, but I actually meant Ben."

"Why do you say that?"

"He's got to be the only Jewish kid for a hundred miles. The others give him endless shit about that."

Interesting. Lisa and her Bible, Ben a Jew. Was there some connection there? Sam knew that some sects were paranoid about Jews, saying they killed Jesus. But then Jesus *was* a Jew, so that line of thinking never made a lot of sense to her. Then her preacher father naturally sprang to mind, and so did the guilt of not being the devout church-goer he'd like her to be. It was annoying how those thoughts could creep into her head without invitation.

11

THE next morning, Sam packed up her gear for the day, tossed Lisa's sketch pad and Bible onto the passenger seat, and headed for the western administration building, which housed the park office closest to her survey area. Arnie Cole was the last person she wanted to spend time with, but as the forest service ranger who had been in charge of Marmot Lake, he was the best source of information about the area's history.

Because no roads crisscrossed Olympic National Park, she had to drive around the perimeter, from one entrance to another, just like all other park personnel. To make matters more complicated, the coastal section of the park was separated from the mountain area by a patchwork quilt of national forest and private lands. Or it had been until the President created a protected wildlife corridor from the Pacific Ocean to the Olympic Mountains by transferring the Marmot Lake section from the forest service to the park service. The creatures still had to cross the two lanes of Highway 101, though; there was no getting around that. She spotted a doe and fawn grazing among the stumps of a roadside clear-cut. With luck, they'd cross at night, when traffic slowed to a trickle.

She spent nineteen miles cursing a logger who insisted on racing his rig just a few inches behind her tailgate, flashing his lights at intervals as if that would make her drive eighty on the fifty-five-mile-per-hour stretch. The truckers got paid by the load, an insane policy that caused them to hurtle around like NASCAR racers. There was no place to pull over. By the time she reached the administration building north of Forks, her nerves were shot. And it was only a few minutes past nine in the morning.

The National Park Service shared the one-story building with the forest service. Although they were both government agencies, sharing quarters sometimes struck Sam as akin to housing cats and dogs in the same cages. Most Americans weren't aware that the United States Forest Service was in the Department of Agriculture, with an emphasis on crops, livestock, and a safe food supply; while the National Park Service was part of the Department of the Interior, with a focus on conservation and energy. Transferring the Marmot Lake acreage from the USFS to the NPS meant changing that area's focus from harvesting to conservation.

Sam waved at the NPS aide on duty behind the counter as she strode over to the forest service offices. She'd just raised her hand to knock on his door frame when Arnie Cole swiveled in his chair and spotted her. "If it isn't Tiny Temporary Ranger Westin!"

When she was introduced to the rail-thin man ten weeks ago, he asked her on a date. She said no. Since then, he hadn't missed a chance to heckle her. It was either his idea of revenge or some sort of adolescent courting behavior he'd never grown out of.

She switched off the radio on her belt so she wouldn't have to compete with it while she talked.

"Sizzling Summer Westin." Cole leaned back in his chair and raised his feet onto the battered metal surface of his desk. An official-looking form skidded from under the sole of his hiking boot and fluttered to the floor.

She hoped he'd lose his balance and fall over backward. No such luck.

"Steamy Summer, Hot Time Summer in the City, Celebrity Summer Westin."

This was getting old. "Did you sleep through the harassment seminar, Arnie?"

His smile dimmed a bit. "I'm just teasing. You know that."

"I guess you've just learned my given name."

"From the TV news, no less. My boss tells me this is the second time you've graced the airways. *And* that you're downright famous on the World Wide Web. And here I was thinking that you were plain old Sam Westin."

"Give it a rest. Please." She perched on the arm of his visitor's chair.

He gave her a lipless grin. "I've been doing research on you. Turns out you're Cougar Lady. Cat Woman."

She groaned. He'd read up on the Zachary Fischer story. "It wasn't nearly as dramatic as the media made it sound."

He raised his elbows and interwove his long fingers behind his head. "Are you going to do a story on us? Are we going to be on the Internet?"

She slid from the arm of the chair down onto the seat. "In case you missed it, I'm not on the Internet anymore. I'm not writing for anyone now. As you pointed out, I'm a temporary contractor for the park service."

"What a comedown. From *Wilderness* Westin. *Wild West.*"

He would have discovered her "cool" name invented by the Save the Wilderness Fund. "Knock it off, Arnie."

"Oh, all right." He retracted his feet and his chair legs thudded into position. "I like your new look, by the way, especially the black stitches. The makeup is from that new line, Bride of Frankenstein, right?"

Ignoring him, she bent to pick up the paper from the floor. He leaned over his desk and rearranged the papers he'd dislodged, staring at her as he tapped pages into alignment. Probably hoping to see down her uniform shirt. "So what's the tiny temp from Interior doing over here in lowly Ag land? Come to learn something about forestry?"

"I already know how to use a chainsaw." Sam handed him the page she'd retrieved. "No, Arnie, I'm here to pick your brain. Since we both know what a minuscule area that is, it shouldn't take more than a minute of your time. What can you tell me about recent activities around Marmot Lake?"

"See," he said, grinning, "You do need me." He rose from his chair and clasped his hands behind his back.

"I keep finding tracks made by ATVs and four-wheel drives," Sam prompted.

"They're just having fun. See, that's the problem with the park service. In the forest service, we understand that maybe a guy wants to drive his Jeep or ride his dirt bike out in the trees sometime."

"Well, there's not going to be any more of that kind of fun out there." She waved a hand impatiently. "Tell me about the history of the area."

"Marmot Lake. When the bigwigs asked which parts of the National Forest they could steal for Parks, I said, please, please, please take *anything* but the area around Marmot Lake. It's the pride of the USFS, I told them. Sure, it's scenic and it's a natural wildlife corridor between the mountains and the coast, but look at all those big trees just waiting to be turned into two-by-fours." He gestured dramatically, his arms raised toward an imaginary audience.

Sam doubted that Arnie ranked high enough to have any voice in the matter, but she let him ramble on.

His gaze came back to her. "Naturally, being the stuffed turkeys they are, they fell for it. Drew the boundary line around it just like that." He snapped his fingers. Then he paced across the planked floor to a map on the wall, and dragged his finger down a red line that partitioned off former National Forest land. "Took half my district."

Oops. "You're not losing your job, are you, Arnie?"

"Not *me*," he said meaningfully, and she wondered who around there was getting the axe. "They're reapportioning the districts; I'm getting a new piece up north." He turned and looked at her. "They didn't hurt me; I was thrilled to get rid of Marmot Lake."

"Why?" Her mind raced now, picturing a toxic waste dump under the lake's placid surface. PCBs, radioactive metals. Not hard to imagine after reading that article on mining and watersheds two nights ago.

"Oh, let me count the whys." Arnie was enjoying this conversation way too much. That meant that he was serious about the problems in the area. He ticked them off on his fingers. "First, there was the hunting, all year round. No attention to seasons or picayune little details like that."

Sam winced at the memory. "I ran into an illegal hunter last Thursday."

"Anytime anyone even thinks they see a bear ass out there, they shoot at it." He grinned at his double entendre. "I mean a bruin butt, not a naked human ass."

"I figured that," she said quickly, hoping to head him off before he segued into an enumeration of other body parts.

"But do all those bullets and arrows whizzing around send our bruins scampering to the backcountry? No, siree. When the pesky beasts aren't ripping apart the family coolers, they're dumping out the trash cans. Or crawling into tents. I figured that was why you closed the campground." He gave her a quizzical look.

"It was closed when I got here." She was told it was NPS strategy for the transition from USFS to NPS. Her management plan was supposed to include advice on whether or not to reopen the campground and picnic area.

"So I guess the bears would be reason number two." He extended a second finger, and then a third. "Reason number three: paintball wars. When the nutcases weren't firing real bullets at bears, they were firing paint bullets at each other. At least half a dozen times each year we'd get a call about crazies crawling around in camouflage, aiming rifles at each other."

That explained the splashes of paint she'd noticed on trees around the lake. She'd figured that they'd been marked for cutting or something.

Arnie pulled down his collar and tapped a circular red scar on his neck. "You probably think paintballs are harmless, but those things hurt! They can put an eye out, even kill you if you get hit close up."

"What did you charge these paintball warriors with?" Did popping a paintball qualify as firing a weapon? Would spattering paint across the scenery count as vandalism, destruction of government property?

His eyes shifted back to the map. "Just ran 'em off."

She guessed that Arnie had never caught up with the gamesters.

He tapped the map. "And that brings us to reason number four: the Lucky Molly Mine, which you discovered the other night."

Aha. "Surely it hasn't been active for a long time."

He snorted. "Someone tries to claim it nearly every year, but they never can make it pay. Most don't last more than six weeks, but there was always blasting or some freaky activity going on back there. We kept filling it in, then some hotshot prospector would dynamite it open two months later. It's on all the old USGS maps."

Great. "What kind of mine is it?"

"Gold, sweetheart. At least that's how it's billed." He raked his long dishwater blond hair with his fingers. "Someone trying to open it up again?"

She shrugged. "I don't know. During that arson fire over there, I sort of stumbled onto the mine. Well, you were there . . ." She frowned, remembering his wolf whistle at the time. "That crater wasn't there a week ago."

"I saw Lindstrom boosting you out of that hole. Wish it'd been my hands instead of his." He bounced his eyebrows.

She ignored his comment. "Do you think someone wants to open up that mine?"

His smile faded. "You'd better hope not, Sam. You don't want an active mine in your territory. We've got one down in our southern section, close to the reservation, and when they're not putting out toxic smoke or leaking cyanide into the streams, they're losing explosives right and left and blaming us for not locking up the woods at night."

"Losing explosives?" That sounded serious.

"Last March, it was a pound of C-4 and six blasting caps."

"What's C-4?"

He greeted her ignorance with a look of disdain.

"I don't blow things up very often," she said. "Unlike the forest service, park employees—even temps—aren't paid to destroy the natural surroundings."

To her surprise, he let that remark pass, and responded only with, "Ever heard of plastique?"

"Sure." That moldable claylike stuff spies and bank robbers were always glomming into keyholes on television.

"You could flatten a city block with a pound of that stuff. Or divide it up and blow up a dozen cars, or a few houses. Or—"

"I get the drift." Jeez. So maybe the boom she'd heard had been a real explosion, not just a firecracker or a rifle shot.

"But why are *you* asking me all this? You're not law enforcement. You're not even—"

"I know, I'm not an aide, I'm not even permanent staff." She was tired of hearing about it. "Look, Arnie, I was hired to document the ecosystem in the new sector and come up with a management plan. So it's my job, at least right now, to be interested in all the flora and fauna and human activity, both past and present, and especially, any *threats* that now exist in that area."

"I'm on *your* side, remember?" He held up both hands in a gesture of surrender, and she realized that she had pounded on his desk.

"Well," she said, for lack of anything better. Illegal hunting. Mining claims. C-4. He'd confirmed her fears and added a new one. Now she was supposed to be on the lookout for bombs in the woods, too? And then there was the arson angle, and Lisa Glass had added kidnapping to the list. What was next? Meth labs, she thought, remembering her conversation with Ranger Paul Schuler near the lake. She stood up to leave, and switched her radio back on. Now she wished she had a partner to accompany her, especially down that newly blazed track. Did Mack or Joe or any of the rangers have cowardly thoughts like that? Probably not. She stiffened her back.

Arnie walked her to the door. "I hear that you stay with Mack sometimes. He's got a girlfriend, you know. That hot red-haired chick. Jodi."

She turned. "Mack and I are friends. I sleep on his couch."

He smiled. "I have a couch, too, Summer."

Was he actually trying to be nice? "I'll keep that in mind," she said. "Thanks."

"It folds out. Into a double bed." His right eye closed in a lascivious wink.

The door had just closed behind her when the radio on her belt squawked. "Three-two-five, come in. Three-five-four."

She pulled it from her belt. "Three-two-five."

"Westin? That you?"

The voice and the radio code were unfamiliar. "This is three-two-five. Sam Westin. Who's calling? Over."

"Oh yeah. Three-four-five. I mean three-five-four. Greg Jordan, at the lookout?"

The poet/firewatch volunteer. Sam grinned at his awkward communication skills. At least someone was sloppier than she was. What's up, Greg?"

"You asked me to call you if anything looked hinky at Marmot Lake? Over."

"Yeah? What's up? Over."

"I think I heard a gunshot, and I can see glints of something shiny now and then. On the west shore of the lake. Should I do anything? Over."

"Stay put and watch for smoke, Greg. I'm going to check it out now."

ERNEST stared at the phone. He'd ripped three pages out of the Greater Seattle phone book at the library and started calling all the landscape companies. On the very last listing, he struck gold: when he'd asked for Allyson Craig, the old guy who answered the phone told him that she was out in the field and would call him back. Ernest couldn't wait to hear his daughter's voice, find out what had kept her away last weekend.

The phone suddenly bleated a shrill note, making him jump. He grabbed the receiver. "Allie?"

"This is Alice."

The voice didn't sound like his daughter, but then she was far away. "Allie, honey, is that you?"

"My name is Alice Gray. Who are you looking for?"

He explained despondently. She sympathized with him for a moment before she hung up. Damn! Another dead end. He reached for the whiskey bottle and found only a sip left in the bottom. What was he going to do now? Call every landscaper in the state of Washington?

He heard ringing, reached for the receiver again, and then realized it was the doorbell. As he hefted himself to his feet, the sound repeated, like an annoying mosquito.

"Coming!" he bellowed. Just how fast did they think a man with a bum leg could get to the door?

A smallish man in a county sheriff's uniform stood on the front steps. The sun glinted from the brass emblem on his hat as he raised his eyes from the little notepad he held. "Good afternoon, sir. Does Allyson Craig live here?"

Ernest felt his heart lurch like it missed a couple beats. *Please God, don't let this be bad news.* "Yeah," he said, "that's my daughter. She works over in Seattle, but she comes back weekends."

The sheriff, or deputy, or whatever he was, held out a thin sheet of paper. "We found a Chevy Nova with this registration in it over by Bogachiel State Park, down by the river, about half a mile north of the public fishing dock."

Ernest stared at the paper. He had to swallow hard before he could say, "Oh God."

The man looked startled. "Sir?"

"Allie never came home last weekend. I thought maybe . . ." He couldn't finish. What *had* he thought? That she'd told him she wouldn't be home and he'd forgotten? That she'd run away from her old drunk of a father? Anything other than this—

The deputy put one hand on Ernest's forearm, and used the other to push the screen door open wider. "If it's all right with you, Mr. Craig, I think I'd better come in."

THE gate barred the road to Marmot Lake. Good, Sam thought, this was a false alarm and Raider wasn't really in danger. But when she reached for the lock, she found that the chain had merely been draped over the posts to make it look as though it were still secure. Her stomach cramped with anxiety. Something hinky, indeed. She drove through, leaving the gate open behind her.

She tried to raise Joe Choi on the radio. "Three-four-seven, this is three-two-five. Come in, three-four-seven." No response. Next she tried the dispatcher. To her dismay, Peter Hoyle responded. "What's going on out there, Westin? Over."

"Where's Joe?" Sam asked.

"Choi is on lunch break. Where are you? Over."

"I'm on my way to check out suspicious activity at Marmot Lake. Someone broke the gate lock again. Over."

"That's a job for law enforcement. I'll dispatch Tyburn to that location ASAP. Turn that vehicle around now, Westin, and go back to the duties you were hired to do. Over."

Sam knew that unless Norm Tyburn was by some miraculous coincidence in this sector, he wouldn't be here for forty-five minutes at the earliest. By that time, anything could happen: Raider could be dead, the forest could be on fire again, some wackos could be torturing another girl.

"Westin? Acknowledge. Over."

She swung the truck into the gravel parking lot, switched off the engine, and intermittently thumbed the Talk button on her radio. "Didn't get that, HQ, you're breaking up. I'm at the lake now. I'll report my findings. Three-two-five, clear." She switched off the radio and slid it back into her belt holster before getting out of the pickup.

She'd parked close to a late-model black pickup, gleaming with stripes and chrome. Jacked up on extra-large tires and adorned with two spotlights mounted above the cab in addition to its four headlights, the vehicle leered down at her like a monstrous black widow about to pounce on an insect. It looked exactly like the sort of vehicle a bear poacher would drive. Or a would-be gold miner. Or an arsonist. Kidnapper. Meth cook. Or maybe just a local backwoodsman; heaven knew she'd seen enough of these in Forks. Whoever it belonged to was, at the very least, trespassing, and deserved to be grilled about that.

She noted its license number on her notepad. After scrutinizing the area to make sure the owner wasn't lurking nearby, she made an undignified climb onto the running board. A quick inspection of the interior revealed little. Two men's windbreakers lay across the seat. A pack of cigarettes on the dashboard. A rifle rack barred the back window. Empty. She prayed that it had been that way when the truck entered the parking lot.

Using the side mirror as a handle, Sam lowered herself to the ground. The loose gravel crunched under her boots. The noise seemed loud in the deserted parking lot. She chewed her thumbnail for a moment. Should she wait for Tyburn? Who knew how long that would take? Go in search of the pickup's passengers? As Hoyle had reminded her, law enforcement was not her job. Still, she was the only ranger here, even if she was only a temporary one.

Pop. Pop. Tightly controlled explosions that, in an urban environment, might have come from a nail gun or a backfiring muffler. But here in the hills, it could only be gunfire. From the far side of the lake. Damn it!

She jogged across the lot and started down the trail. Please let this be paintball, she prayed. Please don't let me find two illegal hunters and a dead bear at the end of this path.

THE deputy listened to Ernest's story about his missing daughter, then borrowed the phone and called his office. He told someone to seal the Nova and call a forensics team. Ernest wasn't sure what that meant, but it didn't sound good.

"I don't know," he heard the deputy say into the receiver. The man's eyes connected with Ernest's for a second, then he turned away and said in a low voice, "It might be related to that other . . . incident. Yeah. Get them on it ASAP, see if there are any, uh, similarities."

After he hung up, the deputy asked if Allyson had ever been fingerprinted.

Ernest shook his head. "No, she's never been in trouble. She is a good girl." *Please, let Allie still be alive and well; let him still be right to say* is *and not* was.

"These days people take fingerprints for all sorts of reasons. Some jobs require them. Some parents get their kids fingerprinted just in case they get lost."

Was the deputy accusing him of being a bad father? Fingerprinting a kid—what was the world coming to? He shook his head again. "No prints."

"Do you know her blood type?"

Oh God, no. "Was there blood in her car?"

The deputy avoided meeting his eyes. "It's just a formality, sir."

"Type O, I think. Same as mine."

The man wrote it down.

"What other incident?" Ernest asked.

"Pardon?" The deputy looked up.

"I heard you say that this might be related to 'that other incident.' What'd you mean by that?"

The deputy's gaze flicked to the tabletop, to the notepad, and finally came to rest on the pen in his hands. He was a young man, clearly uncertain about what to do. "There's probably no relationship, but . . ."

"Just spit it out, man." He could take it, Ernest thought. Christ, he had to take it, didn't he?

The deputy's brown eyes were cool, analytic. His gaze was locked on Ernest's face as he said, "This morning, under the fishing dock, we found a woman's hand."

12

JACK Winner crouched behind a blackened tree and pulled the pistol in close to his chest. After checking the path ahead, he dashed to the cover of the next tree, making no more noise than a chipmunk scampering across the dry ground. Shit, he was good at this.

Leaning against his new cover, Jack chanced a quick look through the branches. King, in camouflage pants and olive T-shirt like his, was in motion, running to the next large tree. King's back was toward him, his eyes fixed on some spot in the distance. Ha! He had him now. King had no idea that Jack was behind him. The man needed to learn to be more careful. Allie had been better, more aware of her surroundings. He'd never been able to sneak up on her like this. She'd even managed to surprise him twice.

He swallowed. Thinking about her made his throat hurt. Best not to dwell on the past. Just look at the news: soldiers were dying all the time in routine exercises, when carrying supplies, in transit to and from the real action. And they were soldiers, he and Philip and Roddie and Allie. She deserved a medal of honor and rifle salutes.

The pain ambushed him in the gut again. It was hard to believe there was not a shred left of Allie, but he'd found nothing; he couldn't even tell where she'd fallen. But as King had pointed out, there were bears around Marmot Lake. And bears were scavengers. From now on, he'd shoot every single one he saw.

Allie had been part of the *real* army, the Americans who knew how to think for themselves, not those poor dupes giving it up in Afghanistan and Iraq, all to make Walmart and Exxon and DuPont even more filthy rich. He could understand bin Laden wanting to take down those monuments to money in New York. Too bad the idiot wasn't better at targeting just the CEOs. He didn't need to kill the janitors and secretaries, too.

He wasn't going to make that mistake. He had discipline. Philip and Roddie always badmouthed the blacks and Jews and Indians and Mexicans, but as far as Jack could see, a lot of those folks were victims even more than your average workingman. He was in charge, and he was going to nail only the ones who deserved it, at the right time, at the right place. The feds wouldn't know what hit them. They'd just realize that suddenly *they* were the endangered species, and they'd better start listening to the real people for a change.

Four members seemed a little pathetic for a branch, but hey, it wasn't like he lived in a big city and could muster up dozens of people. Damn Roddie, or Rocky, or whatever his cousin Rodney called himself these days. The kid came to the meetings, but always had some excuse to get out of the exercises. It was always just him and Allie and Philip out here. And now his group was even more of a twig than a branch: today there were only two.

He ran past the burn line into the green area, aiming for the next clump of trees. He silently lowered himself to the ground. Positioning himself on his elbows under the cover of low-hanging pine bows, he aimed the paintball gun in King's direction. The sights were lined up squarely in the middle of his friend's back and he was about to squeeze the trigger when he noticed King had thrust the barrel of his paintball pistol through the web belt at his waist. Clasped in King's left hand was a nine-millimeter semiautomatic. It was aimed at a woman making her way through the woods toward them.

*   *   *

THE bait was gone, but the trap hadn't been sprung. How the hell had the damn bear done that? Why hadn't the stupid beast climbed into the cage like he was supposed to? Garrett Ford knelt and inspected the side of the cage. He reached through the bars, touched the sticky spot where he had hung the cake of honey-soaked pemmican. Three long scratches were etched into the plywood backboard. Just like that, that's how the damn bear had done it, just reached in and snagged the bait. As Ford pulled out his arm, he noticed a rust-red stain on his sleeve. He rubbed it. Blood. There were spots on the floor of the cage, too. The varmint had probably torn its paw on the bait hook. The drops were drying around the edges, still slightly damp in the middle. Less than an hour old. He'd only missed that bear by minutes.

Mike Martinson sat on the tailgate of his truck, a disappointed scowl on his face. "No bear?"

"Obviously," growled Ford. Teenagers.

"Should I break it down and put it back in the truck, or are we going to leave it here?"

The brush behind him rustled. Maybe the bear was still close by? There was a chance that this trip wouldn't be wasted, after all. He darted to the truck, lifted the rifle from the rack behind the seat. "Stay here," he told the boy in a low voice.

Using the barrel of the rifle to push aside a cedar branch, Ford ducked into the dappled shadows of the forest. He paused a moment, waiting for his eyes to adjust. There, a faint crackle. He crept toward the noise, holding his breath. He might not be so fast anymore, but his hearing was good and he was still an expert tracker.

He followed the sound of scurrying feet through the shadowy woods, pausing behind a tree when the sound stopped. For a moment, all he heard was the drumming of a woodpecker on a hollow tree. Then there was a snorting sound. He peered through the brush. About a hundred yards away, a man, dressed in camouflage pants and T-shirt, leaned against a thick fir. His left hand clutched a sleek black pistol. Looked like a semiautomatic of some kind.

Muscles clenched between Ford's shoulder blades. The guy had damn well better not be aiming at his bear. Ford quickly sidestepped around the barrier of the tree. Farther through the woods, there was a flicker of movement. He recognized the gray-green of a park ranger's uniform, caught a glimpse of a long silver-blond braid.

Summer Westin. Just the sort to be snooping around—the type that never could mind her own business. Her jaw was clenched, her expression anxious, oblivious to the fact that the thug was close by and had a pistol leveled at her chest. Camouflage Man tensed and sighted down the barrel of the nine millimeter. Damnation! Ford released the safety and raised his rifle.

THE hair on the back of Sam's neck prickled under her uniform collar. Something or someone was ahead of her in the woods. Stepping into the shade of a tree, she searched the forest for movement, for the bulky shape of a black bear, for two-legged vermin bearing rifles or paintball pistols. A loud drumming reverberated somewhere above her. *Not now, you stupid woodpecker!* She strained to hear the whisper of footsteps beyond the staccato beats.

A rifle shot cracked ahead of her. She ducked, clung to the Douglas fir. Another bang, this one higher pitched, followed a fraction of a second later. The bullet smashed into the tree above her, showering her with bark and fir needles. A grain of bark caught under her right eyelid. *Holy shit!* Someone was shooting *at* her.

"Ranger!" she shouted. "Stop shooting! I'm a park ranger!" She rubbed frantically at her burning eye.

Another shot cracked through the woods. She dropped

to her knees behind the tree trunk. Muffled footsteps thudded dully on the needle-carpeted forest floor. Sounded like at least two people. The racket moved away from her position. She wasn't about to give chase. They knew exactly where she was, and she hadn't even glimpsed them. She couldn't even see out of one eye. She straightened and brushed her sleeve across her face, wiping more grit onto her cheeks, but dislodging the splinter from her eye.

Tears coursed down her face as she blinked rapidly to clear her vision. About eighteen inches above where her cheek hugged the trunk, a half-inch scar had been plowed through the bark. Her chest tightened. This was not a paintball game.

The intruders were probably retreating to the black pickup, moving down the trail on the other side of the lake. She started to jog back the way she'd come. With luck, she might make it back to the parking lot before they did. With more luck, Norm Tyburn might show up at the same time.

Her heavy hiking boots felt like concrete bricks on her feet. Tears streamed from her right eye, blurring the scenery on that side. She detached the radio from her belt as she jogged, clicked the Talk button, and panted, "Three-one-one, this is three-two-five, Westin here. Shots fired at Marmot Lake. Fired at me. Over."

The toe of her boot whacked against a tree root. She nearly fell, caught herself at the last second. The radio crackled, "Three-two-five, three-one-one. Tyburn's on his way." Sam slowed, shoved the radio back onto her belt, forced herself back to a jog. She wanted to at least get a glimpse of the intruders, even though it might be a blurry glimpse. She rubbed at her burning eye, trying to stem the torrent of tears.

The big boulder was just ahead, marking a half mile from the parking lot. She rounded the rock and slammed headlong into a dark mass blocking the trail. A sound halfway between a grunt and a bawl erupted loudly in her ear. Her kneecap smacked down onto a rock, sending a shock wave of pain up her leg, and she crashed full-length to the ground.

She pushed her head up just in time to see the backside of a bear. The bear turned his head over his shoulder just enough to glimpse her with a fear-rounded eye. He raced down the trail, his rust-tinged rump bouncing as he vanished into the trees. She made out a flash of white on the back of his ear

"Raider!" she coughed, spitting dust.

Blood soaked through her uniform trousers where her knee had struck the ground. Damn, it hurt. She stumbled on down the trail. In spite of the little stabs of pain that jolted with each step, she smiled. Raider was still alive and well. He'd even put on a few pounds if the solidity of their collision was any indication.

When she limped into the parking area, the black pickup was gone. She pulled her water bottle out of the truck and sat on the back bumper, trying to catch her breath between swallows. Maybe the close call had scared the hunters enough that they wouldn't try poaching again. *Yeah, right.*

But Raider was okay, at least for now. She had almost caught her breath when Norm Tyburn finally drove in

"YOU fuckin' shot at me!" Philip King growled.

"Stop whining. It was only paintball. I've shot you plenty of times." After the ranger truck zoomed past, Winner pulled out of his hiding place onto the main road.

"That was no paintball pellet, not the first one. Don't be shittin' me—you hit the tree right beside my head."

"I only took one shot, and it was a paintball pellet," Jack reiterated. "Why the hell were you aiming at Westin, anyway?"

King grinned. "Shit, why not? She was right there. Why not do it now?" He raised his hand, finger and thumb positioned like a revolver aimed at the windshield. "Bang!" He blew on his index finger as if it were the smoking barrel of a gun. "It would have been so easy."

Winner had never realized how ugly the guy's smile was before. A spark of anxiety flared in his gut. He was losing control. First Allie, now King. And Roddie was more interested in collecting a harem of girls than in focusing on the mission. Without control, it would just be chaotic violence without purpose. Like those stupid al-Qaeda guys. And whatever happened would all come back on him. He was supposed to be the leader of this branch.

He swallowed and slowly enunciated each word for King's benefit. "We're not going to kill her now. We are going to save her for the big show, remember?"

The Order was counting on him. Counting on him to be a winner, just like his name. He had promised that he could pull it off. And they promised to pay him when he did. He needed that money. He deserved that money.

The ugly grin was still plastered across King's face. He held his hand pistol out again, made it recoil several times at a line of trees that guarded the road edge. "We'll kill every one of the goddamned tree huggers. They're gonna be the endangered species from now on."

"Get a grip on yourself, man," Winner urged in a low voice. "Have a little discipline. One target on the assigned date."

"That's just the beginning." King regarded him with shining eyes. "It's a holy war," he said. "Bombs, bullets, or knives, it doesn't matter how. But we'll have to kill them all."

Winner turned his gaze back to the road. *Christ,* he thought, grimly gripping the steering wheel, *only a few weeks to go and there's a psycho on my team. A goddamn mad dog.*

13

SAM was grateful that Arnie Cole's office was dark and empty. As she limped past the admin building's tiny break room, she spied Mack Lindstrom folded into a chair. He sat hunched over, his hands pressed over his face. Kneeling in front of him, one hand resting lightly on his thigh, was Jodi Ruderman.

At the sound of Sam's footsteps on the tile floor, they looked up. Their eyes were shiny with tears.

Jodi rose to her feet, and then put one hand on Mack's shoulder. "It's Lisa Glass," she told Sam. "She's dead."

The words thudded into Sam's brain. Dead? "But," she protested, "yesterday she was awake. She had a head ache, but "

"Yesterday afternoon they discovered she was unconscious, bleeding into her brain." Mack's tone was strained. "LifeFlight took her to Harborview in Seattle around six last night. They did emergency surgery, but she didn't make it. She died about three hours ago."

Sam sank into a chair across from her colleagues. "Omigod." She stared at the scuffed brown vinyl floor tiles, but saw only Lisa's hospital room, the disfigured young woman on the bed, her hands pressed to her scalp. *My head hurts so much.*

She'd assumed that Lisa's headache was a convenient excuse to escape her questions. And as always, Sam had been anxious to escape from those sterile corridors, from the beep and hiss of machines performing functions that the attached humans couldn't, from all those sheet-cloaked bodies glimpsed through half-closed doors.

Her mother had succumbed to ALS nearly three decades ago, and still her death haunted Sam. And now Lisa. If she'd only mentioned Lisa's pain to the nurse . . . Such a little thing to do, just a few seconds of her time on her way out of the hospital. If she had done that, would Lisa still be alive?

"What happened to you?"

She raised her head. "Huh?"

Jodi's outstretched finger pointed first at Sam's right leg, where her trousers were still damp with blood, and then rose to a level with her breasts. Looking down, Sam saw that her entire uniform was blotched with dark stains. She raised a hand to her hair. Slivers of bark and pine needles dusted the crown of her head. Her breath caught in her chest as she felt again the thwock of the bullet plowing into the tree trunk overhead, saw again the shadowy figures running through the forest. Had they intended for her to join Lisa in the morgue?

Peter Hoyle strode into the room, several folders tucked under his right arm. Sam had never seen Hoyle anywhere but inside his office in the main headquarters building forty miles away, and Mack and Jodi seemed surprised to see him, too. His gaze raked down Sam's uniform. "You okay?"

Sam straightened in her chair. "I'm fine."

Her boss squinted. "Tyburn radioed that your intruders had escaped."

"I got their license number," Sam said. "They were trespassing and firing weapons."

"So I heard." Hoyle frowned. "Didn't I tell you to clear out of that sector and leave the incident to law enforcement?"

Sam made herself maintain eye contact. "Was that what you said? I couldn't make it out. Reception's really bad in that area."

Hoyle's steely glance told Sam he wasn't buying her story. "I want an incident report. Ask Kowalski for the form." He waited until Sam acknowledged his command with a nod. He cleared his throat, then said, "Guess you all heard about Lisa."

"Yeah," Mack said morosely.

Hoyle sighed heavily. "Westin, I haven't seen that other report I asked you for."

Sam gulped, just now remembering that she was supposed to write down everything she'd learned from and about Lisa. "I'll get on that ASAP."

"See that you do. Now we've got a possible murder on our hands." Hoyle turned and his footsteps faded back down the hall toward the district ranger's office.

Murder. Sam suddenly felt fuzzy with weariness. Her knee burned where blood had melded the khaki fabric to broken skin. Her eye still felt scratchy. After a few moments, Mack and Jodi rose and headed for their lockers. She pushed herself out of the chair and followed them.

The age-spotted mirror in the locker room revealed just how bad she looked. Her face was blotchy and her right eye was bloodred and watery. She'd forgotten about the ugly black stitches in her lip; curiously they didn't hurt at all.

Her right pant leg was ripped across the knee and dark with blood, now dried to a rusty brown color that was nearly indistinguishable from the surrounding dirt blotches. Even if she could patch the knee, she'd never get the stains out.

Maybe she'd be able to salvage the shirt. The khaki fabric wasn't torn, although it was smeared with dirt and bore a large dark bloodstain over her left breast. It looked like she'd been shot in the chest; no wonder everyone had stared. How the heck had she gotten blood from her knee onto her shirt? She frowned. Maybe it wasn't her blood. She summoned up the image of Raider running away. Had the bear been limping? Had he been shot, after all?

In the mirror, she saw the reflection of Jodi leaning against the row of lockers as Mack pulled something from his. Jodi swiped at her cheek. Mack's fingers gently touched her face, and then Jodi stepped into Mack's arms.

It would sure be nice to step into a manly embrace right

now. She wasn't looking forward to returning to the bunk-house. She wasn't feeling strong and adult right now. She wanted hot water, dinner, a glass of cold white wine. Maybe a whole bottle. But most of all, she wanted someone to talk to. Letting herself out the back door, she leaned against the building wall as she tapped a number into her cell phone.

"LOOKS like our holdup artists are right-wingers." Chase Perez stared at the plastic sleeve he held. Inside was an ink-jet printout, dingy with fingerprint dust. On the table in front of him was a pile of similar pages nearly a foot high, the partial contents of the vehicle belonging to their armed robbery perps.

"What makes you say that?" Nicole looked up from her own stack, her eyes meeting his over her reading glasses.

"Council for Conservation of America." He waved the page. "This is an article about government giveaways to illegal immigrants."

Nicole put down a hand-scribbled note she'd been try-ing to decipher. "What, you're not buying into their 'shared moral values of true Americans'? The CCA is on the watch list. *Way* right of center. They might consider me a true American, but you'd probably have to change your last name to pass."

He scanned the article. "Brown stew?" Frowning, he quoted, "If left unchecked, the liberal elite will turn this country into gloppy brown stew."

"Told you."

His gaze leapt to another story on the page. "And guess what? The occupations of Iraq and Afghanistan were money-laundering gambits by Jews and major corporations, who are manipulating world politics for their own benefit."

Nicole took off her glasses, stood up, crossed to his side of the table, and took the page from him. After scanning it, she made a tsk-tsk noise. "Shades of ZOG. Like zombies, aren't they? They never die."

"Yep." Although it had happened long before he'd

become an agent, Chase knew that the Zionist Occupation-
ist Government was a conspiracy plot promoted by militia
groups in the days before Timothy McVeigh brought down
the federal building in Oklahoma City. After that, the mili-
tias got less vocal and less easy to identify, but the people
attracted to their philosophy were always out there, railing
against shadowy international Jewish banking corporations and nonwhites. In recent years, the so-called Patriot
movement was coming back to life with a vengeance. Zombies indeed. The guy who flew his plane into an IRS office
in Austin and the guy who shot up a Congresswoman were
two of the most recent zombie heroes.

Chase noticed marks on the underside of the page
Nicole was holding. "There's something on the back of that
printout."

She turned it over. "Looks like someone used it as a
writing pad." Holding it at an angle to the light, she
sounded out the letters. "Eminen-tur? Eminen-ten? She
held the page out to him.

The one handwritten word was fairly legible, except
for the last letter. E-M-I-N-E-N-T-E-R, or maybe
E-M-I-N-E-N-T-E-N. "A place name?" he asked. "Or a foreign language? Looks like it could be German."

Nicole shrugged. "The techs will deliver their research
on any marks along with the AFIS report on the prints. I
got us top priority, but it'll still take a day or two." She
pointed at his stack and went back to her chair.

He set the page aside in the stack of interesting finds. If
only they'd nabbed the actual robbers instead of their Ford
Explorer, they could be grilling the criminals instead of
sorting through all this detritus. At least the locals had
headed off the robbery this time, but somehow the perps
had vanished into the surrounding woods, along with their
automatic rifles.

A buzzing sensation thrummed against his chest.
Reaching into the breast pocket of his sports coat, he pulled
out his cell phone. His spirits lifted when he saw the readout. *Summer Westin*. Turning his back to his partner, he

pressed the Talk button. *"Querida,"* he murmured in his best sexy voice.

"Chase."

He could tell just by the way she said his name that she was fighting back tears. "Bad day?"

"You could say that."

Yes, there was a definite catch in her voice. "Did they get your bear?"

"No. Actually, that's the only good part of this day. I saw Raider; he's alive. He might have been wounded, but he was running fast and he felt pretty strong to me—"

"Felt?"

"We sort of collided."

"Collided? With a bear?" He glanced over his shoulder at Nicole. She rolled her eyes. He turned back around. This was the *good* part of Summer's day? "Spill it."

She told him about being shot at while investigating gunfire around Marmot Lake. He felt the blood drain from his face, thinking about how close he had come to losing her.

"Give me the license number of that pickup." After she'd read it to him, he said, "Now go have a glass of wine, *querida*. You *have* had a bad day."

"That's not the worst," she said. "She died, Chase."

He searched his memory. "Lisa Glass?"

"Yes, Lisa died this afternoon. From that head injury." He heard a quick intake of breath, and then she continued, "Just yesterday she told me she'd been kidnapped."

The muscles between his shoulder blades were tensing up. "What more could happen out there?"

"Maybe I should mention the C-4."

He came out of his chair. "What about C-4?"

"What about C-4?" Nicole echoed behind him.

"Apparently there's a bunch missing from a mine south of here," Summer said into his ear. "Do you think that could have caused the boom that Lili and I heard? Remember that crater around the mineshaft?"

He remembered it well. C-4 could have easily created the hole. The noise of the explosion would have been heard for miles. C-4 and guns and kidnapping and dead women. What in hell was going on out there on the Olympic Peninsula?

"Summer," he said, "if there's the slightest chance that guys with C-4 are romping around Marmot Lake, you need to get out of there now."

There was dead air for a minute. Then she said, "I was hired to do an environmental survey and develop a management plan for Marmot Lake. That's my area."

In other words, nothing short of a nuclear blast was going to keep her away from Marmot Lake. "Is your job worth your life?" he asked.

There was another long moment of silence. Then she said, "I don't recall telling you to give up your job because it might be dangerous. That's because I've always had the feeling that *your* job was important to you."

Touché. He sighed heavily. "Watch your back, Summer. I want you in one piece the next time I see you."

"So, enough about me," she said, a little too brightly. "How was *your* day?"

"A robbery thwarted, escaped perps, piles of paperwork. Pretty boring stuff. So far the only thing I've learned is that the wars in Iraq and Afghanistan are money-laundering exercises by the Jews and their corporations."

Silence drew out on her end of the phone. "I was kidding about that last part," he added.

"I was thinking it was as good an explanation as any I've heard so far."

"Funny."

"I'll let you get back to the battle. Stay safe, FBI," she murmured, her voice suddenly husky. "I want you all in one piece, too."

He groaned. Just hearing the words *I want you* out of her mouth had an effect on body parts that shouldn't be so sensitive while he was on duty.

"Call me when you can."

"I will. Stay out of trouble, *querida*."

He stuck the phone in his pocket and swiveled around. Nicole's calm gray eyes were focused on him. "This is better than the soaps." She tapped a manicured nail on the table. "Tell me the latest episode."

SAM felt stronger after talking to Chase. The fact that right now her job matched his for excitement filled her with a perverse pride. The bullets and violence and dead people, she could live without.

Most of the time her solitary lifestyle felt tranquil. But at times like this, it was just plain lonely. Mack was with Jodi. Chase was more than a hundred miles away. The same went for her housemate, Blake, who was probably at work, anyway. She couldn't quite picture herself whining about bombs, bears, and dead trail workers to him while he repotted orchids in a greenhouse. Next weekend, she'd trek back to her own home in Bellingham and eat Blake's cooking and pet her cat, Simon. Soft fur and purring made anything—even murder—less horrendous.

She cleaned herself up as best she could in the restroom at the district office, bandaged her knee, combed the bark out of her hair, and changed into relatively clean clothes from the bag she kept in the pickup.

Before heading back to the bunkhouse and the trail crew, she bought white wine and supplies for s'mores at the QFC and then stopped by the local liquor store for a bottle of whiskey. If Blackstock didn't invite her to his truck tonight for a drink, she was going to invite him to hers. She needed to talk to someone old enough to understand all the world's evils.

As she was opening the door to her pickup, a maroon SUV zoomed up beside her.

"We thought that was you," Joe said through the open window.

The passenger door slammed and Lili, dressed in a warm-up suit and cleated shoes, dashed to Sam. "Aunt Summer!" She gave Sam a quick hug, making the bottles clink inside the brown paper bag. "Can you come to my soccer game? Mom has to work tonight."

Sam turned toward Joe, who silently mouthed, *Please*.

"Please, please!" Lili echoed. "It's Forks against Rushing Springs, the division finals. I'm one of the best players. I want you to see me." Her huge brown eyes moved to the paper bag and then back to Sam's face. "Please?"

Sam felt like an alcoholic who had been caught preparing for a binge. Her stomach growled.

"I'll buy you a hot dog," Joe promised. "And we can talk during the game."

She put her hand on the door handle of her pickup. "I'll follow you."

"Yes!" Lili raised a fist in the air as she trotted back to her seat.

LILI was as good a player as she'd promised, and Joe and Sam yelled themselves hoarse cheering as she scored several goals for the Forks Middle School team. They sat at the far end of the bleachers, a little apart from the crowd so they could talk business.

Sitting separate from the community made Sam a little uncomfortable, but she often had the feeling that the citizens of Forks might scoot away even if she plunked herself down in their midst. Townsfolk glanced in their direction and then leaned their heads close to whisper. One handsome dark-haired fellow stared at her. Under other circumstances, Sam might have been flattered, but he was at least a decade younger, and his gaze did not hold even a hint of warmth. A heavyset, graying man with a weathered, pockmarked face and a ragged mustache sat several rows below them and off to the left, but he glanced up and his eyes met hers once before skidding away. The guy from Best Burgers who had glared at her.

"We can't find a single person who knows anything about the explosion or fire," Joe said bitterly. "Let alone about this alleged kidnapping. We can't even find anyone who knew Lisa, outside of the kids on the trail crew."

Joe's dark eyes shone too brightly, and his jaw worked

for a moment before he said, "She was someone's daughter. If I lost any of my kids—"

Sam wanted to put her arm around his shoulders, but was reluctant to provide fodder for gossip, so she settled for a quick pat on his thigh. "I understand."

"And nobody seems to be missing her."

"That is odd." She worried that her own emotions were not as bruised as Joe's. Or Mack's or Jodi's, for that matter. But how much could a woman take in one day?

Joe shrugged sadly. "She was from Philadelphia. The park service gets those types from time to time; kids that want to have an adventure as far away from home as possible. The contact phone number she gave us is bogus. The lady it belongs to finally answered to tell us it was a wrong number; she didn't have a clue who Lisa Glass was."

"Maybe Lisa just wrote it down wrong, by accident?"

"Maybe. Or maybe she's a runaway. We've turned the case over to the FBI in Seattle; I hope they can find her relatives."

Sam thought about her own FBI agent, about how nice it would be to have Chase around to talk to. To touch.

"What kind of a world are we raising our kids in?" Joe shook his head and moved his gaze to the playing field. "There's a guy looking for his daughter down in Rushing Springs. I hear he's a drunk and she's twenty-one, so everyone seems to think she finally had enough and just ran off." He suddenly leapt from his seat as the Rushing Springs team kicked the ball toward Forks's goal. "Block it! Block!"

When he sat back down, he continued morosely, "Running off without a word sounds like something Lili would do."

"Oh, Joe, I don't think so," Sam responded automatically. But that was just her opinion. Or maybe her hope? Lili could be planning to skip town for Katmandu, for all she knew. She'd find a way to ask next time she was alone with the girl.

Joe blinked and cleared his throat. "I hear you had a pretty awful day, too."

After they'd covered her afternoon incident in the

woods, Sam said, "Sometimes I have the feeling that the park service isn't exactly welcome in these parts. Do you feel at home here?"

His gaze met hers briefly before darting back to the field. "For the most part," he said warily. "It helps to have family; I've got the kids in school and Laura at the library. You have to work at it, though."

"Work at what?"

"Being part of the community." He took a sip of his Coke and shrugged. "Don't wear the uniform or drive NPS vehicles off-duty."

Strike one. She often didn't change until she swapped pajamas for the gray-green. Was that the reason for those hostile stares at the burger place? Thank heavens she was wearing civilian clothes at the moment. But her NPS pickup was in the parking lot right now.

"Don't talk too much about the environment or conservation issues."

That was a hard one. She'd made up her mind even as a teenager not to stay mum while people around her cursed tree huggers and government regulations.

"Buy from the local merchants."

That much she could and did do, although Forks had little to offer in the way of shopping, unless you were a fan of the Twilight Series and all things vampirish.

"And go to church."

"Hmmm." It was hopeless, then. She could barely bring herself to enter the church she'd been raised in, let alone a strange one.

On the field, Lili passed the ball to a skinny boy on her team.

Sam asked, "Does Lili like being on a coed team?"

"More than her dad likes her being on one."

Sam laughed. "I'll bet."

"I'm not too sure about her coach."

Sam checked out the bench, where the coach was talking to a girl. "He's the science teacher that she likes so well, right?"

At that point, Lili attempted a steal, then collided with the other player and fell. Joe gasped and rose. She was back on her feet almost instantly, but limping, favoring her right leg. The coach and his teenage assistant ran onto the field and carried Lili off between them.

"She's okay," Sam said. "She was walking."

"I've gotta know for sure. She'll be 'mortified,' but I'm going down there."

Sam stood up. "You wait here. I'll go. I don't want you to embarrass Lili any more than you do every day."

He snorted and then grinned. "Thanks, Sam. She idolizes you."

If that was true, Lili was hard up for role models, Sam thought as she walked to the stairs.

JACK tracked the blonde with his eyes as she stepped down the bleachers. Just like a typical fed, she sat with that slant-eyed ranger apart from everyone else. In or out of uniform, they were like some sort of fungus, the way they clumped together.

She seemed to favor her right leg; she must have hurt it somehow when she ran through the woods after them.

His mother jumped up and cheered as his cousin on the Rushing Springs team scored a goal, then she shouted in joy again a minute later as his youngest brother, Derek, kicked one into the net for the Forks team. When she sat down again, she punched him on the shoulder. "This is great! No matter which side wins, we can celebrate."

Jack had quit cheering a while ago, and instead clapped for every goal. His childhood loyalty was for Forks, his old school, but he lived in Rushing Springs now and some of the people around him were his neighbors. Anyone might be a future customer for his custom furniture business. If it had any future at all.

Throwing her arm around him, his mom gave him a squeeze. "Thanks for coming, Jack. It means a lot to every-

one, you being here." She gave him a little smile before
turning back to watch the game.

Jack wondered if everyone included her new husband,
Ed Tilson, sitting on her left side. Thanks to the land grab
by the park service, Gideon Lumber had to cut back, and in
two weeks, Ed was losing his job as a scaler. There'd be
unemployment for a while, and he was still sniffing around
for another job, but right now it looked like the family might
have to move someplace where they still believed in logging. And then the rambling farmhouse that Jack had grown
up in would belong to someone else. Probably to some
Seattle billionaire who used it only during summer vacation. Jack took another sip of the Bud in his soft drink cup.

Down on the field, Roddie strutted back and forth in
front of the Forks bench, shooting a fist in the air now and
then, lecturing the soccer kids. He was only an assistant
coach, and as a junior in high school, he was way too old
for the middle school girls on the team, but it had to be a
kick, the way they gazed at him like he was some kind of
god. Showboat kid. With his con artist personality,
Roddie—who insisted on calling himself Rocky now—
would end up owning half the Olympic Peninsula. Jack
hoped he knew when to keep quiet as well as when to talk.

"FOR heaven's sake, it's *soccer*, Dad," his daughter com-
plained. "I'm going to get injured sometimes. Coach says
it's only *strained*, not sprained." Lili flipped her braid over
her shoulder. She slid her arm from around Sam's shoulder
and perched on the passenger seat of the SUV while Joe
stood outside, holding the door open.

"I could have finished the game, but no, Coach wouldn't
let me," Lili whined. "I know we could have won by at least
five points, not just two."

"But you won, Lili," Sam said. "And you were great."

"Thanks," Lili said a bit grudgingly, "but George Fishkiller scored the most goals."

"You'll beat him next year, Lili," Joe told her, although he hoped that the big Indian kid would not be on the team next year. It was a little creepy to see such a hulk sitting next to Lili on the bench. He wished the school district had enough students to have separate boys' and girls' teams.

He stared at the elastic wrap on his daughter's right ankle. He couldn't help noticing how slim and shapely her legs were under her skimpy shorts, and how tight her top was. Ever since those female soccer players stripped down to their sports bras on nationwide TV, all the girls thought it was okay to run around practically naked. He always knew his daughters would be beauties like Laura, but he thought Lili would grow into a young woman at sixteen or seventeen. Not at thirteen.

Lili brightened a little. "Martian—I mean Coach—did say I was the best player on the team. He whispered it in my ear."

Joe clenched his jaw. He'd checked Gale Martinson's record in NCIC and with the DMV, and found nothing beyond a parking ticket in Seattle. But that meant only that he hadn't been caught yet. The man always seemed to be surrounded by young girls. And—*Martian?*—the girls had nicknames for him? That didn't sound good.

"A little ice and I think it'll be okay, Joe," Sam said. "Lili's tough."

His daughter shot Sam a grateful look.

"Does Mr. Martinson bandage every girl's leg?" he asked Lili.

"Uh-huh. Helps us get dressed, too."

He jerked his head up. "What?"

She rolled her eyes. "I was *kidding*, Dad. Get a grip. He's the coach." She looked over his shoulder and raised her hand.

Joe turned to see who Lili was waving to. A teenage boy held up his hand briefly, smiling in their direction.

"Scoot in." Joe closed the passenger door, walked to the other side, and slid into the driver's seat.

Lili slouched in her seat and propped her good left foot up on the dashboard.

"Don't forget the ice," Sam said through the open window. "It was fun. Thanks for inviting me."

"What about my writer interview?" Lili asked. "We still need to do that."

"Yes, we do," Sam agreed. "Let me look at my schedule and I'll call you, okay? See you guys later. Lili, you were great."

"I'll be even better next year," Lili shouted at Sam as she walked toward her pickup.

Joe turned the key in the ignition. "Feet on the floor," he said automatically, then he glimpsed a mark on Lili's left ankle. "Wait."

He leaned over and pushed down her left sock. Although he'd halfway been expecting something like this, he could hardly believe it had already happened. "What the hell is that?"

"What does it look like?"

The tattoo was the color of dried blood. An unusual circular design, sort of an upside-down peace sign with a curving vine on each side.

"It looks like a tattoo," he said. "Where did you get this? Don't you know that tattoo needles can kill you? You could get hepatitis or AIDS, And now you're marked for life. When you're a grandma, you think you'll want a—"

"Chill, Dad." She pulled up her sock, covering the tattoo. "All the girls have them. It comes off with baby oil."

At least the last part was a relief. He let out a breath. "Where'd you get it?"

She looked out the passenger window.

"Lili?"

"Five."

What the hell did that mean? "Five what?"

"Five," she repeated sullenly, refusing to look at him.

Fuming, Joe started the car. Lili was only thirteen and already she was becoming an alien. Laura seemed almost as mystified as he was. Maybe Sam could find out what the heck *five* meant in teen lingo these days.

As they pulled out of the playfield parking lot, Martinson and his son and the older boy called Rocky were walking toward the cars, each carrying worn duffle bags full of gear. Lili raised her hand again as they drove past the group. "He *is* hot," she murmured, so quietly he could barely make out the words.

Joe glanced sideways to see Gale Martinson's pale eyes light on his daughter. The man smiled and nodded. Lili grinned in response. Joe's stomach sank to the floorboard.

GARRETT Ford had just opened the door of his diesel pickup when he saw Summer Westin approaching hers. He slid in quickly, hoping to pull out of the spot before she noticed, but she marched over and even had the nerve to smile as she tapped lightly on his window.

He frowned and pressed the button to lower the glass.

"Hi!" Her voice was lower than he'd expected for such a small woman. "I saw you in the stands. Have we met?"

"Never." He narrowed his eyes and did his best to radiate hostility.

Damn if she didn't thrust her hand through the open window. "I'm Sam Westin."

"I know who you are. I've seen you on TV." He glared at her outstretched fingers. Such a little hand. He could just zip that window right back up, bite off her puny trouble-making arm at the wrist. His finger was still on the button.

An uncertain look flitted across her face, and she yanked her hand back outside. "I'm sorry. I didn't get your name?"

"Ford. Garrett Ford."

"Glad to meet you," she said. "I didn't know I was going to be on TV; I was just as surprised as everyone else."

"I'll bet," he said. He turned the key in the ignition.

She stepped back. He rolled up the window and peeled out of the parking lot. In the rearview mirror she looked so bewildered that he couldn't help smiling.

14

WHEN Sam arrived at the bunkhouse, she found the trail crew out back, huddled around a crackling campfire.

"Missed you at dinner," Tom Blackstock said as she sat down next to him. "Guess you heard about Lisa?"

She nodded. The kids were subdued. They all stared into the flames or poked at the coals with sharpened sticks. If they'd been older, she might have offered them wine. In this case, the best she had to offer was dessert. She held up the grocery bag. "I brought the makings for s'mores."

Roasting marshmallows perked up the group. When they were into seconds, Blackstock, in counselor mode, encouraged the teens to talk about what they wanted to do in the future.

"Live on a yacht in the South Pacific," spouted one boy. Several of the others made scoffing noises. Sam frowned at their instant dismissal; she wanted to enjoy the dream of a boat in the tropics for a little while.

"I'm gonna be a rapper," said another. More chuckles. A few gangsta hand gestures flashed around the circle. "It could happen," he insisted.

"I'm moving to Tennessee, gonna drive on the NAS-CAR circuit," volunteered the shaggy-haired youth beside the rapper.

Silence reigned for a minute as the rest of them reflected. Sam wondered what Lisa Glass had planned for her future. Had Tom chosen this subject because of Lisa's abrupt lack of future? Or would this be a lead-in to what was to become of the trail crew after they went home in a few weeks?

Ben Rosen shifted his marshmallow to a more advantageous position over the fire. "I want to be a counselor for people with drug problems," he murmured quietly, keeping his eyes fixed on the fire.

"Great idea," Blackstock encouraged. Others nodded in approval. How many of these kids had a crack-addicted mother at home or an alcoholic father on the streets?

Maya cleared her throat, then said, "I want to be a teacher for kids with learning disabilities." Her gaze traveled around the circle as if daring the boys to challenge that idea. They all simply nodded.

Sam was touched. She'd been thinking of them only as troubled kids, not as the adults they would soon be. Blackstock helped them brainstorm about how best to achieve their goals. They talked a little about school, and while none of them looked forward to going back, they all said they'd stay in class this year or, for the two boys who were over eighteen, get their GEDs.

"Ranger Westin went to college," Blackstock announced. All faces turned toward Sam. "Tell them about what a difference it made in your life."

"Well." *Bad choice, Tom*, she wanted to shout. What to say? "In the first place, call me Sam, not Ranger Westin. I'm classified as a tech, actually, not a ranger, and this is a temporary job for me. I'm only here for three months."

"But you did go to college?" Blackstock pressed.

"Yes." For all the good it did. "I have a degree in wildlife biology."

"So you studied all about wild animals. And what do you do when you're not being a ranger—er, tech?"

She told them about being a freelance writer. None of the teens had remarked on the wildlife biology degree, and nobody said, "Oh, cool," when she mentioned writing about conservation and nature, either. This was her greatest fear—that the younger generation simply didn't care about wilderness.

"How much money do you make?" Ben asked.

Why was that always their first question? Lili had asked, too. "I chose variety and freedom over security," she told them honestly. "I don't make much money. Most of the time I've been okay with that, but now that the economy's bad, it's hard. I'm self-employed, so when I don't have a contract, I have no income. Nowadays I wish I had a steady job and a paycheck hitting my bank account every two weeks."

"Like a steady job's easy to find," one commented.

"To help pay the bills, I have a housemate," she added, so they'd know that everyone didn't have to have an executive's salary. "His name is Blake."

"Housemate. Right." One of the boys nodded knowingly. Another rolled his eyes.

Were they envisioning some sort of sugar daddy? "Blake's gay," she said. Why did she feel compelled to explain herself to these kids? She had to find a way to pay Tom back later for this.

To her surprise, there were no nasty retorts about sharing her home with a gay man. The world had changed a lot since she was their age.

After everyone had showered and retired to their respective rooms, Sam turned to Maya, who sat on her bunk clad in a blue undershirt and boxers, massaging lotion into her feet. "I told everyone about how I ended up here, Maya. How about you?"

"B and E." The girl cracked the joint of her big toe. "You know how there's like a couple hours between the time school gets out and people get home from work? That's a great time to hit houses in the good neighborhoods." She looked up and smiled. "You'd be amazed at the stuff you can pick up."

"I'll bet." Sam was glad she had a housemate with an unpredictable schedule watching over her home.

Maya pulled her legs into a lotus position and sighed wistfully. "Those were the good old days."

"Except for the people you stole from."

The girl shrugged. "Those people had so much stuff that most of the time they never even missed it."

Sam reflected on the families she knew whose garages were so packed with possessions that there was no room for cars, and was inclined to agree with Maya. "Still," she said, "it was *their* stuff."

Maya stood up and grabbed her MP3 player from the top bunk. "I'd never take anything from someone who was poor."

"Nice to know I'm safe." Sam tugged back the blanket and loosened the sheets on her bunk.

"And I don't do it anymore, anyway," Maya added, as if she'd just remembered that she was now reformed. She slid into her bed.

"Good for you. I think being a teacher is a much better plan than being a cat burglar." Sam grabbed one of her pillows and pummeled it, trying to even out the lumps.

Maya laughed. "Give 'em what they want to hear. *Queso* has his reports to do." Pushing earbuds into her ears, she closed her eyes and nodded her head to music only she could hear.

Sam observed her for a moment. Which was the real Maya—the street-smart burglar or the wannabe teacher? They were scary creatures, these teenagers. Good thing she didn't have one at home. A cat was mysterious enough.

"Lights out!" Blackstock called from the hallway. Sam grabbed her penlight, flicked off the wall switch on the way out. They met at the front door, and crept out to his truck for a drink.

A wolf howl startled Sam awake the next morning. Her left foot got hung up in the sheet, and she practically fell out of the bunk, banging her injured knee on the bed frame. The invisible wolf howled three more times as she groped her way toward the little table that held her cell phone and charging unit.

"Westin," she croaked.

"Hey, Summer! I didn't wake you, did I?"

Who in the hell? She waited, rubbing her bandaged knee, blinking sleepily in the dim room. Her head ached and her mouth tasted like a possum had denned up there overnight. She licked at the stitches in her lip.

Maya's bunk was made and her hiking boots were gone from the alcove that served as their closet. Sam felt a little uneasy; she hadn't even cracked an eyelid as her roomie had dressed for the day. Maya and her burglar buddies could have stripped the room and she would not have known.

"Hello?" the male voice said uncertainly.

"Who is this?"

"It's Richard Best, your old friend at *The Edge*."

"Of course. The guy who told me to get lost."

It took him only a second to recover. "I'm the one who *hired* you. And then I gave you a little rest break, but hey, that's the business, you know? Now I'm hiring you again."

"Where'd you get my cell phone number?" Hoyle wouldn't give it out.

Her call waiting signal beeped and—speak of the devil—it was Peter Hoyle calling. She decided to let him go to voicemail and deal with it later.

"I'm hurt that you forgot to give me your cell number," Best was saying. "Anyway, where's that contract for the endangered species gig?"

"What do you care about this 'endangered species gig'? What happened to spas and rich people?"

"It's supposed to be a big conference, and the press will be there. Believe it or not, people still remember you from that cougar thing last year. And we took a poll. You'd be surprised how many of our target audience are environmental types."

"No, I wouldn't."

He ignored that. "Did you sign the contract? Is it in the mail?"

The chill of the old wooden floor was seeping through her thin pajamas. She stood up. "You really want to hire me just to write a paper and speak at a conference?"

The contract stipulated less than a week's worth of work. With everything going on around the park, a speech seemed almost too inconsequential to bother with. But then again, her contract with the park service was up in a few weeks. And unless Blake had collected phone messages from clients that he hadn't yet shared with her, there was no other work waiting for her in the wings.

"I suppose we could cover expenses, too," Best said. "But it's local, so really, there shouldn't be anything more than maybe a meal or two."

Her head ached, making her regret the bottle of wine she and Blackstock had downed in her truck last night before turning in. It had seemed like a good idea at the time, a natural accompaniment as they shared their feelings of guilt over Lisa's death.

"Summer? You still there?"

"You need to cover your butt, don't you? You already told the media I'd do it."

He laughed. She couldn't tell if it was forced or not. "We were sure that you'd want to, and you weren't here to ask. It's your kind of thing; it's a *wildlife* conference."

It crossed her mind that she might not need *The Edge* at all; she could probably just contract with the conference organizers. Whoever they were.

As if he could read her mind, he added, "If this goes well, we might start a weekly column about outdoor adventures."

She noticed he didn't actually *promise* any work beyond the conference. Public speaking was not her forte. As a matter of fact, most of her encounters with a microphone and the public had been disasters. But, she argued with herself, she'd be prepared this time. It was another payment on the mortgage for her cabin. What could happen at a conference, for heaven's sake? The greatest threats would be overbaked salmon and watery coffee.

The Edge might surprise her and come through with other offers. At the very least, once her name was out there again, she'd get a few more writing assignments from the

conservation organizations and maybe some of the outdoor
sports magazines as well. And the park service and forest
service and BLM had publications, too; maybe some of
those could be a new source of revenue after those organizations knew about her.

"So, is the contract on its way?" Best prompted.

She sighed, resigned to her fate. "As soon as I get to a
post office."

"Just fax it."

"All right," she told him. "Work on that weekly column
idea. And don't make any more promises to the media on my
behalf." She pressed the End button. The phone sang its voice
mail waiting ditty, and she switched over to voice mail.

"Westin?" Hoyle sounded more annoyed than usual.
"Where are those reports I asked for?" Click.

Whoa. She'd better hightail it to the district station and
type up the reports first thing this morning. Right after coffee and a shower. As soon as she'd set down the phone, it
howled again. She stabbed the Talk button. "What?"

"Maybe I'll just call back later."

She smiled at the familiar voice. "No, it's okay, Blake. I
just haven't had my coffee yet and my phone keeps howling
and there are creeps in the woods and people are dropping
dead—"

"*More* people? I read about that poor trail worker girl in
the paper this morning."

"Well, then, not *more* people, I guess." How had she
managed to make Lisa's death sound trivial? "Hey, you
called me. What's up?"

"I don't want to add to your woes."

"But?"

"The kitchen sink's dripping."

"You mean the piping under the drain's leaking? Or is
water running down from the faucet? Or the sprayer? Or
is it a fitting around the garbage disposal?"

"How would I know?"

"Well, you have to dry everything off and then watch
where it's coming from."

There was a long silence, then he finally said, "Or I could just call a plumber."

In rural Kansas, people knew how to fix things. Especially men. One of her grandfathers had done his own welding, for heaven's sake; the other constructed whole buildings out of rock. Her father had built wheelchair ramps and installed railings and shower seats for her mother. And her grandmother had helped him. How could any adult male not know how to fix a leaking sink?

"Never mind," she groaned. It was her house, after all. And she was not about to foot the bill for a plumber. "Stick a dishpan under it. I'll fix it when I come back in a day or two."

"Okey-doke," he said.

Okey-doke? That didn't sound like one of Blake's expressions. "Have you been talking to my father?"

"Just the once, a couple of days ago. He said he was praying for me; I told him, likewise. Didn't he call you?"

"Yeah," she said, remembering. "About the wedding. Any other calls for me?"

"Does a solicitation from The Red Cross count?"

"Definitely not."

"Then no. Go get that coffee. Don't bite anyone." He hung up.

While pawing through her daypack for her hairbrush, she uncovered Lisa's Bible and her mind abruptly leapt back to the case at hand. Guns, mines, explosives, terrified bears, and a young woman, dead. Garrett Ford—was he simply an irritable local rattler she had run across, or was he up to something? Did any of these pieces fit together? Maybe Paul Schuler had been right; if you hung out in the woods long enough, you'd encounter every form of shady activity.

She decided she'd left her hairbrush in her truck and padded to the kitchen. A cup of coffee, a few minutes to pack, and she'd be on her way to the Marmot Lake area. The sheriff's department and the park rangers would pursue interviews about Lisa's kidnapping and the illegal gunplay in the area. At least she hoped they would. The FBI would handle the autopsy. They had the resources to track down Lisa's relatives and associates.

Sam was tired of chasing shadows. Like the plumbing in her house, the wilderness was her domain. She knew how it worked. Eventually, she would make Marmot Lake give up its secrets.

When the caffeine kicked in, she remembered that today was the first day she could have her stitches removed from her lip. She drove to the tiny emergency clinic in Forks. The brief pain of having the stitches plucked out was well worth the reward of no longer looking like the bride of Frankenstein.

On to the next onerous task—creating Hoyle's reports. In the mailroom at the division building, Sam faxed the signed contract to Best, hoping that the transmissions weren't logged and she wouldn't be reprimanded for using government equipment for private business. Then she forced herself to sit at the desk she'd been assigned to. She and several other temps shared access to an ancient computer. As the technological dinosaur warmed up with its usual coffee-grinding noises, she scrubbed a layer of fine dust from the keyboard and screen. She should have brought her laptop from home. But then, that had been part of the appeal of this assignment, to get away from the insane pace and chaos of hi-tech.

Outside the window, wisps of ground fog floated along the ground like ghosts gliding among the trees. She loved the mysterious moist cloak of clouds that rolled in from the ocean. Snagged by the forest and dammed in by the high peaks of the Olympics, the fog would lay hushed in the hollows like a cold-blooded beast that had to be warmed by the sun before it could move.

Fog was a rarity in the rolling hills of southeastern Kansas, where she'd grown up. To walk through a cloud-shrouded forest was a special joy: trees dripping in primeval moisture, muffled wingbeats of birds flying invisible overhead, diamond chandeliers of spiderwebs stretched between the fern fronds.

By noon, the fog outside would be gone. Turning the squeaky chair toward the keyboard, she set about typing as fast as she could. First, the Lisa report she'd promised Hoyle. She entered all her conversations with Lisa Glass, as well as her trailside interview of the girl's coworkers and her inspection of Lisa's dorm room. Then she worked on the report for the incident at Marmot Lake. Reduced to words on the screen, she definitely did not come off as a professional investigator. She left out her collision with Raider, but noted a sighting of a large male bear, possibly wounded. Under "Conclusions": she typed, *Trace license plate, continue investigation of lake area.*

She e-mailed both files to Hoyle, then clicked the flashing mailbox icon at the top of the screen. Most messages were from the Division Office, standard instructions about proper usage of forms or distribution of funds or about yet another reorganization of high-level NPS managers nobody had met. One message, from Peter Hoyle to all employees, contained advice about dealing with Lisa Glass's death; it was mainly a warning not to talk to the press. Another to Sam alone suggested how to represent herself at the upcoming conference. She squirmed in her chair, already fretting about the speech she was now committed to do. It was not an event to look forward to.

And there was her father's wedding to get through before that. High heels and church ladies and unrealistic pledges of forever. Although, now that she thought about it, since her father was in his mid-sixties, forever might not be all that unrealistic. She was suddenly ashamed of herself for dreading his marriage. She needed fresh air and bird songs to sweep that malicious dust out of her brain. She peeked outside. Dang, the fog was nearly gone.

She called Tom Blackstock and told him she would not be returning to the bunkhouse tonight. Arnie Cole caught her in the supply room as she was lashing a tent onto a backpack. "Well, well. Sizzlin' Summer Westin. I'll bet you're camping out at Marmot Lake."

"There's something weird going on out there."

"I heard about the gunplay. There's always something going on out there, just like I told you."

"I suppose you heard that Lisa Glass died, too."

"Was that her name?" He looked genuinely stricken, and for a moment she thought she may have misjudged him.

"I think there's a connection between what's still going on out there and what happened to Lisa." Sam pulled a nylon strap through a metal-toothed buckle and snugged it up tight. "We're never going to discover what it is with law enforcement just responding to calls." She stood up.

"You're camping out there by yourself?"

No way was she going to tell him that. She hefted the backpack.

"Need protection?" He bounced his eyebrows at her. "I'm available."

"I wouldn't risk it if I were you, Arnie. I have a gun, and I'm a little jumpy these days."

JACK Winner stood on Ernest Craig's rickety front steps, holding a postcard and pretending hard that it was from Allie. His throat was closing up fast. When Ernest answered the door, the old man also had a postcard in his hand.

"So you got one, too," Ernest said, blinking. The hand in which he held the Universal Studios card trembled like a leaf in a breeze. Without Allie's paycheck to fund his habit, the old sot probably had the DTs by now.

Ernest noticed him looking and slid his quivering hand, along with the postcard, into his front pants pocket. "It just doesn't seem like Allie to run off to L.A.," he said. "But it says she met this guy Steve—" Ernest's gaze met Jack's at that point, and he paused. "Anyhow, I'm so glad to know she's alive, aren't you?"

Jack wasn't sure he could speak at all for a few seconds, so he just nodded. Finally, he croaked, "Mr. Craig, I—"

"Ernest."

Jack cleared his throat, then said, "Ernest, I don't know

how you'd feel about this . . . I don't even know how I feel
about it, but—"

The old man interrupted, "I don't understand about the
car, though."

Jack blinked at him. "What car?"

"Allie's car. How come she left it at Bogachiel State
Park if she was goin' to L.A.?"

Oh, God. He'd forgotten about the car. Jack racked his
brains for an explanation. "Maybe she hitched a ride."

"Too dangerous." Ernest shook his head. "Allie wouldn't
hitch."

"Mr. Craig—Ernest—it seems like Allie did lots of
things that you never thought she would."

The old man deflated like Jack had just slugged him.
"Yeah," Ernest finally managed to get out. "I guess so."

"Things we both thought she'd never do," Jack said.
"Maybe this Steve guy gave her a ride. Maybe they drove
his car to L.A." He liked to think that sometimes, that a
nice guy had stolen Allie away and they lived happily ever
after. In his imagination, this Steve looked a lot like Jack
Winner but had a lot more money. He could see the two of
them now, driving south on 101 in a convertible, enjoying
the sun and the ocean views.

"You were gonna ask me something?" Ernest said, jerking Jack's thoughts back to the present.

"Yeah." Jack paused a beat before adding, "Allie asked
if I'd send her a few of her things."

The old guy's eyes lit up. "You got an address for her?"
He sounded eager and hurt all at the same time.

Damn. Of course he'd need an address. Why the hell
hadn't he thought of that? Then inspiration struck. "It's a
general delivery post office box; you know, a place to pick
up mail and packages, until she gets settled. I'll write it
down for you." He didn't know how long a post office
would keep general delivery mail these days, but he figured that even if Ernest's letter got returned, the old man
would assume that Allie had just moved on. That was how

he tried to think of her now, too. Like she'd moved on to someplace better.

Ernest let him in. Jack could hardly believe the place. It was almost as clean as if Allie were still living there. The old man had scrubbed the kitchen and even vacuumed the living room. The stains were still there on the carpet, but the place smelled like orange cleaner instead of sour whiskey now.

Ernest watched as Jack wrote down a fake P.O. box address on the back of an envelope. Thank God the zip code for Hollywood was on the back of his postcard.

"I'm gonna write to Allie," Ernest told him. "Tell her I'm cleaning up. You'll tell her that, too, won't you? It'll be better around here now; she won't have to be ashamed. I'm gonna get me some sort of job, even if it's just a dishwasher at the diner. I'll find an AA group and I'm really gonna go this time."

He sounded so hopeful. When the old man's quivering hand landed on his shoulder, Jack wasn't sure he could take it. "You'll tell her, too, won't you?"

Jack had to swallow hard before he could answer. "Sure, Ernest, I'll write her that when I send the stuff. But I don't know if she'll listen to me." His voice broke then and he had to stop. Had Allie died because she'd listened to him too often?

"Why d'you think she asked *you* to send her things?"

Jack shrugged. "Probably because she didn't want you to have to make a special trip." He nodded in the direction of the man's bad leg.

"'Course. She always did baby me like that." Ernest turned and looked toward the bedrooms. "What kind of things did she want? I hope it's not the paintings I got in my bedroom. She did those when she was just a little kid, and I sorta need 'em. I gotta have—" Ernest choked then.

"No, it's not paintings." His chest felt like it was caving in on itself—was twenty-four too young to have a heart attack? He couldn't wait to get this over with. "A couple of her photos." He glanced at his postcard like he was reading from it. "A marten on a log? And a full moon at Rialto Beach." He'd been with Allie when she'd taken those. He understood what Ernest was talking about when the old man said he needed some of Allie's things.

"I guess that'd be okay. They're in her room." He preceded Jack there, and now Jack realized why he'd never seen Ernest Craig around much before. His limp was painful to witness. No wonder the man had taken up whiskey. Allie said her dad was wounded in Vietnam but the VA had said his leg problem was not service-related; which was just what you'd expect of the feds. Plenty of tax breaks for the rich but no medical care for a man that couldn't work anymore. That was why Allie had wanted to blow up the VA Building in Seattle.

Ernest took Allie's incredible purple moonlight photo down from her wall, and then the one of the bright-eyed weasel that stole a chicken leg from their picnic at Marmot Lake. He handed them to Jack. Then the old man put an arm around his shoulders. Jack couldn't keep the tears from spilling over, and they both stood there for a minute, pretending they weren't crying, neither one looking at the other.

Jack had no idea what the others had planned for Eminenten, but he'd make his part spectacular. For all the soldiers who came home broken, and for all the ones that didn't come home at all. For all the hardworking folks who got ripped off. For Allie and her dad.

15

AFTER scouting the Marmot Lake area to make sure no surprises awaited her, Sam set up camp in thick woods beyond the burn zone, hiding her tent beneath the low-hanging branches of a red cedar. All evidence indicated that intruders had so far been active only near the lake shore. Her camp would be behind them, out of their sight. At least she hoped so.

It took her half an hour of throwing rocks and ropes over high limbs to string up a bear line and suspend her food from it. Then she set off, using her GPS to guide her from the lake to the coordinates where she'd left the illegal track days ago. If she'd had wings, it wouldn't have taken long, but she had to divert around massive firs, battle through meadows of thigh-high ferns and salmonberry brambles, and wade glacier-melt creeks that made her whole body ache. As her private expedition entered its third hour, she had new respect for the hardy explorers who first hacked into the Olympic Peninsula in the 1880s. Although the area she was traversing had been logged twice, hiking off-trail was still tough going.

As she scrambled over a moss-encrusted log, she dropped her GPS locator, which slid into a pocket of rot at the cedar log's base. She gritted her teeth. While she could reconnoiter roughly with her compass and map, she wanted to meet the track exactly where she'd left it before. She knelt, groaning a little at the pain from her injured knee. After digging under the log and jamming a splinter up under a fingernail, she finally fished out the handheld. The screen was blank.

"Dammit!" She banged it on her thigh several times, pressed a few buttons. Finally, thankfully, the LCD blinked back on. Then she heard footsteps in the forest on the other side of the log.

She flattened herself on the ground. Poachers? She was not eager to feel bullets whiz by her head again.

A black and yellow centipede crawled through a miniature grove of orange gumdrop fungi a couple of inches from her nose. She closed her eyes, praying the creature wasn't attracted to body heat. The steps neared her position. Small snaps and rustles came from several directions. Damn; it was a whole group. Now it sounded like someone was standing on the other side of the log. The skin on her back crawled with the expectation of a sudden blow. Another minute passed. She heard the crunching of twigs beneath heavy feet, not more than a yard away.

Raising her head, she chanced a look across the top of the log. Startled brown eyes stared back at her from a long mournful face. A drooping stalk of greenery hung from the elk cow's mouth. They gazed at each other for a second.

Then Sam burst out laughing, although she knew she shouldn't. Three long-legged calves grazed among more adults, not far away, and elk could be violently protective.

The cow snorted and wheeled around, starting a minor stampede. Sam concentrated on counting the herd before they crashed out of sight. Five cows or yearlings—hard to tell from their backsides—and three calves only a couple of months old. She jotted down the numbers and position in her notebook. When she continued her quest, her mood was much happier.

After fifteen more minutes, she met the tracks where she'd left them two days before, and then followed them forward into the woods. The vehicle clearly had four-wheel drive because the tracks went over rocks, mud, and uneven ground. She mourned two red-bellied salamanders flattened in a tread mark. A little farther on, a native pink-and-green frog had been reduced to two dimensions by the right-side tires. The ruined plants were too many to keep track of.

Wouldn't it be a piece of luck if Garrett Ford's pickup tires matched the tread pattern on the ground? The man gave her the creeps. She wouldn't be surprised to find he was behind all the THIS LAND IS YOUR LAND signs.

After a forty-five-minute walk, the rough road ended in the midst of a thicket where the tracks made a three-point turn to double back on themselves. At first she was turned around, but then she realized that the splash of brightness glimpsed between tree trunks far to the west had to be Marmot Lake, shimmering in the sunshine.

According to the GPS, she was now not even a half mile from her tent. In the midst of the three end points, where the same vehicle had clearly been parked multiple times, Sam found boot prints from two people, a large rectangular area where the grass had been flattened by something heavy, and an oblong rust red patch, thick with flies. Blood. Lots of it, now mostly absorbed into the ground. Her heart sank further as she found claw marks slashed through drying mud, and then, a couple of feet away, a clump of rough black fur.

Something terrible had happened to a bear here within the last few days. She scraped up some of of the blood-soaked soil into one of her sample bags in case the rangers wanted to test it. Then she walked a widening spiral out from the turnaround, sniffing the air for the scent of decay. No bear carcasses. No remains of bait piles. The poacher hadn't been out just for the gall bladder and paws, but had taken the whole bear, meat and fur and all. Not that it made any difference to the murdered bear.

And—some consolation—she knew the victim hadn't been Raider. This had happened more than twenty-four hours ago. But goddamn it, this was a protected area now and all the bears in it were supposed to be safe.

She couldn't raise anyone on her park service radio. She was in a dead zone. A death zone. Feeling a little sick, she jotted down the GPS coordinates and marked an *X* on her map, then headed back down the tracks. In a spot where the right wheel of the vehicle had dropped off a rock outcropping into a depression, she maneuvered a large pyramid-shaped rock onto the down side of the outcropping.

With luck, the driver would never see the rock, and when the tires inevitably dropped into the hole, the sharp rock would do major damage to the vehicle's oil pan or transmission. Hopefully, the driver would be stuck here, clearly trespassing, with his vehicle covered in evidence of major criminal activity. Transmission fluid hemorrhaging from an illegal hunter's pickup; now that was a nice image.

Her trap set as best she could, she hiked back through the forest toward the lake and her tent. It was evening by the time she got there. She called in her findings to the dispatcher, and then, after checking the mine shaft and seeing no changes in the depression there, she circumnavigated the lake, verified that the parking lot was empty and her truck still hidden among the trees. She found no signs of Raider.

She hadn't been lying when she'd told Arnie she had a gun. Six months ago, Chase had given her a Glock pistol, saying she might need it someday. What she didn't tell Arnie was that it was still hidden in her bedroom closet back in Bellingham. For the first time, she wished it were with her. She was planning to spend the night in an area crawling with illegal hunters. A place where a woman had been fatally attacked, if Lisa's story of kidnapping was true. But she hated guns. Bullets traveled long distances and killed creatures not even aimed at, and Sam had survived for thirty-seven years without ever carrying a weapon. Her radio and cell phone worked here. If anything happened, she would be in place to observe and call for assistance. With luck, the element of surprise would be hers.

She lowered her food bag from the bear line, removed her dinner from it, and carried her meal to the lake shore. Hanging a pair of binoculars around her neck, she settled onto a rock and munched her bagel and peanut butter as she watched night settle over Marmot Lake.

With darkness came a slight breeze. Water lapped gently against the rocky bank, a continuous whisper in the darkness. The soft breath of air was welcome against her sticky face, but the water's murmur was a little bothersome: the noise could cloak human footsteps or the padding of a bear.

She raised her binoculars. Through the stand of slender vine maples at the far edge of the lake, she could see the dim outline of her NPS truck. No lights, no movement there. She traced the shoreline around which she had walked. A hundred yards away from the parking lot, a dim shape moved through the shadows. Tensing, she squinted. The shape was too big for a raccoon. Not solid enough for a bear. Big enough to be human. Or maybe two humans, side by side. She rotated the binocular dial but couldn't sharpen the focus. A slender head and neck emerged from the tree line. The creature stepped hesitantly to the water's edge, dipped its muzzle into the liquid. The blacktail buck raised his head, his large ears swiveled in her direction.

She continued scanning. In the growing darkness, detail was fast disappearing. The moon was rising over the mountains, but its light would be filtered through the tall forest for an hour yet.

Three ducks bobbed in the shallows not far away, quacking softly now and then. Mallards. The two drakes paddled close to the hen like teenage boys flocking to a cheerleader. Sam was reminded of the kids at the soccer game yesterday. Even though it was no longer mating season, the ducks definitely had sex on their minds. Maybe the kids did, too. Maybe Joe was right to worry about Lili.

She sipped from her water bottle and savored the gentle quiet. Small shapes flitted back and forth over the lake, skimming the air just a few feet above the water. Maybe swallows; but more likely, the little brown bats that nested in rock crevices and under the loose bark of trees. One tree frog tested its throat, then another. The song swelled to a chorus of amphibian voices.

Sliding to the ground, she pressed her back against the rock, closing her eyes to soak in the night music. The symphony rose in volume, then suddenly stopped. A throaty *"hunh"* from the far shore punctuated the abrupt silence. Sam jerked her binoculars to her eyes.

A dark shape padded down to the water, waded into the shallows. An elongated head stretched toward the liquid, sniffed, then sank toward the surface. Raider! The bear curled his paw, swirling the water around him. He slapped at a tiny wave he'd created, snapped at the droplets that flew through the air from the splash, his teeth flashing white in the darkness.

A wild animal playing always made her smile. Raider looked fat. With a grunt, he sat in the water, raised the other forepaw. Spreading two-inch claws into a fan around his muzzle, he licked the leathery pad of his paw, nibbling delicately, as if trimming a ragged hangnail. A wounded foot?

A duck squawked. Raider rose on his hind legs and peered intently toward the sound. It was an eerily human posture, paws clasped to his barrel chest like some burly logger. He remained upright for only a moment, then sank back to proper bear form on all fours and climbed up the bank. Sam watched his bulky silhouette disappear into the shadows, content to see that he was limping only slightly.

She lowered the binoculars and leaned against the rock again. How had Raider been injured? It couldn't have been their collision—had that really happened only yesterday? He might have had a squabble with another bear, or maybe it was just routine bruin clumsiness, a run-in with a thorn or a sharp branch. Or he might have been grazed by a bullet like the one that had barely missed her. The thought of the puddle of blood in the turnaround rekindled her anger.

She slapped a mosquito on her cheek. Her face felt gritty under her fingertips. The rest of her body was grimy, too. Sometime during the day the scab on her leg had broken;

the skin of her knee was once again glued to the fabric of her pants. She didn't miss her bunk, but she sure missed the hot showers at the bunkhouse.

Nine thirty. No sign of intruders. The lake water was pewter silk in the waning light. She couldn't resist any longer. She pulled off her clothes and waded into the shallows.

The water temperature was lower than she'd expected, but after the initial shock, its cool kiss was welcome. Placing her hands palms down on the smooth rock bottom, she extended her legs and stretched her weary muscles. Lowering her face into the water, she drank in huge gulps, savoring its earthy freshness. The heck with warnings about giardia. Right now, she was a wild creature of the night, like the deer, like the frogs, like the ducks, like the bear. She pulled the elastic band from her French braid and freed her hair, then sank beneath the surface and swam out into the brightness of the silvery moonlight. Liquid gurgled past her ears. Curious fish brushed against her in slippery whispers, trying to identify this huge new creature in their domain.

The deep water was cold. She blew the air out of her lungs and inhaled quietly, treading water. There was no sign of movement along the banks, no lights, no sounds but the symphony of tree frogs and lapping water. Turning onto her back, she floated, her thoughts wandering happily through the infinite beauty of stars and moon and water and plants and animals.

Then the hum of tree frogs stopped. A screech owl shrieked. With a flutter of wings, the ducks took off noisily, flapped only inches above her, then settled near the far side of the lake. Exhaling, Sam sank beneath the water, leaving only the top of her head above the surface as she turned to peer at the bank. Owls didn't hunt ducks, at least not in her experience. Something had spooked the birds. She held her breath and treaded water. The frogs started singing again. It was probably just Raider, or maybe another deer. She searched the shoreline.

There. A blackness too solid to be the shadows of tree limbs. A solid hulk, unmoving. Right next to the rock where she'd left her clothes.

She treaded water as quietly as she could. The black shadow didn't move. Definitely not an animal, then. It had to be a man. Should she swim to the far side of the lake? He'd still have a good chance of shooting her there. Fleeing naked through the woods was too humiliating to consider. On foot, it would take hours to reach help.

Oh, hell. He could have shot her by now if he'd wanted to. She was cold. Moving her hands in a modified breast-stroke underwater, she pulled herself toward the shallows and felt for a loose rock, a broken branch, any kind of weapon. Her fingertips identified only a smooth ledge of stone beneath the water. Damn! She could feel him watching her. She could barely breathe. He was less than fifty feet away. How long before he'd make his move?

"I'm a ranger," she said softly, surprised she could hear her own words over the thundering heartbeats in her head. A naked ranger. A naked unarmed ranger. And not even a *real* ranger. Some threat.

"I know," a low voice hissed, the words clipped.

Well, shit. This situation hadn't been covered in the NPS employee handbook.

"Stand up. Walk toward me."

The voice sounded vaguely familiar. "I will not!" she retorted indignantly. "Is that you, Arnie? You goddamned pervert . . ."

His laughter caught her off-guard. The black form stood up and walked forward into the moonlight, revealing familiar features.

"You're a pervert, too, Starchaser Perez," she growled, this time in a softer tone. She knew he was grinning, because his teeth gleamed softly in the moonlight. Now she recognized the clipped quality of his words as sup-pressed laughter. She gathered her feet beneath her. "Turn around."

He folded his arms across his chest. "No way." He looked like he was willing to stand there all night.

She pushed herself out of the water and stalked up the bank. "You're a louse, Chase," she said as she passed him.

He gave her a soft wolf whistle.

With her back to him, she struggled to find the legs of her jeans. "I should have known you Indians could creep through the woods without a sound."

His warm hands touched down on the cold skin of her naked hips, making her gasp. "We Mexicans can, too," he said softly. "Comes from long practice sneaking across the Rio Grande. I'm a credit to both sides of my heritage." He wrapped his arms around her shoulders and pulled her back against the solid warmth of his lean body. "'Course, it helps a lot if the person you're sneaking up on is swimming underwater."

"I'll bet."

He gently kissed the top of her head while his hands glided slowly over her wet skin to cup the underside of her breasts.

"Now is not the time, Chase."

His voice was a low murmur in her left ear. "If not now, then when?"

Good question. But she was soaking wet, and it couldn't be more than sixty degrees out. Her left foot was in the soft mud of the lake bank, while her right was stuck in the leg of her jeans. "I'm freezing, Chase."

"All right, then." He let go and stepped back.

Simultaneously relieved and regretful, she bent to pull on her jeans over her wet skin. She had them halfway up her legs when she was suddenly lifted off her feet. "Hey!"

Jerking the jeans off, he laid her down on a bed of warm flannel and cushioned nylon. He lowered himself beside her, now naked from the waist up.

The hard pectoral muscles of his chest pressed against her chilled breasts as he wrapped himself around her. His lips were warm and gentle at first, then increasingly hot and demanding as he kissed her thoroughly, moving from lips to jaw to ear, neck, shoulder, breast. His left hand was knotted into her hair; his right caressed her hip and then stealthily slid lower on the taut skin of her abdomen. His lips and hands left trails of fire as they glided over her body.

They broke for air. "Whoa, Starchaser," she gasped. "You do know how to take a woman's breath away."

"Still freezing?"

She shook her head. His breath was fast and warm against her cheek. His eyes were black in the night. "Moon goddess," he whispered, tracing a fingertip across her right nipple.

She groaned. Why had he surprised her like this? "Chase, I'm not . . . uh . . . prepared."

"I am." He blew softly across her breast with a warm breath. "In triplicate."

Of course. He would be. He probably had women falling down in front of him wherever he went.

He pressed his warm tongue to her left nipple, making her gasp, then raised his head and repeated, "If not now, when?"

"My thoughts exactly." She reached for his belt buckle.

"WOW," Summer panted into Chase's ear a half hour later. "You weren't kidding about being a *special* agent."

She'd hardly been a passive partner herself. It had nearly given him a stroke to hold back for so long, to wait until he felt her rising toward the crest along with him, and not until then did he thrust them both over the edge. The sex had been every bit as good as he'd imagined. He'd suspected that when Summer Westin committed herself to something, she would give her all, and he was right. He shifted most of his weight to one elbow and a knee, gently lifted a strand of silver-blond hair from her forehead and smoothed it back along her temple. He stared into her eyes. "It was my pleasure, ma'am."

"Mine, too."

He lay half-curled around her, one leg thrown over hers. The skin that shared contact with her was still hot, but his outer edges were cooling fast. The moon and stars overhead were brilliant, and the tree frogs chirped in surround sound. It might have been incredibly romantic if his backside weren't so damned cold.

She ran one hand over his shoulder, and the other idly stroked the fabric beneath them. A more focused look replaced the dreaminess in her glass green eyes. "This is a sleeping bag," she said.

He laughed. "Nothing gets past you, does it?"

She grabbed and half twisted his ear, then brought her face up and kissed him on the mouth. She tasted like lake water.

When she released him, he said, "I was hoping you'd provide a tent."

It was her turn to laugh. "My, aren't we presumptuous?"

"We," he echoed, "are getting frostbite."

"It's not *that* cold." Her warm fingers pressed down on his buttocks, which naturally pressed other parts together, too. Her eyes widened. "I sense that hypothermia has not set in yet."

He was suddenly hot for her again, and all too ready. But he wanted to make love to her even more slowly this time. Groaning, he pushed himself off her and helped her to her feet. Now his front was as chilled as his back, and the effect was as dampening as a cold shower. "The tent?"

Laughing, she grabbed her clothes and took off running barefoot and bare-assed through the woods. He barely had time to snatch up his clothes and sleeping bag to follow her before she was lost in the shadows of the trees. He dropped a boot along the way, and stopped to pick it up. When he straightened, she was nowhere in sight.

Then a light flicked on among a group of tall ferns, and he made out a green ripstop nylon tent half hidden under a big cedar. When he dived inside, she had her sleeping bag thrown open, waiting for him.

16

AT daylight, Chase was startled to find himself alone in the tent. How the hell had she snuck out? Why hadn't she awakened him? Summer Westin was one slippery woman. Gritting his teeth, he pulled himself from his sleeping bag and dressed, cursing the lack of space in the tiny tent.

He unzipped the screen door and crawled out, then straightened to his full six feet and stretched. Summer stood, back to him, about a hundred yards away. He walked to her position. As he neared, he saw she stood at the lip of the mine shaft crater, a cup of steaming coffee in one hand. "That looks good," he said.

She handed him the half-filled cup.

"Thanks." He took a sip. He usually took his coffee black, but it was a darn good thing hers contained creamer, because she'd cooked up some kind of wilderness espresso that would eat the enamel off his teeth without something to mellow it. "How'd you get dressed in that baggie without waking me up?"

She laughed. "I didn't; I took my clothes outside."

"Why didn't you wake me up?"

"It wasn't even six. You looked so . . . asleep."

It was disconcerting to think she'd watched him as he slept, crawled over him without waking him. He was used to being the one who left at dawn. The one who left when he was ready.

"You should have woken me. What are you doing out here, anyway?"

"I'm thinking this is where that missing C-4 went," she said, staring at the bottom of the crater. "I'll bet that was the explosion I heard on the night of the fire."

"It's possible." He looked at the hole. "But this would account only for a very small part of it."

Discussing explosives wasn't how he'd imagined his early morning hours with her. He yawned and stretched elaborately. Maybe she'd take the hint and come back to the tent with him. "We could be in a nice warm sleeping bag right now."

She ignored him and said, "Lisa could have been hit by a flying rock."

He sipped the coffee, pulling his thoughts out of the torrid sleeping bag scene playing in his mind. He considered the possibility of flying debris due to an explosion. Yes, possible; he nodded. "But how do you account for the fire? And Lisa's story of abduction?"

She sighed and folded her arms across her chest. "I haven't gotten there yet."

He scratched his jaw and was reminded that he hadn't brought a razor with him. He wasn't accustomed to driving for hours and hiking a couple of miles to make love on the cold ground and spend the night cocooned in a tent, either. He hoped this wasn't going to become a habit with Summer.

His mind flashed on the murdered game warden he'd learned about when he talked to the Seattle bureau about suspicious events on the Olympic Peninsula. The reason he'd come out here. Well, one of them, anyway. "Summer, I have some disturbing things to tell you."

She took the coffee cup from him, looked inside it, and then raised her gaze to his. She had such beautiful eyes, so clear and gray-green and bottomless. "I can tell from that tone that we're both going to need more coffee," she said.

He followed her back toward the tent. A few feet away, she had set up a small camp stove and prepared a tiny coffeepot. Overhead a blue nylon stuff sack was suspended from a cord stretched between two trees. A bear bag. Bears. A potential hazard that hadn't even crossed his

mind last night when he shucked his pants by the lake.
God, wouldn't Nicole laugh if he came back unable to
sit through meetings because of claw marks on his backside?

Summer knelt, took a lighter from her pants pocket, and
fired up the stove. As she bent over, her T-shirt pulled out
of the back of her pants, giving him an enticing view of
bare flesh. "Breakfast?" she asked. "Bagel and peanut butter, or oatmeal with walnuts and dried apricots?"

As soon as she'd set the pot on top of the flame, he
pulled her into his arms, sliding his hand onto that patch of
exposed skin at the top of her buttocks. "I'd rather have *you*
for breakfast."

Bending down, he pressed his lips to hers. When he let
her go, she acted self-conscious. "Is something wrong?"

"I'm not used to a surprise visit in the wilderness from a
horny FBI agent. I'm not sure what's supposed to come
next."

This was hardly the reaction he'd hoped for. Was that all
he was to her—a horny FBI agent? "You mean a surprise
visit from your *lover.*"

"Lover." She seemed to be testing the word to decide if
she liked the taste of it. His stomach clenched for a few
seconds before she said, "I like *that.*"

Placing a hand on either side of his head, she pulled him
down for another kiss. His thoughts moved back inside the
tent, back into the sleeping bags. "And as for what comes
next," he said, his face still close to hers, "I'm hoping for a
lot more of what we did last night."

She smiled.

He brushed her T-shirt-covered breast with a finger. "I
have a two o'clock meeting in Seattle, so we'll have to be
quick."

"Not too quick, I hope." She turned off the stove and
pulled him into the tent.

Over an hour later, she lay sprawled across his chest, her
hair streaming over his neck and arm, their legs still entan-
gled. He wanted to stay this way all day, but he had to get

on the road, and soon. He was starving, too. His stomach growled to announce it.

She laughed. "Hungry?" The word brushed softly against his chest hairs close to her mouth.

Resting his stubbly chin on the crown of her head, he stroked his fingers through her hair, combing out the tangles their activity had created. "I've got to leave in a few minutes."

"I know." She raised her head. Her right cheek was rosy where it had been pressed against his chest. "You still have to tell me your news. And I need to show you something before you go."

He slipped a hand down to cup her firm buttock. "I'm not sure I can deal with another show from you right now."

She slid off him, taking half the sleeping bag with her. "You'll cope. What I need to show you is outside." Leaning over, she kissed his left nipple, her soft lips giving him an electrical zing that rushed right through his belly and all the way to the end of his cock. But before he could grab her again, she tossed his khakis onto his stomach and climbed out of the tent, her clothes in hand.

He managed to pull on his underwear and pants inside the tent, then joined her outside. As he finished buttoning his shirt and putting on his boots, she took down the food bag and smeared two bagels with peanut butter.

Handing one to him and then crooking a finger in his direction, she walked off through the trees, her pale hair shining as she flashed in and out of patches of early morning sun.

He snatched up the water bottle and followed her to a large cedar. When he had nearly caught up, she vanished under its prickly foliage. Ducking, he joined her in the cave formed by the drooping branches. "Your favorite make-out tree?" he teased.

"It was pretty huggable when bullets were flying two days ago." She pointed to a groove dug into the bark at her eye level. "Fortunately, I was down here." She demonstrated by briefly crouching against the tree.

Anger surged through his midriff at the sight of her pressed against the trunk. The bullet blaze was less than two inches above her head. Some trigger-happy numskulls had come so close . . .

She straightened and pointed higher. "But here's what I wanted to show you. I just noticed this yesterday." About six inches above the blaze was a number hacked into the reddish bark: 14.

"Fourteen? What does that mean?"

She shook her head. "Not a clue. There's more."

Taking his hand, she pulled him to another tree, into which was carved 8128. The numbers were crude and slanted to the right.

"And look at this alder." She dragged him to yet another tree, one with white bark. He would have guessed it was an aspen.

"Some sort of code?" she asked.

4-19. The numbers on the alder made his blood run cold. "This one could be a date." A date imprinted on every federal agent's mind.

She stared at it. "What happened on April nineteenth?"

"Waco."

She thought for a moment. "That was a long time ago, wasn't it?"

He nodded. "Nineteen ninety-three—the FBI showdown with the Branch Davidians. And then, on April nineteenth of nineteen ninety-five, the Oklahoma City bombing." He took the pad out of his shirt pocket and wrote down the whole series of numbers.

"Good God." Her mouth took on a grim line. "But that's ancient history now, and these carvings look fresh."

"To some groups, those dates are sacred. Let's hope I just have a suspicious mind and four-nineteen means something else," he said. "A lot of people were no doubt born, married, or died on April nineteenth, too. And maybe, at age fourteen, someone got lucky under that other tree?"

She raised an eyebrow. "Sex at fourteen?"

"It happens. Or it could mean fourteen times. Or number fourteen on the football team."

"But 8128?"

He shook his head. "No clue. Probably just a personal code." He sounded more optimistic than he felt. He had a bad feeling in his gut; too many coincidences were piling up in Washington State: 4-19. The Council for Conservation of America. The antigovernment propaganda his team had recovered from the robbers' SUV. The missing C-4. The gunplay in the woods. The murdered game warden. He remembered he hadn't yet told Summer about her.

"I'm glad your contract is almost up," he said. "I'll feel better knowing you're not wandering around the woods here."

She flashed him a dirty look. "Well, that makes one of us."

Oh, yeah. She'd be without a job after her contract was up. But she was smart and resourceful; she'd find something.

"There are ugly things going on around here," he said.

She raised an eyebrow. "Gee, ya think?"

"I mean even more than you know about." He described the antigovernment literature he and Nicole had uncovered from their robbery suspects' vehicle.

She shrugged. "That was in Blaine."

He told her about the game warden who had been murdered on the Olympic Peninsula.

She put a hand up to her mouth as if she felt nauseous. Finally, something he said had made an impression on her. "That's all they found?" she asked. "Just one hand?"

"So far. Someplace called Skylark Slough."

"That's about forty-five miles away. Just over the border between the park and National Forest."

He touched her shoulder. "Maybe now you can understand why I'm worried. A group may be targeting lone women, or they may be targeting government agents, or both. If they find, uh, more . . . the agency will compare the corpses to see if there are similarities."

"More corpses?" Her expression was shell-shocked.

"More of Caitlin Knight—the game warden, so they can compare her corpse to Lisa Glass."

"Oh yes, Lisa." She caught her lower lip between her teeth for a moment before continuing. "I'm still not used to thinking of her as dead. You suspect that Lisa was a victim of the same killer?"

"There's not enough evidence to conclude that. Yet. The two incidents could be totally unrelated, or we could have a serial killer on the loose. All I know right now is that I want you to get out of the woods." Realizing she was likely to bristle at the last sentence, he added in a gentler tone, "I can't sleep at night knowing you're out here with no protection. Why don't you carry that Glock I got you?"

"We don't all sleep with firearms." She gave him a flirtatious look. "Some of us sleep with armed men instead."

He pulled her close. "And which armed man would you have slept with if I hadn't come along?"

"I'll never tell." She kissed him.

When she leaned back, he said, "I really wish you'd go back to the bunkhouse."

"I know you do."

She was unbelievably stubborn. Particularly when there were animals involved. "Look, Summer, you can sleep at the bunkhouse and look for that bear during the daytime, can't you?"

"I saw him at the lake last night, just before you showed up."

That close? It gave him a jolt. Turning his head, he studied the dense foliage around them, seeing how a bear could be hidden from view. How any number of dangers could be hidden from view.

She made a scoffing sound. "You chase criminals armed with automatic rifles. How can you be scared of a little ol' bear?"

He squeezed his arms around her. Her body was lean and solid, but so small. Muscles and intelligence were no match for bullets. Or claws and teeth. "I'm scared of them all," he told her. "You should be, too."

* * *

AS Sam walked Chase down the trail back to the parking
lot, she told him about the way Garrett Ford had glared at
her at the soccer game and the burger place.

"Sounds a bit like that Ferguson guy in Utah," he said.

Her thoughts precisely, but then again, both men were
woodsmen and she was in the woods, after all. "If they
weren't fairly common outdoor types, a girl could almost
get paranoid about it. The park has had some threats
against personnel and you've just got to wonder—"

He grabbed her arm. "What threats?"

How should she phrase it so it wouldn't sound so bad?
"Apparently, threats against rangers are not unusual. But
I've been told that the number of threats picked up after the
news report about the upcoming wildlife conference."

"Wildlife conference?"

"It's for federal employees and environmental groups,
and its focus is endangered species this year. I guess it
didn't help that I was featured on the same news broadcast, too."

His brown eyes blazed. "You? Why?"

She sighed. "With his typical unmitigated gall, this guy
at *The Edge* promised I would speak at the conference, so
the TV news stuck a photo of me in there, too, along with a
summary of the Zack Fischer story from last year."

"*You're* speaking at a federal wildlife conference?"

She made a face at him. "Well, you don't need to sound
quite so surprised, Chase. I can be presentable when I try."

"Of course you can."

She stared at him. Did that mean he thought she needed
to try more often?

He caught her look and said, "I mean, you always are.
Presentable, that is."

She laughed at his backpedaling. "Oh, for God's sake,
don't be *polite* with me. Half the time you've seen me, I've
been swimming in muck or I've got stitches on my face and
half my hair's burned off."

"Are you telling me that's not normal for you?"

A small snort escaped from her nostrils.

"It's just that I never knew you did public speaking," he explained.

She sighed. "Unfortunately, it's the only gig I've been offered after I finish 'wandering around in the woods here,' as you put it." She walked on, and he followed.

When they reached the parking lot, she retrieved Lisa's Bible and sketchbook from her truck and handed them to him. "Give these to whoever's working on Lisa Glass's case."

He raised an eyebrow. "How did you—"

"The bunkhouse, remember? I'm sleeping in Lisa's bed. And yes, I've been pawing through them; I never realized that these might become evidence. I was going to take them to her in the hospital, and then I heard—" *It's Lisa Glass. She's dead.*

"Anything of interest in these?" he asked.

She swallowed hard, and then continued. "The inscription in the Bible mentions her loving family, which seems weird, given that nobody can find any of her relatives. There's also a scrap of paper with addresses in Wyoming and Seattle."

"Those might be meaningful."

"I hope so. The sketches on the pad are mainly of the trail crew. She seemed to focus heavily on one kid, Ben Rosen."

He frowned. "You think that's significant?"

"I don't really know." She chewed her thumbnail, considering. "Ben has olive-colored skin and black hair, and Lisa described one of her attackers as dark with swarthy skin."

"Swarthy? Who uses a word like *swarthy*?"

"It is odd, isn't it?" she agreed. "Sounds archaic. Lisa was only nineteen."

"Most likely she was repeating someone else's words." He held out an olive-skinned hand and studied it. "So I'm swarthy? I've been called a spick and a redskin and one time a Cuban—"

"Hey, I think swarthy is beautiful." She took his hand in

hers and pressed it to her cheek. "The only reason I brought up Ben Rosen is that he's darker than the average Scandinavian around here, and he's on the trail crew because of some juvenile conviction, so he's not exactly an innocent. Plus, Lisa drew a sketch that looks quite a bit like him. Maybe she was trying to tell me Ben was in on the crime, whatever the crime was."

"I'll check him out." He tossed the items she'd given him onto the passenger seat of his rental car, and then wrapped his arms around her. "I don't want to leave you here with all this going on. Come with me."

Was he kidding? She pulled back. "To an FBI meeting in Seattle?"

"I was thinking more about the hotel afterwards."

Really? Sounded a little slutty, but inviting, too. "Can you promise there'll be a hotel afterwards?"

Chase hesitated. Probably thinking about the possibility of being ordered to travel after the meeting. He seemed to be perpetually on the road.

His arms felt so good. So strong and safe and warm. With her head pressed to his shoulder just above his heart, she could hear its reassuring rhythm. For some unaccountable reason, it made her want to cry.

"That's what I thought," she said into his jacket. "I think we both know I'm not a wait-in-the-car kind of woman." There was never enough time. "I don't want to make you late," she reminded him.

His arms fell away. "I'll get the Seattle office to work on Lisa's case," he promised. "And I'll check out Garrett Ford and Ben Rosen. You better call me whenever you can." His gaze lingered on her face. "Please move back to the bunkhouse, Summer."

Although she knew that he had her best interests at heart, she still found his insistence a little annoying. "I'll think about it," she said.

The look he gave her said he knew she was lying. He pulled open his car door. "Well, watch your back. Stay safe, *mi corazón*."

What did he expect her to call him? "Chase" seemed too brotherly now. "Lover" seemed tacky. She'd always hated "Honey" or "Dear"—they seemed like fill-ins used by people who couldn't be bothered to remember your real name.

"Watch out for the bad guys, *querido*." The Spanish word sounded a little clumsy, but a lot less frightening than English.

He grinned, and she felt ridiculously happy to know he was pleased. Then his lips brushed hers one more time, and he was gone.

She walked the trail back toward her camp and paused at the edge of the lake. A loon plowed a wake into the still surface near the far shore, a rare sight that would normally have made her heart soar. But she wished Chase were still there to share the moment.

It was not, precisely, a welcome feeling. It was as if a part of her had driven off with Chase. Did other women feel like this about their men? Some days she was positive that she knew more about butterflies and tree frogs than about her own species.

She walked through the forest—half black, half green—back to her tent. Last night, before Chase had shown up, she'd been so happy to be alone. Now, as she passed the trees and thought of the mysterious numbers hidden beneath their branches, her solitude felt ominous.

Sam worked on her field notes and cooked herself a brunch of reconstituted stew before heading out to do her survey work. She drove as close as she could to the eastern border of her area and then hiked in. Then she spent five hours patrolling, sampling, and noting species of animals in a sector she hadn't yet documented. The rust-bellied salamanders and six-inch banana slugs and fuzzy-eared Douglas squirrels were common, but always a welcome sign of a healthy ecosystem. A porcupine munching the bark on the lower limb of a pine was a pleasant surprise: she hadn't seen one for years. She did her best to list the plants, too, knowing that Mack would eventually follow up with a more thorough botanical survey.

She found no illegal signs tacked on trees, no ATV trails ripped into meadows, not even a rifle casing. The undamaged forest definitely lifted her mood. This had always been her dream, to get paid for exploring the wilderness, communing with plants and animals. Animals had never caused her even a tiny fraction of the grief that people did.

First it had been her father, insisting that she should give thanks to God that her invalid mother had lived as long as she had. Sam had never been in the least grateful. Would she make it through his wedding without adding more demerits to her abysmal record?

Then there were the illegal hunters and nasty sign posters of the world: the people who saw wild plants and animals either as pests or commodities. And the labelers, who took one look at her and named her a liberal intellectual feminist environmentalist, all descriptions she was proud to own in the Pacific Northwest, but which had somehow become epithets in other places.

But not every human was a disappointment. She did have friends. Mack and Blake and Joe up here, and in Utah, Kent and Rafael. She didn't see any of them often enough; when they weren't at work, they were understandably occupied with wives and children, or girlfriends. Or in Blake's case, the occasional manfriend.

Mud squished underfoot as she crossed the wetland close to her parking spot. Yes, most people were more trouble than they were worth. But there was Chase. She couldn't help smiling at the mere thought of him. Then again, he was trouble of a sort, too. He lived in Utah, she in Washington, and they both worked long days at weird and hazardous jobs. Would they ever truly get together? Did he really want to?

What did he see in her, anyway? Chase had plenty of women pursuing him. She'd noticed longing looks cast in his direction more than once.

It was frustrating to have no close female friends to talk this sort of thing over with. Laura Choi seemed nice, but they mostly talked about Joe and Lili. Which reminded her—she still needed to find time for that talk about writing careers with Lili. Maybe she could find a way to get more information from the kid about those damned signs, too.

WHEN she crawled into her sleeping bag that evening, Sam noticed it smelled like Chase. Where would she be tonight if she'd gone with him? In a hotel, having steamy sex? A delicious thought. Or more likely, sitting alone in a government car or sacked out on a couch in a nondescript office, waiting for Chase to come back from some rendezvous or surveillance activity. Pathetic. She didn't want either Chase or his partner Nicole to think of her as some sort of groupie along for the ride.

The one place she knew she would be, had she gone with him, was out of work. Peter Hoyle would can her in an instant if Sam wasn't absolutely diligent about wrapping up her three-month contract. Heck, Hoyle would probably fire her if he found out that Chase had stayed with her in a restricted area last night.

Chase probably hadn't really meant that invitation, anyway. It was just a polite thank-you for sex. And such great sex, at least from her perspective. She closed her eyes and focused on the memories of making love with Chase.

JUST before midnight, something woke her. Maybe the brightness of the moon? The skies were crystal clear, rare near the Olympic Mountains, and moonlight spilled in through the tent's mesh window. She lay still and listened for a minute. A snapping sound, like someone had stepped on a dry stick. A couple of quiet thuds, muffled against thick forest duff.

After stuffing her penlight into her pocket and pulling on her pants and boots, she unzipped the tent as quietly as she could and slipped out. She crouched in the shadow under the fir, watching and listening.

A crunching among the ferns to her left drew her attention, and she briefly flicked on her light and aimed it there, highlighting a thicket of legs among the greenery, then a little higher up, luminous globes of eyes. A trio of deer. They stared at her, trying to decide if she was a predator or a competitor, or maybe just hopeful that she'd provide entertainment. She turned the penlight off, but could feel their eyes still on her.

There. A splash of light in the burn area. Her breath stopped for a minute as she stared hard at the dark forest, trying to sort out the shapes. Had she imagined it? She saw it again, a bright spot flickering past blackened trunks. A flashlight. Someone was walking near the Lucky Molly Mine.

17

IN his loaner cubicle in the Seattle FBI office, Chase booted up his laptop. What a long day of meetings and comparing notes; it was nearly midnight and he was only now processing the latest reports on his own case. On the other side of the padded blue cubicle wall, he could hear Nicole's keystrokes as she studied evidence assembled from robberies across the country. Pulling up Google, he typed in *eminenten*, the mysterious word he'd come across a couple of days ago. A list of URLs and descriptions in what looked like German appeared, with words similar to *eminenten* highlighted.

At the bottom of the list was a URL with no description: *www.poeagle.org*. When he clicked the link, his laptop screen displayed a video of a bald eagle flying as the red, white, and, blue of the American flag rippled in the background behind it. Clever animation, but what was the point? And where did *eminenten* come in? The only words on the screen were "Let Freedom Ring!"

He clicked the center of the screen, then the words, tried moving his cursor around the screen to see if it changed over a hot spot link in the graphic. If there was a hot spot, it was tiny. He tried the bird's eye, and congratulated himself on his brilliance as the screen displayed three horizontal strips laid out like odometers. The top one was labeled "Profits of Top Ten U.S. Corporations This Year." Numbers in that row were flipping so fast that his eyes could barely focus on them. The numbers in the second row, labeled "Number of U.S. Citizens Living in Poverty," rolled over more slowly, but the total was consistently increasing. And the sum in the bottom row, "U.S. Dollars Spent Overseas," was growing nearly as fast as the Profits counter.

In the lower-right corner was a pumpkin-colored square that read "In the Know? Make Some Dough. Apply for Eminenten Grants Now."

Eminenten, finally. Leaning forward, he eagerly clicked the orange square. The screen redrew for the third time. His spirits dampened when he saw the Members Only message, followed by fill-in boxes for name and password. He took a couple of guesses. His third brought up a threat: This Is Not A Game. You Are Now Registered As An Intruder. Try Again and Penalties Will Result. He'd barely finished reading the words when the speakers made an exploding sound and the screen went completely blank.

"*Chingada suerte!*" he cursed.

Nicole rounded the cubicle wall. "Found something interesting?"

"I'm making progress," he said.

"Right." She stared at the blank screen. "I can see that."

SAM considered turning on her radio to report the intruder in the woods, but that would be easily heard in the hush of night. The interloper would probably flee, and then she'd be no closer to finding out who was skulking around this area at night and what he was up to.

After she was sure it was only one person, she stealthily made her way toward the glow of the flashlight. Even with the moonshine, it was slow going without her own light; the ground was rough and clumps of giant ferns and hurdles of fallen logs barred her way. She groped along, trying to make as little noise as possible.

When she was about fifty yards away, the flashlight ahead winked out. She crouched behind a tree, afraid she'd been discovered. But after a minute she heard snuffling noises, and peeking around the tree trunk, she could barely make out the dark shape of a man.

He was simply standing there, barely moving. She froze. After another moment, he threw something away from his body. She could tell from the motion that his back was turned toward her. She crept closer.

His flashlight suddenly blazed again. The beam swept overhead. Sam pressed herself to the ground alongside a fire-blackened log, hoping her clothes and hair and skin were now filthy enough to blend into the scenery. She was afraid to breathe.

What the hell had she been thinking, anyway? If the intruder had a gun—and hadn't the paintball warriors of a few days ago been armed with real bullets as well as paintballs?—he could easily fire a couple of bullets into her prone form. After another pass, the light flicked off again. His shadow remained still. Moving slowly and silently, she drew herself into a crouch behind the huge stump of an ancient cedar.

What now? She listened for a minute. Was that a sob? She peered around the charred and crumbling cedar. The man's head was now softly lit by a patch of moonlight. He had dark hair, and she had the impression that he was young. That and his husky shape was all she could make out.

She pressed her back to the stump and waited. Suddenly the horrible thought flashed into her mind that he might be waiting for his comrades, in which case she'd made the worst possible choice she could have by sneaking up on him. As she debated her options, the distant rumble of a truck engine joined his quiet snuffling. Someone was driving up the track she'd hiked yesterday.

A pair of lights flickered in the far woods. Headlights. The fellow behind her noticed too, because he growled, "What the fuck?" and turned away from the mine pit. The snap of a twig told her he had stepped in her direction.

Oh jeez, not now. The adrenaline coursing through her veins urged her to run, but instead she stayed in place, raised her hand to her mouth, and bit down hard on the knuckle of her first finger. *Oh God, don't let this be some sort of poacher rendezvous, with me in the middle.* Why hadn't she brought the Glock? Why hadn't she gone with Chase, even if she had to sleep in the car?

Her heart pounded so loudly in her ears that she was surprised to hear the crash of metal against rock. The movement of headlights stopped. She heard muffled thumps of heavy doors opening. Her booby trap had worked.

The footsteps behind her came closer.

Shit! She pressed herself harder against the stump, willing herself invisible. If he were focused on the vehicle in the distance, he'd pass right by. And he must have, because she could no longer hear him moving. She heard two angry male voices, interspersed with the grinding of gears and whine of wheels spinning against the ground.

She took a deep breath, crawled to the nearest tree, and pulled herself up with shaking fingers, staring toward the dim glow of headlights through the trees. It occurred to her that if the intruders wanted to hike out, the trail around Marmot Lake was the closest route back to civilization. They might walk right past her tent. If the sniffling man by the mine was waiting for the others, they'd surely come her way, because he had to have a vehicle parked at the end of the lake trail. Why hadn't she thought of this before?

She waited for the confrontation of the three men. Instead, she heard the thuds of two doors closing, and after a painful squeal of metal against rock, the headlights backed away. The engine noise of the departing vehicle was loud in the night.

Did she dare move toward her tent? The throb of the engine died away, leaving only the rhythmic sigh of the wind. But she didn't feel even a whisper of breeze. It hit her in a rush that she was listening to *breathing*. Her own breath stopped at the thought. Bile rose into her throat, burning and bitter.

She could feel him close, just behind her right shoulder.

"I could kill you right now." His voice was surprisingly gentle.

"What's stopping you, then?" She was amazed to hear her own voice come out so brazen. She wanted to step out and confront him, go down like a fighter, but she couldn't make her body move away from the solidity of the tree trunk.

"It's not yet time."

She heard him move away like a rattlesnake uncoiling and slithering into the brush. After a few seconds, she let her legs collapse under her and sat down hard on the ground. In the distance, the intruder's flashlight flicked on. He was on the trail around the lake. He was taking his time, knowing that even if she called for backup, he'd still make good his escape.

After five minutes, her breathing slowed and her shaky legs would hold her again. Yeesh, she was a wuss. How had Caitlin Knight worked as a game warden, facing down armed hunters for a living? What had her last moments been like? Sam shivered.

She turned on her penlight and walked unsteadily to the edge of the mine pit. A white rose lay at the bottom of the crater, its half-opened petals a pale bloom against the dark rock.

The rose could only be for Lisa Glass. At least it proved that someone did miss her; she hadn't been completely alone in the world. Unless, of course, the man was one of her killers and this was a show of remorse for his heinous act. He had certainly talked more like a killer than a lover.

As she walked back to her tent, every sound unnerved her. The tiny rustle of leaves now sounded like a stalker instead of a mouse; that thump a footstep instead of a pine-cone dropping to the ground. But every time she flashed her light around, she was alone. At her tent, she found her radio and called in the two intruder incidents, more for the record than in any hopes of capturing the culprits. Maybe they could identify the guy on the track by damage to his vehicle.

Taking the sleeping bag from her tent, she carried it to the cover of another big cedar, just in case the whispering intruder had spotted her camp. In the second before she ducked under the drooping boughs, a primeval yell resounded through the forest. *"Ka-ka-ka-ka-wow!"* She held her breath as she waited for another savage to acknowledge the attack signal. When the answering call, farther away, came in the form of *"Hoo-hoo-hoo! Hoo-hoo!,"* she realized that she was listening to a conversation between two great horned owls. Damn that sniffling rose man! He had ruined a magical moment for her.

Providing she survived the night, she was heading home for a breather. She needed a cat in her lap and the security of a night in her own bed.

Pulling the bag over her, she awaited dawn with her back against the tree, opening one eye every time a chipmunk scurried through the pine duff.

18

BONE or taupe? She couldn't decide. Both pairs of heels clomped on the polished wooden floors of the cabin. Or maybe they clunked. Whatever the noise was, it wasn't attractive. Surely other women didn't make this sound when they walked in heels. Normal women would be able to put into action verbs other than *clomp* or *clunk*, verbs like *float* or *drift* or *sashay*. Sam tried to sashay across the living room, watching herself in the full-length mirror on the back of the coat closet. She swung her hips like a runway model, swishing the full skirt of her only good dress, the draped little coral number that Adam had given her a couple of years ago. The man may have been a self-centered social climber, but he had taste.

Blake opened the front door, his arms clasped around a full grocery bag, and stopped, studying her. She waited for his smart remark. Simon bounced off the couch with a meow of greeting for him.

Her housemate strode into the room, leaving the door open as he moved toward the kitchen, Simon following at his heels. As he passed, he said, "Hot dress."

"I concur."

She turned back to the door. Chase, clean-shaven and blue-suited, leaned against the frame, grinning.

It was funny how she was getting used to him showing up unexpectedly in all sorts of places. For once, luck was with her; she was freshly showered, her hair was combed and lay shining around her shoulders, she'd shaved her legs and armpits, and she was fully dressed. Smiling, she gestured him in.

"A *very* hot dress," Chase reiterated. "On a *very* hot woman."

"But I clomp."

"I'm sure your clomping is hot, too." He shrugged off his suit coat and deposited it on the couch. Crossing the room, he came up behind her and put his arms around her. They regarded themselves in the mirror. His shoulder holster and gun added a thuggish note, turning them into a petite blond Bonnie and a tall dark Clyde.

"I'll bet Nicole doesn't clomp." Sam turned in the circle of his embrace and lifted her face for a kiss.

"True." He dipped her backward so far she would have fallen on her ass if he hadn't been holding her. "But then, Nicole is never *hot*."

He hauled her back up and she stood on tiptoe as their lips met. He smelled of lime aftershave and his chin and cheek were smooth against hers, not stubbled with whiskers as they had been in the woods—had that really been only three days ago? Marmot Lake seemed a world away instead of only a four-hour journey.

"Got time for dinner out?" he asked.

"Unfortunately, no." She pointed toward the open door to the laundry room, where one load rumbled in the dryer, one was rotating in the spin cycle in the washer, and another pile of dirt-encrusted clothes waited on the floor. She'd spent yesterday finding parts and fixing the leaking drain pipe in the kitchen, and was just now getting around to her laundry.

Blake rounded the refrigerator, a bunch of Italian parsley clutched in one hand, a paring knife in the other. "Stay," he commanded, looking at Chase.

"Yes, sir." Chase dropped onto the couch and tugged at his tie.

Sam kicked off her left shoe and slid her foot into one from the other pair. "Bone or taupe?" She turned slowly sideways, gazing expectantly at her housemate.

Blake responded, "Don't ask me. Heels are not my style at all."

"Mine, neither," she replied.

"Dress color?" Chase asked.

"Aqua." She frowned at herself in the mirror. "I hope it turns out to be closer to turquoise than sea green. Pastels make me look like a corpse."

"Go with taupe. More versatile." The blue-patterned tie slithered from around Chase's neck, and he stuffed it into a pocket of his suit coat.

"Dinner is nothing fancy," Blake told him. "Ravioli and salad. And this wonderful sourdough herb bread I found at TJ's."

"Sounds like heaven." Chase stood up. "What can I do?"

Blake stepped out of sight and then returned a second later, holding a corkscrew and a large chopping knife. "Choose your weapon."

Chase yanked a bottle of wine from the pocket of his folded sport coat, crossed the floor, and took the corkscrew. "I'm basically a nonviolent type."

"Then ditch the gun." Blake disappeared behind the refrigerator.

"Deal." Chase unsnapped the holster from his belt, and tossed it onto his jacket on the couch. Giving Sam a wink, he, too, vanished into the kitchen.

She'd fretted about whether her macho FBI agent would get along with her gay housemate. Now she was starting to feel like a third wheel in her own home.

"I'll make the salad," she yelled. "Be back in a minute." She dashed into her bedroom to change.

She felt short without the heels but more like herself in worn blue jeans and an orange cotton sweater and flip-flops. Chase reclined against the blue-tiled counter, sipping a glass of red wine and regaling Blake with a story about thieves who chained a cash machine to the bumper of their pickup. Blake stirred a pot of tomato sauce.

She took the salad makings to the table and started chopping. Chase moved into the dining area, handing her a glass of wine as Blake slid the bread into the oven. She glanced at the wine bottle on the counter. What were the odds that Chase just happened to bring Chianti when they were having pasta? This had to have been prearranged. Maybe the men had met at the grocery store?

"Blake," she said, "have you heard teenagers say 'five'?"

"Five what?" He knelt and took a large pot from a lower cabinet.

"Nothing, just 'five.' Like a smart-ass answer to a question." At least that's the way Joe had explained it to her when she'd stopped by the district HQ to tell him about the rose and the headlights last night. "You know—'what are you up to, kiddo?' 'Five.'" She mimicked a teenage voice on the last word.

"Hmm." Blake considered as he filled the pot with water. "I've never heard Hannah say that, at least not yet. But she's only twelve." He shot a glance at Chase. "Hannah's my daughter."

Chase didn't even blink. Maybe he knew a lot of gay men with children.

"Well, this girl's thirteen," Sam told them both. "Ranger Joe Choi's daughter, Lili."

Chase guessed, "Maybe it's some kind of teenage shorthand for the Fifth Amendment."

"As in "taking the fifth'?"

"That's the only part most people have heard of." He launched into a quotation. "No person shall be held to answer for a capital, or otherwise infamous crime, unless on a presentment or indictment of a Grand Jury, except in cases arising in the land or naval forces, or in the Militia, when in actual service in time of War or public danger; nor shall any person be subject for the same offence to be twice put in jeopardy of life or limb; nor shall be compelled in any criminal case to be a witness against himself, nor be deprived of life, liberty, or property, without due process of law; nor shall private property be taken for public use, without just compensation." He finished with a swig of wine.

Blake looked stunned. "Good grief. Who knew all that other stuff was in there?"

Sam quartered a small tomato and tossed it into the bowl. "You think a thirteen-year-old would know the Fifth Amendment?"

"Oh, man," Blake said, "Never underestimate what they know. Hannah informed me yesterday that plants bend toward light because the side away from the sun grows faster. I work in a friggin' greenhouse, and I didn't know that. It's kind of scary."

Sam laughed. "I know what you mean. Lili told me 'Aunt Sam' sounded like a transvestite."

They both turned toward Chase.

"You don't want to hear any of my stories about the baby monsters I've encountered, believe me." He set down his wineglass, picked up a quarter of tomato, and tossed it into his mouth. " 'Five,' huh?"

She knew that he was thinking about the numbers carved into the trees. "Kind of weird how all these numbers keep cropping up, isn't it?" she said.

"It's downright hinky." He grinned.

She cleared the salad makings from the table.

"Silverware? Plates?" Chase asked.

Sam pointed to a drawer and a cabinet. "And placemats in that drawer over there."

It seemed so natural to have Chase there. How did he do that, just slip into place wherever he found himself? She watched with admiration as he discussed cooking with Blake throughout the meal. Chase favored fiery Asian and Mexican dishes. Blake was studying French cuisine right now at the culinary program at Bellingham Technical College. They found common ground in French-influenced Vietnamese food. Her own cooking didn't extend much further than grilled cheese sandwiches, so she wasn't able to contribute much other than her opinion as a taster.

After dinner she left the men to clean up while she attended to laundry. Simon kept her company from the top of the dryer, paws curled under his chest as he supervised the transfer of wet clothes from the washer. He took offense when she moved him aside to press the Start button. She was cuddling him against her neck and apologizing when Chase came in with a serious expression on his face and a manila envelope in hand.

She looked up from Simon's fur. "What's that?"

"Autopsy results. Lisa Glass."

"Anything unusual?"

"We got a match on her prints."

"So you know where she's from? You found her family?"

"We don't have a verified identity yet. Her prints match those found on the padlock of the mine shed the C-4 was stolen from."

"*Lisa* stole the C-4?" Sam yelped. The girl had seemed so young and vulnerable. "I suspected she wasn't telling the whole truth about what happened at Marmot Lake, but . . . that's a surprise." Now it seemed probable that C-4 had been used to open up the mine. What went wrong? Who set the fire? "What else?"

"Lisa died of bleeding into the brain. Apparently it was too slow to be caught at first, and by the time they realized her confusion wasn't just smoke inhalation, it was too late." He opened the envelope and thumbed through some photos, selected one, and thrust it toward Sam. "She had a tattoo on the back of her left shoulder."

The image gave her a start. An upside-down peace symbol, or perhaps a stylized tree, surrounded by curling ivy. "Was this a permanent tattoo?"

"Henna; I'm told that can last as long as three weeks." Chase raised an eyebrow. "Why do you ask?"

"Joe Choi's daughter has this same tattoo. Can I take this?" She waved the photo in the air.

Chase looked startled. "Uh . . . no. I shouldn't even be sharing this file with you."

She took the photo to her office, woke her computer and scanner from hibernation mode. She quickly scanned the photo and printed it on her color copier. Chase followed her in and frowned at her actions, but said nothing. She handed the original back to him. "What does that tattoo mean?"

"We don't know yet. We've got a tech running it through the data banks. Of course, it might just be a popular design, like dragons and angels."

Dragons and angels. Some days Sam felt like she was living in a foreign country.

"And remember that slip of paper you gave me from Lisa's Bible? The Seattle address is the Veterans Administration Office."

Sam raised an eyebrow. "What would Lisa be doing with the VA?"

Chase shrugged. "Who knows?"

"And the other note, Frazier in Wyoming?"

"We're still working on that." He returned everything to the envelope. "I may find out more tomorrow."

They went back into the living room and watched a sci-fi show with Blake. Sam liked the way that the women characters were warriors equal to the men. She liked even more the fact that Chase and Blake either didn't see anything remarkable about that, or at least chose not to comment on it if they did.

Chase showed no sign of leaving. Surely he and his partner were booked into some hotel. During a commercial, she asked, "Where's Nicole?"

"San Juans again," he said. "With hubby, 'til Tuesday."

"That must be nice."

"Must be." He made a face. "She left me to deal with the task force meeting in Seattle tomorrow at eight thirty."

At ten o'clock, she yawned and stretched elaborately, raising her arms over her head. "I've got to be back at work by ten tomorrow morning. I have my alarm set for five," Sam told him. "I was planning on an early night."

Beside her on the couch, Chase stretched, too. "Sounds good to me. Seattle's a two-hour drive."

She wasn't sure what to make of that and she couldn't bring herself to ask with her housemate not twenty feet away. She stared at Chase and tried to divine what was going on behind his clear brown eyes.

Blake snorted from his recliner. "Do you two need *instructions*?"

When Sam stopped laughing and could breathe again, she stood up and held out her hand to Chase. "Coming?"

"I thought you'd never ask. Good night, Blake. Thanks for dinner."

"Any time, Bro."

Bro? Now she was sure that these guys had colluded. What personal details had Blake shared with Chase? Even more worrisome, what had Chase asked?

Thank goodness that her sheets were newly washed and the room was in reasonable condition, her sunflower quilt smoothed over the queen bed, and her old sweats kicked into the closet.

"An honest-to-God bed," Chase remarked happily. "I was beginning to think you didn't own one."

The cat observed from her bookcase headboard as they undressed, but she nudged him out of the bedroom before she stripped off her underwear. Chase slid between the sheets, and she climbed in after him, pulling herself up on top of him, relishing the warm hardness of his chest against her bare breasts. Putting an arm on either side of his head, she pressed her lips to his, and felt his instant reaction hard against her inner thigh.

"*Mi corazón,*" he groaned, his hands cupping her backside.

"*Querido.*" This time it came out sounding natural. With enough practice, she could get used to these endearments. And she would certainly welcome getting used to the other feelings she was experiencing right now.

After their lovemaking, lying on her side with Chase snuggled up against her, she wondered if the noises she'd made had been as loud as the hallelujah chorus ringing in her head. She wavered between wanting to drift into a cozy sleep and wanting to repeat the performance. Who knew when they'd meet again?

Chase was still awake. She could tell by the firmness of his arms around her, although his breathing was slowing. He shifted a hand, pulled back her hair, and blew softly across her sweaty neck.

Suddenly she was back in the dark woods, a madman close enough to touch. *I could kill you right now.*

"What's the matter?"

She rolled over to face him. "After you left, I stayed Thursday night at Marmot Lake."

He sighed. "I knew you would. What happened?"

She told him everything: the bear-kill site, the booby trap she'd set, the intruder and the white rose and the terrifying encounter.

"'It's not yet time'?" Chase echoed, rising up on one elbow to peer down at her. "What the hell does that mean?"

She shivered. "I don't know."

"God, Summer." He stretched out beside her again and pulled her over against him, spooning. "You *are* going back to the bunkhouse, aren't you?"

"I am," she promised. "At least at night."

"Two more weeks out there?"

"Yep." Two weeks until unemployment. And then the trip to Kansas; her father's wedding. Things to look forward to.

"Do you know a man called Jack Winner in Rushing Springs?" Chase asked.

"I don't know anyone over there except for park staff. Who is he?"

"The owner of the truck you found in the Marmot Lake lot. Your friend Choi went to see him on Friday."

That chafed a little, that neither Chase nor Joe had told her. "And?" she prompted.

"Winner said he didn't know the area was off-limits now. He has no criminal record. He owns a small business, a little furniture-making shop. But according to Choi, he was sweating like a racehorse after the Kentucky Derby, so he may be hiding something."

"Jack Winner," she repeated, memorizing the name.

"Leave it to law enforcement, Summer. Stay away from him."

"Of course I will." *Yeah, right.* Winner could be responsible for the explosion and fire, for the bullet that barely missed her, or for that pool of bear blood at the end of the track. Jack Winner could be Lisa Glass's murderer.

"You could stay out of the field, couldn't you?" Chase asked. "Just work in the office?"

Good thing he couldn't see the expression on her face. "I could." But she wouldn't.

"You have a management plan to finish." He caressed her cheek lightly with one finger. The tingling sensation made it difficult to maintain the sharp edge of annoyance she'd felt just a second ago. His finger brushed over her lips and slid down her neck. "You have a speech to write," he added.

The speech. The conference. Anxiety bubbled up, warring with the delicious sensation of his fingers on her skin. "Thanks for reminding me," she groaned. "Now I'll never get to sleep."

"I know a great way to relax." He pressed his body full length against hers.

When the chimes of her alarm began at 5 A.M., Chase was still curled up at her back. For once she was reluctant to leave civilization and return to the woods.

19

TWO double lattes and two and a half hours later, Sam drove off the Kingston ferry and headed west. As soon as she crossed the Hood Canal bridge onto the Olympic Peninsula, she called Joe Choi.

"Morning, Joe."

"Sam? Why are you so chirpy? It's only seven thirty. I just walked out of the house."

"I wanted to catch you before you get busy, or out of range or something. Anything on that vehicle I reported Thursday night over at Marmot Lake? The bear poacher? Probably a smashed oil pan or a dented axle?"

"Slow down, girl. How much caffeine have you had, anyway? We're still checking it out."

"Are you checking on Garrett Ford like I suggested?"

In the background, she heard the engine of Joe's truck start up. "I had the Forks police drive by his place," he said, "but he wasn't home all weekend. Just FYI, we haven't had any previous run-ins with him."

She'd bet that Ford was holed up somewhere working on his truck. "Can you check the repair shops in Port Angeles and Sequim for his truck?"

"Maybe."

Why did he sound so reluctant? She said, "If I were you, I'd check his phone records to see if he called park headquarters on the dates threats were made against the staff."

"Whoa, Sam. As far as I know, Ford's an upstanding

member of the community. Do you know something that incriminates him?"

She had to admit that she didn't. "It's intuition."

"That sounds like something Laura would say. Law enforcement generally requires more . . . like evidence."

"That's what I'm looking for," she said, annoyed. "Did anyone check that illegal track over the weekend?"

"A bunch of us barricaded it off with brush Friday afternoon."

"Good." Of course, that didn't mean that a new track wouldn't be blazed into the area, but maybe the barricade would slow them down for a while.

"And before you ask, we're checking the gate to Marmot Lake a couple of times a day," he added. "Where will *you* be today?"

"In the office, working on my management plan." Just thinking about being closed up all those hours while the sun was shining made her antsy. At least she'd brought her own laptop from home, so the computer work would go a little faster. Surely she could salvage a couple of hours. "I thought I might pick up Lili later and take her out to the beach for that other interview I promised her. Think she'd go for that?"

"In a heartbeat. Laura's taking Lili to school right now. You can probably catch Laura on her cell." He gave her the number.

"I'll call. Joe, what do you know about Jack Winner?"

"You and Perez teaming up on me?"

"What?"

"He called five minutes before you did."

That was interesting. Did the two of them know something about Winner they didn't want to tell her? "What'd he want?"

There was a long pause, then he said, "Come to our house for dinner, Sam. Six o'clock."

Something he couldn't say on a cell phone? That seemed ominous. But one of Laura's home-cooked meals would be

a good deal. "That sounds great, Joe. I'll call Lili and
Laura now. See you at six."

On the front door of the district headquarters was a
poster asking for the public's help in solving the case of
Murdered USFWS Enforcement Officer Caitlin Knight.
Sam studied the photo beneath the headline. Caitlin had
been a large-framed, square-faced woman with long black
hair; the type of woman that people called handsome instead of pretty. Her dark eyes stared confidently at
the camera. She looked like a fighter, and Sam couldn't
help wondering what her last moments had been like.
The text neglected to mention that only Caitlin's right hand
had been found so far. *Be on the lookout for other body
parts* was probably too grim a message to print in a public
notice.

She lugged her laptop to her desk in the NPS/USFS district headquarters. In her box in the mailroom, a fax waited
for her. It was from Richard Best at *The Edge*, asking when
he would receive the draft of her speech.

Sam bristled. Best wanted to censor her words? She
supposed he did have a right to at least read them, since his
company was paying her to do the speech. She decided to
send it to him at the last minute so she could ignore any critique he had to offer.

So far the speech consisted only of a few notes from
newspaper articles about attacks against environmentalists. The discovery of a hit list of activists in Montana was
the latest news she had stumbled across. Had Caitlin
Knight been just a name on a list to someone? Were there
more murders to come?

It's not yet time. She shivered, again feeling the rose
thrower's breath on her cheek. But those words could mean
anything. He might be some wacko who believed in the
Rapture, when only the enlightened few would be taken up
to heaven. Her name certainly wasn't on *that* list. The
thought of religion reminded her of her preacher father,
although he was not a fundamentalist type. The trip to
Kansas was only two weeks away. She needed a haircut.

Did she even possess a slip or a pair of pantyhose anymore? She'd have to check the bottom of her lingerie drawer.

She clenched her jaw, poured herself a cup of sludge from the communal coffeepot, and sat down at her desk. If she didn't focus, she'd never get anything done today.

Because she used her own laptop from home and up-to-date software, her work on the environmental report and management plan went faster than she'd expected. She decided that the best tactic to protect the Marmot Lake area from illegal hunters and ATVs would be to again open up the picnic area and campground to the public. New latrines, bear-proof trash containers, and food-hanging lines would have to be installed. To start, she tackled the issue of public access: first, widen the trail around the lake into a nature loop accessible to wheelchairs and add educational signs about the ecology of the area; then, as soon as possible, blaze connector trails to meet up with the major east-west hiking paths that led out to the ocean beaches and up into the rugged valleys of the Olympic Mountains. She used a scanned map and a paint program to sketch out the suggested routes, making sure to avoid areas that were elk calving grounds and prime bear habitat.

What to do with the Lucky Molly Mine was her biggest quandary. According to the map provided by the park service, the mine shaft opening was now on the national park side of the boundary and therefore off-limits to mining, but the old tunnel extended to the forest service side, which meant that there, it was fair game for prospectors. If the current crater was filled in and all signs of the mine's existence removed, would people stop looking for it? That hadn't stopped them so far. Or would it be better to fence off the opening, make the mine a feature of the area, and install a plaque detailing its unsuccessful history? That could be an opportunity to educate the public about the mining laws. But that could backfire, too: a new awareness might inspire a fresh crop of prospectors to take advantage of those laws.

Except for the desk clerk out front who dealt with the

public, Arnie Cole was the only other person in the building. She took the risk of approaching him in his office and asking his opinion.

"Ah, I knew you'd be back," he said with a grin. "Why not sell passes and let the yahoos dig for gold? They're gonna do it, anyway; might as well make some money from it."

In other words, he was no help. To make matters worse, after that he cruised by her desk every fifteen minutes. "Need any more help?" he asked. He tried to read her laptop screen over her shoulder. By one o'clock, she was desperate to escape from the building.

After eating her lunch of cheese and crackers at the picnic table in back of the building, she returned to her laptop and checked her online resources for Jack Winner's address. If Chase and Joe weren't going to be forthcoming about what Winner was up to around Marmot Lake, then she was going to find out for herself.

According to the map on her computer screen, Rushing Springs was a tiny dot just off Highway 101, about fifteen miles south of Forks. She should be able to easily make a round trip and still pick up Lili at the library at three thirty.

THE dot on the map represented a gas station/quick market hunkered on a gravel pullout next to the highway. The rest of Rushing Springs was a collection of tumble-down cabins and manufactured homes scattered through the woods.

Jack Winner didn't answer the door of his cheaplooking but tidy double-wide manufactured home. Its windows were too far off the ground for her to do any snooping there. She had to content herself with peering through the dusty windows of the remodeled barn out back, cupping her hands to the sides of her face to block the glare. Only a few items of furniture seemed to be in progress: a handful of dark-stained lecterns and various pieces that might eventually be a desk of some sort. Winner Woodworking didn't look like a prosperous business, at least not from this angle.

"You lookin' for something?"

Startled, she turned to find a man at her side in faded jeans and flannel shirt, with longish graying hair. He was older than she'd expected—around sixty or so. His tennis shoes had holes over his little toes. He didn't look like the type to drive the monster black pickup. "Jack Winner?" she asked.

"He's not home, I guess, or you wouldn't be back here."

She wasn't sure what to say to that.

"Ernest Craig." He held out a trembling hand.

She shook it, pretending not to notice how hard it was shaking, then told him her name. "You're a neighbor of Jack's?"

"I live back there through the woods." He pointed down a gravel track, but she couldn't see anything but trees. "I was taking a walk. Not much place to go around here, but walking keeps me from . . . well . . . it keeps me out of trouble."

Craig's watery gray eyes remained glued to her face with a fierce intensity. He didn't appear to be in very good shape, but he had at least eight inches and sixty pounds on her. Maybe she should have told someone she was coming down here.

His expression suddenly brightened. "I *know* you," he said.

"I don't believe we've ever met, Mr. Craig."

"From TV, I mean. I seen you on TV. It was over at the bar, oh, a week or so ago."

That had to have been the KSTL program Peter Hoyle had mentioned. The one about the conference and speech.

"I remember because this one guy there wasn't too happy to see you."

She knew it was Garrett Ford even before Craig described the man. Nobody else except Mack and Joe knew her around here, but Ford had known her on sight. She decided to cruise past his place as soon as possible.

See if there was a big dent in his pickup or a bear skin drying on the clothesline.

Focus, she reminded herself. Winner's truck was in the lot at the time of the shooting incident at Marmot Lake. That had started off as a paintball game. "Do you know if Jack and his friends like to play paintball?"

"Yeah. I've seen 'em heading out with boxes of those paint pellets and coming back all colored up."

"Can you tell me the names of some of his friends?" Maybe she could get some information from this guy that Chase and Joe didn't have.

Craig stared up at the trees and thought for a minute. "There's a Phil somebody, I don't know his last name. He works here sometimes. I should know, really I should . . ." He looked embarrassed, and ran his fingers through his shaggy hair.

"That's okay. I can't say that I know my neighbors very well, either." Blake was the chatty one; she was the hermit writer.

Craig was still thinking. "I know Jack's got family up in Forks. His mom lives up there."

He made it sound like Forks was in another state instead of fifteen miles up the road. A sorrowful expression crept onto his face. "You work for the park?" he asked.

She was wearing an NPS uniform shirt and name tag, so she could hardly deny it. "Yes."

"That girl who got hurt in the fire, she died, right?" Tears glittered in the fellow's eyes.

"Yes. She died last week." Why was he so interested? "Her name was Lisa Glass. Did you know her?"

"No," he said. "But I have a daughter just two years older. She ran away to Los Angeles. She didn't even say good bye. That other girl's family is gonna miss her something terrible."

He seemed so mournful; she wasn't sure what to say. "There's going to be a memorial service for Lisa Glass on Wednesday, up on Hurricane Ridge," she offered.

"Will her family be there?"

Sam shook her head. "I don't think so, Mr. Craig. So far none of her family has been located."

The man looked like he might cry. "That's a terrible thing," he said. "My daughter loves wild places, just like that girl did."

Personally, she was dreading Lisa's memorial, but perhaps this man wouldn't. Her father always said that funerals brought closure and comfort. She put a hand on Craig's arm. "Maybe you'd like to come to the service?"

"I think I would. Thank you. I think I'll do that." He passed the back of his hand quickly over his eyes. "Want me to tell Jack you were here?"

"No," she said quickly. "That's okay. I'll catch him some other time." She hadn't decided what she'd tell Winner if she confronted him. She just wanted to lay eyes on him, to see if he could be the illegal hunter she'd encountered. Or the rose thrower. "Mr. Craig, do you think Jack knew Lisa Glass, the trail worker who got killed?"

Craig seemed surprised at the thought. "I don't know. I guess he could have. I'll ask him."

"You can tell him about the memorial service, too. The public's welcome." Maybe Peter Hoyle would give her extra credit if she showed up with guests for Lisa's service.

"HOW do you decide what you want to write about?" Today, Lili wore her hair in a complicated arrangement of a bun on each side of her head, wrapped with strings of red and black beads that clicked together in the salty breeze blowing off the Pacific.

Sam, sharing a seat on a wind-polished driftwood log, smiled at Lili's refreshing naïveté. She shifted her gaze away from the rolling swells to look at the girl. "If you're writing for money, usually someone else *tells* you what they want you to write. You get assignments, just like in school."

Lili frowned, disappointed. "Really? That sucks. I thought being a writer meant you were free." She looked toward the ocean. "I'm going to be a hairdresser; at least that's creative."

Sam stifled a smile. "There aren't many jobs that allow much freedom. I'll bet most salon customers tell hairdressers how they want their hair done; they rarely let the hairdresser do whatever she wants."

Lili pulled thoughtfully on a string of beads dangling from the side of her head. "Maybe."

"Freelance writers do have more freedom than writers with permanent jobs. You can decide that you want to write about something, and then pitch that idea to a print or online magazine or newspaper. Sometimes they go for it. But you still have to do your homework so you know when and where to pitch your article, because they usually plan to print pieces that complement what they're selling at the time."

"You mean they sell the story?"

"No, I mean that they want the story to help them sell other goods or services." It was sad that the world was so commercial, but Lili would learn this sooner or later. "For instance, a magazine might buy an article about hiking for an issue where they'll have advertisements for boots and backpacks."

Lili's big brown eyes were unblinking. Either she didn't understand or she was already bored into blankness.

"Like that magazine." Sam pointed to the copy of *Max Girl* that protruded from Lili's daypack. "May I?"

Lili nodded, and Sam pulled the magazine out of its pocket. She flipped through the pages. "See, here's an article on how to put on eye makeup. And see all these ads for eye makeup? They hope that the article plus the ads will make you buy makeup."

Lili's brow wrinkled. "So they're, like, manipulating us?"

Sam laughed. "I'm glad you recognize that."

"So when you write articles, you're manipulating people, too."

It was Sam's turn to make a face. "Most of the time, it

feels more like the magazine's manipulating me." Organizations like *The Edge* always seemed to hold all the cards. Now they'd manipulated her into becoming a public speaker.

She pulled her thoughts back to Lili. "Do you ever feel like anyone tries to manipulate you, Lili? Does anyone try to get you do something you wouldn't usually do?" *Like have sex or nail up illegal signs in the woods?*

The girl tossed her head. "Of course."

Sam hadn't expected it to be so easy. "Who does that?"

Lili gave her an odd look. "Duh. Mom and Dad? That's their job." Abruptly, she pointed to a pudgy shape in a blue-green wave. "A seal!" She dashed toward the surf.

Sam followed, eager to see the harbor seal again, too. A walk on Rialto Beach felt much more satisfying than trying to pump the child for information. How she was going to miss this—the scents of salt water and cedar, the seals and bears and birds wheeling overhead. In two weeks, she'd be shut up in her tiny home office again, pounding out words on a computer and fretting about the next paycheck. Her only consolations were that she would have her cat, Simon, to share her confinement and Blake's dinners to look forward to.

After inspecting the orange and purple starfish clinging to the exposed rocks and marveling over the microcosms in the tide pools, Sam drove Lili home. They sat at the Chois' kitchen table as Sam told what little she knew about novelists and screenwriters, types that were more interesting to Lili than article writers who worked on assignment.

Laura checked the delicious-smelling chicken enchiladas in the oven, then told Lili to set the table for dinner.

"But we haven't finished my questions," Lili whined. "I'm supposed to ask about money and job opportunities and all that."

Sam grimaced. Money and job opportunities—two things she was always short of. But kids needed to know the realities. "We can meet after school again, Lili. And you can always call me on the phone."

The girl's face fell. "Believe it or not, I don't have a cell phone."

"Believe it or not, regular telephones still work," Laura said. Turning to Sam, she said, "Thanks for offering to take Lili out after school. The other two are in day camp, but with summer school . . ." She shrugged. "She gets awfully tired of hanging around the library with me. The truth is, I don't have a clue where Lili is most of the time between two and six."

Lili frowned. "I'm with my friends, Mom, like I've told you a hundred times."

"Where? Doing what?"

The girl stood up and slapped her books into a pile, muttered an F-word barely louder than a whisper.

Laura fisted her hands on her hips. "*What* did you say?"

Yanking her books from the table, Lili stomped out of the room.

"Did she say what I think she said?" Laura demanded.

"It sounded more like 'five' to me," Sam said.

"Which means?"

Sam held up her hands to show her ignorance of teenage numberspeak. "Talking to a thirteen-year-old seems like negotiating a minefield."

Laura slipped a potholder onto her hand and turned toward the oven. "Welcome to my war."

20

TALK over the dinner table was family chitchat, focusing on Lili's soccer, Tamara's upcoming role as Cinderella in her day camp play, and little Joseph's newfound love of T-ball. After dinner, Sam asked Lili if they could talk in her room.

"Girl talk," Sam said when Joe raised his eyebrows. Lili gave her father a smug smile.

When the door was closed on the bedroom Lili shared with Tamara, Sam said, "I want to ask you about your tattoo, Lili."

"Not you, too! I *can't* take off the tattoo, I just can't." Her eyes filled with tears. She threw herself onto a twin bed filled with stuffed animals.

Sam sat on the corner. "I wasn't going to ask you to take it off."

"Well, thank God for that, then. Dad bugs me about it every day."

"But it's just temporary, right? Why is it such a big deal?"

"Well . . ." She squirmed, plucking at the flowered bedspread instead of looking at Sam. "It's like . . . the tattoo shows I'm in the club."

Ah, that teenage desperation to be part of a group. Sam understood. She still remembered what it felt like to be an outcast. First she'd been the preacher's daughter with a sick mother, and then the preacher's daughter with a dead mother. Only after her grandfather had given her Comanche and she'd joined the 4-H Range Riders did she have the experience of being part of a special group. "Being in a club sounds pretty cool," she said.

Lili looked up. "It is."

"What sort of club is it?"

The girl hesitated. She pulled a stuffed seal from the pile and played with its flippers, making it clap.

"Honors club?"

Lili rolled her eyes. "Like I need to be associated with *that*."

Sam tried again. "Secret girls' club?"

A sly smile crossed Lili's face. "It's secret, but it's not just girls. But only girls can wear the tattoo. It's a life sign. We can have babies, so life continues through us."

Damn! Was this about sex? Sam searched to find a way to ask the question. "That tattoo *is* pretty," she said, staring at the design on Lili's ankle. "Do you have to do anything special to earn one? Could I get one?"

Lili chuckled. "I don't think so. You're a fed."

"A fed?"

"Feds can't be in the club." Clutching the seal to her chest, Lili leaned back against the pile of stuffed animals. "I'm lucky they let me in, what with Dad being a fed."

So a fed was a government employee. "I'm just a temporary fed," Sam told her. "I won't even be one in two weeks."

"Yeah, but it still counts against you." Lili squirmed, pulled a purple unicorn from behind her back, and tossed it to the floor, then leaned back again, seemingly satisfied with the adjustment.

"But I know a fed who had the same tattoo you do," Sam said. "You know, that trail worker who got killed. She had that tattoo on her shoulder."

She pulled the scanned page from her pocket and unfolded it to compare with the design on Lili's ankle. Except for color, they were identical.

"Omigod." Lili pointed to the photo. "Is this a picture after she's dead?"

Sam had momentarily forgotten about the corpse under the tattoo. "Um, yes. See, she had the same tattoo."

A frown knitted Lili's dark brows. "That doesn't make any sense. I'll have to ask Rocky—" Her eyes widened and her hands flew to her mouth. "Forget I said that."

"Okay," Sam said. Lili had also mentioned Rocky during their conversation in the firewatch tower. "Can anybody who's not a fed join the club? Do you have to do something special?" Now that Lili had brought up the boy who she thought was *fine*, it seemed more likely than ever that this club had something to do with sex.

"Well," Lili said hesitantly, "it's not what you have to do; it's what you know."

That sounded better. "So this is like a brainiac club?"

"You mean nerds?" the girl scoffed. "It's not for nerds. You have to know something *valuable*. Something that Roc—the leader thinks is valuable."

This game of twenty questions was getting old. Sam still had to find her way back to the bunkhouse and clear off her bunk and get a shower before lights out. "What do you all have to know?"

"It's all different. Like, Deborah knows about planes because her dad has one; and Emily knows about locks and stuff because her dad's a locksmith. And George, his dad has a fishing boat."

"So it's a club where people talk about their fathers? You talk about your dad?"

"Yeah, that's my special knowledge. I can teach about what rangers do." She traded the seal for a black beanbag puppy, flopping it across her thigh.

Sam grabbed an orange kitten toy and stroked its soft fur. None of this made any sense. What did plane owners and bank managers and rangers have to do with each other? And why would teenagers think any of this was interesting? Maybe it was like Explorer Scouts? "You talk about this stuff to figure out what you'd like to do when you grow up?"

"No." Lili shot her an irritated look, and Sam realized that she probably considered herself grown up already. "We learn things, and go for walks in the woods. And we make stuff."

Sam couldn't resist. "Do you ever make signs, Lili?"

The girl's face darkened. "I told you I don't know anything about those signs."

"What kind of things do you learn?"

Lili frowned. "That's secret. Just forget I said anything about it, okay? We just talk and do the tattoos and stuff. It's just for fun."

Sam stared at the stuffed kitten's blue plastic eyes for a minute. She couldn't think of a way to broach the subject, so she cut to the chase. "Is this club about sex?"

"Sex!" The girl burst into laughter. "Why do grown-ups think everything's about sex?"

Sam laughed then, too. "I don't know. But if I can tell your dad that the tattoo has nothing to do with sex, I think he'll let you keep it."

"But don't tell him anything else, okay? I mean, he's a fed. And he's sort of a cop, too."

"Okay," Sam said, having no intention of keeping that promise. "Lili, what's this 'five' business? Does that mean, like, 'I plead the Fifth'?"

"Huh? Pleat the what?"

Sam smiled. "Never mind."

Lili leaned forward. "*That's* what it means."

It was Sam's turn to be perplexed.

"Like, 'Never mind' or 'None of your business.' That's what 'five' means. Like, 'I don't have to talk to you.'" Lili flipped a strand of beads over her shoulder to demonstrate the proper disdainful attitude.

"I get it," Sam said. "I think."

"So you'll talk to Dad about the tattoo?"

"Sure. Is there a number code for saying 'sure'? I think it sounds like an eight. Eight, I'll talk to your dad."

"You're weird." Lili leaned forward and hugged her.

"Thank you, Aunt Summer. I really, really can't go back to being a mud girl."

"DEBORAH and Emily and George Fishkiller? That doesn't make any sense." Joe handed her the casserole pan he'd just washed. Sam rinsed it under the faucet before setting it in the drying rack. Beside them, the dishwasher thrummed in its wash cycle.

"And everything you did at thirteen made sense?"

Joe smiled. "Point taken. But we did think about sex. A lot." He handed her a saucepan. "Pretty much all the time."

"When I was thirteen," Sam confessed, "we believed that aliens would land on a night of the full moon to take all the young women to their planet for procreation purposes."

He looked surprised. "So you hid under your bed every full moon?"

"*Au contraire, mon ami.* We had our suitcases packed. We were ready to create the brave new species."

He groaned. "So you did think about sex."

"But only in the most noble way. We weren't thinking about the local boys. Too common." She stacked the saucepan on top of the casserole dish in the drainor, and then leaned back against the counter. "We were reserving our virginity. For the aliens."

They were still chuckling when Laura came in. "I want to trade kids' bedtime for kitchen cleanup. You guys sound like you're having way too much fun in here."

"Perfect timing." Joe swept out his hands to emphasize the spotless kitchen.

"Thank you for talking to Lili," Laura told Sam. "She looks up to you. Maybe she'll decide to become a writer or a ranger."

"Probably not a ranger. It sounds like feds are not in favor among Lili's peers right now."

Laura grimaced. "That attitude seems to be going

around. I'm putting together an exhibit at the library on the federal employees that the kids never think of, like test pilots, CDC doctors, and the Army Corps of Engineers. Mack is going to give a talk about botany. Show the kids that federal employees are more than cops. Not that cops aren't wonderful." She gently punched Joe in the arm.

"Speaking of cops." Sam turned to Joe. "You said Chase called you today?"

"He wanted to know about Jack Winner's associates." He pulled out a chair from the kitchen table and offered it to her.

"So do I."

"Coffee?" Laura waved a mug in the air.

"No, thanks," Sam said. Somewhere around age thirty-two, Sam had found she could no longer drink coffee after 4 P.M. and get to sleep before 2 A.M.

Laura took a seat at the kitchen table. Taking his wife's hand, Joe told Sam, "I get most of my local information from Laura. She knows who's who around town a lot better than I do."

Laura sipped her coffee. "It's one of the benefits of being the town librarian."

"Anyhow," Joe continued, "most of Winner's associates are relatives—more Winners, and the Jorgensens. All okay as far as I know. But there's one bad apple."

"Philip King." Laura grimaced. "He comes in to use the Internet computers once in a while. He gives me the creeps."

"He should." Joe took a sip from his cup. "He's the guy I wanted to warn you about. King's only twenty-six and he's already done time for assault and attempted robbery, and that was after he graduated from juvie, where he landed after stabbing a teacher's aide with a knife. A real sweetheart. Now that we know his history, we'll keep a close eye on him."

Sam decided that she wasn't camping out alone again before the end of her contract. "What does he look like?" She wanted to be able to identify Philip King on sight.

"He looks like a weightlifter," Laura said. "Wears muscle shirts most of the time."

"Blond crew cut. Five-nine. About one seventy pounds." Joe added. He removed a photo from his shirt pocket and slid it across the table to her. "Here's his last booking photo."

Sam studied the picture. He wasn't the rose thrower; that guy had dark hair. He might be the illegal hunter she'd met in the woods a couple of weeks ago. It was hard to say, since the guy had worn a cap and camouflage makeup, and her main focus had been his rifle. She passed the photo back. "Did you tell Chase all this?"

Joe nodded. "We wanted you to know, too, especially now with Caitlin Knight . . ."

"Got it." Sam flicked her hand to indicate he didn't need to elaborate. "What about Garrett Ford?" She'd driven by his place but there'd been no vehicle in his carport.

"Still not home."

In other words, nothing had been resolved. Anywhere. With anyone. Sam stood up. "I'd better get to the bunkhouse. Thanks for the meal, Laura; those enchiladas were wonderful. I want the recipe." She'd give it to Blake. She looked at Joe. "You'll let Lili keep the tattoo?"

"For now." Joe made a face. "But I still don't like it. I don't understand why it's so important to her."

Sam shrugged. "Peer pressure. She said it shows she's part of the club, that she's not a mud girl anymore."

"Mud girl?" Laura's back went rigid.

"Is that a soccer thing?"

"I sure hope so," Laura said.

"'Mud people' is racist slang for anyone who's not white as snow," Joe explained. "Blacks, Indians, Latinos, Asians."

Sam abruptly felt ashamed of being one hundred percent Caucasian. "Maybe 'mud girl' doesn't mean the same thing to thirteen-year-olds as 'mud people' does to adults."

"I hope Lili's never even heard of 'mud people.'" Laura sipped from her coffee mug. "I'll find a way to ask her tomorrow."

Sam fished her keys from her pocket. "I'd better get back before the kids short-sheet my bed."

On the drive to the bunkhouse, Sam used her cell phone to check her voice mail and was delighted to find a message from Chase. "*Mi amor,* I was just thinking of you. Sorry I missed you. *Te amo.*"

I love you. It was the first time he'd said that. How could three words—or only two in Spanish—be so thrilling and so frightening at the same time?

She was thirty-seven. She didn't really believe in happily-ever-after endings anymore. She couldn't remember if she ever had. But the thought of Chase always gave her the warm fuzzies, as Blake would say. She speed-dialed his number, and got a recording saying he was not available. She tried not to think about all the possible reasons he didn't answer.

"*Querido,*" she murmured to the recorder, "I'm sorry I missed you, too. I'm sleeping indoors tonight, and I hope you are, too. Stay safe, lover."

The bunkhouse was dark and quiet when she let herself in. It must have been a hard day for trail breaking; it was barely ten and even Blackstock was snoring in his bunk. After getting up at five thirty, she was bleary-eyed, too. She sat at the kitchen table for a few minutes, sipping shiraz from her commuter cup, inhaling the leftover aroma of chili, and watching through the window as clouds swallowed the stars. She missed the warmth of a cat on her lap.

After brushing her teeth, she changed her clothes in the bathroom and slipped into bed. Overhead, rain now pattered against the metal roof in a steady rhythm. She didn't envy the trail crew their job tomorrow. Working in the rain guaranteed staying damp all day long, either wet from the downpour without rain gear or swimming in sweat inside it.

Before closing her eyes, she put the phone to her ear and played Chase's message again. *Te amo.*

"I think I love you, too," she whispered softly to the darkness.

"That's nice," Maya's voice, raspy with sleep, emanated from the other bunk. "But you're really not my type."

21

IT was still raining the next morning, making parts of Sam's drive from the bunkhouse to the district headquarters a slippery affair. Inside the building, she shook out her raincoat and hung it on the peg in the big shared office. Another fax was waiting in her box. Hoyle wanted to know how her management plan was coming along and whether he could take a look at her speech for the upcoming conference.

The nerve! *The Edge* was paying her to give that speech, and she wasn't about to let Richard Best control the content, let alone Peter Hoyle, who had absolutely no authority over her, or at least wouldn't in ten days. Besides, all she had written was the first line of her speech, and she wasn't even too sure about those four words.

She flipped open her laptop, fuming as she waited for it to boot up. By the time she remembered that the office did not have wireless service and switched the phone line from the ancient desktop computer to her laptop, she'd calmed down a little. She'd worked alone for too long; Hoyle *did* have a right to check up on her in her current position, especially when she was so close to the end of her assignment.

She logged in to the NPS mail system and sent the assistant superintendent a message that all was going well, promising that she'd have a draft management plan in a couple of days, and asking if Hoyle wanted to see it then via e-mail attachment or courier. She didn't offer to drive the sixty miles to deliver it to Hoyle's office.

She'd already sent that message when she had the bright idea of admitting that she hadn't progressed very far on her speech and asking for Hoyle's suggestions. She didn't have to take them, after all. It might be instructive to know what was in the head of an NPS honcho these days on the topic of environmentalists as an endangered species.

Hoyle's response came back almost immediately, asking for the draft plan via e-mail and suggesting a historical approach for the speech, including early environmentalists such as Teddy Roosevelt and John Muir. *Ask what the country would be like today if their opposition had triumphed*, Hoyle wrote.

It was a damn good idea. Sam could see how she could start the speech off that way, and work up to the struggles in current times, showing the importance of environmental and conservation champions in shaping America's landscape and history. She was embarrassed that she hadn't thought of it first. Hoyle should probably be giving this speech instead of her.

Dynamite suggestions—thank you! she replied. For once, she could be sincere with her boss.

She hadn't been working on her draft plan for more than five minutes when Hoyle sent a list of web links and a note saying that he would give Sam a folder of articles after Lisa Glass's service on Wednesday.

She clicked a link about John Muir and brought up the web browser. Interesting. She knew about Muir and The Sierra Club, but she hadn't known that Muir had been so influential with Teddy Roosevelt and largely responsible for the creation of many of the Western parks. The things you could find out on the Internet.

Inspired, she brought up the search engine and typed *life symbol*. She could research Lili's tattoo design from here. Sure enough, there were sites explaining various life symbols, including trees of life and ankhs and Celtic crosses. She waded through the list, brought up the second page of links. The second item there was *A Visual Data-base of Extremist Symbols, Logos, and Tattoos.* Extrem-ists? She remembered Joe's "mud people" comment. With a sense of dread, Sam clicked the link.

Hate on Display. Cripes, there was a whole database. She clicked *Graphic Symbols.* There was Lili's tattoo, the very first symbol in the list. A life rune, according to the description, an ancient symbol that originally signified life, creation, rebirth, and renewal, used by the Nazis on the graves of SS soldiers, and used by racists to denote "Giver of Life" status for women in the white supremacist movement.

Oh, no. The connection between Lisa's comments and Lili's was starting to make an ugly sense now. Pulling out her cell phone, she dialed Chase. Miraculously, he answered.

"Chase, I've got it! The tattoo, swarthy, mud people, Lisa's Bible, the drawing of the Jewish kid—it all makes sense now."

"I'm glad to hear that, *querida.* Now, take a deep breath and then explain to me what the heck you're talking about. Mud people?"

Realizing that she was close to hyperventilating, she took that deep breath. "Sorry. Where are you?"

"Just outside of Boise."

So he was getting farther away by the minute. "Is Nicole with you? What happened to the meetings in Seattle?"

"Nicole's driving. Seattle was yesterday."

It was a reminder that her world was much smaller and slower than his. She wasn't ready for him to leave. But he'd return. Eventually. When it was convenient.

"What's this about the tattoo?"

"It's a life rune, Chase. I found this website that says it's a symbol used by"—she checked the screen—"the National Alliance."

"I thought the National Alliance was dead." He sounded grim. In the background, she heard Nicole say something in response, but she couldn't make out the words.

"I suppose it could be just coincidence—I mean, it *is* an ancient symbol—but remember Lisa's Bible and how she talked about the one Jewish kid and used the word *swarthy*? That word is all over this database. And Lili Choi's got the same tattoo and last night she was talking about not being a mud girl anymore." Sam switched the phone to her left ear so she could use her right hand to mouse over to *Number symbols*.

"Mud girl?"

"Well, I think it's a version of mud people, which is white supremacist jargon—"

"I'm familiar with the term."

He would be, she supposed, being half Latino and half Lakota. She stared at the new page that came up. "Five, Chase. I'm looking at it. Five stands for 'I have nothing to say.' Oh jeez, there's a fourteen, too. Hang on."

Broadband would have been handy right now, but she was stuck with the NPS dial-up connection. Finally, the screen redrew. "Fourteen stands for: 'We must secure the existence of our people and a future for white children.' Coined by David Lane from The Order." She clicked the Back button. "The numbers we found on those trees are some kind of racist code."

"Give me the URL of this website."

While she waited for the screen to display the last page, she read him the address at the top of the browser. The list of numbers finally reappeared. "There's no 8128, Chase."

"That'd be too easy."

"The descriptions here sound very antigovernment, too."

"Most white supremacists hate all forms of government."

"But Joe's a ranger. And he's Korean." Now *she* was sounding racist. "Korean-American, I mean. What I really mean is that Lili's dad is a federal officer and she's a quarter Korean—how can she be in a white supremacist group?"

"They adapt, Summer, just like all other groups. Maybe

they're taking partly brown people with law enforcement relatives now, figuring they can breed out those impurities."

She groaned. "Hate never dies, does it?"

Arnie came out of his office. On hearing her words, his expression brightened with curiosity and he sauntered toward her desk. She pressed a key on her laptop to activate her screensaver, and then swiveled in her chair, turning her back to him.

"You've got that right," Chase replied. "I'll do some checking around on known hate cells in your area. But don't say anything to anyone, Summer. We don't want to flush any quail out of hiding before we're ready to shoot them. Or at least net them."

She felt Arnie hovering behind her. "You mean your organization would do that?"

"Is someone in the room with you?"

"Yes," she answered. "That's right." She heard Arnie remove his rain jacket from the rack on the wall.

"Hate groups are FBI business. I'll get someone on this."

Arnie walked out the door, which thumped closed behind him.

"He's gone now," she told Chase. "But I can't figure out how Lisa Glass and Lili Choi both ended up spouting the same sort of drivel. They both have . . . had . . . the same tattoo. Lisa was from back East somewhere. I'm sure Lili doesn't know her."

"These groups are often nationwide. Maybe Lisa Glass came out there to meet up with someone."

"Maybe." She'd look at everyone with suspicion now. Jeez. Illegal hunters in the woods, murderers roaming the river banks, white supremacists all over the place?

On the poster, Caitlin Knight had long black hair. She asked Chase, "Was that murdered game warden Native American, by any chance?"

"Good question. I'll have to check. Ethnicity could be a possible motive."

She wanted to call Joe, drive to the reservations to warn members of the Quileute, Hoh, and Quinault tribes. Oh God, there were the Ozettes and Makahs up north, too. This was like finding a cockroach under the sink; it made her want to spray the whole area with insecticide.

"Remember, Summer, don't flush those quail. Don't talk to *anyone*."

"How can you read my mind like that?" It really was disturbing.

"We're kindred spirits." She heard voices at his end of the phone, then he said, "I've got to go. Are you sleeping at the bunkhouse?"

"With the rest of the delinquents." She liked the way he laughed at her jokes, even when they weren't that funny. "Where are you off to?"

"Can't say. I'll call you later. Be careful."

The connection ended before she could say, "You, too."

She spent the rest of the day struggling to focus on her management plan and decipher the latest NPS regulations, when she really wanted to head out to Marmot Lake with a hammer and chisel to obliterate those awful numbers from the trees.

JACK was appalled to find Ernest on his doorstep again, looking pitiful with rain dripping from his ragged graying hair. Now that Allie was gone and her father had decided to dry out, Ernest was around more than ever.

"That ranger was here yesterday looking for you," Ernest said.

"Ranger Choi again? What the hell did he want?" They couldn't have uncovered anything else about the paintball games or the C-4. Dammit, if King was shooting his mouth off—

"Not a *he*," Ernest said. "That little blond ranger, you know, the one that was on TV?"

"Westin?" The back of Jack's neck prickled. Why would Westin come here? It was like she was haunting him.

"I don't know her name," Ernest said. "She told me they're having a memorial service for that trail worker girl tomorrow, up at Hurricane Ridge."

"Yeah, it was in the paper. Look, Ernest, I'm just getting dinner . . ." He half turned toward the inside of the house. He had a sandwich partially made on the kitchen counter.

Ernest caught the screen door and took a step closer. "I'm going. Want to ride with me?"

Now what the hell was this about? "Why would I want to do that? Why would *you* want to do that?"

It'll be a fed roundup, King had pointed out. *Good place to do a little demolition work.* It had taken Jack twenty minutes to talk the idiot out of the idea. Deferred gratification was a concept King had apparently never heard of. The money was the only thing that finally convinced him.

"I thought I'd pay my respects," Ernest said. "Jack, that girl was two years younger than Allie."

"Yeah, well, that doesn't make up for *who* she was. You wear the uniform, you're one of them." Jack crossed his arms and leaned back against the inner door, swinging it wider. "Feds take our land, our money—they sent the whole national treasury to Iraq and Afghanistan, for chrissakes—they spent billions of dollars a week over there, did you know that? So the freakin' ragheads can have 'democracy' "—he drew quote signs in the air around the word—"so they can have the right to free speech and the right to criticize *their* government. But tell the truth about the bastards running our government, and they'll slap you in Guantanamo—"

"What's that?" Ernest interrupted. His gaze was no longer on Jack. He pointed toward the bedroom.

Shit. Ernest could see the purple moonlight photo through the open doorway.

"You said you were sending those photos to Allie," the old man said.

Jack swallowed, thinking fast. "Ernest, you know how you said you needed those paintings Allie made when she was a little girl?"

The man's eyes shimmered with sudden tears. "Yeah."

"Well, I decided that I need these photos." He let the silence hang painfully between them for a minute. "You can understand, can't you?"

Ernest's jaws worked like he was considering an argument, but then he said, "Yeah, Jack, I guess I can. I miss her so much. I sent her a letter at that address you gave me, but I haven't heard anything back yet."

"Let me know when you do, okay?" If Jack had to look at Ernest's sad grizzly face any longer, he'd get all choked up, too. With the sheeting rain, he felt like he should offer the guy a ride home. He knew Ernest's car was dead and Allie's was in some impound lot. But he didn't want to continue this any longer than he had to. Besides, it wasn't far and the old man was wearing an old Army surplus poncho. "I'm sorry about yelling at you. I know you feel the same way about the feds as I do."

"Yeah, well." Ernest backed up, letting the screen door bang shut between them. "Night, Jack."

"Night, Ernest." Jack closed the door and watched the old man shuffle off through the dripping trees.

Ranger Westin was sniffing around for him? She was the last person he wanted to show up at his door. Probably the Marmot Lake trespassing thing again; she couldn't possibly know anything else. She couldn't have made him from the other night. Still. He turned on his computer and brought up the web page, logged in, and left a message on the bulletin board. Then he turned the machine off, pulled out the hard drive, and replaced it with a new one. After eating his sandwich, he buried the old drive in a plastic bag under his compost heap.

22

IT was still raining on Wednesday when Ernest drove up to Hurricane Ridge. The trip took longer than he'd planned on, because he'd been amazed to find a gate across the road and an attendant who wanted a ten-dollar entry fee. Then the young woman embarrassed them both by asking if he was a senior when he was only sixty-one. Finally, she just waved him on through without paying after he said he was on his way to the memorial service.

The service was already in progress and the single pink rose he'd bought at the grocery store in Forks was wilting in his hand as he limped down the aisle. They'd set up outside the visitor center under a huge portable awning to shield them from the downpour. Up front was a table and a speaker's stand, and behind that, a chaplain. Just like Jack had predicted, the folding chairs held an army of gray-green uniforms, with only a few people in regular clothes scattered among them. He saw a silver-blond braid in the middle of the pack that might be that little ranger who'd come looking for Jack a couple of days ago.

He took the first empty folding chair he found, next to a teenage girl with chopped-off red hair. Beside her sat several tough-looking boys. Although their faces and hands were clean, their pants were wet to the knees and stained with mud; they'd clearly been working outside. The girl beside him smelled of sweat and he was glad for the open-air chapel. The dead girl had been part of a trail crew, he remembered. These must be her comrades.

Up front he could see a photo of Lisa Glass hanging on the speaker's stand, just above a spray of lilies. She had light-colored hair; that was all he could tell from here.

The chaplain was going on about how Lisa loved the woods and being outdoors. His speech reminded Ernest of all the field services in 'Nam, where the poor schlub with the cross around his neck was just as confused as the rest of them, but since it was his job to conjure up something nice to say, he talked about how the guy who'd had his guts ripped out by machine gun fire had been a high school football player or loved his dog or something.

". . . and so Lisa chose to work on the trail crew to be close to nature," the chaplain was saying now.

"What a crock," the red-haired girl beside him murmured.

He glanced sideways at her.

"She did it for the money," she told him, wiping tears from her freckled cheek with the back of her hand. "It was the only job she could find. Her family was poor."

"Shhh." A man in front of them turned and glared at the redhead. In response, she stuck out her tongue. She wore four earrings in the ear he could see. He wondered if her other ear had four holes, too.

"Sounds like Lisa was nice," he whispered.

"Not particularly." The girl's muscular shoulders lifted, then dropped. "But she didn't deserve this."

He couldn't think of anything else to say. There was a rumor that Lisa Glass had been murdered, and another one that she was drunk and accidentally set the fire. The truth was probably somewhere in between, but the redhead was right—it didn't really matter, because nobody deserved to die. Not at nineteen years old.

How old was that poor murdered game warden? Had anyone held a service for her? That wasn't park service. That would be—he couldn't come up with the branch of government—but he hoped she had friends and family to honor her memory. God, it was a terrible world, with young women dying all alone in the woods.

Then the service was over. Some people slipped out the

back and sides while others went up to lay things under the photo of the girl. He followed the red-haired girl toward the front, carrying his flower in both hands so it wouldn't look so droopy. The redhead placed a big pinecone on top of the pile of stuff under the photo. He laid his limp rose next to it. There were a couple of tiny Beanie Baby animals in the pile. Allie had collected those when she was about ten years old.

Ernest looked at the picture to see if the dead girl was a pinecone type or Beanie Baby type or a rose type. It was a lousy photo, all in shadow. She was tall and blond and holding a shovel. Under the hard hat she wore, her face looked a lot like Allie's. They said everyone had a double somewhere in the world, and this girl looked like she could be Allie's. Squinting hard, he put his face close to the photo to study her eyes.

It hit him then. More sudden and more excruciating than when the shrapnel had smashed into his leg in 'Nam. A moan started up from somewhere, soft and far away at first and then getting louder and closer. When he realized that he was making the horrible noise, he clapped a hand hard across his mouth. He staggered back from the photo.

How could Lisa Glass be Allie? Oh God, how could this dead girl be his Allie?

He felt a hand on his arm. "Are you all right?"

The flowers and Beanie Babies and pinecone swirled like a cyclone, dark and mean, roaring around him, taking his breath away. He thought he might never be able to talk again.

"You all right, sir?"

He could barely hear the voice through the awful roar, and he turned to see why the man was speaking so softly. The guy wore a ranger uniform. CHOI, it said on the brass nameplate over his pocket. He had a pistol on his hip.

"Allie," he managed to croak. But it couldn't be Allie. It couldn't.

"Maybe you'd better sit down."

Not Allie. She was in L.A.

But she hadn't said good-bye. And she hadn't called or written. And that just wasn't like her.

Although he had no memory of how he got there, Ernest found himself sitting in a chair in the front row, staring at the photo.

The Choi fellow was sitting beside him now. Only the two of them were left in the tent. Choi's slanted brown eyes looked kind. He asked, "Did you know her?"

Did he know her? He knew the smell of her hair, the crooked tooth she had in front, the scar she had on her knee from when she fell on the garden hoe. He knew she loved art and English and hated math and could take photos as good as any pro. He knew that Cheeseburger Macaroni was the kind of Hamburger Helper she liked best, but she always added mushrooms and green beans to make a balanced meal.

"Did you say something about an alley?" Choi asked. "Lisa Glass was found injured in the woods, not in town."

How could Allie be here and be dead when she was supposed to be in Los Angeles? She'd written him and Jack . . . But she'd never called. And Jack had kept her photos. Oh God.

He buried his face in his hands. God no, not Allie. Not his girl. Not dead. *I'm getting clean, Allie, so you won't be so ashamed of your old man, so you'll come back. I got a job today at the grocery. Just stocking shelves, but you won't have to work so hard anymore.*

"Did you know her, sir?"

He knew she worried about her weight and wished she were skinny instead of sturdy. He knew she wanted to go to college. But he didn't know what she'd study when she got there. Allie had a lot of secret dreams.

How could it be Allie? Now he really *wanted* her to be in Los Angeles, wanted her to be anywhere else. But Christ, it all fit. The forest fire was the same night that she didn't come home. And even when he wasn't sober enough to know it at the time, Allie had always come home.

Jack had hung her photos on his bedroom wall instead

of putting them in the mail. The bastard had known all along. What had Jack done to his daughter? Ernest sat up and grabbed the ranger by the arm. Choi looked startled, laid his hand on the butt of his weapon.

"I know her," Ernest croaked. "I need to talk to you."

LISA'S memorial service cast an understandable pall over the trail crew, and the kids were quiet during dinner at the bunkhouse. It was too wet for a campfire, so Blackstock divided them into teams and had them play Trivial Pursuit. Thank heavens they had the popular culture version; Sam couldn't quite imagine these teens competing in geography and history.

Sam retired to her room and made a few notes about her morning's fieldwork and its implications for her management plan. Then, bored, she pulled out her quilt blocks and estimated how many more it might take to make a quilt, trying to concoct various designs for a finished product. Nothing that she came up with was pleasing, and the whole idea was starting to seem narcissistic to her. She didn't really have the skill to make a quilt. She didn't have children to pass one on to, either, what was the point in documenting her life in needlework? Still, she thought, running her fingers over her mother's and grandmother's embroidery, it would be a shame not to honor these beautiful pieces of art. Maybe she'd just frame them. She shoved them into their plastic bag, tossed it onto the top bunk, and since the boys were all involved in the game, commandeered the bathroom and took her shower.

When she returned to the room, she found Maya sitting cross-legged on her own bunk, the quilt blocks spread out on the blanket around her. "Sorry," the redhead said, glancing at Sam, "but I couldn't resist. These are *sweet.*"

"You think so?" Sam slung her towel onto a hook on the wall. A tough girl like Maya, enthralled by embroidery?

"What are they for?"

Sam explained the album quilt.

"Your mom and grandma made these for you?" The girl fingered the square of Sam and Comanche galloping through the fields. "You had a horse?"

Maya's tone was so wistful that Sam felt guilty as she nodded yes.

23

THE continuing rain made it a little easier for Sam to sit at her desk researching NPS regulations and vocabulary and finessing her management plan all the next day. She was headed north on 101 back to the trail crew bunkhouse, when she just happened to look in her rearview mirror in time to catch the flash of white turning east on Forest Service Road 4312. A big pickup.

Not Garrett Ford's—his neighbors told her his was black. Only this morning she had cruised his house to see if by any chance there was a wreath of bear claws on his front door or a pool of blood leaking out of the garage, but nobody was home and his truck was gone.

Road 4312 was the one from which the illegal track took off to infiltrate the Marmot Lake area. There were no campgrounds along 4312. It was dusk. Odds were that the occupants of the white truck were up to no good.

She stomped on her brakes, hydroplaning a little, and then made a U-turn. By the time she got back to the turn-off, the vehicle was nowhere in sight. She drove down the dirt road, checking pullout areas and side roads. She saw only piles of rubbish dumped by yahoos too lazy or cheap to drive to the county dump.

She reached the beginning of the illegal track. The brush that rangers had piled across the track had been heaved aside, and new tread marks embossed the mud. She parked, checked her watch—Joe was on duty for another fifteen minutes.

He didn't sound thrilled to hear her on the radio. She

gave him her location; told him that it looked like they had activity on that illegal track into Marmot Lake.

"Are they in the NPS area?" he asked.

"I'm just off 4312—I can't tell. I can't see them from here. I'll check."

His "no!" was loud and definite, even over the staticky radio connection. "You're a civilian—stay out of there."

A loud crack resounded through the dripping woods. Sam's heart leapt into race mode. "I just heard a gunshot, Joe. I have to see what's happening." Sliding the pickup into four-wheel drive, she started down the track.

"No! Stay put! I'm on my way."

"But Raider—"

"Remember Caitlin Knight."

That brought her up short. Hikers had found the poor woman's torso, still dressed in her uniform, this morning along the beach out where the river emptied into the Pacific. Her arms, legs, and head were missing. They couldn't be sure of the actual cause of death without the rest of her body parts, but the bullet hole in the back of her USFWS uniform shirt left no doubt that she'd been murdered.

"She died on the job. Just like this, Sam."

"Okay." She took a deep breath, put the truck into park, and turned off the lights. She tried to take comfort from the fact that she'd heard no more gunshots. Maybe the prey had gotten away. But then again, maybe the first bullet had been sufficient.

Joe arrived seven minutes later. She climbed into his truck. There was now a wide swath cut around the rock trap she'd devised, and they took that detour, too, crashing through the brush. "They'll hear us a half mile away," Joe groaned.

A few hundred feet from the end of the track, he parked and shut off the engine. He took a key from his belt and unlocked the overhead rack, pulled down a rifle. As he reached for the door handle, he said, "Stay here."

"Like hell I will." Sam slid out.

They crept through the woods, one on each side of the track, trying to keep sight of each other in the growing darkness and sheeting rain. Sam's entire body prickled with dread.

The clearing held two pickups, one black and one white. No men in sight. There was a steel cage near the tailgate of the black pickup, with a huge lump of black fur lying motionless inside. Her heart in her throat, Sam heard Joe's hissed "no" from the nearby woods, but she rushed to the cage, anyway.

It *was* Raider. His once-lively black eyes were filmy, his tongue lolled out of his mouth, lifeless. Rage flooded her veins.

"Goddamn it!" She slammed a fist on the cage frame.

"Come on out, guys," Joe yelled from his position. "You're not going to get away. We have your license numbers; I've already radioed them in."

That last part was a lie; they hadn't been able to see license numbers until now. And she knew they were in a radio-free zone. Would Joe's bluff work? Would the poachers walk out of the woods with their hands up? Staring angrily at the lifeless black heap that used to be a bear, she hoped it wouldn't happen that easily. It would be nice if Joe was forced to shoot at least one of the murderers.

"I know these trucks belong to Garrett Ford and Gale Martinson," Joe yelled. "We can either do this peaceably right now, or we'll impound your trucks and pick you up later."

After a tense moment, a teenage boy walked out of the woods, his hands held out to his sides. "Michael Martinson?" Joe said. "What in the hell—"

A branch cracked. The bulky form of Garrett Ford in a rain poncho materialized next to his pickup. He held a rifle in his right hand. "Don't blame Mike," he said. "He's just helping me load."

"Drop the weapon!" Joe barked.

Ford seemed to consider whether or not this was a good idea. Sam wished for the second time she'd brought her Glock with her. What was she going to do if bullets started flying?

She heard Joe click the safety off his shotgun. "Put down that rifle!" he yelled again.

"Never leave the safety on myself. Too slow." Ford continued to point his weapon at Joe. He lowered his head as if aiming down the sights. Rain dripped from his graying forelock.

A flash of headlights and the groan of an engine announced an approaching vehicle. Sam's blood suddenly chilled. Did Ford and Martinson have armed comrades on the way? She looked to Joe in alarm. His gaze was locked with Ford's. She glanced at Mike Martinson, who looked as uncertain as she felt.

A rivulet of rain ran down the side of her neck. There was a sizable rock next to her right foot. Should she chuck it at Ford? Mike studied the ground around him as though he might be weighing the same consideration. Except she was pretty sure that *his* target would be Joe.

All four of them flinched when a voice came from the darkness around them. "Dammit, Garrett, what are you up to now?"

Unbelievably, it was Arnie Cole, and he had a rifle trained on Ford. A rustle on the other side of the circle brought her attention to another forest service ranger. He, too, had a rifle pointed in the same direction. "Three to one, Ford. Give it up," he said.

Finally making up his mind, Ford laid his rifle on the ground. Joe ordered Mike Martinson to sit on the ground, hands under his buttocks. Then he patted Ford down for other weapons.

Arnie pointed his rifle skyward as he clutched the poacher's arm. "Just two miles north and four more days, you dumb shit, and you could have been hunting legally."

"How could you?" Sam spat at Ford. "How could you kill this bear, in a protected zone, for no good reason—"

"I don't kill them," Ford grunted.

Sam frowned, squatted, and thrust a hand through the bars of the cage. The carcass was still warm. Now that she had her hand pressed to his furry flank, she could feel that Raider was still breathing, although barely. "He's not dead." Her voice was squeaky with surprise. "They darted him, Joe."

"Why?" Joe asked. Pulling handcuffs from a pouch on his service belt, he manacled Ford's hands behind his back.

"I want a lawyer." Ford frowned at Sam. "I shoulda just let him shoot you."

She blanched. "Let *who* shoot me?"

"Don't let him yank your chain, Sam." Joe turned to the boy. "Stand up, Mike." He pulled a zip-tie out of his pocket and motioned for the kid to turn around. "Aren't you only fifteen? You can't even drive legally yet."

"Fifteen and a half. I got my learner's permit."

"Not anymore you don't. Why are you darting bears, Mike?"

"Five," the boy said.

Joe rolled his eyes.

Arnie's grin was so wide that his teeth were visible in the dim light. "Forest service saves park service ass again."

The other USFS ranger nodded. "Typical."

Joe shot Sam an apologetic look. "I had to call them. I didn't know what jurisdiction we'd end up in."

"Well, well, well." Arnie's boots made sucking sounds in the mud as he strutted around her like a rooster. "I shoulda known hot-time-in-the-Summer Westin would be in the middle of some bear business." Leaning close, he gave her a wink. "Told you Marmot Lake was trouble."

Since the park service had jurisdiction and nobody had a backseat, Joe decided to load the prisoners into the bed of his pickup. Ford was sullen and silent. Mike Martinson protested, "But it's raining."

"Funny how you didn't mind that a little bit ago," Joe told him. "If you want to tell me what you were going to do with the bear, I might reconsider."

Mike's chin went up.

"Five," Joe said simultaneously with the boy.

"You NPS folks speak a weird language," Arnie said.

"We need to take the bear," Sam said.

Everyone turned to look at her. She gestured toward the cage and repeated, "We need to take the bear. To make sure he wakes up okay. Unless"—she looked at Ford—"you have the antidote with you."

Ford stared at her, his eyes cold.

"I didn't think so," she said.

The three men lifted the bear crate to the bed of Joe's pickup. It was a tight squeeze with Garrett Ford and Mike Martinson in the back. Raider didn't stir as they shifted him.

It was an odd feeling, driving through the woods with two criminals and a crated sleeping bear in the back. "I hope he didn't overdose Raider," she told Joe.

He glanced sideways at her. "What do you think Ford was going to do with that bear?"

Sam grimaced. "Notice how he said 'I don't kill them'? He could mean that he keeps them alive and milks them for their bile."

"You can do that?"

She squirmed uncomfortably. "I've read about the way they do it in China. It's the worst kind of torture—they keep a tube inserted through an incision into the bear's bile duct. They sell the bile that drains out and hope the bear will produce more before it dies." It nauseated her to think about it. "I'm worried that he said, 'I don't kill *them*.' That means he's done this before. He might have bears in cages somewhere."

They arrived at her truck. She reached for the door handle.

"I'll dump our boys off at the jail, but what am I going to do with the bear?" Joe asked.

"Does the park service have a vet?"

He winced. "In Port Angeles."

An hour and a half away. She considered. "I'll take him to the bunkhouse," she said. "At least for now, I'm a biologist in the park service. The trail crew kids might get a kick out of having a bear with us tonight."

She backed her truck up to Joe's, and with a great deal of shoving and pulling, they finally managed to push the crate from Joe's pickup into hers. Raider still wasn't moving, but when she felt his throat to make sure he was breathing, he seemed to be holding his own. His black eyes were dull and still at half-mast, though. Worrisome. "Got some eye ointment in your first aid kit, Joe?"

He did. She squeezed a thread of ointment across the bear's eyes to keep them from drying out, and stuck the tube in her pocket for later.

She followed Joe back to Road 4312, trying to ignore the icy glares Ford and Martinson aimed at her. She would have turned on her high beams to irritate the two if the bright lights wouldn't have tortured Joe, too.

What had they been planning to do with Raider? And where? 'I don't *kill* them,' Ford had said. Her hands, wrapped around the steering wheel, were white at the knuckles. Garrett Ford reminded her of another man who earned his money guiding hunters to wild animals. Wait a minute. She clenched the wheel even more tightly. Had Ford said, '*I* don't kill them'? Maybe he was more like Buck Ferguson than she'd imagined.

When they reached 4312, she jerked the wheel right instead of left. In her rearview mirror, she saw Joe's truck stop. "What are you up to, Sam?" her radio said a second later.

"I'm just following a hunch, Joe. Go on, I'll let you know if it pans out."

"No way. I'm coming, too."

She saw him turn around, and then his headlights were following her. The USFS pickup turned, too. This would be really embarrassing if her hunch led nowhere. But Road 4312 was perfect—an unmaintained road that went way back into the forest where nobody had good reason to go anymore. There was no active logging going on here now. The road grew increasingly rough, and she kept her four-wheel drive in gear as she drove, slowing to check the side tracks. Mercifully, the rain slacked off and visibility was marginally improved.

Finally she saw what she was looking for—fresh tread marks leading into dense woods. She followed them, grind-

ing over rocks and through a little stream. She could hardly
believe it when her headlights lit up a bank of cages. Leaving the lights on, she climbed down from the truck to
explore. A handsome five-point buck blinked at her from
his enclosure. Two mountain goats cowered in a corner of
their cage. A black bear stood on its hind legs and clawed at
the heavy mesh that imprisoned it. An enraged snarl split
the darkness. Dear lord, was that a cougar?

Joe and the forest service rangers caught up with her.

"Unbelievable," Joe said, climbing down from his truck.

"What made you think this might be here?" asked the
other USFS ranger, who'd introduced himself as Hauser.

"I know this hunting guide in Utah," Sam told him.
"He makes big money leading yuppie hunters to trophy
animals. And I suddenly realized that Ford could hardly
drive through town with a caged bear in the back of his
truck."

"This is downright entrepreneurial." Arnie paced the
line of cages. "How better to guarantee a trophy animal
than to keep one for when you need it? Then you just let it
out and lead the hunter to it. And since it's the National
Forest instead of some Texas game ranch, the hunter will
think you're a helluva tracker." He laughed. "It's brilliant,
Garrett!" he yelled toward Joe's truck.

"Fuck you," Ford yelled back.

"It's criminal," Sam groaned.

"Oh, I don't know about that," Arnie said. "He wasn't
going to kill them until hunting season, I'm sure. He's got
less than a week till bear season out here." He looked
toward Hauser. "Is there a law about imprisoning animals
in a national forest?"

"Damned if I know." Hauser scratched his chin. "Maybe
something about operating a commercial enterprise without a permit."

Sam walked toward a stack of hay she spied under a
tarp, peeled off a few flakes, and thrust them into the buck's
and goats' cages. The animals fell on the hay hungrily.

"Should we let them out?" Hauser asked.

"I want all these animals released in the national park," Sam said.

Arnie frowned. "We don't know where they came from. That fella"—he pointed to the buck—"could have come from around here. He'd make a mighty nice hat rack." He made his hand into a gun and pretend-fired at the buck.

Now Sam wanted to yell "Fuck you" at Arnie.

"It's a while until hunting season," Joe said quietly, putting his hand on her arm. "And they could very well end up in the park then." He turned to Hillser. "Can we agree to leave this until tomorrow? This is a crime scene. We need to get back here and take photos and evidence in daylight. Both NPS and USFS are involved. Fish and Wildlife, too, maybe."

Sam poured some dog chow into the bear's cage and, since she didn't see anything better to feed it, into the cougar's as well. She made sure they all had water, checked Raider again—he was breathing a little more deeply now—and then they all left, in convoy again.

By the time she reached the trail crew bunkhouse, both she and Raider were staggering; she from fatigue, and he from the anesthetic still flooding his system. The bear kept trying to get to his feet, only to collapse onto his side again, shuddering from the effort.

"Calm down, buddy," she murmured. "You're safe with me." She took a chance on opening the cage door just enough to push in a bucket of water, then tossed a tarp over the top of the cage to protect him from the rain.

"Sleep tight." She knew *she* would. It felt good to have finally accomplished something positive. The paintball crazies were still out there, that C-4 was still missing, Caitlin Knight's murderer was still on the loose, and Lisa Glass's death remained a mystery. But her bear poacher would sleep behind bars tonight.

She helped herself to bread and peanut butter in the kitchen, sluiced off the worst of her grime in the bathroom, then headed for her bunk. As she was pulling off her shirt, Raider bawled outside.

Maya sat bolt upright in her bunk. "What the *fuck* was that?"

"Shhh," Sam murmured. "It's only a bear. He's locked up in my truck."

"Of course, a bear. Why didn't I think of that?" The girl collapsed back onto her pillow. "Just a regular day here in Disneyland."

24

WHEN Sam wandered into the kitchen the next morning, she found two notes from the trail crew. *No pets allowed*, from Tom Blackstock, and an arrow pointing to a sealed envelope. A single page with a question mark written on it—that had to come from the kids. Teens seemed to be into symbols and abbreviated communication these days. She wrote, *Y not?* after the question mark, preferring to remain a source of mystery a little longer. At their age, she would have thought that packing a bear around was pretty cool. Hell, she still thought packing a bear around was pretty cool.

She opened the envelope. Inside was another note from Tom. *I've been called up; can you believe it? My unit ships out to Afghanistan at the end of next week. Know anyone who can take over for me here for the last three weeks?*

She stared at the writing, stunned. The news *was* pretty unbelievable; Tom had to be nearing fifty. Thank God Tom hadn't asked her if she'd do it. She really wasn't the den mother type, especially not for a crew that included six adolescent boys. She searched her memory banks for men she knew, and came up with one she thought might work out. But would the park service accept him? She'd have to talk to everyone concerned. Stuffing the note into her pocket, she walked out to her truck.

Weak sunlight filtered through the dripping trees this morning. Raider was wild-eyed and rambunctious when she lifted the tarp on his cage. After checking her watch—

it was only a few minutes after seven—she drove to the Chois' home. Joe had already left for work, but Laura and the kids were still at breakfast. She brought them out to her truck.

"Lili, you said you wanted to see a bear." She threw back the tarp. Raider let out a bawl, which made Lili's younger siblings squeal and stumble backward. The bear rushed to the other side of the cage, slamming into the bars and nearly tipping it over. He hunkered down in the corner and eyed them warily.

Lili put a hand on the pickup fender, her eyes filled with concern. "He looks so scared."

"He is. Last night someone shot him with a tranquilizer dart, so now he's probably even more afraid of people than he usually would be."

Six-year-old Joseph pulled himself up on the back bumper. Laura grabbed the back of his belt so he wouldn't get too close to the cage. "Why'd they shoot him?" he asked.

"To make him sleep," Tamara told him, showing off her ten-year-old wisdom. "A tranquilizer is like a sleeping potion."

"So they could take him to a zoo?"

Sam glanced at Laura. She didn't know how much reality the younger Chois could handle.

Looking at her kids, Laura said, "Some bad guys wanted to take the bear to a place where some other guys could shoot him."

All three children appeared stunned by this news. Sam wondered how Laura explained legal hunting to the kids.

"Remember how Daddy got home late last night?" Laura asked. "He and Aunt Summer were catching those bad guys and rescuing this bear."

Sam basked in the glory of that statement for about ten seconds.

Joseph asked, "Can we keep him?"

"No," Sam laughed. "This is a wild bear. He needs to live in a wild place where there aren't so many people around. Laura, can I borrow Lili for an hour to help me? I'll drop her off at school afterwards."

"Oh, sweet!" Lili chirped excitedly, turning toward the house. "I'll get my backpack."

"Finish your toast and brush your teeth," Laura yelled after her, shepherding the younger children back into the house.

The two of them didn't talk much on the way to Marmot Lake. Lili kept her head turned most of the way, watching Raider through the back window. Today the girl had her hair loosely twisted up into a bun and secured with a painted Chinese chopstick, and Sam could see the lovely young woman that Lili was fast becoming. It was a little unnerving to think of all the decisions this thirteen-year-old had ahead of her. She understood why Joe and Laura would fret over the possibilities.

They'd climbed down from the truck. Sam asked, "Want to touch him?"

"Can I?" Lili's eyes gleamed.

Sam scrambled up onto the fender and swung her feet into the truck bed. Raider lunged to the far side of the cage. "I'll distract him from here. You go around in back and touch him very softly through the bars. Just with your fingers, don't put your hand into the cage."

She clasped her fingers around the bars and leaned her face close, talking loudly to cover the sound of Lili's footsteps. "Hey, Raider, my bad boy, my bear buddy, I'm so glad you're still alive. I'll bet you are, too. Ready to get out?"

The bear's ears swung forward; he looked confused. Then suddenly he lurched forward, looking back suspiciously over his flank at Lili.

"Wow," she said softly. "He's so warm. And his fur is so soft." She walked back to join Sam, sniffing her fingers. "That was so cool, Aunt Summer."

"Ready to let him go?"

Lili nodded.

Sam let down the tailgate and told her to climb up,

swing open the cage door, and stand behind it. In less than a second, Raider leapt from the pickup and disappeared, leaving them staring at the quivering greenery he'd vanished into.

"Do you know who shot him with the dart and dragged him into the cage?" Sam asked, not looking at Lili. When the girl didn't respond, she answered her own question. "A man named Garrett Ford. And a kid named Mike Martinson was helping him."

"Were they really going to let someone shoot him?"

"Yep," Sam said. "For the right price, of course."

After a mournful moment, Lili said, "Well, shit."

The Chois didn't allow their children to swear, but this situation seemed to call for it, and Sam wasn't Lili's parent, anyway. Putting an arm around the girl's shoulders, she said, "Sometimes people aren't who they pretend they are."

"Some fine boy he turned out to be." Lili's expression flitted between anger and sadness and then back to anger again.

Sam drove her to school, stopping the truck in front of the old brick building. "This is the last week of summer school, isn't it?"

Lili nodded, her hand on the door handle. "Did I say thank you for helping me with my report? I'm turning it in this morning, a whole day early. I think it's pretty good."

Sam put a hand on the girl's purple backpack to delay her a few seconds longer. "I'm proud of you and that report. You should be proud of yourself, too. Don't ever let anyone make you do something you know isn't right. Don't ever let any nutcases say that you or your family is not as good as they are."

An uncertain look crossed Lili's face. Had she lectured too much? Sam lifted her hand from the pack.

"Got it," Lili said, sliding out. "Ciao!"

Sam returned to Marmot Lake and walked the trail to the mine, envisioning her plan for a picnic area near the parking lot, a hike-in campground in the forest on the other side of the lake. If only she was going to be here to help make it happen. She stared at the crater of the Lucky Molly Mine for a few minutes. The white rose was a lump of moldy petals and leaves floating in a puddle at the bottom. In her memory, the mine would always be associated with the explosion, fire, and Lisa's death.

This morning she'd heard on the radio that another amendment to the 1872 mining law had died in Congress.

Finally, Sam made up her mind to recommend that the park service eradicate all signs of the Lucky Molly; fill in the crater and sow native plants on top of it to disguise its existence. Maybe eventually it would disappear from the USGS maps and nobody would remember it had ever been there.

"ALLIE used to complain about how old that thing was." Ernest nodded toward the computer Ranger Choi sat in front of, tapping on the keyboard with latex-covered fingers and staring at long lists of words on the screen.

They were in Allie's bedroom. Today Choi wore jeans and a flannel shirt instead of his law enforcement ranger uniform and gun. Just in case Jack or one of the other neighbors saw him, their cover story was that Choi was Ernest's AA mentor. Ernest had thought of that himself. He might have enjoyed this cloak-and-dagger business if there'd been a different reason behind it. He sank back down onto Allie's bed and stared sadly at the high school graduation photo in his hand.

"Bingo!" Choi leaned toward the monitor. "Do you know Frieda Frazier? Or an organization called Justice for Veterans?"

"No. But Allie had a lot of computer friends, and she was always trying to get the VA to do something more for me." Whereas he'd given up on the VA a decade ago, and he'd done most of his socializing with Jim Beam and Jack Daniels.

Choi started up the inkjet and printed off a couple of e-mail messages.

"You found something to show Jack's guilty?" Ernest asked. He wanted to make sure that bastard paid for getting his girl killed.

"Not directly, no." Choi picked up the printouts. "There's a message to this Frieda Frazier five months ago about getting supplies—that's probably the C-4. And then one on July twenty-second, about going out for a practice run."

"July twenty-second?"

Choi nodded. "Eleven thirty-two P.M."

"Oh, sweet Jesus." Ernest felt like his head was going to explode. He put his left hand up over his eyes.

"Are you all right, Mr. Craig?"

"Ernest," he croaked. "It's just . . ." He wiped the tears from his eyes. "She did come home that night; that proves it. I was probably passed out on the couch in front of the TV. Oh God, she was here and then she went out again and I never said good-bye."

As the printer screeched away, Choi wandered around the bedroom studying Allie's photographs, taped to the wall with cellophane.

They were beautiful pictures. He should have bought frames for them, Ernest thought, to let Allie know how proud he was of her photography. On her shelves were trophies from junior high and high school track meets. In between two brass statues was a little glow-in-the-dark angel from that church his sister and brother-in-law had introduced Allie to before they'd moved away.

He looked at Allie's high school graduation photo again. She was so beautiful, her blond hair streaming over her shoulders, her blue eyes shining and so full of hope. She'd grown up listening to everyone bad-mouth the government—especially him. He thought about all the times he'd gone along with the talk just to be sociable, all the times he'd agreed that anyone associated with the government had to be a crook. And his girl had taken it all in, and that was why she was too ashamed to tell him about her new job, the best-paying one she could find. "Oh, Allie, I didn't really mean it. I was *always* so proud of you."

He must have said it aloud, because Choi turned and glanced at him, then shifted his eyes to the printer, embarrassed. Allie's face in the photo blurred as Ernest's vision filmed with tears. He'd always thought of Rushing Springs as nowhere. The end of the world. Such a depressingly hopeless place, where everyone blamed their troubles on someone else. But now he realized that, for Allie, it had been home. It was the only world she'd ever known.

ON her last day with the park service, Sam got up early to share breakfast and good-byes with the trail crew. She and Maya exchanged phone numbers and addresses. Then she strolled around Marmot Lake, hoping to catch a glimpse of Raider. Aside from the myriad little brown birds that always flitted through the trees, she saw only a rabbit high-tailing it for the brush, and a pair of wood ducks cruising majestically across the placid water. She visited each of the defaced alders and ran her fingers over the numbers carved into their bark. She hated having to leave that mystery unsolved. Next, she cruised Garrett Ford's house and caught him carrying a garbage can to the curb. He saw her and raised his middle finger in her direction, which was exactly what she'd expected from him. Then, after a quick glance around to make sure he wasn't observed, he narrowed his eyes and drew his hand across his throat in a theatrical slashing motion, ending with his index finger pointed at her. Now *there* was an unmistakable message; maybe it *was* a good thing that this was her last day. All his imprisoned animals had been released back into the wild, and she hoped they'd stay within the safe park boundaries. She put her foot on the gas and drove out to Rialto Beach to soothe her jangled nerves.

After an hour of walking close to the crashing surf, she felt calm enough to say her good-byes to the staff of the western division headquarters. Arnie, naturally, took advantage of his bon voyage hug to give her a resounding kiss on the lips. She grabbed his earlobe and twisted until he howled, much to everyone else's amusement.

From there, she drove up to Hurricane Ridge to admire the panorama of the highest Olympic peaks. The afternoon was clear enough that she could see Vancouver Island to the north. And to the south, endless mountains and tree-lined valleys. Damn, she wanted to stay and belong in this spectacular place.

Finally, she couldn't delay it any longer. She drove down the mountain to complete her exit interview with Peter Hoyle.

"You did a good job on the management plan," Hoyle told her. Sam thought he sounded a bit grudging about it. "And thanks for finding a replacement for Blackstock on the trail crew."

Sam thanked him for his suggestions for the upcoming speech. She waited for some hint of future work. No such luck. Hoyle relieved her of her NPS identification card and the keys to the truck, shook her hand, and ushered her out the door.

"Always a bridesmaid," she muttered to herself as she tramped across the parking lot to her ancient Civic. She seemed destined to get only tantalizing tastes of interesting jobs before being dumped back out on the street.

At least she'd caught the bear poachers. Garrett Ford might be out on bail, but he'd racked up thousands of dollars in fines. His court appearance in three weeks was circled in red on her pocket calendar. Mike Martinson was also in big trouble, but he was still a juvenile. If he got a lenient judge, he might be working off his penalty on the trail crew next year.

She hated to leave with so much unresolved: Lisa's death, the missing C-4, and Lili still enmeshed in some hate group. Chase assured her that the law enforcement authorities were working on all these issues. She suspected he and Joe knew a lot of things they weren't telling her. But it was no longer her business; she'd already been shoved to the outside of the circle. Her only business right now was to work on her speech and get through her father's wedding next week.

ERNEST found it hard to believe that Tom Blackstock had been called to active duty. The guy had gray hair, for God's sake, just like him. Blackstock was fifty-one. But here he was, in uniform no less. He said his Army Reserve unit was shipping out for Afghanistan tomorrow.

"One of the summer rangers will oversee your trail work every day, but Ernest here is your new *queso grande*," Blackstock told the assembled group of teens. He punched Ernest in the arm to show they were both he-men.

Ernest punched him back, hard enough to make Tom stagger sideways, and the kids laughed. They seemed like good kids—a little tough, but basically good. He liked Maya's quiet strength and Ben's jokes. Tony acted like a hard case, but Ernest guessed he was hiding some sort of pain. Someone had to have done something awful to the kid to make him stab an old lady at age fifteen.

Tonight, after the kids got back from their work, they'd make Allie's Cheeseburger Macaroni casserole together. And a salad. And bread; those boys would probably eat half a loaf apiece. Then they'd go out back and have a campfire and roast marshmallows or, if it was raining, make brownies in the kitchen. Outdoors or in, they'd talk. He was going to pick a different subject every night. They would all say what they thought about it, and he'd set them straight when they didn't understand the truth. He'd tell them how it really was, the good and the bad. Everyone had a right to his or her opinion, but there'd be no bullshit in this cabin. Not on his watch.

25

"THE dog wouldn't stop barking, and I went out to see why. That's when I found this possum in the corner of the yard," Stephanie Faber said, carefully positioning a silver knife and spoon on a folded blue cloth napkin.

Sam set a dinner plate on the floral tablecloth. A bead of perspiration rolled from the back of her neck down between her shoulder blades, where it joined a hundred others in the swamp of her bra strap.

Her father and Zola had chosen an informal potluck for their prewedding dinner. This was déjà vu, setting tables on a sweltering summer evening with the church ladies and their kids. Except that then, she'd been one of the kids, and now, the church ladies were the girls she'd gone to high school with. She envied the easy camaraderie of the women. They all knew each other so well that they didn't need to clarify what they were talking about. They included her because she was one of them by birth, but she could no longer share in their stories. So far there'd been a discussion of how expensive school supplies were now and whether or not an elderly woman who was ill would appreciate them cleaning her house or be insulted by the gesture.

"When I looked close, I could see that the possum was giving birth," Stephanie continued.

Sam was jealous. She'd like to be off somewhere watching an opossum in labor. Opossums gave birth to half-formed babies that crawled into their mothers' abdominal pockets to complete their development. Or did the mama opossums somehow move them there? However it happened, *that* would be something to see.

"Madison," Stephanie directed her preteen daughter by her side, "the napkin?" She nodded at the proper place beside the next plate.

"Was John home?" asked Zola's daughter Julie, simultaneously with Cathy Wakebutter's prompt of "So what did you do, Steph?"

Stephanie continued, "The dog wouldn't be quiet, and John wasn't home, so I got a shovel from the garage and started beating on the possum."

"What?" Sam stopped in mid-table setting, half a stack of plates cradled in her arms.

The three women and the little girl all stared at her, surprised by her outburst.

"Is *that* what you're teaching your children? To beat innocent creatures to death with shovels?" Sam glared at Stephanie.

Madison glanced from her mother to Sam, back to her mother, and then back to Sam again, as if she were following volleys in a tennis match.

"Summer." Her father materialized out of the sweltering background to take the plates from her. "Zola needs you inside."

Sam stalked toward the house, fuming, trying not to clomp in her new sandals. She was wearing the coolest of her three dresses, a flowered sundress that she'd bought in her college days. She'd worn it on previous visits, but hoped that her high school chums wouldn't remember.

A drip of sweat slithered down in front of her left ear. She hadn't been this hot since the forest fire, or this uncomfortable since she'd sat in the hospital with Lisa Glass. She'd arrived the day before yesterday, and already her head throbbed as if a migraine were settling in for the next decade.

Last night one of her father's friends had commented on how remarkable it was for Sam to work as a ranger at her age. This morning her father and Zola took her to breakfast at the Red Roof Café, where, naturally, everyone stopped by their table to share news and say hello. One farmer commented on the numbers of Toyota Priuses passing through town, laughing about an invasion of Californians. But then, thankfully, Zola's nephew said, "Maybe a hybrid's a good deal now that gas prices are skyrocketing. The cost of filling a pickup's almost enough to give a man a stroke."

They all commiserated on that. They also remarked on the tragic death of the local boy whose Army portrait hung in the front window, but agreed that it was a good thing to fight the terrorists in the Middle East instead of here. Sam had kept her jaws firmly clamped together, determined not to advertise her alien mind-set. But now she'd gone and blown it with her opossum comment.

Letting herself into the kitchen through the screen door, she leaned against the food-laden counter for a minute, taking a deep breath.

Zola entered, her newly silvered curls gleaming softly under the kitchen lights. "Enjoying yourself, dear?"

Was her father's fiancée being sarcastic? Sam couldn't tell. "The table is just about ready. Dad said you needed me?"

"I want to show you something before we sit down to eat, Summer." Taking her by the hand, Zola pulled her toward her father's study.

The air held the welcome chill of the air conditioner, which had been on until half an hour ago, when the locals decided it had cooled off enough to be pleasant. Her father's oak desk still faced the window that overlooked the river, although the desk now sported a computer. The bookcases to the side seemed unchanged, still full of philosophy texts, various versions of the Bible, history books, and classical literature.

The unexpected addition was a man in a lightweight sport coat and khaki trousers. He stood with his back to her, staring at a photo on the wall.

"These are incredible." Turning toward her, Chase Perez held out a hand as if they were in mid-conversation.

Behind her, Zola murmured, "Surprise!"

Sam closed her mouth and swiveled to smile at the older

woman, then turned back to Chase and took his outstretched hand in hers. He reeled her into his arms and
planted a breath-stopping kiss on her lips.

While she was getting used to his abrupt appearances in
Washington State, she was positively shocked to find him
here on her native rural soil. But she couldn't have been
more delighted. She hungrily kissed him back. "What are
you doing here?"

"I was invited." He nodded toward Zola, who still stood
behind her. "Thank you."

"Our pleasure." Zola beamed.

"But how did you know?" Sam asked her.

"Blake told us," she responded. "We invited him, too."

"He sends his regrets," Chase said.

Sam was pretty sure that her housemate had few regrets
about turning down the invitation to face a conservative
church crowd. Her father's church was hardly fundamentalist, but there would still be plenty of disapproving
frowns and behind-the-hands whispers if an openly gay
man attended. Blake had shared several phone conversations with her father, and later reported that Reverend Westin had hope that Blake would eventually understand God's
love. Which Blake chose to interpret as meaning that he
was not worthy of God's love in his current form, and
which Sam chose to ignore completely.

"Well, I'll leave you two for a bit," Zola said. "Dinner in
ten minutes." She vanished through the doorway.

Chase put his arms around her again. "Surprised?"

"Astonished." She hugged him tightly. He smelled
faintly spicy. "I'm *so* glad you're here. You can keep me out
of trouble." She rose on her tiptoes for another kiss.

"Like I've been able to do that so far." He kissed her,
then turned back toward the wall. "I'm learning all your
secrets."

Perplexed, she followed his gaze and was astounded to
see that in place of the serene landscapes she remembered
were photos of herself. As a toddler with her mother, taken
when Susan Westin could still sit upright; herself as a

young girl in Easter dress and beribboned blond pigtails; as a slender teen in bell-bottoms and halter top; as a high school graduate in cap and gown.

"This is my favorite." Chase pointed to a photo of her in a tall-grassed pasture, the sun shining though her curtain of straight blond hair as she leaned forward to plant a kiss on the outstretched muzzle of a pinto gelding. Her grandparents had given her the horse for her tenth birthday, a few months after the death of her mother.

"Comanche." Sam raised her hand to the photo. Her throat tightened, even after all these years, at the sight of the gelding. She'd loved that ornery old red-and-white horse like nothing else, and had felt so guilty when she left for college and had to give him to a neighbor girl.

Despite Chase's outwardly calm demeanor, tension radiated from him in waves. She could practically feel him vibrating. "Why are you *really* here, FBI?"

"For you, *querida*." He ran a finger down her cheek. "I have something to tell you."

Zola peeked in through the doorway. "Dinner, you two."

"Later," Chase whispered before he turned away. "This is a lovely room, Zola."

"I can't believe this." Sam gestured to the wall. "I've never seen some of these."

"Your father had all those photos squirreled away in his desk drawers for as long as I can remember. I thought it was about time they got framed before he wore them out with all his fingerprints. C'mon. Food's on the table now."

Sam fretted all the way to the table about how to introduce Chase. What would her father's colleagues and her old high school cohorts make of her lover? She finally settled on saying simply, "This is Chase Perez."

She needn't have worried about anything more, because as usual Chase took charge of the situation, charming all the ladies present, complimenting their cooking, and answering questions about the FBI.

Several of the husbands present exchanged steely glances. One asked if Perez was a Mexican name. Chase responded with a tale about his grandfather, who had been a logger in the Sierra Madres of northern Mexico before emigrating to work in Idaho. All the women seemed thoroughly enchanted, and in the rare moments they lifted their gazes from Chase, both Stephanie and Cathy shot green-eyed glances Sam's way. Now *this* was a novel feeling, to have her old high school chums jealous of *her*.

There would be gossip at the café later, but if the church ladies accepted him, then Special Agent Starchaser Perez would be welcome. Still, Sam suspected that he might be classified more as an exotic entertainment than a regular man.

After an hour, Chase showed signs of feeling like an entertainer who was waiting for the second act to relieve him. He'd emptied his water glass twice, and kept grabbing for Sam's hand. Little Madison, sitting across the table from him, asked where his gun was.

"That's a secret," he said. "You don't need me to arrest someone, do you?"

The child giggled. Chase said, "I've hogged the conversation long enough. We're here to celebrate the upcoming wedding of Mark Westin and Zola McAfee. I've just had the pleasure of meeting them, but most of you have known them for years, and now *I'd* like to hear some stories about the two of them."

Well done, Sam thought. She spoke up. "Let's go around the table. Stephanie? Why don't you go first?"

Stephanie blushed, embarrassed to be caught with nothing to say. In Sam's opinion, it was not an adequate punishment for an opossum basher, but it was the best she could come up with at the moment.

"DAD, Zola. Chase and I are going for a drive." She stood on the front porch, one hand in Chase's.

"Now?" Her father cast a look at Zola, sitting beside him on the porch swing. "It's almost ten o'clock."

"Summer and I are still on Pacific Time," Chase countered. "It's a lovely night. And you two no doubt have lots to talk about in private."

The air had, thankfully, cooled to a mere eighty-five degrees. The warm night vibrated with the hum of locusts in the trees. At least everyone always called them locusts when Sam had grown up. Most everyone outside of Kansas called the insects cicadas.

"We'll be back in an hour or two," Sam said.

"Chase, I already made up your bed on the sofa in Mark's study," Zola told him.

His dark eyes glinted as he nodded. "Perfect. Thank you. We'll see you two in the morning."

"Church at ten," her father reminded her.

"Night," Sam called over her shoulder as she followed Chase to the driveway. Her rental car was a low-priced something-or-other manufactured somewhere in Asia. His was a sleek convertible.

"Is the FBI paying for this car?" She finger-combed her hair loose from her French braid and let her hair fly in the breeze as they rattled down the gravel road.

He grinned. "That's top secret. Where's this lake you told me about?"

She directed him for the five and a half miles of open road. Then she had to get out to open the gate across the cattle guard to let him drive into a pasture. They drove slowly through a herd of curious Hereford cows, then crested a small hill and cruised down the rough road to the lake.

The lake looked smaller than she remembered, but no less magical, shimmering among the black oaks and cottonwoods, the half-moon and stars reflected in its placid surface. Chase cut the engine and they sat, staring through the bug-encrusted windshield at the dark water. The locusts seemed even louder out here, their song a deep primal hum in the night.

"Nice," Chase said. He wiped a drip of sweat from his forehead. "Is it always this hot?"

"In August? Oh, yeah. We're lucky. It barely broke a

hundred today. Chase, you said you have something to tell me?"

"I'm working up to it. Give me a minute."

Sam rested her head on the back of the seat and stared at the sky. It was rare to see so few clouds and so many stars at her home in western Washington. In the far distance a coyote howled. She threw back her head and let out a loud *"Arrooooooooo! Yip, yip, aroooooooooooooooooo!"*

A different coyote answered, this one a little closer than the first.

"Sweetheart, is there something you need to tell me about your Kansas heritage?" Chase's face was deadpan. "Some trend that runs in your family that comes out on the night of the half-moon?"

"Sorry," she laughed. "I've been wanting to do that all day."

"And I've been wanting to do this all day." Hooking a hand behind her head, he pulled her close for a kiss. "For three weeks, actually."

His lips were hot and insistent against hers, and they clung together for a long, intense moment. Sam felt a little breathless when they parted. "Chase, I am *so* glad you're here." She started to unbutton the front of her sundress. "I'll race you."

"No fair getting a head start!" He unbuttoned the top button of his shirt, then yanked it off over his head, following it with his T-shirt, tossing them into the backseat. He'd just unbuckled his belt when she stepped out of the car, letting her dress and underwear fall to the ground in one move.

"Summer?"

She dashed across the dry grass and splashed into the lake. The water was only slightly cooler than the air, silky smooth against her skin. She waded out until the water was up to her neck, and then turned onto her back. She was floating quietly, looking at the Milky Way, when she felt his hands come up under her shoulders and buttocks. "I win," she said.

"You must have been a terror in high school." He propelled her gently through the water.

"I am the preacher's daughter; I have a reputation to uphold."

He kissed her right breast. "Feeling better?"

"Mmmmm. Cooler, anyway. That feels wonderful. But I'm not going to forget; you still haven't told me your news."

His lips moved to the other breast. Then his grip on her abruptly tightened, and his head jerked up. "What was *that*?"

"What?" Had he heard something?

"I felt something move against my ankle."

She giggled.

"Something just grabbed my toe!" He dropped her and fell back, thrashing.

She floundered into an upright position and grabbed his forearm. "Relax, Chase."

"There's something in the water with us!"

"There are all kinds of things in the water with us." She pulled him to his feet and put her arms around his waist. "Fish. They're the toe grabbers." She kissed the smooth skin between his nipples. "Frogs."

"Frogs?"

She slid her hands over his muscular buttocks. "Turtles."

"Turtles?" He tensed in her arms. "Like *snapping* turtles?"

She smiled at the nervousness in his voice. Sometimes she forgot that he'd grown up in the suburbs. "Snapping turtles are possible, city boy." She moved her hands to his shoulders. "But not likely."

"That's city *man* to you, swamp sister."

"There's nothing here that's going to hurt you. Fish, frogs, turtles—tonight we're all just creatures of the night, creatures of the lake." She pulled herself up and wrapped her legs around his waist.

"You preachers' daughters are merciless." Staggering a little on the mossy lake bottom, he carried her out onto the grass.

26

AS Chase buttoned his shirt, he caught a glimpse of something in the darkness. "Uh, Summer?"

They were in the front seat of the car, putting on their clothes. She looked over her shoulder. Four white-faced heifers stared at her from behind the convertible, their large dark eyes barely visible in the gloom. Laughing, she turned back. "Don't worry, they're curious, not carnivorous." She pointed to a button that he was pushing through a mismatched buttonhole, and he huffed in exasperation and yanked it out again. "When do you have to go back to Salt Lake, Chase?"

"I leave tomorrow at two P.M.," he said. "But I'll be in Seattle on Wednesday."

"You're coming back to Seattle?" Yes! That was a lot sooner than she'd expected. "Another task force conference?"

"I need to be at the Western Wildlife Conference on Friday."

Uh-oh. Was this what he'd come to tell her? He probably thought it would be a pleasant surprise. But she really didn't want him to watch her give her speech. More than likely, she'd make a fool out of herself. She cupped his face in her hands, looked into his deep brown eyes. "Chase, that's really sweet, but you don't need to—"

"Oh, I do." Picking up her hair elastic, he motioned for her to turn around in the seat. Then he ran his fingers through her damp hair, pulling it back to the crown of her head and starting to braid it. She didn't want to think about how he'd learned to weave a French braid; hopefully it was from his sister and not a long string of girlfriends.

More of the cattle herd had gathered around the car now. She was starting to feel a little self-conscious; she'd forgotten how silly one could feel with a rapt bovine audience.

Chase's supple fingers stroking her scalp felt heavenly; it was hard to concentrate on what she wanted to say. "I'm flattered that you want to come, *querido*, but I'm not sure I want you in the audience. It might make me nervous. I mean, more nervous."

"I'll be backstage. But you won't see me. Because you won't be there."

"Of course I will; I'm the keynote speaker."

He snapped the elastic onto the end of her braid. "Summer, we found a list."

She turned to face him. "A list?"

"Frazier was the key."

"That scrap of paper in Lisa Glass's Bible?"

"You mean Allyson Craig's Bible."

She blinked at him for a second. "Are you telling me that Allie Craig and Lisa Glass are—were—the same person?"

He nodded. "Looks like Allyson took the trail crew job to make some money. She didn't want anyone to know she was working for the government."

"Oh, no. Who's going to tell her poor father?"

"He found out at Lisa's memorial service. He came to us. To your friend Joe, actually. He thought his daughter had been murdered by her boyfriend, Jack Winner. But it looks like her death was an accident."

"It was the C-4, right? They blew open the mine." She knew that Lisa—Allyson—hadn't been telling the whole truth about that night.

He nodded again. "Allyson must have been in the wrong spot at the wrong time. That branch that the rangers picked up? One side had Allyson's blood on it; the other had explosive residue—it had to have been lying on top of the mine crater at the time, and then was propelled by the explosion."

"But the fire?"

"It was probably set to cover up evidence of the explosion. Either her cohorts thought Allyson was dead, or wanted to make sure she did die. In either case, they left her there."

"That's so . . . cold." Poor Lisa; what could she have thought on waking up all alone? "Why didn't anyone come to see her in the hospital?"

"Get this: they never knew it was Allyson. The newspaper only mentioned a park service employee."

"And her ID said she was Lisa Glass."

"And Allyson was a member of the Patriot Order—the P.O.b. note in her Bible referred to a Patriot Order branch, not to a post office box. The Patriot Order is an antigovernment group. None of her friends would think to look for her among park employees."

The girl's tattoo, her accusation of a big-nosed Jew. "Is the Patriot Order a white supremacist group, too?"

"Parts of it have that tendency, yes. Looks like the skinheads have joined forces with the old militia movement."

In the hospital, Lisa—Allyson—seemed so vulnerable. So sweet. It just went to show: you could never know what was going on another person's mind. She'd felt sorry for this terrorist-in-training? A dark thought suddenly leapt to mind. "Oh jeez, is Allyson's father part of this Patriot Order, too? I got him a job with the trail crew—"

Chase shook his head. "Ernest Craig had no idea what his daughter was up to."

"That poor man." Sam's head was spinning. The cows, lured by their quiet conversation, had moved closer now. She could hear one chewing its cud near the right rear fender. "You said Frazier was the key?"

"Frieda Frazier was an Internet friend of Allie's. Head of a group called Justice for Veterans. Its mission is to put pressure on the government to take care of veterans' health and unemployment problems."

Ernest Craig's limp immediately came to mind. "That sounds worthwhile," Sam said. Maybe Lisa—Allyson—wasn't quite the terrorist Chase was making her out to be.

"Except that the group's idea of pressure isn't merely political. Frazier was also a leader in the Patriot Order, and it looks like she and Allie were hatching a scheme to blow up the VA building in Seattle."

Sam twisted to study Chase, and the closest cow shied back with a snort. "*This* is what you've been working on? I thought you and Nicole were assigned to those robberies."

He popped open the glove compartment and yanked out a piece of paper, turned on the light on the bottom of the rearview mirror. "We matched the fingerprints of one of our armed robbers to a security guard at a warehouse in Carbonado, Wyoming. We found this in a recycle bin there."

Judging by the faint lines that ran vertically down the photocopy, the original had been shredded and then pasted together again. It was a table of letters and numbers, labeled EMINENTEN GRANTS at the top.

"Grants?" she asked. "Is this some sort of scholarship list?"

He chuckled. "I guess you could say that. The money from the robberies is meant for the payouts."

"Payouts? What for?"

"You'll see."

The columns on the page were headed by the letters *B*, *T*, and *O*. The squares under *B* were filled with numbers; those under *T* and *O* contained letters.

B? *T*? *O*? Only the letters in the *O* column looked remotely familiar—IRS, SSA, NOAA, USFWS . . . "What is this?" she asked. "A list of government organizations?"

"Check out the row with NPS in the last column."

She read the row backward. A heifer crowded her side of the car again; the animal's breath was hot on the back of her neck. It felt as if the cow were reading over her shoulder. "*O*—NPS. *T*—SW." She looked up at him. "*O*, Organization. What does *T* stand for?"

"We think it stands for 'Target.'"

She stared at him, open-mouthed. He answered her unasked question. "And we believe SW stands for Summer Westin."

27

"BUT I'm *not* part of the National Park Service. I was just a temp. Again." The heifer at her elbow blew a puff of warm air as if to emphasize the point.

"Apparently they don't know that."

The locusts, receiving some silent, invisible signal, began to hum again from the nearby stand of cottonwoods. "What happened to blowing up the VA building?"

"That was Allyson's plan. Guess the plan changed after she died."

It's not yet time. Her stomach did an odd little flip-flop.

"These are huge organizations. It took a long time to link these initials with dates and come up with names of individuals." Chase pointed at the letters next to IRS. "RO is Robert Orso. After thirty-five years of service, the IRS office in San Diego is giving him a retirement party on August twenty-eighth." His index finger moved down a couple of squares. "Natalie Seger is the public affairs officer for the U.S. Marshals service in Atlanta. She's hosting a medal ceremony on August twenty-eighth. Ralph Guze is a customs inspector. As far as we know, he'll be at work on Friday, on the docks in Baltimore."

She stared at him in horror. "The number we found on the tree—eight-one-two-eight? It's not eight-one, is it? It's eight-slash, as in forward slash, as in August twenty-eight. Eminent-ten," she gasped. "How cleverly obscure. An eminent man could also be called an august man, although that usage is pretty archaic; ten is two plus eight. August twenty-eight."

"Too bad you weren't on our team earlier," he said. "It took Nicole and me a long time to figure that one out."

August 28 was the opening day of the conference. The date of her speech. The date that had been grouped with the number 14 and the anniversary of Waco and Oklahoma City. The locusts seemed to reverberate inside of her skull instead of singing from the trees. "There must be close to a hundred people on this list."

"Exactly one hundred. There were references to a hundred points of light in some e-mails. *B* probably stands for branch; we've been calling them cells. This appears to be a coordinated event, scheduled to happen on the same day all over the country."

Unbelievable. She was holding a domestic terrorist hit list. And her initials were on it. She slid the sheet of paper onto the dashboard and wiped her sweaty palms on the front of her dress. Thank God the FBI had figured it out before it happened. "But now you know, so you can stop it. You have your robbers, right?"

"Not yet." He took her hand and looked deep into her eyes. It might have been a romantic gesture except for the grim set of his mouth. "We know who they are, and now we know what they're funding. It looks like each branch that pulls off a hit will get fifty thousand dollars. We've identified most of the intended victims on this list."

Most? She swallowed hard.

"We've got agents all over the country working on this. We'll know all the targets by the twenty-eighth."

"Good," she said. "You'll have everyone rounded up before then."

"Here's the hard part." His grip tightened on her fingers. "We'll know the targets—and they will have protection— but we don't know all the perps. We're not arresting anyone until the twenty-eighth."

She turned to him, incredulous.

"This is our big chance, Summer. We've never had an opportunity like this to expose a nationwide terrorist network in one sweep." His eyes gleamed with excitement.

"We can't afford to alarm anyone. We need to catch them in the act so we can put them all away for good. Otherwise a bunch of them will get only a slap on the hand for weapons charges and they'll go underground again."

Her lips were dry, and she had to lick them before she could speak. "So all of us—targets—we have to do whatever we're scheduled to do on August twenty-eighth." She had a sudden ridiculous thought of forming a support group for terrorist targets. It would be nice to meet Robert and Natalie and Ralph. Before the twenty-eighth. Just in case.

"That's why you won't be at the conference. We're searching for a lookalike stand-in now."

"To give my speech?" She thought about it. "That won't work. Where are you going to find a gorgeous five-foot-two blond, buff woman like me?" She held up her arms and flexed her biceps.

"Summer . . ." He shook his head. "I can't . . ."

"They know me. You have no choice. They *picked* me." She smiled stiffly. "I feel so special. I bet the others do, too."

He didn't smile back. "We're pretty sure that we know who is after you, Summer—at least, we know two of them: Jack Winner and Philip King."

How long had they been watching her? Had they been the shooters at Marmot Lake? "I have to do it," she said. "The odds are they know me on sight. You'll keep me safe. Right?"

He nodded, his face grim now. "We'll do our best. But I'm still looking for that stand-in."

"No. If I don't show up, they might choose another target." He didn't disagree.

"Why did they pick me? Just because I gave Winner's truck license to the rangers?"

Two cows stood near the passenger door now, chewing their endless green gum, waiting to see what the denouement of this drama might be. Another stood not far away from Chase's door. Several had quietly moved in front of the car, down to the water's edge.

"You've been on television in NPS uniform, you're going to stand up in front of a big government audience and talk about endangered species, another sore point with the anti-government crowd. This whole project is designed to make a statement—I don't think there's anything personal involved."

"Well, that makes me feel a lot better." She frowned. "Philip King—Joe told me that he has a record of violence."

Chase nodded. "We found his fingerprint on Caitlin Knight's belt buckle."

A chill prickled across the back of her neck. King's print on the murdered game warden's belt buckle most likely meant that he'd raped her before he shot her. Or after. Sam struggled unsuccessfully to wipe the awful image from her imagination. "So you have enough evidence to put him away?" *Please tell me he's already behind bars.*

He nodded again. "We have the evidence but we don't want to grab him yet. That might cancel their big plans."

Their big plans to kill her. The new knowledge that the FBI let known murderers wander around free gave her chills. Sam listened to the cows slurping water and stared beyond them at the shimmering lake, wondering what else her government was pretending ignorance of.

Chase raised an eyebrow and jerked his thumb over his shoulder, calling her attention to the cows that crowded his door.

"Ignore them," she told him. "They're just being cows."

"Weird." He twisted in his seat to stare back at them. With a flurry of hoof clops, they backed up.

She thought about the unkind stares she'd received in Forks. "How many people in Washington State belong to this Patriot Order?" she asked.

Lili's "club" must have some sort of link to it, but it couldn't be too overt or Lili would never have fallen for it. Were the other government employees safe? She couldn't stand the thought of anything happening to Joe. Or Mack. Jodi. Peter Hoyle. Even Arnie Cole. "Why didn't you and Joe tell me?"

"We didn't piece it all together until two days ago. And like I said, we want them to think they're getting away with it."

What else hadn't he told her? "So how are they planning

to get me?" She couldn't bring herself to say the word *kill*. "The C-4?"

He winced. "Maybe, but that was Allyson's plan, so it might be something else. We're still working on that."

We're still working on that? The words didn't exactly inspire confidence. And sure, the FBI knew Winner and King, but how many others were out there? The Bureau had figured out the Oklahoma City bombing only after the fact. Then there was 9/11. She swallowed hard. How had her throat become so dry? She believed that Chase would do his utmost to keep her safe, but her trust in the efficiency of government organizations was near zero.

Two heifers still stood beside her door, their liquid eyes fixed on her and Chase. They belched fermented grass, their constant chewing interrupted only by an occasional tail swish. Sam Westin, an underemployed nature writer, the target of a group of antigovernment terrorists? It seemed too far-fetched to be true. She was pretty sure that was the cows' opinion, too.

"I'll be there, *mi corazón*. And there'll be others. We won't let anything happen to you."

He'd given in pretty quickly to her demand to speak at the conference. They both knew it was the only strategy that made sense. She pulled one of her hands free from his and put it on his cheek. "Can you make them like my speech?"

"Want us to wave our guns and demand applause?"

"I'll let you know." She sighed. "And now, I suppose, we have to go back and pretend that none of this is happening."

"Right." Putting his hand on the car key, he gazed at the herd surrounding the car, and then gave her a questioning look.

She rolled her eyes. "Move it!" she yelled, banging the side of the car with her open palm. The cattle snorted, wheeled around, and disappeared into the darkness. She wanted to disappear with them.

28

THE church was almost exactly as she remembered it. The same oak pews, polished to a smooth gloss by decades of skirts and pants. The same three stained glass windows up front, depicting the wise men visiting Jesus in the manger, Jesus healing the sick, and her favorite, Jesus surrounded by children and animals. She'd spent hours staring at that one, wishing she could get animals to come to her by raising her hand that way.

She was glad to have Chase's hand to hold, to feel his strength sitting beside her. The flooring, she realized as she studied its pattern beneath her taupe pumps, had been replaced since her last visit. And she couldn't recall the pulpit behind which her father now stood. It was a lovely honey-hued oak with a cross on the front and carved tendrils of leaves and grapes twining up the sides, and the book rest at just the right height for him.

Her father looked confident and handsome this morning, his silver hair still bearing the marks of his comb, his tanned face beaming at the crowd. His congregation. The organ music died down and the crowd hushed, expectant.

"Today," he said, "we're going to have a wedding. My wedding. I'm so happy to have you all here to celebrate with Zola and me, and I'm thrilled that my good friend, Reverend Martin Heath from First Methodist in Clear Lake, will officiate." He nodded toward a suited man in the front row.

"But first, my thoughts for the day, otherwise known as the sermon. Today's will be short." He looked down at his notes on the pulpit, waited for a beat, and then asked, "Why did God give Man dominion over the Earth?"

Oh no. Chase glanced her way. Had the words actually come out of her mouth? She leaned toward him and whispered, "If smoke pours out of my ears, please drag me outside before my head explodes."

He nodded solemnly, but she could see a glint of amusement in his dark eyes.

"Today's scripture reading is from the book of Genesis," her father said. " 'So God created the great creatures of the sea and every living and moving thing with which the water teems, according to their kinds, and every winged bird according to its kind. And God saw that it was good. God made the wild animals according to their kinds, the livestock according to their kinds, and all the creatures that move along the ground according to their kinds. And God saw that it was good.' "

"In Psalms, it says, 'The earth is the Lord's, and everything in it, the world, and all who live in it.' And God says, 'every animal of the forest is mine . . . I know every bird in the mountains, and the creatures of the field are mine . . . the world is mine, and all that is in it.' "

He looked up at the congregation. "Sounds to me like God has staked a claim to wildlife, doesn't it?"

A murmur ran around the sanctuary. Sam waited for a Biblical verse that could be interpreted as divine permission to flatten opossums with shovels.

"What, then, are we to make of this next passage from Genesis? 'God said to them, be fruitful, and multiply, and replenish the earth, and subdue it and have dominion over the fish of the sea, and over the fowl of the air, and over every living thing that moves upon the earth.' And another from Psalms: 'You made him a little lower than the heavenly beings and crowned him with glory and honor. You made him ruler over the works of your hands; you put everything under his feet: all flocks and herds, and the beasts of the field, the birds of the air, and the fish of the sea, all that swim the paths of the seas.' "

" 'Under his feet,' " he reiterated, "meaning under humanity's feet. So, *we* are the rulers over the creatures of the Earth."

Sam cringed inside. She'd often been accused of caring more about animals than people, and for the most part, that was true.

"We have the power of life and death over all other living things on this planet. But why did God create all this beauty and entrust it to our care? Did He want us to use it only for our own benefit?"

Reverend Mark Westin knew how to use silence. He paused a long minute to let the audience ponder the question. Sam was surprised at the direction the sermon was taking. She'd grown up among a lot of farmers who thought uncultivated land was wasted land and all wild animals were varmints.

"In Revelation, there is a promise of destruction for those who destroy the earth. We would do well to remember that promise."

"We live in a wondrous universe, on a beautiful planet. Let us not forget that as well as flowers and trees and fruit and human beings, God created hummingbirds and grizzly bears and wolves and blue whales . . ."

And opossums, Sam added in her head.

"And God called all His living creatures 'good.' God gave us the gift of love. So let us celebrate His works by appreciating the beauty and the worth of the living world around us; by loving and caring for each other and loving and caring for all His creations, each and every day. Let us pray."

As her father raised his head after the short prayer, he caught Sam's gaze, and they exchanged a smile. The sermon was his gift to her. "And now," he said, "let's have that loving wedding so we can start caring for some of Stephanie Faber's incredible fried chicken."

The congregation laughed and clapped as Mark Westin gestured for his colleague to take his place and stepped down from the pulpit. He pulled off his robe, revealing a white tuxedo, and took his place on the right side of the aisle, gesturing for his close friend Gavin to stand beside him as best man.

Sam stood up. "Break a leg," Chase whispered.

She grimaced. "Gee, thanks. I probably will."

"You look wonderful. And the shoes are perfect."

She made a face at him, then walked quickly up the side aisle to the back of the church. Peeking through the sanctuary doorway, she saw Zola, in a lovely ivory linen suit, waiting in the reception hall, flanked by her twin daughters, Jane and Julie, who wore dresses identical to Sam's turquoise sheath, except that Jane's was a shade lighter, and Julie's paler still.

Jane handed Sam her small bouquet of yellow and white roses.

"Ready?" Sam asked.

All three nodded. She centered herself in the doorway, took a deep breath, and signaled the organist to begin.

As she slow-stepped down the aisle in time to the music, Sam felt like a trick pony in a show. Why did people do this to themselves? She felt a slick of self-conscious perspiration forming between her skin and the dress. She raised her chin and focused on her father waiting up front, but she could feel the burning gaze of the entire community assessing her.

How was she going to give a speech in front of hundreds of people? Or would it be thousands? Would she know that she was safe by then, or would she be waiting to see the glint of a weapon in the audience? By the time she reached the front of the church, she was wondering where she could score some Valium before Friday. She turned to watch Julie and Jane and Zola finish their march.

The ceremony was simple but heartfelt, statements of love by people who'd known each other for decades. Sam's mother had died twenty-eight years ago. Her father had known Zola forever, along with her husband, Bill, who had died seven years ago. Mark Westin had waited a long time to find happiness with another woman.

When Sam joined the crowd outside in the heat, Jane and Julie swooped down on her, giving her hugs and introducing her to their children, who had been absent from dinner the night before. "We're sisters now," Julie told her.

At age thirty-seven, Sam hadn't imagined that her father's marriage would expand *her* circle of relationships, and she certainly had never dreamed that anyone would consider her a sibling. She found herself inviting them to visit her at home.

"We wish we could be there for your big speech," Jane said.

Sam scoffed in surprise. "No, you don't. It'll be pretty boring." *Oh, and there is a chance that I'll be killed.*

Zola pressed a small flat box into Sam's hands. "Bridesmaid's gift. Open it later."

Sam blushed. "I believe I'm supposed to give you gifts."

"And you have, dear, just by being here." She gave Sam a hug. "I'm thrilled to have another daughter."

"Everyone really likes Chase," Jane said.

Sam followed her gaze and spied Chase chatting with Julie's husband, the visiting minister. She knew they hoped for an explanation about who Chase was to her, or—God forbid—some sort of announcement about their future together. That was as much a mystery to her as it was to her new relatives.

29

ON the plane home, Sam opened Zola's gift and immediately burst into tears, much to the consternation of the plump woman in the next seat.

"Why are you crying, honey? I think it's beautiful." She gently touched a painted fingernail to the embroidered quilt block on Sam's lap. "Is that a mountain lion?"

"Yes," Sam said. "I think it's beautiful, too." Zola had stitched a scene of a woman carrying a small child through a canyon. On the cliff above was the silhouette of a cougar against the setting sun.

"There must be a story behind this." Her neighbor studied Sam for a few seconds, and then grabbed her forearm. "I saw you on TV, a few weeks ago! You're that woman who went after that kid in Utah, when everyone else was saying that the cougars killed him."

Sam nodded. If she hadn't been belted in, she might have hugged the woman for saying it that way. Some people remembered little Zack Fischer disappearing, and others remembered that she'd protested shooting the cougars, but not many remembered that it had all happened in the same incident.

She hoped that her conference speech would not also make the headline news.

THE day before her speech, Sam approached the conference center, her nerves on fire. Was this what death row inmates felt like on their way to the electric chair? Her skin felt crawly, like someone was watching her. Her instincts were not wrong. Clearly, someone observed her approach from the parking lot, because Nicole Boudreaux arrived at the entrance door at the same time she did. Sam was surprised to see Chase's auburn-haired partner instead of him, and even more surprised to see Nicole wearing a badge that said FACILITIES COORDINATOR. Following Nicole's lead, she shook hands and they introduced themselves as if they were meeting for the first time.

Just inside the door, an armed guard was posted at a sign-in station. Was that standard procedure for all conference setups or something special the FBI had arranged? The guard copied the information from Sam's driver's license, and when Nicole explained that Sam was with her, he noted that, too.

While she had been in Kansas, the conference schedule arrived in her mailbox, complete with a four-color ad on the back that said, *Take It to* The Edge: *Your Source for High Adventure and Luxury Travel*. In her experience, high adventure and luxury rarely went together. Luxury implied comfortable surroundings and gourmet food, didn't it? She'd found that high adventure was most often accompanied by falling rocks or sucking mud or, occasionally, terrifying torrents of water. And if there'd been any food at all on her adventures, it had been only an antique protein bar or a strip of tough jerky.

Nicole walked with Sam down echoing, highly polished hallways to lecture room A, which turned out to be the largest. The number of chairs already arrayed in rows around the room made Sam's chest tighten with anxiety. On the left side of the room, several workers were unfolding even more. On stage, a man in coveralls glanced at them briefly over his shoulder before he went back to attaching a horizontal brass cylinder to the front of the podium.

A tiny stand, a huge expanse of stage. Could she really stand up there and deliver a performance tomorrow with any shred of grace? Her speaking skills were untested. And then there was...that other little problem. That someone planned to kill her.

The lectern looked so lonely, so exposed. Her throat felt tight and dry. She wouldn't have an attack of desert mouth tomorrow, would she? God forbid.

"Is everything all right?" she whispered to Nicole.

"It will be."

Not the response she was hoping for. "Where's Chase?"

"It's important that you're not seen together," Nicole said, her voice a soft murmur Sam had to strain to hear. "We're filming everything and everyone." Nicole's gaze flitted suggestively to the projection room over their heads, and Sam looked up briefly, but saw only a dark window.

"I don't see anything." Taking the cue, she kept her voice low.

"With luck, neither does anyone else."

"Have you noticed anything suspicious so far?"

Nicole's expression was frustrated. "No."

Sam sighed. "Maybe it's all a big hoax."

"We can't assume that, Summer."

Sam looked around at the various workers in the room. "Shouldn't you be doing more than just filming?"

"After everything is set up and everyone's out, we'll do a complete sweep for explosives and hidden weapons."

Sam's heart hammered with the realization that she could be in the same room with a bomb or a hidden cache of guns. Her gaze flicked nervously around the room. The fat guy taping down a cable looked legit, but wouldn't they all? The guy fiddling with the lectern on stage tossed another glance at them over his shoulder. Sam tensed.

Nicole touched her arm gently. "Loosen up. You look scared to death."

"That's because I *am* scared to death."

"Well, try not to look it. What are you wearing tomorrow?"

Why did Nicole care what she wore? Richard Best had wanted her to don a signature TAKE IT TO THE EDGE!

T-shirt, but she'd drawn the line there. They might be paying her to expose herself in front of a giant audience, but she had to preserve some personal dignity. "Pants, silk blouse, jacket," she said.

"The jacket's good," Nicole replied. "Make sure your blouse is loose enough for the Kevlar vest."

"What?" Sam squeaked. The other woman tightened the grip on her arm in warning, so Sam said in a quieter voice, "You're not exactly inspiring confidence, Nicole."

Nicole tucked a wing of shining auburn hair behind her ear. "We plan for all contingencies."

In that case, Sam thought, she should wear a helmet or demand a bulletproof shield like the Pope used. She was short enough that most of her body would be hidden behind the podium, but wouldn't her silver-blond hair make a nice bright target under the lights?

Sam gestured toward the stage. "Can I go up?"

Nicole nodded. "Let's do it."

As they walked up the steps onto the stage, the man on stage jerked a cord, unfurling the banner from the cylinder he'd attached to the front of the podium. Green and white silk proclaimed, THE EDGE PRESENTS SUMMER "WILD WEST" WESTIN. TAKE IT TO THE EDGE!

"Oh, crap," she groaned. "I'm going to kill Best. Can you take that thing down?"

The worker shook his head. "I just got it attached, like my boss told me to do. But it rolls back up." He demonstrated by pulling the cord again, and the offensive banner disappeared into the brass cylinder. "So it'll only show when this Wild West person is up here."

"Wonderful," she said wryly.

While Nicole inspected the wings, her heels clicking across the polished floor, Sam positioned herself in back of the podium and looked out at the vast room. She already felt nauseous, even though the place was empty. Tomorrow, she'd probably faint. She rested her arms along the podium's edges, trying to find a comfortable position.

Anyone in any of those chairs would have a good, clear

shot at her head. Chase would never let that happen. Right? She couldn't help remembering all the times she'd prayed for a shining knight to gallop up and save her. It never happened. Not once. But this time her knight was not alone, she reminded herself; he came with a whole contingent of armed personnel from the U.S. government. The FBI would keep her safe; they'd keep everyone at the conference safe. Right?

She shifted her weight, curled one hand around the podium's mitered edge. Every stance felt awkward, yet somehow, the smooth dark wood and attached long stemmed reading light seemed familiar The sense of déjà vu was unnerving. She'd only stood behind a podium a few times in her life, and she'd certainly never touched this particular one. But—

A memory flooded her mind. She jerked her hands from the polished wood surface. "Nicole!"

Nicole approached from the left flank of the stage, her eyes brightening, one sleek eyebrow raised in a question.

"It's the podium!"

"Look out at the room," Nicole directed, whispering. "We're not alone."

Frowning, Sam followed her lead. Shit, she was lousy at this pretending business.

Leaning close, Nicole pointed up to the projection window, and then waved a hand around the room as if demonstrating its features to her. "Now tell me—softly—why you said that."

"Jack Winner owns a woodworking business. I saw a podium like this in his workshop. Actually, I saw several."

"I see." Her gaze flitted to Sam's face briefly. Then she nodded, reached over, and bent the reading light down a fraction of an inch.

"Don't touch it!" Sam hissed. "It might explode or something." Her imagination conjured up the crater of the Lucky Molly Mine. She suddenly pictured a similar hole right where she stood.

"The C-4, Nicole. The C-4 stolen from the mine over on the Peninsula." Her hands began to shake.

"I understand. Calm down." Nicole smiled and took her hand, gently pulling her toward the steps at the edge of the stage as if she were reassuring a hysterical celebrity. "Tomorrow's the big day, Summer. We'll have it all under control. If there are explosives in this room, we'll find them tonight."

Sam certainly hoped so. Now she'd scared herself so badly she was quivering like a hypothermic Chihuahua.

"Get a grip on yourself," Nicole told her in the parking lot. "And don't say anything to anyone about this." Then, raising her voice, she called, "See you tomorrow," and waved cheerily as she headed back for the building.

Sam sat in the car doing deep breathing exercises for five minutes before she felt calm enough to drive the eighty-five miles home.

FIVE hours later, she was sitting in the dark at the kitchen table, listening to her most tranquilizing Andean flute tape on her ancient Walkman and sipping her third glass of wine when Chase finally called. "You were right—the podium was packed with C-4 and a nifty little detonation device."

"Did you check them all? Did you check the seats, too?"

"Of course. But only yours was rigged. The conference schedule's been out for a couple of weeks now, so they knew which room you'd be in."

"That makes me feel *so* much better."

"It's safe now."

Was that really true? "Any sign of Jack Winner or Philip King?"

"No. We made sure the place was clear before we did our sweep. Winner's company set up the electronics in the podiums a couple of days ago; it was in the Winner Woodworking contract. They or some of their cohorts will probably show up tomorrow."

"Probably? Some of their cohorts?" His vagueness was ratcheting up her anxiety level.

"Summer, listen. This is important."

There was more to come? She took a gulp of wine.

"Are you *drinking*?"

She swallowed. "What makes you think I'm drinking?"

He sighed heavily. "Are you sober enough to remember what I tell you?"

"I'm way too sober, believe me." She thunked the wine-glass down on the tabletop. A drip splashed over the rim. She swiped at it with a finger tip.

"The explosives are gone. We replaced the detonator with a receiver in the podium, rigged up to a little red light—you'll see it at the edge of the book platform. When the receiver gets the signal to set off the bomb, the light will blink. At that point, we want you to raise your right hand and run your fingers through your hair."

"But you'll know who it is, right, Chase?" *Just in case the guy has a Plan B, like a gun in his pocket?*

"We might need confirmation. When the light blinks, raise your right hand and run your fingers through your hair. Got that?"

"Got it," she replied grimly.

"We still want you to wear the Kevlar. Be at Door F a half hour ahead of time. A female agent will be there to help you with the vest."

He seemed much more an FBI agent than a lover now. She was having a hard time remembering how safe she'd felt in his arms. "Where will you be?"

"Around. These people might have seen me with you before. We don't want them tipped off."

He was right; Winner, King, various cohorts—whoever that might be—could have seen her with him in the woods, in her truck, in the fire tower, at Mack's apartment. Seeing her with him might blow the whole deal. And it might make him a target, too. "Shit."

"You okay, *querida*?"

"I could sure use a hug." She upended her glass, filling her mouth with the last of the wine.

"That'll have to wait until tomorrow night. Sleep tight, Summer. *Te quiero.*"

She had to swallow first, so he'd already hung up by the time she got the words out. "Me, too."

Blake appeared next to the refrigerator in his pajama bottoms and T-shirt. "Did I hear a request for a hug?" He held open his arms.

"Oh jeez, yes." She hugged her housemate tight.

"Don't get too invested, Sammy," he murmured into the top of her hair. "Chase Perez is a nice guy, but he's the love 'em and leave 'em type."

She pulled back to look at Blake. "And how would you know that?"

"How many times has he breezed through here so far? How many times have you two made plans and then he didn't show up?" He tweaked a strand of her hair. "I don't want you to get hurt."

"Thanks for caring." She hugged him again. He wasn't being exactly fair. Criminals didn't work on a set schedule, so neither did Chase, and a lot of what he did was necessarily secret. But Blake had precisely named her fear. Could he read Chase better than she could?

Before falling into bed, she scribbled out a will of sorts, leaving Blake the cabin. Just in case her speech didn't end well tomorrow.

30

SAM felt like she was wearing a corset. Was the Kevlar vest too tight, or was this the crushing squeeze of anxiety? She would be murdered by terrorists, or pummeled by rotten fruit thrown by a disappointed audience. One way or another, she was sure she was going to die. And she had to sit in this chair at the edge of the stage and pretend that this was a normal day.

The conference host introduced some guy she'd never heard of, a bigwig in the Department of the Interior. As this stranger read the ridiculously overblown introduction provided by *The Edge*, she scanned the crowd. It looked like there were thousands out there. What were they hoping for? Entertainment? Enlightenment? Clothing ranged from T-shirts and jeans to suits and blazers. The men in ties were a tad overdressed for Seattle. These employees from at least a dozen government agencies had no idea that a group of thugs wanted them all dead. Or maybe, like Peter Hoyle, they were accustomed to receiving death threats, and she was the naive one.

Conservation groups were also in attendance. She recognized a face from World Wildlife Fund, another from The Nature Conservancy, and two from the Save the Wilderness Fund. A cluster of people sported Sierra Club shirts. A couple other familiar profiles were in the room, too. Wasn't that the silver brush haircut of Jerry Thompson, Superintendent of Heritage National Monument in

Utah? He looked up in that instant, met her gaze, gave her a thumbs-up.

She blushed. The summary of her exploits in his park made her sound like some kind of superhero. In fact, the introduction made her sound like an award-winning out-door adventure writer instead of a mostly unemployed one. What an imposter she was. But maybe, if she pulled this speech off, she'd become that successful writer. Assuming there was a future.

She took a deep breath, tried to relax her shoulders. Why was she doing this? She wasn't a soldier who could be court-martialed; she was free to leave. The exit door back-stage pulled at her like a magnetic field. But if she walked out, then they'd get away, at least some of them. Or maybe they'd kill someone else here. Or kill her another day. She wiped her damp palms on her pant legs.

Similar scenes were playing themselves out all over the country right now. It was 10 A.M. here on the Pacific Coast. How many murders of government personnel had already been attempted in the East? How many had succeeded? *Suck it up, Westin.* She licked her lips for the hundredth time. Her lipstick had probably disappeared fifteen minutes ago.

Up front were a couple of print reporters with cameras around their necks and pads and pens in hand. In the center aisle was a television camera on a stand, manned by a guy with a shaved head that gleamed softly under the lights. He covered a yawn with an upraised hand. She hoped he'd stay bored.

There was no station tag on the TV camera. It was probably a private operation, then; the conference was probably being taped for later distribution throughout government agencies.

In the second row, Richard Best was seated beside a young woman with a bright pink camera strap around her neck. He gave Sam two thumbs-ups and mouthed "Knock 'em dead." An unfortunate choice of words. She saw no sign of Jack Winner or Philip King. Chase had shown her multiple photos of the two men. But would she recognize either one in disguise? She doubted it. And if "one of their cohorts" had come to kill her, it could be *anyone* out there.

The bomb was gone, she reminded herself. She tried not to think about how much better the FBI was at solving crimes than at thwarting the plots in the first place. *You never hear about the crimes we succeed in preventing,* Chase had argued.

Where was Chase, anyway? She glanced toward the door backstage again. The big red EXIT light above it seemed like a command. Exit! Now!

"Please welcome Summer Westin."

The crowd clapped. Time to get it over with. She stood, amazed that her legs still obeyed her, and walked to the podium. The slick of nervous perspiration under the Kevlar was chilly against her skin. Her hands, too, were cold and damp; they stuck to the pages as she spread her notes across the dark wood. Where was the light Chase had mentioned? There, a tiny bulb in the upper left corner.

So far, so good. Still alive. She could do this. She looked up at the audience. An ocean of expectant faces.

Oh God, that bearded man at the back of the room! What was that in his hand? Something metallic, something small. Her heart hammered. The man lifted the device to his ear and pushed his way toward the door. A cell phone.

Get a grip, Westin. She released the death hold she'd taken on the podium edges, flattened her hands on top of her notes. She'd rehearsed this speech so many times, Blake had taken to wearing his iPod around the house. She could do this talk in her sleep.

Get on with it, then. Taking a deep breath, she leaned toward the microphone, and began. "I am an environmentalist."

She paused for effect, as she'd practiced. A few uncertain claps filled the void. Better than the gunshot she'd feared. She flinched as the flash of a camera went off close by, then another. Suddenly her vision was filled with blinding white. Now, when she most needed to see everything!

She forced herself to say the next lines. "Today, that statement means different things to different people. Some automatically believe I'm a noble person who seeks to protect the natural environment for the good of all . . ."

The white fog finally dissolved, revealing a man up front punching a handheld gadget! Oh God, was it Philip King? King was blond; this guy had wheat-colored hair. But this man wasn't looking at her. King would want to watch her die, wouldn't he? The guy punched more buttons, using his thumbs. A smart phone, then. A nice, normal modern phone.

She realized she wasn't breathing. Or talking. Where had she left off? Had it really been mid-sentence? They'd think she was an idiot. She *was* an idiot, a stuttering, blithering idiot. She made herself continue, "But there are others who believe that I am an enemy to be stopped, even killed."

The bulb in the corner flashed red, and her words slammed to a stop. Someone was signaling the detonator. It was really happening. Just like Chase had said it would. Her gaze swept the crowd. Shit, it could be anyone, anywhere! She raised her right hand, which now shook violently. She raked her fingers through her hair.

If the bomb was still here, she'd be dead. They really wanted her dead. The light continued to flash. She continued to comb her hair with her fingers. Where the hell was the FBI? Had something gone wrong? Please God, don't let the terrorists have a Plan B.

B for Bullet. It suddenly occurred to her that the TV camera aimed in her direction might not be *only* a video cam. She stared at it. Could a rifle be disguised as a camera? That glass lens could shatter at any moment, and the bullet would smash into her skull . . . Damn her overactive imagination! She peeled her gaze away from the camera's fixed glassy eye, forced herself to scan the audience again.

"How did we get to this point?" she said into the microphone. It was the next line in her speech, curiously appropriate right now. How in the hell had she arrived at this point in her life? She wasn't a representative of the government, for chrissakes. She wasn't a ranger. She was no longer sure what she was, other than a total wreck.

A muffled thump issued from the projection booth overhead. Glancing up, she saw a brief flash as a man hit the window. Blue jacket. Black baseball cap. Was that a pistol in his upraised hand? Several hands were smashed against the window, gripping his upraised arm, his shoulder. Then they all slid out of sight.

Was it over? Did they have the bomber?

The flashing stopped. Good. That meant they had him, didn't it? The situation was under control. She was so tired of being frightened. Quite a few of the audience were twisting in their seats, trying to get a look overhead. An ordinary-looking man appeared behind the Plexiglas. He briefly flashed what looked like a law enforcement badge and then gave her an okay signal.

She took a deep breath and smiled woodenly, trying to reassure the crowd. Just as she'd planned, the first photo appeared on the screen behind her, an old sepia-tinted photo of a lone scout on a cliff overlooking a vast territory below. Taking a deep breath, she plunged into the history of the environmental movement, beginning with John Muir

She described the constant opposition—ranchers, miners, hunters—and from the country's beginning to the current day, the rich who wanted to reserve spectacular sites for themselves. Moving into righteous anger mode now, she talked about what the West would be like today if conservationists had not succeeded in preserving federal lands. No Yellowstone, no Yosemite. A privately owned Grand Canyon? Slides appeared in succession on the screen behind her, showing mountains, deserts, rivers, and animals preserved because of the efforts of the courageous and dedicated few. She was proud that many of the slides featured were her own photos.

"Poachers. Toxic waste dumps. Smugglers. Meth labs." She ticked off a litany of dangers faced by field personnel,

knowing her list was far from complete. She named the
wildlife protection officers who had been murdered in the
line of duty just in the last two years: a BLM ranger in
Nevada; a fishing boat observer in Alaska; two NPS rangers in North Carolina and Arizona; U.S. Fish and Wildlife
Officer Caitlin Knight in Washington State. The photo editors at *The Edge* had montaged photos for this part—shown
along with photos of the victims were yellow-taped outdoor crime scenes, heaped flowers left at a makeshift
memorial, a flag flying at half-staff before a federal
building.

A buzz of appreciation rippled through the audience.
Their empathy carried her along. The final three photos
were her favorites. The two beautiful sweeping landscapes
of Heritage National Monument in Utah and Rialto Beach
on the coast of Olympic National Park flashed up behind
her. "No matter how much opposition we may face, never
let us forget: saving the environment is a noble cause.
Clean air, clean water, wildlife, and wild places are always
worth fighting for."

The warm orange glow that reached into the first rows
let her know that the final slide was up now. Against the
backdrop of her famous photo of a cougar standing on a
natural rock bridge against a flaming sunset, she con-
cluded, "We are the good guys."

The applause was loud. She was so grateful that it was
finally all over. She'd done it. She'd survived both the
speech and the assassination attempt. Her legs quivered
with relief as she walked toward the wings.

The host brushed past her on the stage en route to the
podium, and right behind him, a boy walked out of the
wings toward her, a large bouquet of lilies in his hands.
Stargazers—she could smell the strong scent two yards
away. What a nice gesture. So unexpected. Or was it common to receive flowers after a speech? It wasn't as if this
was a routine experience for her.

The delivery boy was a handsome youth, with slicked-back black hair, in white shirt and tie. "Flowers, Miss Westin." He smiled at her as he held them out.

Was she supposed to take them and bow to the audience or something? Was there a protocol she had missed? Nobody had told her what to do after she had finished talking.

The delivery boy's face seemed familiar. It took a second to place him—Rocky, Lili's mentor. How odd to see him here. The overhead lights glanced off a metallic blade in his right hand

All she managed to get out was the word "No!" before she felt a blow to her chest. She staggered backward

Then her attacker crashed facedown on the stage with Chase on top of him. The audience collectively gasped. It sounded like the building was breathing. An absurd thought, she knew. But the whole world seemed a little absurd just then. Camera bulbs flashed, as bright as fireworks. She stood alone in the spotlight, clasping a perfumed bouquet and staring with disbelief at the knife that protruded from her chest just above her heart.

31

THE host hustled Sam off-stage. Nicole removed and bagged the knife, and then unbuttoned Sam's blouse and ripped off the Velcro tabs that held the Kevlar vest in place. To Sam's surprise, there was blood above her left breast and now she felt a small stab of pain.

"Only a nick," Nicole pronounced. "Sorry. I should have tightened it up more; the blade went through the strap just above the armor." She took a bandage from the first aid kit someone produced and pressed it across the wound. "Still, you should see a doctor."

Sam could hear the anxious roar of the audience outside and the coordinator begging them to please keep their seats and not panic. "I have to go out there." She pushed away the helpful hands and rebuttoned her blouse.

When she appeared from behind the curtain, the audience hushed, then began to clap. She approached the podium and borrowed the microphone from the coordinator. "I'm okay, folks. I told you we were the good guys."

"And the good guys always win!" Richard Best shouted from the second row. "Way to take it to *The Edge*, Summer Westin!"

Blushing furiously, she told the audience, "The bad guys are in custody. You are all safe. Enjoy the conference." They clapped as she exited backstage and into Chase's waiting arms.

* * *

THE nick on her chest needed five stitches, but she was glad that it was no worse than that. Three government employees had not been so lucky—two had been killed and one was in critical condition from a gunshot wound.

"The attack was nationwide. We're not flawless," Chase said.

"Now you tell me," she groaned.

"Nicole and I are heroes. We couldn't have done it without you, *mi corazon*."

After a quick kiss, he was gone, swept back into the maelstrom of meetings and investigations. The FBI's discovery of Eminenten netted 132 antigovernment activists across the United States. More arrests would come later, Chase assured her. She tried not to think about how many had gotten away.

Sam wrote an article for *The Edge* about her experiences. It was picked up by the *Seattle Times* and thirty-two other newspapers across the country. Five conservation nonprofits called to ask about her availability for projects. While it was nice to have employment again, the offers seemed sort of anticlimactic after Eminenten.

JACK Winner stared through prison bars at the dingy hallway. The lights were out in his cell. He'd chosen the lower bunk because it was darkest, but they never turned the lights out in the hallway—how was a man supposed to sleep?

Nothing made sense anymore. The feds told him that the park service trail worker who had died was Allie. But that had to be wrong—Allie wouldn't be caught dead working for the feds. But if Lisa Glass was really Allie, then—oh, God—that fucker King had lied to him and Allie hadn't been dead when they'd started that fire. They said she'd been in the hospital for three days after. But she'd never called. No, that story had to be a trap. The feds were capable of anything; just look at Guantanamo, all those ragheads held for years without a trial—they probably fed them lies along with their beans and rice every day.

According to the papers, King had killed that game warden. That, he did believe. That sounded like King. What a waste. If there had to be killing, it should be advertised and it should be for a reason. What an incredible screwup King turned out to be. And Roddie or Rocky or whatever he called himself these days, well, he'd tried his best, but he was just a kid.

The gutless media had sidestepped the truth as usual, so now the feds looked like the good guys again, and *nothing* had changed. The government was still handing millions of dollars to thugs overseas every damn day, and every damn day hardworking Americans found it harder to put food on the table. No matter what his lawyer said, at his trial he was going to take the stand and shout the truth at the top of his lungs. Then the goddamned papers would have to print it. Maybe he'd even make the television news.

He bunched up his pillow under his head. The mattress was surprisingly comfortable, better than the one on his bed back home. The food, too, beat his own cooking. It was ironic that the feds were paying all his expenses right now.

32

FOR a month after Sam and Chase parted, she received only brief e-mail messages and voice mails from him. She tried not to worry. He was overworked, constantly traveling in multiple time zones, perhaps even overseas; it was hard to connect. When Chase finally called from Maryland, their conversation was anything but romantic, although it started off well enough.

"I miss you," he told her.

"Not as much as I miss you." She instantly relived the feel of his arms around her. Simon was a welcome warmth in her bed each night, but a cat couldn't take the place of her lover.

Then Chase went and ruined the mood.

"I found your name on a Homeland Security watch list," he said.

"What?"

"You've made donations to Greenpeace and Environmental Defense."

"Of course I have." Were the feds spending their time tracking donations of average citizens? "Did they mention World Wildlife Fund and The Nature Conservancy, too? Defenders of Wildlife?"

"And what's this about a protest at the Department of the Interior?"

She snorted. "We delivered a bunch of petitions to the National Park Service in downtown Seattle, Chase, and for once the press covered it. The administration is taking comments on the management policies for the parks. Some groups are pushing for multiuse revisions, and my conservation group wanted to squelch those suggestions."

"Didn't your protest piss off your buddies in the national parks?"

"You think they became rangers to chase dirt bikers and guard oil rigs?"

"Guess not," he sighed. "Well, *mi corazon*, you might want to cool it for a while."

"Environmentalists can't just stay in the shadows, Chase, because then the other side will win."

That statement hung in the air between them for a tense minute. What was he thinking? Was he getting heat because of his association with her? Did he want to cool their relationship for a while?

"So," she finally said, trying to lighten the tone, "will you come visit me in Guantanamo?"

"Of course, *querida*. I'll bring you a hacksaw in a key lime pie."

It was hardly the response she was hoping for.

She'd barely ended the call with Chase when the phone rang again. "Sam Westin," she answered.

A sound halfway between a sniffle and a sob floated over the airwaves.

"Hello?" Sam raised her voice. "Lili?"

A sniff. Then a female voice said, "I love it."

It wasn't Lili. "Maya?" Sam guessed. "Are you all right?"

"I love this sewing picture thing you made for me. I don't care what my foster mom says about nails, I'm hanging it on my wall."

A few days ago Sam had sent her a simple cross-stitch picture of a red-haired girl swinging a pickaxe along a trail among tall evergreens, and added the date and Maya's name. "It's called a sampler. I'm not much of a seamstress, but I'm glad you like it. How are you doing?"

"I'm good. School seems better this year." Maya paused. "Do you think maybe sometime you could teach me how to do this kind of sewing? Is it really hard?"

"If you can thread a needle and make an *X*, girl, you can do it. I'll drive down to Tacoma and show you."

"Could we do it at your place? I could come up on the train."

Let a delinquent into her house? Ex-delinquent, she corrected herself. Sometimes you had to extend a hand, even if it might get bitten off. "You can stay overnight with me and Blake and practice. You'll be a cross-stitch expert when you go back home."

"Really? I could come tomorrow."

Sam glanced at the calendar on the wall. "Maya, isn't tomorrow Thursday?"

"Yeah. The train runs every day. I checked."

"Isn't Thursday a school day?"

"Oh. Yeah. That."

"See you *Saturday*, Maya."

"Saturday's cool."

A week later, Sam explored the woods behind Marmot Lake. At the first of October, the park service had opened the area to visitors again, and she had trekked back to Olympic National Park, hoping to lay eyes on Raider. She found only a pile of bear scat, and that wasn't even fresh. Which was probably a good thing, because it meant he'd adapted to the wild and was staying away from the campground. Still, she was disappointed.

She was due at Joe and Laura's for dinner in an hour, and she needed to set up her tent first. She had just begun to snap together the frame when her cell phone howled. She pulled it from her pocket. CHOI, JOSEPH.

"Hi, Joe. Need me to bring something for dinner?"

"Lili's missing."

Sam heard the anxiety in Joe's voice. "How long has she been gone?"

"About four hours. We thought she went to Deborah's after school, but it turns out Deborah told her mother that they were coming over here. And now it's getting dark."

Sam's thoughts jumped to the worst-case scenario. The FBI had netted three members of the Patriot Order in the Forks area, but who knew how many more were out there? What if they wanted revenge? She knew Joe was thinking the same thing.

"Thanks to the mixed classes in summer school, she now knows kids who are old enough to drive," Joe fretted. "If only we'd gotten her that cell phone. Any idea where she might be?"

"Best Burgers, maybe?" It was clearly a teen hangout.

"Oh, yeah. I'll go there now."

"I'll check a few of the other places she and I went together."

"Thanks, Sam. Call me back."

Sam tried to think like a teenager in Forks. A small town famed for sexy vampires and werewolves vying for a young girl's love. Mysterious dark woods, beautiful beaches. Sam chose the most romantic place she knew of. After dashing to her car, she headed for the beach.

As she drove, her imagination ran wild. She envisioned Lili as a hit-and-run victim, lying in the drainage ditch alongside Highway 101. Lili running away with a wild older boy like Rocky. Lili kidnapped by thugs and dragged off into the woods. By the time Sam arrived at Rialto Beach, her brain had cooked up a dozen horrible scenarios.

The gate to the parking lot was closed, but there were several cars parked on the shoulder nearby, and it was easy enough to sneak over the hill to the beach hidden to the west. Sam parked and carried her binoculars to the crest of the hill. She focused on a large beach fire to the north. Then she sat down on a giant driftwood log and called Joe. "Found her, Joe—Rialto Beach. I'll wait here for you."

The tide had just passed its lowest level for the day. The surf crashed far down the steep sloping beach, leaving a shimmering wake and the pleasant rattle of stones as each wave retreated. The rhythmic motion and whispering sounds were soothing, and she wished she had set up her tent on a beach tonight instead of in the woods.

She heard a vehicle arrive and then footsteps coming in her direction. She turned on her penlight and placed it on the log next to her to mark her location. When Joe thudded into place beside her, she handed him her binoculars and pointed at the bonfire down the beach.

After a quick look, Joe said, "Let's go."

Due to the surf noise and their own revelry, the teens didn't hear Joe and Sam until they were only a few feet away. A blond girl was the first to look up. "Uh-oh," she said, "Busted."

"Got that right," Joe said. "You know that fires are illegal this close to the parking lot. And this area of the beach is closed after dark."

"Dad!" Lili whined, giving the word two syllables.

The other teens said nothing, but they all stood up, and one of the boys started kicking sand into the flames to put them out. Joe stared at the pile of wooden signs fueling the bonfire. THIS IS YOUR LAND.

"Where did you get those?" Joe asked his daughter.

Lili shrugged. Sam was willing to bet that most of the signs had come from the Marmot Lake area. She hadn't seen any today.

Joe turned and looked at her. "Sam, do you know anything about this?"

Sam hesitated. Joe was her friend and he was a concerned parent. But Lili was her friend, too, and the girl was cleaning up her mistakes. Finally, she said, "Five."

Lili pressed her lips together, stifling a smile. Deborah laughed out loud.

"Five?" Joe echoed, fuming.

"That's my story and I'm sticking to it." Sam turned and looked at the surf line. A dark shape materialized out of the foam. Seal? No, it was an otter, with a wriggling fish in its mouth. Moving silently, the lithe mammal loped up the beach and vanished into a pile of driftwood.

"Sweet," she and Lili said simultaneously.

Turn the page for a preview of
Pamela Beason's next Summer Westin Mystery . . .

UNDERCURRENTS

Coming soon from Berkley Prime Crime!

BY the time Sam finally stepped into the brilliant sunshine of the Galápagos Islands, she felt like she'd toured the entire Western Hemisphere in one day. She'd driven to Seattle in the wee hours of the morning, boarded a plane for Houston, then another for Guayaquil, and then another for Puerto Ayora. She'd barely had time to introduce herself over dinner to Dr. Daniel Kazaki before she'd fallen asleep. Now, only sixteen hours after touching down, she was preparing to jump into the Pacific Ocean with him.

She had looked forward to sun, but she wasn't quite prepared for the contrast between the Pacific Northwest and the equator. Daylight in the Galápagos was blinding, even from behind the polarized screen of her sunglasses. She blinked at the surroundings, feeling like a mole that had been suddenly unearthed. She hoped she wouldn't feel similarly exposed in the water. She'd passed her diving certification course with flying colors and had done well in the underwater photography class, too. But today was the real test.

Her first posts at Out There were due tomorrow. She had one day to pass herself off as an underwater pro, or at least not reveal herself as an inept pretender. Last night at dinner, when she told Dan that all her dives had been in the Pacific Northwest, he said ominously, "Good, then you'll have no problem with the currents here."

She studied the water around their boat. Unlike the Pacific Northwest, there were no fields of bull kelp fronds here to indicate the water's flow. "Have you explored this location before?" she asked Dan.

"Several times," he responded, without looking at her. Clad in a wet suit unzipped to the navel, neoprene sleeves tied around his waist, he leaned against the side of the cabin cruiser. Dan nibbled the end of a pen, his brow wrinkled in concentration as he studied the clipboard he held. "It's easy, great for gear checkout."

Easy. Hallelujah! She picked up her digital camera and zoomed in on him. While he did have a kind smile and a few shallow wrinkles around his hazel, almond-shaped eyes, Dr. Daniel Kazaki was in no way the gray-bearded academic she'd imagined. In fact, he was a few years younger than she was, and his muscles would have been the envy of many a high school gym class. Sam prayed that she'd be able to keep up with him.

She pressed the shutter button. Dan looked up. He pulled the pen from his mouth and frowned at the tooth marks that dented the plastic. "Bad habit. You're not putting that on the front page?"

"It's a blog. It's up to the editors where the photos go. I'm just a peon."

"Impossible. I refuse to have a peon for a partner." He grinned. "Ready to go in?"

"Almost." She checked her regulator and buoyancy control device vest—BCD for short—for the tenth time, twisted the valves on her main cylinder and emergency pony bottle to be sure they were fully open, studied the readout on her dive computer, and breathed from her safe-second mouthpiece again to assure herself that she could use it in the event her primary mouthpiece failed. It was like preparing for a space walk.

She straightened and gazed at the surroundings, trying to postpone the dive a few minutes longer. A short distance to the east, a spear of rock broke the mirror glare of the Pacific. To the north and west lay the Santa Cruz Islands and the town of Puerto Ayora, where they had slept last night.

"Zip up," Dan told her, shrugging into the sleeves of his wet suit.

Key Corporation had supplied her with a sleek black wet suit that featured neon green and yellow insets and "Get Out There" in fluorescent yellow script across her breasts. It made her look quite the dive diva, if she did say so herself. They had it fabricated just for her, so it perfectly fit her muscular five-foot-one inch frame. For a woman resigned to spending her life rolling up cuffs, the perfect fit was a rare luxury.

The air temperature had to be over ninety degrees Fahrenheit and she was not eager to enclose herself in thick neoprene. "Do we really need these wet suits?" she asked.

"You'll see." Reaching behind his back, Dan pulled up the cord attached to his zipper, stretching his wet suit tight across his upper torso. Centered in the middle of his chest was a rectangle of gray duct tape, peeling at the edges. Curious. The rest of Dan's gear looked to be in excellent shape.

Dan tugged up his hood, buckled on his fins and then reached for his tank. As he hefted the strap of his BCD over his right shoulder, Sam snapped another photo. "Marine Biologist at Work," she named it aloud.

"Save the film for the sharks."

"There's no film." She snapped the camera into its waterproof housing and mounted the lights she would need below the surface. Then she caught up with the end of his sentence. "Sharks?"

"If we're lucky, we'll see a nice big hammerhead."

Nice big hammerhead? Perched on the starboard side next to Dan, Sam reluctantly harnessed herself into her equipment and tugged on her fins. She pushed her regulator into her mouth and took a quick suck of metallic-tasting air.

Dan tethered a small handheld computer to his left wrist with a black cord, and then patted himself down, checking equipment. "Time to blast off." He looked toward the boat cabin. "Ricardo?"

A dark-skinned man in khaki shorts and a green shirt emerged. A red can of cola sweated between his callused fingers, and a pair of sunglasses perched on top of his head.

"We're going in now."

Ricardo's gaze focused on the duct tape on Dan's wet suit. "You have a rip?" He stepped forward and pulled at a loose flap of tape. "I have glue. I can fix."

"It's no big deal." Dan quickly smoothed the tape back down over the circular NPF logo Ricardo had exposed.

"N-P-F?" Ricardo pronounced it with Spanish letters, *ennay-pay-effay.*

Dan shrugged. "They gave me the wet suit. I'm a university professor."

Ricardo frowned. "Pero . . . but NPF—"

"Could you hand Sam her camera?" Dan interrupted. "We should be down less than an hour. No need to move the boat—we'll circle and come back here."

Ricardo nodded. Then he pulled his sunglasses over his eyes, cloaking his gaze. Sam recognized the mirrored lenses as a brand that gang members were killing each other for in the United States—PCBs. PCB was a hip designer, not the toxic compound found in Environmental Protection Agency cleanup sites, but the idea of poisons apparently also appealed to the gangster crowd. The glasses seemed out of place here.

It was too risky to leap into the water holding the expensive camera, and on this small boat, there was no platform to gently step off from. Sam folded the attached lights against the camera and handed it to Ricardo.

"Let's do it." Dan shoved his mouthpiece into place, pulled down his mask, and backflipped headfirst into the water.

You can do this, Westin. After a last longing look at the sunny surroundings, Sam stretched her mask strap over her French braid, then held her face mask and regulator with one hand and followed Dan's lead. The jade-green water closed above her. *One step down.* She rolled to the surface again to take the camera from Ricardo's outstretched hands, then exhaled and sank into the foreign world.

A school of silver fingerlings, scattered by her splashdown, regrouped in a swirl around her. Sunlight stabbed the water in bright beams that reflected from the pearlescent scales of the tiny fish. *Beautiful.*

She took a breath. The canned air didn't taste bad, although it was as dry as the desert. It was the sound of her breath that rattled her nerves, amplifying the intake and outflow of her own lungs like a ventilator. A vision from her childhood welled up in her imagination. *Tubes and wires and pump, breathing for a woman who was more machine than mother.* Sam willed the dreaded hospital memory away. She was not her mother, nor the nine-year-old girl watching her die. She was thirty-seven now, a strong woman on an adventure.

First rule of scuba: breathe slowly and continuously. She tried to relax and do exactly that. The glittering surface receded as she descended, pinching her nose and puffing air into her sinuses to equalize pressure in her ears. Her computer readout marked fifty feet below the surface. So far, so good. She'd been down to seventy on her training dives. Rolling to a horizontal position, she spotted Dan twenty feet below her, gliding over the coral-encrusted seafloor. She sank down to join him, remembering at the last second to add air to her BCD to prevent a crash landing.

Dan plucked a tube-shaped creature from the rock and held it out. She nodded to show she recognized the sea cucumber, one of the overfished creatures NPF was especially interested in counting.

Dan gently repositioned the animal on the rock. Another of the orange-and-white species crawled a short distance away, side by side with a pale yellow one. She watched Dan tap the count into his handheld computer.

A school of bullet-shaped silverfish, each at least a foot long, surged just ahead of them. Bigeye jacks? She'd have to look them up later in her Galápagos wildlife encyclopeıia CD. Dan held up ten fingers three times, then two fingers on his left hand.

Crap. She forgot she was supposed to be helping. Taking a quick glance at the gray blurs disappearing into the blue, she nodded, agreeing with the count. The look in Dan's eyes told her that he knew she was faking.

He pointed into the murk. Sighting along his finger, Sam spotted a dark shadow headed in their direction. *No.* She wasn't ready for a shark. As the creature approached, she concentrated on breathing slowly.

The shadow transformed into a spherical beast with wings. A turtle, flying underwater. *Whoa.* The sight was amazing. Dan returned to his examination of the ocean floor—he'd probably seen hundreds of sea turtles. Sam swam closer to the marine reptile. Its dark eyes were huge and soft, almost spaniel-like. Black spots freckled its pale green beak and neck. The turtle ignored her, gliding past with powerful thrusts of its long flippers. She took a photo with the turtle in the foreground and Dan hovering over a cluster of starfish in the background.

She finned back to Dan, who obligingly plucked a mottled red-and-white lobster from among the starfish and held it out toward the camera. As she centered his figure in the frame, his head jerked and a cloud of bubbles burst from his regulator. Alarmed, she curled the fingers of her right hand into an "okay" sign. Another burst of air bubbled from his regulator, then he quickly jabbed a finger at his throat, and returned the "okay" sign. Just coughing.

It was understandable. The compressed air was dry; her own throat felt tight and scratchy. As she reframed man and lobster in the viewfinder, she noticed a torpedo shape in the blue gloom beyond him. *Uh-oh.* She took a breath and pressed the shutter button, exhaled, and then pointed.

After a quick glance, Dan thrust his fingers into a vertical fin on top of his neoprene hood. Scuba sign language for shark. *Crap.* There was no mistaking the dorsal fin on its back, the flattened profile. It was indeed a shark. Sam hovered uncertainly in place. What was a diver supposed to do to avoid looking like food?

Dan held his hands out, two feet apart. A little shark? As it swam closer, she saw that he was correct. It was bigger than two feet, but probably no longer than three. Its sleek hide was an intricate mosaic of shaded patches. A leopard shark. Harmless, gorgeous, and best of all, alone. As the shark swam upward, she followed with the camera, capturing a shot of the shark suspended beneath the triangular shape of their boat. Even as she snapped the photo, Sam knew she shouldn't have glanced up. She had a perfect view of all the bubbles streaming upward from both regulators. There was fifty feet of water between her and normal air.

Her breathing sounded mechanical and forced now. *Calm down*, she told herself. In—hiss. Out—bubble, bubble, bubble. *You signed up for this.*

She looked down. Below, Dan stared at her and coughed again. The display on her computer was flashing, the technological equivalent of a stern teacher shaking a warning finger. She'd been down with Dan, up after the turtle, down with Dan again, and then up after the shark. Yo-yoing. A definite no-no. Letting air out of her buoyancy vest, she slowly sank again, holding out her arms in an underwater shrug, then pointing to her camera, hoping he'd read that as being an overly enthusiastic photographer. If her fingers trembled, maybe he'd attribute it to the water's chill. He had definitely been right about the wet suit. Her computer registered seventy-two degrees Fahrenheit, which was surprisingly cold when suspended in liquid for thirty minutes.

With another burst of bubbles, Dan turned away, circling over the algae-mottled seabed, searching for more marine life. She followed, gliding a yard above the rough black lava, delighting in the marvels of a red-and-white cushion star and a psychedelic display of orange cup coral.

Suddenly the rock floor beneath her fell away, and she found herself suspended above a deep chasm. Dan was below her, his form made hazy by a shoal of tiny blue fish between them. His bubbles streamed up between the darting shapes. One air globule hit her mask squarely in front of her right eye, and clung there like a droplet of mercury until she turned her head and it rolled away, continuing its journey to the surface.

She was suspended in blue-green space. It felt marvelous and frightening and astounding, all at the same time. Her air gauge showed almost a thousand PSI left. She was breathing well, not too fast. She was gliding through the liquid womb of Mother Earth with fish and reptiles and— what *was* the proper classification for sea cucumbers, anyway? Echinoderms? Her wildlife biology studies had focused on mammals, so she needed to brush up on the cold-blooded classifications.

She came face-to-face with an exquisite purple lace fan. On land, she would have said it was part of the fern family. Down here, coral? She wasn't sure. According to her books, corals came in many shapes, sizes, and colors. So did sponges. To make identification even more confusing, other creatures mimicked plants. Bryozoans? She didn't yet know which name applied to which creature. Or even if it was one creature she was staring at. Some marine organisms were actually groups of animals. *Mind-blowing.*

They'd been down for nearly forty minutes now. Hadn't Dan told the boat pilot they would circle? They hadn't. Unless her underwater navigation skills were seriously flawed, they hadn't traveled very far at all. Shouldn't they be swimming more, counting more? Beneath her, Dan listed slightly to starboard. His computer dangled on its wrist cord in the slight current. He floated facedown, barely moving. Sam joined him to see what was so mesmerizing. Unable to detect much of interest within his range of vision, she tapped him on the shoulder. When he didn't react, she tugged at his arm.

His body rolled toward her like a mannequin. Behind the face mask, his eyes were dull, his eyelids at half-mast. She flashed the "okay?" question at him.

Dan floated listlessly, unresponsive.